SECRETS

Books authored or coauthored by Blaine M. Yorgason

Secrets
Prayers on the Wind
Namina: Biography of Georganna Bushman Spurlock (private printing)
The Life Story Of Roger And Sybil Ferguson (private printing)
Obtaining the Blessings of Heaven
To Mothers and Fathers from the Book of Mormon
Receiving Answers to Prayer
Spiritual Survival in the Last Days
Into the Rainbow
The Warm Spirit
Here Stands a Man
Decision Point
KING—The Biography of Jerome Palmer King (private printing)
Pardners: Three Stories on Friendship
In Search of Steenie Bergman (Soderberg Series #5)
The Greatest Quest
Seven Days for Ruby (Soderberg Series #4)
The Eleven Dollar Surgery
Becoming
Bfpstk and the Smile Song (out of print)
The Shadow Taker
Tales from the Book of Mormon (The Loftier Way)
Brother Brigham's Gold (Soderberg Series #3)
Ride the Laughing Wind
The Miracle
The Thanksgiving Promise
Chester, I Love You (Soderberg Series #2)
Double Exposure
Seeker of the Gentle Heart
The Krystal Promise
A Town Called Charity, and Other Stories About Decisions
The Bishop's Horse Race (Soderberg Series #1)
And Should She Die (The Courage Covenant)
Windwalker (movie version—out of print)
The Windwalker
Others
Charlie's Monument
Tall Timber (out of print)
Miracles and the Latter-day Teenager (out of print)

SECRETS

BLAINE M. YORGASON

AND

SUNNY OAKS

DESERET BOOK COMPANY
SALT LAKE CITY, UTAH

First printing in hardbound edition 1992.
First printing in paperbound edition 1999.

Library of Congress Cataloging-in-Publication Data

Yorgason, Blaine M., 1942–
    Secrets / Blaine M. Yorgason and Sunny Oaks.
        p.   cm.
    ISBN 0-87579-657-5 (hardbound)
    ISBN 1-57345-477-X (paperbound)
    I. Oaks, Sunny. II. Title.
    PS3575.O57S38   1992
    813'.54—dc20   92-33959
                                                                          CIP

Printed in the United States of America   10246-6401
    10   9   8   7   6   5   4   3   2   1

Staley
401 Belmont Ave
Bellefontaine oh
43311

937-592-8363

For the children

Acknowledgments

We wish to express heartfelt gratitude to the men and women who have shared with us as we have prepared this manuscript. Some have given freely of their education and knowledge, all have given of their time, and many have willingly shared their most horrible, gut-wrenching memories and experiences. To each of you, and you each know who you are, we can say no more than "Thank you."

We also express thanks to the staff and management of Deseret Book Company, specifically Ronald Millett, Sheri Dew, Jack Lyon, Richard Erickson, Craig Geertsen, and Tonya Facemyer, who have labored patiently with us as this manuscript was being prepared. Special appreciation is extended to Terri Young, who wrote the poems "Latter-day Gulls" and "Benediction," and to Dean Byrd, associate commissioner of Social Services for the LDS Church, who gave many hours both in critiquing and in enhancing the manuscript.

BOOK ONE

THE WOUNDING

PART ONE

PRAYING FOR MY ENEMY

He flung
His fiery darts
Against my heart
Wounding
My precious
Child
Devouring
Innocence
Crushing
Purity

Is this the
Enemy
For which I am
To pray?

And
If I do
What then — ?

1

TUESDAY, MAY 28

10:15 A.M.

Bishop Frank Lee Greaves paused for a moment in front of the window overlooking the playground of the Nephi S. Southernland Elementary School. It was morning recess, and frenzied, giggling children in bright-colored shorts and T-shirts darted happily around the play equipment, filling the air with their squeals and excitement. With the window open Frank could feel their anticipation and hear their shrill chatter. The warm spring air was alive with their excitement.

So, too, was it alive with the scents and colors of late spring as the world outside moved effortlessly into summer. It was a wonderful time of year, his favorite, and for a moment Frank closed his eyes and breathed in pure delight.

Of course as a teacher with sixth-grade graduation coming up, Frank had his own excitement — arrangements to make, parents to call, certificates to fill out, report cards to finish — all that in addition to completing each child's cumulative folder to send on to junior high.

Every year as school ended for the summer Frank faced this anticipation, feeling the heady excitement of seeing his kids beaming in front of their parents as they completed elementary school. With a painful joy he accepted their almost tearful good-byes, and with tender pride he watched them move on. Of course he knew that some of

5

them would continue to grow and succeed, but he was also concerned that a few others, well, just wouldn't. If only he could just graduate and go on with them.

Turning away from the window, Frank stared around him. On the walls of the room were posters of the countries of the world with their capitals. The board was filled with the words for the final spelling quiz. Looking down the rows of desks, Frank saw that they were all cluttered with pieces of paper taped to the sides. And the name tags, once bright and new, were now tattered and covered with stickers and doodles. Those desks would soon be empty again, and the room would take on the smell of summer varnish.

With a sigh Frank glanced at the magazine in his hand, thinking again of the article he had just read.

"Frank, how did you get out of reffing the softball game?"

Turning around, Frank was startled to see his good friend and the school principal, Kent Bailey.

"Mrs. O.'s covering for me today," he replied easily.

"Taking advantage of that sweet cousin of yours?" Kent teased, knowing full well that Frank and Mrs. O., another sixth-grade teacher, frequently traded days out with the children at recess.

"What's family for if you can't lean on them once in a while?" Frank teased back, setting the magazine to one side.

"So, how are you set for graduation?" Kent asked good-naturedly.

"Piece of cake." Frank smiled. "You know Mrs. O. She's doing most of it."

"You really lucked out when she came here to teach," Kent responded. "Every other teacher is running around looking like they could chew nails. And look at you, taking it easy and reading magazines."

"Comes from clean living," Frank teased, his hazel-gray eyes dancing.

"Did you see Andy Bartelli?"

Frank nodded. "I did. He's getting tall, isn't he."

"Well, he should be. Ninth grade next year. Mrs. O. says he's doing well, too."

"I'm glad to hear that."

Kent sighed. "Yeah, it was a rough situation. Sometimes I find myself wondering how many more of our students are being abused like he was."

"So do I," Frank agreed as he reached over and picked up his magazine again. "Here," he said as he opened it and handed it to his principal. "I read this last night. Take a look and tell me what you think."

"What is it?" Kent asked as he took the proffered magazine.

"A Church magazine."

"For bishops?" Kent questioned sincerely as he dragged up a chair.

"For everybody."

"Hmmm." Kent looked appraisingly at the page. "Abuse, huh? Interesting, especially considering the fact that we both see Andy today." The principal shuddered. "I'm just glad we're not dealing with that case anymore."

"Yeah." Frank agreed simply.

"When I think of all the garbage dragged up by that boy's lying parents—"

"It got pretty ugly, didn't it," Frank agreed.

"There's nothing pretty about the things those parents did to that boy. How that's possible, I'll never know."

Kent began skimming the page. Then, looking up, he smiled. "You didn't know I was a Sunday School teacher in my church, did you?"

Frank was surprised.

"Yeah," Kent went on, "I figured if you could be a

bishop and teach school, there was no reason why I couldn't teach Sunday School and also be a principal."

"Makes sense," Frank agreed.

"This is good," Kent nodded, referring to the article. "He says here that healing from abuse can only come through the Lord Jesus Christ. And if this healing doesn't occur, victims will experience fear, depression, guilt, self-hatred, destruction of self-esteem, and alienation of normal human relationships. Sounds like he's describing Andy, all right. And listen to this! 'If aggravated by continued abuse, victims will feel rebellion, anger, and hatred, which can be focused against self, others, life itself, or even God. These feelings can lead to drug abuse, immorality, abandonment of home, and even suicide. They can also lead to despondent lives, discordant marriages, a complete loss of trust, and even the transition from victim to abuser.' Sounds like he knows the Bartelli family personally!"

"Or he knows abuse," Frank responded. "For some reason, that article just jumped out at me."

"Mrs. O. tells me Andy is still in therapy," Kent said as he continued to read.

"Well, Kent, he was a mixed-up kid for a long time. Mrs. O. is also working with him, though, so he'll be fine."

"That's right. Andy's the one who got her going back for her graduate degree, isn't he."

Frank nodded. "She's worked hard, too. The sabbatical helped, and she tells me she'll have her Ph.D. in family therapy by the end of next year."

"I hope she doesn't leave us then," Kent said. "She's a real asset." And then, looking back at the magazine in his hand, he read for another moment or two.

"This article leads me to wonder—you must deal with abuse problems in your church."

"We're people like everyone else, so I'm sure of it. But, thankfully, we don't have any in my ward, at least that I know of."

"Ward?" Kent asked, puzzled.

"The term for a Latter-day Saint congregation, a ward being similar to a parish. The Church is divided into wards, then stakes, and then the Church at large."

Kent nodded his comprehension. "But you don't have any abuse in your—ward?"

"I don't think so. Oh, we have our share of problems, don't get me wrong. But by and large my ward is filled with great people. We have a city councilman, several university professors, corporate executives, wonderful parents, and some of the finest kids you've ever known. Just last week, Amy Nelson received a National Merit Scholarship—"

"Amy's a Mormon?" Kent asked in surprise. "I'm impressed."

"She comes from a great family. Her dad's an outstanding man, and her mother is a real fireball—two of those people who seem to know what they want and how to get it."

"Speaking of getting things you want," Kent asked, "what have you planned for the summer?"

"Well," Frank leaned back with a wide smile, "I'll be working on my degree after we get back from visiting Jeanee's son Tony. He and Megan are expecting their third child, you know."

"They're not wasting any time. Well, congratulations, Grandpa."

Frank ran his hand through his thinning hair and grinned lopsidedly.

"And how's that other son of yours? The baseball player."

Frank smiled. "Erik? He's doing great—impatient to get his driver's license, but what sixteen-year-old isn't?"

"He's your boy, isn't he?"

"As far as I'm concerned. Actually, he's Jeanee's, but he was so young when his father died—"

"And Angie? She's yours?"

Frank nodded, beaming.

"She's in one of our first-grade classes, isn't she?"

"That's right. On the early morning schedule."

"So that's why you get here so early."

Again Frank nodded. "That's why I'm looking forward to next week."

"Yes. And speaking of that, I'm going to be doing some remodeling on my family room, Frank, and I was wondering if you might have time to do my cabinet work for me?"

Frank ran his fingers over his desk. "What kind of wood are we talking about?"

"The wood you made your desk out of is just what I want."

"A light oak?"

"That's right. Do you think you'll have time?"

"Well, maybe," Frank said with a grin. "If I can use the scraps to build a telephone stand for my office here."

"If I could just cut through all the red tape to *get* you that phone"—Kent raised his arms in frustration—"you would have had it months ago. But don't give up on me—"

The jangling of the bell interrupted Kent, and with a sigh he rose to his feet, magazine still in hand. "Well, back to work. I appreciate your time. Listen, would you mind if I made a copy of this?"

Remaining seated, Frank shook his head. "Heavens, no. Copy the whole magazine if you want."

"Thanks." Kent smiled as he turned away. "I just might do that. See you at lunch."

"And I'll get back with you on that cabinet project," Frank called.

Turning then, he watched as the sixth-grade classes filed off the playground. They were such a great bunch of kids. If only—

"Mister Greaves?"

Spinning, Frank looked at the girl who stood in his doorway. "Hi, June. Something I can do for you?"

June McCrasky smiled, her dental braces flashing metallically, and Frank wondered briefly if anything could ever be worth wearing such a mouthful of metal.

"You have a telephone message," June stated thickly. "It says here that you are to call Mrs. Martin, from church. Here's her telephone number."

Abby Martin, Frank thought as he took the message from June's outstretched hand. Sad, but she was fast becoming one of the "regulars." *I wonder what crisis has impelled Abby to call me at the school?* he thought. "Sure would be nice," he mused as he hurried toward the administration office, "if Kent could get that private telephone for my room."

11:20 A.M.

Sunlight rippled across the aqua-blue of the pool, splashing the water with silver fingers of light. Just beyond, above the juniper tams, two white butterflies played tag for a moment and then disappeared into the blue-white of the sky. Along the fence, daisy buds seemed ready to burst, and pink-purple daphne blossoms sent fragrant sweetness into the air.

Carefully Jeanee Rae Greaves breathed in the beauty and stillness of her yard. Then, reaching over from the chaise lounge, she turned on the soft music of Zamphir's Pan Flute. Once again she lay back, this time with eyes closed and body relaxed as the music floated her concerns away. It took a concentrated meditation to keep the twinges of guilt from interrupting her thoughts. It had, after all, taken her husband's death and the massive insurance settlement to make these wonderful surroundings possible. Strange, she thought, that all the years she had been married to Earl had been such a struggle. And now, because he was gone, she had a better life than she had ever hoped to have, and it was with someone else. It was an irony that she couldn't resolve, so regularly she pushed it out of her mind.

Late morning sun warmed her face as she let her thoughts drift to vacation plans. She needed to get Angie's swimming suit finished, and two matching Sunday dresses for her granddaughters, Amber and Nicole, and finally some maternity casuals for Megan. Jeanee loved to sew for her family.

"What a good life I have," she smiled to herself. "In just ten years, so much has changed."

The flutter of a bird interrupted her thoughts, and Jeanee opened her eyes to watch its flight past the lilac bush and into the neighbor's backyard.

"Just ten years ago," her thoughts continued. "Is it possible for so much to change so fast? Am I really here? Is my past really behind me?"

In all her life Jeanee had never known the security she was now feeling. Never before, as a child, a teenager, or a woman, had she known the kind of love she now knew. And she would not do anything to risk losing that love.

"Oh, Frank," she whispered in her mind, "you just don't know how my life has changed. You with your wonderful laugh and your beautiful, honest eyes. Life has always been so simple for you."

Thinking back to when they had first met, at church, Jeanee thought of the one heartache Frank had experienced. His wife, Christine, had passed away after years of fighting a losing battle with cancer. A month later, they had met. Yet even then, with grief in his eyes, there had been something untouched about him. Jeanee couldn't comprehend his ability to just accept the loss and go on with life.

"How does he do it?" she wondered half aloud. "With no bitterness? It took me years, and I still don't know—"

The jangle of the telephone startled Jeanee. Sitting up, she reached for the remote next to her.

"Hello?" her voice was soft.

"Hello? Is anyone there?" came the reply, sounding very distant.

"Yes, I'm here." She cleared her throat. "This is the Greaves residence."

There was a short pause. "Jeanee?"

"Yes. Is that you, Sarah?" Jeanee recognized the voice of her stake president's wife on the other end of the line. "Is everything okay?"

Another pause.

"Jeanee, could you please get a message to Frank?"

"Of course. Sarah, is something wrong?"

"It's Mother Stone," came the reply. "She's gone. We have to be out of town for a couple of days. Arrangements for the funeral—you know—"

"Oh, Sarah, I'm sorry."

"And Dick wanted me to call and say the Tuesday night meeting—"

"Is canceled." Jeanee finished the sentence.

"Yes, that's right. Could you tell Frank? Just in case Brother Heath can't get hold of him before tonight?"

"I'll tell him, Sarah. You tell the president that you'll all be in our prayers."

"Thanks." Sarah's voice quavered. "This has been an ordeal. Maybe it's best this way."

"I'm certain it will be. You take care, now." Jeanee hung up the phone. Uneasy with death, even now, she tried to focus on the thought that this change of plans meant that she would have a rare evening with her husband.

"And we know that all things work together for good . . . " She quoted the first part of a favorite scripture to herself. "Even death. Remember that, Jeanee. Even death.

"Oh, Frank, how do you do it? With all the burdens you carry every day, as bishop, how do you keep it from bringing you down?"

Unlike her husband, who seemed to have a talent for taking life as it came, Jeanee had to make a concentrated effort just to keep a balance. Over the years she had learned that the only way to do that was to clear her mind of worry every day and just let it float for a few minutes.

Quickly she French-braided her longer wisps of honey-blond hair and clipped them under. Then, in one smooth running motion, her body propelled itself into the cooling, cleansing resistance of the water. Deep beneath the surface she plunged, arching slowly upward only after she had touched bottom.

With a whoosh she surfaced, feeling exhilarated from the shock of the cool water. Smiling, she closed her eyes and sank her face beneath the surface one more time. Then she pushed forward, reaching out to the silky smoothness of the water, lapping the pool again and again as she blocked every thought and care from her mind. Finally her only thoughts were of her breathing and of the cleansing rush of blood through her veins as a resisting wall of water massaged every muscle.

Harder she pushed, water churning around her, until she felt the release that always came when she forced herself to go beyond comfort.

"Oh, yes!" she laughed aloud. "Yes, yes!"

Then, relaxing every muscle, she let her body rise to the surface like a figure in a ballet. Floating to the top, she lay suspended in the liquid womb of the pool, water caressing her face, sunshine warming it. Every other part of her was submerged just beneath the silky bed of water as she floated, relaxing, submitting to the rhythm of her own breathing.

For a moment nothing existed for her but this place. Her labored breathing was her only awareness—in, out, inhaling, releasing. Suspended in timelessness Jeanee allowed her mind to float, to think of nothing, to feel nothing but the coolness of the water and its gentle splashing against her face.

At that moment she was at peace, connected with herself, and totally free. It was so incredible to her, this ability to relax. And it had not come easily. Nor had she discovered it before she had married Frank. Even as she floated, he became real there beside her, his love reaching out to her as had nothing she had ever experienced before.

"Frank," she found herself wondering, "what would you do if I told you everything? Would that be a mistake? Have I been right to keep it to myself all these years?"

From the patio, above the sound of the pan flute, the timer signaled that it was time to go in.

"It can't be noon already," she thought to herself. "I just got started."

With a sigh Jeanee swam to the edge of the pool and stepped out. "Back to the real world," she sighed as she picked up her towel. "Time to get on with the stuff of living."

But, oh, she felt wonderful! As she toweled her hair and headed up the stairs, she wondered how she had ever lived before she started swimming. "Whoever said life begins at forty," she thought to herself, "must have had a pool."

As she was slipping into a pair of powder-blue sweats, the telephone rang again, and she wondered as she reached for the receiver if it might be another crisis.

"Hello?"

On the other end Jeanee heard a sob being sniffled back. "Hello?" she repeated.

"Jeanee?" There was a pause and another sniffle. "Are you . . . are you Jeanee Rae Pyper?"

Suddenly uneasy, Jeanee stared straight ahead. "I . . . I used to be," she heard herself saying.

"Oh, thank goodness I found you. I . . . I'm sorry to bother you, but I have to talk to someone before I go crazy!"

"Of course," Jeanee reassured. "Who . . . am I speaking with?"

"I'm sorry. How can you remember after all these years? It's Marie, Jeanee. Marie Winston—at least, that used to be my name. I knew you in high school. Remember?"

Another sniffle.

"High school?" Jeanee's mind raced. "Marie Winston. Oh, yes! Marie! My goodness, it's been years!"

"Marie," she probed, "are you all right?"

"Yes, I . . . I'm fine." Marie forced a laugh. "I'm just having a little nervous breakdown."

"What can I do?" Jeanee was instantly concerned.

"Do you have a few minutes?"

"Yes, I . . . well, I'll make them. Would you like to meet me somewhere? Are you in town? Should I pick you up?"

"No, I mean yes, I'm in town. I'll come over there. I mean, if that's all right."

"That's just fine."

"If we could just talk. Do you have some time—today?"

"Hey, right away is fine. Can you be here at 12:30?"

Marie forced another laugh. "That would be just fine. You're sure this isn't putting you out?"

"Are you kidding? I'm looking forward to seeing you again."

"You're sure?"

"Marie, I'm here by myself. The family's in school, and I would love to visit. Let me give you directions—"

"That's okay," Marie interrupted. "I know where you live. In fact, you can't believe how many times I've driven past your house, hoping it was yours, wanting to stop and make sure but being afraid."

"Oh, Marie—"

"Well, now it's done. I'll drive over. And Jeanee? Thanks."

As she hung up the phone, Jeanee felt an old trembling coming back into her body. There had been something in Marie's voice . . .

Picking up the blow dryer, she began styling her hair.

"What is it?" she asked herself. "I haven't felt this way in a long, long time."

Looking into the mirror, she wondered at the uncertainty she saw in her own eyes. Every time she was reminded of the past, it was as if an invisible shadow had entered her life.

"And we know that all things work together for good . . . " Jeanee again repeated the first part of Romans 8:28. "Whatever is coming, Jeanee, remember that even this will work together for your good."

2

TUESDAY, MAY 28

12:20 P.M.

It was lunch recess, and eleven-year-old June McCrasky
sat alone on the lawn outside her school, a book open on
her lap. Though other children were paired or in groups
around her, she was not really aware of them. If she allowed herself to become aware, the pain of loneliness came,
and June was so tired of pain that she did her best to avoid
it. One way, she had discovered, was through dreaming.
And so now she sat wrapped in dreams—thin, wispy
threads of nonreality that gave solace and comfort to her
soul.

These were not big dreams but little ones, of flying
away to a place of beauty where people spoke quietly and
where everyone was nice to everyone else. She dreamed
of soaring effortlessly through the air as the poor earth-
bound kids stared upward in awe and wonder. She felt
great power as she flew easily above the others, and she
knew she could do anything she wanted to them, anything
at all. Of course she did not want to hurt anybody. There
was already too much hurting—

"June, June, pickled prune," two boys chanted as they
ran past, and June squeezed her eyes tightly against their
mocking laughter. The chant was as old as the third grade,
and it didn't bother her as much as . . . as some of the other
things that were said. And even those would end in another
three days, when school closed for the summer.

Yet, in spite of her loneliness, June loved school. It brought her relief from what was happening at home, and it gave her the opportunity of truly pleasing someone. And she did! Every day she outstudied and outperformed everyone else in her class, and it felt so incredibly wonderful when her teachers noticed that. Now she was even being allowed to help in the office and to run errands for the principal, and that too was fun and exciting.

For a moment June thought of that, her eyes again open as she watched some girls who were giggling nearby. She could not hear what they were saying, but she knew their laughter was concerning her. It always was. Somehow, though she had never determined exactly how, she was different from all the other kids in school. Whatever it was, it was not a good difference, either. Had it been, the others would have liked her. But they didn't, and so she was alone — alone except for her dreams and the teachers who liked her.

Next year she would be in the sixth grade, and it would be the best year of her life. She knew it. In spite of the fact that she was different, people would love her — her teachers would love her, especially if she could get Bishop Greaves. She would get perfect grades from him; she would work hard to help him in class, she would —

But first, June McCrasky had to find a way to get through the next three days that stretched so painfully before her.

12:25 P.M.

"Bob, what is the matter with you?"

Bob Nichol looked up at his wife, his anger seeming to have a life and will of its own. "The matter with *me?*" he stormed, his voice getting louder. "Nothing's the matter with me!"

Jumping to his feet, he slammed his magazine to the

floor. Then he stalked to the window, his entire body trembling with rage. "I'm telling you, Claudia, if that idiot kid doesn't start doing what I tell him, then you'll *really* see some anger. Look at this lawn out here! I told him two days ago that it needed to be cut, and he hasn't touched it."

"But . . . he hasn't had time."

"Time? What does he have to do with his time? Nothing. Just goof off, and you know it. Here he is seventeen years old, and he doesn't even have a job."

"Bob, its the end of school, and he's in the middle of finals. Besides, he's been looking for work for over a month now."

Bob Nichol laughed harshly. "Yeah, like I look for ulcers. That kid's got some hard lessons ahead of him, Claudia, and if I don't pound a little sense into him, he'll never make it."

"But . . . but you don't have to do it with such anger, honey. You don't have to be mean to him."

Incensed at his wife's accusations, Bob turned on her. "Who do you think you are, telling me how to raise my son? I preside in this home, and don't you forget it! You've pampered and mollycoddled Robby from the day he was born, and I've had it with you every bit as much as I've had it with him. That kid needs to learn a few things, and since you can't see it, I'm just the guy to teach him."

Angrily Bob Nichol stormed out the door to return to work, leaving his wife sobbing and his lunch uneaten on the table. "Serves her right," he muttered angrily as he started the car and accelerated rapidly out of the driveway. "She can eat her own crummy food for a change."

12:30 P.M.

With a sigh Mel Blodgett put down his half-eaten hamburger, saved the data on the computer, and walked to the ringing telephone. "Blodgett Engineering," he said after he had lifted the receiver and cradled it against his shoulder. "Oh, hi, Frank. What's up?"

For a moment Mel listened, unconsciously working to wipe his scrupulously clean hands on a rag he had found lying on the counter. "Abby Martin, huh? . . . No, I haven't heard anything. . . . She says John's not making his child-support payments again? Well, it doesn't surprise me. He deserves to be horsewhipped for the pain he's put Abby and those kids through."

Listening again, Mel's mind diverted for a moment to the lathing problem he was struggling to program on the computer. Blasted thing should have been programmed and tooled up yesterday, and he still couldn't get it up to specs —

"What's that?" he asked sheepishly as he realized Frank Greaves had asked him a question. "No, my mind wandered, Frank, and I didn't hear you. Besides, the radio in here is on so loud. . . . Busy? Well, I'm just under a little pressure, is all. I was supposed to have some work done yesterday, and one of my engineers has been sick for the past week, so I'm stuck trying to get it done. . . . Yeah, I know. Too much office work has dulled my skills. That's no kidding, either. The rain we had last week put our sample crew behind, up at the new dam. The soil's been too wet for samples, and the people have been screaming for days. Anyway, yeah, I'm a little busy. But that's all right. It's only time. Now, what was it you asked?"

Soberly Mel nodded. "Sounds like she needs a visit, all right. I've heard some other rumors, too. . . . Oh, I'd rather not say until I can check them out. . . . Yeah, I could break away for a little while and run over there. . . . No, Frank, don't worry about it. I know you can't just walk away from school. Besides, what's a counselor for? I can squeeze it in. Did you get hold of Terri? . . . Same old story, huh? Well, she's a dandy Relief Society president, even if she is hard to get hold of. . . . Oh, now that's a good idea. Does Jeanee have time?"

Mel laughed. "Yeah, I know what you mean. You're lucky to have found her, Frank. I hope you know that. . . . Yeah, sounds good. I'll get on it right away."

Slowly Mel Blodgett hung up the phone; then with a soft curse he threw his rag back onto the counter. Time? Yeah, right. Well, he'd make time, just as he always did. His mind churning, he walked to the sink and began washing his hands. Like the other bishops Mel had served under, Frank Greaves had acknowledged that he'd never had a better counselor. And it was going to stay that way, Mel declared to himself as he scrubbed. No matter what it took, even if it meant neglecting his business, it had doggone well better stay that way.

Now, if he only had another ten hours in the day. . . .

12:35 P.M.

Quickly Jeanee drank the glass of water. Then she leaned against the counter, trying to calm her trembling body. Through the window she could see Marie seated on her patio, fidgeting with her long, prematurely gray hair. She had grown into a beautiful woman, with long artistic fingers and soulful blue eyes, eyes that even now were holding back tears.

"What am I doing?" Jeanee asked herself. "Of all times to have a trauma! Get a grip, Jeanee! Go back out there and say something."

Taking a deep breath, Jeanee reminded herself again that she was now a healthy woman. Then resolutely she placed the glass on the counter.

"I'm sorry," she said to Marie as she walked back out and sat down. "Something got caught in my throat."

"It should have caught in mine," Marie declared softly. "I'm sorry, Jeanee. I shouldn't have dumped on you. You have a life of your own to live, and you don't need my dirt to clutter it."

Marie picked up her bag, as if to leave.

"No, no," Jeanee insisted. "Don't go. Really, it's okay. I just had no idea. I mean, when I used to go to your house, everything seemed . . . so . . . normal."

"Yeah, real Norman Rockwell stuff!" The sinister edge on Marie's voice cut like a knife. Jeanee cleared her throat to cover her uneasiness.

"Do . . . do you remember what he did?"

"That's the worst part!" Marie agonized. "The memory is almost there, in flashes, like turning the channel on TV real fast. But then it's gone, and I can't remember. I'm so confused and disoriented. And I feel so guilty! Like it's my fault."

Jeanee looked out over her backyard. The ripples in the pool and the sound of windchimes gently tinkling had a soothing effect she was grateful for. She took another deep breath.

"Tell me," she said softly. "When did this start?"

"What? The stuff with my dad?"

"No, this recent—"

"That's the crazy part." Marie laughed nervously. "It started after Dave and I were married, about three years ago."

"Did you have problems? I mean . . . did he upset you?"

"That's just it," Marie moaned. "He's wonderful. He's a good provider. We have meals on the table, clothes in the closet, a beautiful home, even a condominium up on the lake. He's good to the children—"

"How many do you have?" Jeanee interrupted.

"Five!" Marie rolled her eyes. "Me, with five kids. Can you believe it?"

"Are any of them Dave's?"

"No . . . but you'd think they were. I mean, he spoils

them. I honestly think if something happened to our marriage, they'd rather stay with him than with me. How does that make me feel! I mean, my own kids . . . "

Jeanee leaned forward and reached out to cover Marie's hand with her own. "Does it look like something's going to happen to your marriage, Marie?"

Marie didn't respond. Instead she sat motionless, as if moving would open a floodgate of emotion that she would be unable to stop.

"This is really hard for you, isn't it."

Marie's lips began to quiver, and she sniffed hard to hold back the tears. But it was no use. Pulling her hand free of Jeanee's, she began fumbling in her purse for a tissue.

"I . . . I've never had it so good," she sobbed. "Anything I want. I mean anything! Dave gets it for me. He can afford it, he's got the money. But besides that, he's such a good man, and . . . and . . . Oh, Jeanee," she wailed, "I think I'm losing my mind!"

"It's okay, Marie. Don't hold anything back. It's just you and me. We're safe. Say anything you need to say. I'll listen, and I'll hear you."

"Safe!" Marie exclaimed. "I've never been safe in my life — until these past three years. And now that I think I have a man I can finally trust — I'm losing him! Make sense out of that one."

"It doesn't have to make sense," Jeanee whispered, almost to herself. "When feelings are so strong, sometimes all you can do is accept the fact that you feel them."

Marie blotted mascara from under her eyes and looked up, puzzled. "You do understand, don't you?"

"Maybe, a little." There was a silent exchange as their eyes met.

"Tell me," Jeanee continued, "how did it start?"

Marie took a deep breath. "At . . . first it was the nightmares, ugly dreams about being chased, and running, always running. Then the ground would give way, and I'd start sinking—and . . . Oh, Jeanee, it was terrible! And the dreams kept coming back and coming back—"

"And you were afraid to go to sleep at night because you didn't want to fight the dreams?"

"How . . . how did you know?" Marie asked, puzzled.

"Tell me," Jeanee paused, trying to get comfortable with the boldness of her next question. "Tell me about Dave. What is your personal life like? I mean, is he thoughtful of you . . . as a woman?"

"You mean intimately?"

"Is that too personal?"

Slowly Marie shook her head. "No. And I've thought of that. But he is, and so there isn't any reason for me to be feeling this . . . this crap! Do you realize that sometimes—" Marie picked up her bag again and clutched it to her for security. Then her voice changed, becoming almost childlike. "Jeanee, this is scary, but sometimes I feel like I'm sharing my body with someone else."

Marie waited for a response, and, when none came, she continued, her voice very still. "I lose chunks of my life."

"You mean that you forget things?"

"More than that. I've had people I don't even know come up and talk to me about things they have no way of knowing about. And they know me! I have no memory of them, but they insist that we know each other well.

"Besides that, I forget promises I make to my children. I forget to pick them up from school. I go to the store and can't remember what I went there for. It's like I've lost part of me somewhere. I just wish—"

Both Jeanee and Marie jumped at the loud ringing of the telephone.

"Excuse me," Jeanee said as she stood. "This will take just a minute. I'll be right back."

Jeanee was concerned about leaving her friend at a time

like this. Always the telephone was interrupting. But that was part of being a bishop's wife, being there for the emergencies and messages that needed to get to her husband. Still, after two years, she wasn't used to it.

"Hello? Oh, Frank. What a surprise!" Jeanee smiled, watching through the window as Marie fidgeted nervously in her chair.

"No, that's okay," she continued. "I was just visiting with an old friend from school. . . . Of course. I'd be happy to do that. I'll just make a double batch of what we're having tonight. . . . No, I don't know Abby very well. Maybe it's time I reached out to her, huh? . . . Okay. Oh, and your meeting tonight has been canceled. Sad news. . . . That's right, President Stone's mother has passed away. . . . I know. I feel bad too. . . . Okay, sounds good." A wide smile brightened Jeanee's face. "I'll plan on that."

Marie was walking into the kitchen as Jeanee hung up the phone. "Maybe I should be going?" she asked.

"No, that's fine," Jeanee said reassuringly. "That was just Frank, asking me to help out with one of the sisters in the ward. We can visit while I throw something together for dinner."

12:45 P.M.

As quickly as he could, Frank hurried down the hall. He knew he was already late for class, but he didn't want the kids getting so rowdy that other classrooms would be affected.

"Thank goodness for Jeanee," he said to himself as he moved. "I guess there are advantages in having her serve as compassionate service leader. Of course, Jeanee is so giving that even without the calling she'd be doing it — "

A small boy darted in front of him, running somewhere, and Frank dodged awkwardly, avoiding the child but almost losing his balance in the process. Feeling foolish, he was thankful when he glanced back that the hall was deserted. It was bad enough being so big, but add clumsy to the list and Frank shuddered at the mental picture he had of himself.

Unlike his first counselor, Mel Blodgett, who hadn't put on an extra pound his entire adult life, Frank considered himself anything but in good form. Mel could eat all he wanted and still remain trim. He was athletic, articulate, and well educated, and his sense of humor was renowned. Sometimes it was difficult being around him, he seemed so self-assured and in control.

Why, Frank wondered, had he not also been blessed with such grace and dignity?

"Mr. Greaves?"

Looking up, Frank identified the girl standing in his doorway down the hall.

"Coming, Alicia," he called back. And then, sucking in his somewhat bulgy abdomen, he strode forward with even greater alacrity.

3

TUESDAY, MAY 28

1:00 P.M.

"Enough garlic? What do you think?" Jeanee offered the large spoon to Marie for a taste test.

"Delicious. And so fast! You really are a little 'Molly Mormon,' aren't you. Perfectly clean home, little positive-thinking plaques all over the walls. And you whip up delicious dinners at the drop of a hat."

A wink let Jeanee know that Marie was just teasing.

"And how many children do you have? Twelve?"

The last comment hit a tender spot. For Jeanee, childbirth had been very difficult. And so when she said nothing, Marie sensed that she had said too much.

"Forgive me, Jeanee. I put my foot in my mouth on a regular basis, but this is too much. I'm really sorry."

"Oh, no, it's fine," Jeanee lied. "If you want to get the stuff in the crisper, I need to tear up a large salad. Oh, and the rolls in the freezer—would you get them out? Two dozen should do it."

"Two dozen? Somebody has a large family."

"Abby Martin—and no husband to support them." Jeanee poured a steaming mountain of egg noodles on top of the turkey stroganoff sauce and began stirring them together in a large canning kettle.

"I guess I'm pretty lucky, aren't I?" Marie acknowledged as she carried the salad vegetables to the sink to wash. "I should count my blessings. Isn't that what that old hymn used to say?"

"Still does," Jeanee answered, dividing the huge pile of noodles into two casserole dishes. "Marie, are you still going to church?"

Marie laughed harshly. "You got me there! I guess I'm what you would call a Relief Society dropout. Only I dropped so far that Relief Society wasn't the only thing I quit."

Marie's tone was cynical, though Jeanee didn't look to see her expression. Instead she topped the casserole dishes with foil and put them in the fridge. She was walking toward the sink when Marie started singing, "When upon life's billows you are tempest-tossed—"

"You still have a beautiful voice," Jeanee declared, ignoring the obvious irreverence in her friend's attitude.

"Oh, yes—beautiful Marie." Then the woman grew very quiet. "That's what *he* said," she abruptly whispered. " 'Beautiful Marie. You are so beautiful that I can't stop touching you.' And . . . and he kept touching me!"

Marie dropped the lettuce in the sink and began scratching at her arms with wet hands. "If I could just KILL that memory!"

Jeanee put her hand on Marie's shoulder. "We can finish the salad later, if you want to talk some more."

Marie looked at the ceiling for a moment, fighting to regain composure. Then she reached for a paper towel to dry her hands.

"Why is it," she pleaded, "that I have always felt different from other people? What is it about me that is so strange?"

"Marie," Jeanee motioned her friend to join her on the bar stools, "whatever happened to you has left you wounded. You just need help sorting through your feelings."

"And what *are* my feelings?" Marie almost moaned. "I

don't know! It's like they are hidden in this darkness I feel inside. It's like no one else can comprehend the crazy things I feel. Admit it, Jeanee. You used to think I was weird, didn't you."

Jeanee seemed stunned.

"You did! I know you did. Especially when you asked me to go places with you, and I always came up with excuses."

"That's right. I remember now. You were always getting headaches or something."

Marie shook her head. "I was just hiding, afraid that somehow you would notice the darkness in me and turn away. I was so afraid of getting close to anyone."

Jeanee understood only too well what her friend was saying. But she continued to listen in silence, nodding and encouraging Marie to keep talking.

"Even today, I feel like when I'm talking with people, it isn't really me that's talking. I feel like I'm standing apart, just listening. Am I going crazy, Jeanee? Am I the only one that feels this way?"

"Marie, we all have dark secrets we don't want others to know about. Another who has experienced what you were forced to endure might not have handled it as well as you have."

"I don't know that I've handled it that well. You don't know me, Jeanee. Not anymore. In fact, I don't know myself, and that's a big part of what's scaring me. There's a secret part of me, a darkness growing inside, but it's like it's growing out of control till I can't hide it any longer. And even though I'm obsessed with 'down-to-the-bone' clean, I feel so dirty. No matter how many times I shower each day, I can't wash my shame away.

"Did you know that after my first date—remember Thurl Riggs?"

Jeanee sat at the counter nodding compassionately.

"Well," Marie continued, "I dated him, and nothing

happened. Absolutely nothing. He just put his arm around me. And it felt so good, it scared me to death! I went home and scoured myself so thoroughly with a pumice stone that I had no hair left on my arms, and I was even bleeding in places. It took three months to fully heal. I even peeled my skin off in places where my dad touched me, hoping that would make the black spot go away. But it always grew back."

"Do you still do that?" Jeanee was concerned.

"No. Now I just drink the memories away. I get to feeling so good I don't much care what happened when I was a kid. Does that shock you? See? I told you I was a dropout."

Marie searched Jeanee's face for a reaction. "You're not shocked, are you?"

"Are you trying to shock me?" Jeanee smiled.

"No." Marie looked out over the pool. "I guess I'm just testing, to see if I can trust you."

"And how am I doing?"

"Like I thought you'd do. I don't know how I knew it, but I was certain I'd be safe talking with you."

"Safe?" Jeanee questioned.

"Yeah, safe. Something I want more than anything else in my life. To know that no one is going to hurt me or leave me or not believe me."

"You're safe with me," Jeanee encouraged.

"Safe enough to tell you the worst?"

"Safe enough to tell me anything you want to tell me."

"But it's terrible! And it keeps getting worse."

"And I'm your friend, Marie. Unless you can talk it out, it will keep eating at you until you won't have any sane moments left."

There was silence except for the steady dripping of the faucet on the iceberg lettuce in the sink and the tinkling of the windchimes.

Marie took a deep breath and looked off in the distance,

beyond the French doors in the dining room. It was as if she wasn't seeing what was before her but, instead, a scene from yesterday, releasing itself from the corners of her mind.

"It was after work," she began, a distant tone in her voice. "Remember when I worked at the Dairy Queen my junior year?"

Jeanee nodded.

"It was January, and I was calling home from the phone booth outside the Dairy Queen. You remember that phone booth?"

Jeanee nodded again.

Marie looked at Jeanee and then suddenly away, as if eye contact would silence her courage to go on.

"Suddenly from out of nowhere these guys had a knife at my throat. They took me to their truck and made me lie down in the back, and I just did what they said. I was too afraid even to scream.

"I don't remember how long it took to get to the little park where they stopped. I just froze in the back of the truck. It was like it wasn't real. It wasn't happening. So I just lay there waiting until they dragged me out and threw me on the ground."

Marie was silent for a moment, her eyes glazed over, almost as if she wasn't mentally present. Jeanee didn't move or speak.

"I remember the ground," Marie whispered. "It was so hard and so cold. There wasn't any snow, just icy-cold grass and dirt, frozen hard. And I just kept digging my fingernails into it all the time they were hitting me, and cutting me with their knife, and saying horrible things. I can still feel that icy ground."

Marie began wiping at her fingertips as if she were cleaning away the grass and dirt from those many years ago.

"And that's how I kept from feeling — I just kept digging

into the dirt while they . . . they—Oh, Jeanee! What they *did!*"

Tears were escaping down Marie's face. But still she fought the heaving sobs that were trying to come out with numb denial. Then her voice, suddenly monotone, continued.

"And all the time it was happening, I didn't scream. I didn't even cry. I was like I wasn't in my body. My body was there, but I wasn't connected to it. And I didn't scream."

"Marie, I'm so sorry." Jeanee reached her hand to her friend again. But this time Marie pulled away.

"Afterward they threw me over the bridge into the river," she continued. "I remember thinking, 'They killed me, they killed me!' And even then it didn't really matter. I knew I deserved it, so it made sense for them to kill me."

"I landed half on the bank and half in the ice and water. And when I came to, a big chunk of my hair broke off, because I tried to get up and it was frozen into the ice . . . " Marie's voice trailed off.

"What happened then?" Jeanee pressed, encouraging her friend to finish.

"My parents didn't believe me, but I had to do the police thing anyway. I could hardly remember the rape. It was like my mind turned off. But the police examination. With their photographs and everything, it felt like I was being raped all over again.

"What a farce! They poked and prodded and wrote things on their charts. But they didn't care. *Nobody* cared! And I didn't cry. I just let them do what they wanted to do—and I wouldn't let myself feel it.

"Anyway, that's been the story of my life. I can't feel— not what I'm supposed to, anyway."

"Oh, Marie, I'm so sorry. I had no idea." Jeanee's voice was tender, and she was holding back tears.

"And three husbands later"—the sarcastic edge returned to Marie's voice—"I'm losing it."

"Three husbands?"

Marie nodded. "The first was a jerk! We split after one
kid and one year of marriage. The next jerk lasted ten
years and four kids. Then he just took off one night and
never came back."

"He left you with five children to take care of?"

"That's right, and with no job."

"When did you stop going to church, Marie?"

"Oh, that was way back, after the rape. I've tried a
couple of times to go back, but I don't belong with all those
goody-goody little Mormon women who bake bread and
quilt"—Marie looked around Jeanee's kitchen—"and
make casseroles for other women whose husbands have
left them. What am I doing here? I'm talking to one of
them. Oh, my gosh, how can I be baring my soul to the
epitome of all I can never be?" Marie laughed a deep,
throaty laugh. "This is really crazy!"

Jeanee ignored the masked pain in Marie's outburst.
"Tell me," she asked, changing the subject, "is your Dave
at all understanding of what you are going through?"

"Oh, no way!" Marie was emphatic. "He just gets angry,
says I'm flipping out and need a good shrink. To tell you
the truth, I think he's right."

"Do you have someone to go to? Someone to help you
through this?"

"Why? Do you know someone?" Marie almost chided.

Jeanee smiled. "I know a couple of 'someones.' Actually, three, if you count the One who's done me the most
good."

"Done you the most good? What are you telling me?"

Jeanee looked Marie squarely in the eye. "I'm telling
you that I understand, Marie. Because I do. It's no coincidence that you came to see me."

"What do you mean?" Marie was finally quite serious.

Abruptly Jeanee looked at the clock. "Oh, dear, look at the time! I'm sorry, Marie. I do want to talk more, but I can't today. Are you okay with getting together later in the week?"

Slowly Marie nodded agreement. "Here," she said as she reached into her bag. "Here's a card with my phone number and address."

Jeanee smiled when she saw the address. "Hey, I think you're in our ward boundaries. How long have you lived here?" She tacked the card on the bulletin board next to the fridge as Marie answered.

"About six months. Is that good?"

"Probably bad," Jeanee said half jokingly. "I should have known you were living here, and I didn't. On the other hand, my husband is your bishop now."

Marie rolled her eyes and then winked. "Well, if he's anything like you, he'll be an improvement over the last stuffed shirt I talked to."

Jeanee looked wounded.

"Look, Jeanee, thanks for putting up with me." Marie gave her a hug. "I know I've dumped on you. I promise it won't be like this next time."

Jeanee smiled her warmest smile. "Great. I'm so glad you came to see me, Marie. Really. Call me anytime. I'll be here for you."

Marie looked cautiously out of the corner of her eye. "Are you real?" she teased as she headed for the door.

Jeanee didn't know how to respond, so she just shrugged and gestured with her hands. "We aim to please."

"Don't bother to see me out. I know my way."

And with that, Marie was gone into the afternoon, leaving Jeanee to tear up her salad and sort through some difficult feelings of her own.

1:10 P.M.

Mel Blodgett was fit to be tied. There were not enough hours in a day, and it seemed like everything was going wrong. Now that the ground was finally dry enough to take samples from, the dumb guy who was working for him had gone and broken the rig. Talk about stupidity! If he had just watched what he was doing—

Then the one remaining engineer at work in his firm had just called him on his mobile, telling him the computer model Mel had been working on all week had faulty data. It might work if they started all over again, but that would take at least another day, and probably two. Of course there had been no choice, but Mel wanted to scream, he needed that contract so badly.

Mel was also frustrated with his visit to Abby Martin's home. "Blast it, Frank," he muttered softly as he drove, "you ought to have known I couldn't do anything there! What Abby needs is a food and furniture order, and that takes you and Terri Elder, not me. Now I've got to remember to call you after school and tell you all this, and you should have been there in the first place."

Pressing his lips together, Mel shook his head. Actually, he admitted to himself, what was really bothering him wasn't his visit with Abby Martin. It wasn't even the fact that things were all going wrong at work. No, his real problem was with his wife, and that was what he couldn't find a way of dealing with.

Actually, they had fought over the telephone less than an hour before, while he had been on his way to visit Abby. Blast these mobile phones, he thought. They gave a man no peace. Nor did his wife. She was always on his case about something or other, and it had finally reached the point where they sometimes went days at a time without speaking. She was so doggone pious it was sickening. No-body was really like that, of course, unless maybe it was

God and her. And sometimes, he thought with a wry grin, God probably took lessons from her. But still, he could hardly stand it the way she lorded her righteousness over him.

Oh, he had tried to talk with her from time to time, hoping to get a little compassion for his weaknesses. But she was so blasted busy with the kids and church callings and every other little thing that she didn't have time to understand, even if she had wanted to. So, for the past few years, Mel had shared very little with her. And that was just fine with him. At least his daughters were there for him.

Still fuming, Mel found himself driving toward the junior high school where his two eldest daughters were in class. "I wonder if they're as miserable as I am?" he mused as his car seemed to slow down of its own accord. "I'll bet they are. And I'm the only one who can help my girls find a little joy in life. Its a darn sure thing my wife can't help them. Or help me either, for that matter, the pious soul. Yes sir, that's what I'll do! I'll check one of them out of school for the rest of the afternoon, and we'll go have a little fun together."

Pulling into the school turnaround, Mel got out of his car and walked toward the school, utterly forgetting that Bishop Greaves needed to be called about Abby Martin.

1:20 P.M.

"Pain, pain, go away! Come again some other day!"

Elaine McCrasky sat in front of her console at the office, gently massaging the sides of her head, breathing her version of the old nursery rhyme over and over, trying to will it to happen. Oh, how she hated these headaches! Ignoring the ringing in her ears, she took two more aspirin, washing them down with her diet drink. Then she forced her eyes to open wide against the pain, and once again she attacked the document on her screen.

Sitting for eight hours in a tiny cubicle staring at a computer screen was an impossibly difficult job. But the money was good, and, combining it with Ralph's income, she was somehow able to make ends meet.

They'd been married three years now, and she still didn't know if she had made the right decision. Ralph was a good man, but he was never home. He needed to work if the business was going to be a success, but sixteen hours a day seemed a bit much. And when he was home, he still left the family problems on her shoulders.

Then there was June, Ralph's eldest child. Elaine had tried with her, but the little girl glared rejection whenever she tried to be kind, and her defiant attitude was rubbing off on the younger children.

Again Elaine squinted her eyes shut against the pain. "Dear Heavenly Father," she breathed, "please take this pain away from me so I can get my work done."

1:30 P.M.

"Wh-when do I get my furniture back?" Abby Martin stood with the telephone to her ear, her entire body trembling with fear as she waited for her husband to respond. Around her stretched a practically empty home, stripped of all the furnishings that very morning while she had been at work. Still numb from shock, and still reeling from the ordeal John Martin was putting her and their seven children through, Abby was now doing her best to conquer her fear and face him squarely.

"Your furniture?" John Martin repeated.

"Yes, and my childrens' furniture."

John laughed. "That's crazy talk, Abby. You know as well as I do that I bought that furniture, not you. You haven't produced a lick of income in sixteen years."

"And you haven't done a lick of housework, John Martin, or anything else around this home!"

"Oh, come on, Abby, don't be stupid! In the division of labor you and I agreed on years ago, my task has been to provide a means of living for my family. I paid for that furniture and everything else you have, while you sat around writing stupid poems. Besides, you should have been there with the kids this morning. I could have you prosecuted for abandonment."

"But . . . but —"

John laughed. "Listen to you, stammering with guilt. You'd just better hope I don't prosecute. You know, Abby, the longer I'm away, the happier I am that you drove me out."

"I *what?*"

"You heard me. And stop screaming! You're out of control again."

Tears streaming down her face, Abby did her best to regain her composure. "John, I never drove you out, and you *know* it!"

"Obviously," the man's voice retorted calmly, "we have a difference of opinion. Since I now have the furniture as well as the income, and things are going so well for me, I would say that was an indication of which of us has the correct opinion."

"But John, think of your children! What are they to do?"

Still the man's voice remained calm, almost automated. "You should have thought of them earlier. And that reminds me. Isn't this about the time you buy the kids their summer clothes?"

"Yes, but —"

"Well, I want to put you on notice, Abby. I called the bank yesterday and canceled your VISA card. I assume they'll be contacting you about the outstanding balance. I told them that was your responsibility."

"But you already lowered the credit limit two months ago. Besides, those charges were for family expenses."

John laughed again. "According to you. But again, Abby, you should have thought of that before you drove me out. Now you're on your own, and as far as I am concerned, you deserve nothing more."

"John," Abby said, breathing deeply as she fought for sanity, "you can't do that! I have no means of supporting these children — your children. You know that! You must help me."

With a sinking feeling she listened as her husband laughed his quiet, measured laugh and then hung up. Then, with tears falling freely, she slowly hung up the phone and sank into the one remaining living-room chair, powerless to stop this thing from happening!

"Mom?"

Looking down through tear-filled eyes, Abby saw that her next-to-youngest son was gazing up at her, a worried expression on his face. Reaching out, she lifted him onto her lap, and then for a few moments she hugged him close, rocking her body back and forth.

"You okay, Mom?" he finally asked.

"I . . . I'm fine, Michael."

"Was Daddy mean to you, too?"

Sharply Abby looked down at her son. "Daddy was mean to you?" she questioned.

Michael nodded solemnly. "When those men came this morning, Mark tried to stop them from taking all our stuff. Daddy yelled at him, and then he yelled at all of us. He said some nasty words, too. Just like before."

"I . . . I'm sorry, Michael," Abby whispered, her head swimming with pain. "I don't think he means to talk like that."

"Then why does he?"

"I . . . I don't know."

For a moment there was silence, and then Michael sat

up. "You know, Mom," he said as he looked around the room, "I kinda miss having a couch to sit on. But at least I have you. And that's better!"

1:35 P.M.

Claudia Nichol stood at the sink washing dishes, her mind numb. Her husband's food remained on the table, not because she wanted it to be there, but because she hadn't decided if she dared remove it. If she did and Bob came back home for it, he'd be angry, and that terrified her. Of course, if she didn't remove it and he came home later to find it still cluttering the table, he'd be angry over that. So Claudia stood at the sink, her hands woodenly performing their tasks, her mind trying to sort out what she should do next.

Eighteen years she had been married to Bob Nichol, eighteen years that were now a blur in her mind. Oh, she could remember good times, many of them, especially during their first year together. But gradually Bob had changed, growing more and more angry and inclined to violence. The worst part for Claudia was that she felt responsible for Bob's change. She had racked her brain again and again trying to discover what she had done. She had even asked Bob about it — once. But she wasn't about to go through that sort of pain again.

"If only I was smarter," Claudia scolded herself. "Before I started making mistakes with the checkbook, things were much better."

Drying her hands she began wiping the counter. "But I thought he was taking care of the bank balance. I just paid the bills. I wasn't extravagant, and he was earning good money!"

As Claudia sat down, she thought of Bob's anger when the overdraft notices had started pouring in. Not only had he taken her checkbook but he had put her on a terribly tight budget, and he had begun excluding her from other aspects of life as well.

Claudia looked on the wall at the baby pictures she still kept of Robby. He had been such a cute little tyke. Even though he had had so many health problems, he had brought such happiness into her life. But the closer she had grown to Robby, the more controlling Bob had become. He had even limited her budget to ten dollars a week, which had been impossible even that many years ago. With that she was supposed to buy food, gas for trips to the doctor, and everything else she needed.

Then Bob had put a lock on the mailbox so she couldn't touch the mail until he got home. She had become more and more isolated, and Bob had become incredibly critical of everything she did.

The one good decision she had made in those early years of her marriage, she now knew, had been to stop having children. And even that decision had been made almost by default. Bob's bedroom behavior had grown bizarre, so much that Claudia had become terrified of even having him home. When she had finally withdrawn from him, the beatings had started. Once, after she had been five minutes late getting his dinner ready, he had knocked her down the stairs. She had been unconscious for an hour, and so he had finally taken her to the hospital, where he had told the doctor she had slipped, bruising her face in the fall.

Bob's anger had begun to shift after that, and within a year or so Robby was taking the brunt of it. Claudia had hated it, but she had been so relieved to be free of pain that she had dared do nothing to protect her son. Of course she knew she was a terrible person for that, a very terrible person. But she had been so afraid —

"You're such a cowardly woman," Claudia muttered to herself as she straightened the pictures on the wall. "When Bob hurts you or Robby, what do you do? You never dare stand up to him! All you ever do is pray, asking God to solve it for you."

Prayer had worked, too, she thought ruefully. At least a little. Bob didn't beat them as much as he had once. Instead, when he had his temper tantrums, he usually just broke things around the house, blaming Robby for it once it had been done.

But the strangest part of all was that Bob's violent nature somehow continued to remain hidden from others. Neighbors and what few friends they had didn't suspect. Even at church they were treated as normal ward members. And Bob had a gift, he truly did. He was smart, and he knew all the right words. He frequently bore his testimony, and several times he had been Gospel Doctrine teacher, wowing the people with his great knowledge.

That had bothered Claudia, for she wondered how Bob could have the Spirit with him. And yet he must have it, or he could not impress so many really fine people. No, it was her—weak, stupid Claudia—who had been the problem in their marriage. And she was going to change things, too. Just as soon as she could decide what to do.

But first, she had to decide whether or not to remove Bob's food from the table.

4

TUESDAY, MAY 28

1:45 P.M.

With a final stroke, Frank completed the single page of writing that, with a little work, would become his next bishop's message in the ward newsletter. Pulling the page free of the typewriter, he quickly scanned it for typos. One, he finally concluded. Not bad for an old man who typed with just three fingers.

Thinking back, Frank recalled vividly how he had come to understand the concept he had just written of. He knew he had a gift for getting along with kids. His students trusted him, and he was a fairly popular teacher. But a few years before, his popularity had become a real threat to another teacher, who began trying to undermine him.

Feeling bad about that, he had spoken about it to Jeanee, who had immediately pointed out that the other teacher had placed herself in the position of being his enemy. Then his wife had shown him a couple of scriptures about praying for enemies, and with a sly wink she had challenged him to memorize and then live them. Frank had done just that, and by the end of the school year he had been astonished to realize that the other teacher had become his staunchest friend and ally.

Now this lesson had become a bishop's message to his ward. Glancing down, he read the scripture he still had memorized from so long before. It was from the 33rd chapter of Alma in the Book of Mormon:

3 Do ye remember to have read what Zenos, the prophet of old, has said concerning prayer or worship?

4 For he said: Thou art merciful, O God, for thou hast heard my prayer, even when I was in the wilderness; yea, thou wast merciful when I prayed concerning those who were mine enemies, and thou didst turn them to me. . . .

10 Yea, and thou hast also heard me when I have been cast out and have been despised by mine enemies; yea, thou didst hear my cries, and wast angry with mine enemies, and thou didst visit them in thine anger with speedy destruction.

"Brothers and sisters," Frank had then written, "if a person gains an enemy, it is easy to be angry and even to hate. But the promise is clear; if we gain an enemy and then sincerely pray for him, in his own time God through His Son will bring to pass one of two things. Either He will turn our enemy back to us in support and friendship, or He will visit him with speedy destruction. Is such a promise not worth our casting aside our anger, our slights and wrongs, fancied or real, and joining in prayer for our enemies?"

The message concluded with Frank's personal testimony, which was short and to the point. Frank wasn't certain why this particular message seemed like the right one, but he didn't question his inspiration, either. He had learned more than once during the past two years the importance of acting on the spiritual promptings he was given.

"Life is simple," he thought, smiling, "when we simply live the gospel."

1:50 P.M.

"Busy, Frank?"

Spinning in surprise, Frank knocked his jar of extra

pencils to the floor. "Hi, Mrs. O.," he said, smiling lamely, "I didn't hear you come in."

"And I didn't mean to startle you," Mrs. O. replied by way of apology as she stooped with Frank to pick up pencils. A friendly, outgoing woman, Mrs. O. had announced when she had transferred to the school that though she had a first name as well as a rather lengthy last one, she was quite comfortable being called Mrs. O., by students and teachers alike. Frank had started calling her that, and now his use of the name had become a habit.

"Only," she continued, "you looked so engrossed."

Frank smiled. "Bad habit of mine. In a kid it's called daydreaming. I think I'm supposed to have outgrown it."

"And you haven't?" Mrs. O. teased.

"Not hardly. I guess that means I'm still just a big overgrown kid."

"That's what makes you so popular! I knew there had to be a reason, but I always suspected bribery."

Frank laughed. "I'd do that, too, if I could."

"Me too." Mrs. O. smiled. "You know, as much as I like the kids, I really enjoy this PE time."

"Yeah." Frank smiled. "They say a break is as good as a rest, and to me this is both."

"Agreed. What are your plans for the summer?"

Frank sighed. "Do you have a lot of time for an answer? First, we're going to see our son and his wife. I'll finally be able to spend some time with my grandkids."

"That's right, you are a grandfather. I'd forgotten."

"Scary, isn't it." He grinned.

"I'll say. Frank, I was wondering if you were planning on going to school."

"I'm afraid so. I hope this will be my last summer on that graduate degree. Why do you ask?"

"Oh, I'll be up there too, and I'm going to need a private study room —"

"And you want me to be your roommate. Right?"

Mrs. O. nodded. "If we both applied, I think we could get one this year."

"Great idea! Let's do it."

"All right, Frank. I'll apply." Then Mrs. O. looked out the window. "Say, isn't that June McCrasky over there, sitting alone?"

Frank looked at where Mrs. O. was pointing. "That's her, all right."

"She's in your ward, isn't she?"

"She is. I'll tell you what, Mrs. O., that little girl is the best-behaved kid in our Primary. Whichever one of us gets her next year is really going to have a star pupil."

"Maybe she'll be a star pupil, Frank. But I'm very concerned about some other issues."

Surprised, Frank turned to look at the other teacher. "What do you mean?"

"I mean," Mrs. O. responded tentatively, "that I'm afraid poor little June has some difficult emotional problems."

"I wouldn't have guessed that," Frank stated instantly. "She's a hard worker, concerned about others, and always trying to find out what more she can do in the ward to help out. She also works hard around her home. Add to that the straight A grades she has this year, and you can see what I mean."

"Oh, I see what you mean, Frank." Mrs. O. smiled. "I don't think you see what I mean, though."

"Then run it past me another time," Frank said.

"Have you noticed how she always sits alone?"

"Yeah. She's studying."

"Have you ever seen her with friends?"

"I . . . well . . . she sure leads the kids in Primary."

"Do any of them sit by her?"

"Well, I . . . uh . . . "

"You haven't noticed, have you."

Slowly Frank shook his head.

"Did you know her mother was killed in an accident when June was in first grade?"

"I knew that, but it was quite a while ago, before they moved into our ward."

"I think that's related to her loneliness now."

Frank shook his head. "Mrs. O., I respect what you're saying. But that's four years ago. Kids get over things like that. They forget. Besides, that little girl does *everything* right."

"Which is precisely why I'm worried, Frank. June isn't a fun-loving little kid like she's supposed to be. Instead, she's a worry-wart adult in a little girl's body." Again Mrs. O. looked out the window, open in the early summer heat. "Just look at her and think about her. She's a lonely little adult-pleaser, all because she thinks of herself as an adult and wants us to accept her as one."

"Interesting," Frank declared, impressed by the observation. "And you think this is related to her mother's death?"

"Probably. I believe a great pain, most likely her mother's death, has caused June to abandon her childhood, and now she's a lost little girl trying to be an adult who doesn't know where to cry for help."

"I wonder if her family is helping her with that?"

Mrs. O. looked disgusted. "Frank, you're their neighbor. Answer your own question."

And sadly, Frank did. Sister McCrasky. Who in Frank's neighborhood could fail to recognize that woman's voice? Through his back fence and two doors down, she stood all too often on the wooden deck overlooking her backyard, berating some or all of her children. It was not done quietly, it was not done discreetly, and it was certainly not done with the idea of enhancing the childrens' self-esteem. Instead it was like a personal attack, and Frank hated to be forced to listen to it.

"So you think June's problems go back beyond her family situation?" he asked, sobered into considering it.

"I do."

"Well, that really gives me something to consider—"

A noisy scuffle in the hallway took Mrs. O. scurrying through the door, and Frank was left alone to watch the little girl who had suddenly become an enigma.

2:15 P.M.

Jeanee stopped the car in front of the address Frank had given her over the phone and reached across the seat to the box with the dinner she had prepared. As she closed the car door and walked up the cracked cement walkway to the house, she felt strangely unsettled.

Why hadn't she reached out to Abby Martin before? Was it the uncomfortable feelings she had about Brother Martin that had stopped her? She didn't know. She had felt the same hesitancy to open up to Carol Blodgett, and she had felt guilty about both situations. Unconsciously, without realizing her natural protective tendencies, Jeanee had avoided making friendships with both women.

Once she was at the door, she took a deep breath. Then, balancing the box of dinner against her hip, she reached up and knocked.

Relieved to see the dirty little face of Michael Martin as the door opened, a broad smile crossed her face. Jeanee always felt comfortable with little children.

"Is your mommy home?" She smiled down at the little child.

"Are you my mommy's friend?"

"I hope so." Jeanee smiled again as Abby Martin came around the corner from the kitchen, wiping her hands on the front of her shirt.

"Jeanee Greaves! What a surprise!" Abby smiled against

her own embarrassment. Then she turned to the little boy and urged him to go wash up in the bathroom.

"This isn't much, Abby," Jeanee declared, attempting to be at ease. "But it's what my own family has to put up with tonight."

Abby watched her little boy walk slowly down the hall. Then she turned to Jeanee, who appeared to feel more awkward than did Abby.

"Are you okay?" she asked.

Jeanee brushed the concern away. "It's just a busy time for us. We're getting ready for vacation, the kids are getting out of school, and that sort of thing. There's just a lot to be done. You know. Do you mind if I just put this in the kitchen?"

Abby pointed around the corner and then followed as Jeanee walked to the refrigerator and placed the dinner inside, not seeming to notice how bare the shelves were. Shutting the door slowly, she turned to look directly into Abby's eyes.

"I want you to know, Abby," she almost whispered, "that although we haven't had a chance to become close friends, you do have a friend in me." The words seemed to come from another source. And the feelings of love Jeanee was suddenly experiencing were so profound she felt almost overwhelmed. Without even considering her previous misgivings, Jeanee reached out and took Abby's hand. "Life doesn't always give us the breaks we deserve, Abby. And you and the children deserve far better than you are getting. I want you to know that."

Now it was Abby who was at a loss. Her nose began tingling. And try as she would, she couldn't pull her eyes away from Jeanee's soft, penetrating gaze. A tear escaped, then another, and immediately Abby was shaking with emotion.

In an instant Jeanee's arms were around her. "It's okay,

Abby. It's okay to cry," she comforted. "You don't deserve this. You truly deserve far better."

"I . . . I don't understand," Abby sobbed. "Why did this happen? I had no idea that John was even thinking of leaving us. And now, this? Look at my house. It's stripped! My children . . . we have nothing! And where do I turn?"

"I know, I know," Jeanee continued softly. "Sometimes things are hard to understand. I won't even try to tell you you're better off without him. I just want you to know that you deserve better than this. And better is on its way, Abby. You just hang onto that thought. Better is on its way."

The warmth of the experience filled Jeanee with a sense of peace and conviction. And Abby, trembling in her arms in her barren little kitchen, was suddenly a sister.

"Did Brother Blodgett get hold of you today?" Jeanee asked, recognizing that Abby's need was for more than just an evening meal. "Frank told me he asked him to drop by."

Abby sniffed her tears back, embarrassed at her outburst. "I . . . I'm sorry, Jeanee. I just—"

"Don't apologize, Abby. It's just that we all want to be sure that you and the children are taken care of."

Abby bit her lips and looked out the kitchen window, tears streaming down her cheeks. "Yes, Mel came over. He was very—" Then Abby's voice broke again. "I don't believe this is happening," she said. "I've always been the strong one."

"And it's so hard to accept help," Jeanee added.

"But the children—" Abby wiped her tears with the back of her hand. "They can't live on the little bit of nothing John has left them. How can a man do something like this? To his own children?"

"It's amazing what some men are capable of doing to their children," Jeanee whispered. Then, suddenly realizing that she was being too transparent, she turned so Abby couldn't see her eyes.

"Abby," she stated as she fought to keep her focus, "you're not alone. You have friends. Maybe some of them haven't let you know yet that they're there for you. But you'll see. You haven't been utterly deserted."

Then she turned back and looked into Abby's hollow eyes. "I'm sorry I haven't been closer to you in the past. I guess I've been wrapped up in my own little family and the busy schedules that Frank keeps. I don't know. But I'm here now, Abby."

"It's okay, Jeanee. I know you're busy . . . " Abby's voice trailed off.

"But I'm not too busy for you," Jeanee assured. "I'll be here anytime you need me. Day or night. Do you understand?"

Abby was shaken by Jeanee's open invitation of friendship. But she agreed.

"I hate to do this," Jeanee apologized, "but Angie's going to be home from school any minute, and I need to be there. I'll talk to you soon?"

Again Abby agreed.

"And you'll call me if I can do something?"

"I . . . I'll call," Abby agreed with a nod. "And thanks, Jeanee, for the dinner. It will help—a lot!"

As Jeanee drove away, she couldn't shake the feeling that something significant had just happened. What had been the invisible barrier that had kept her from getting close to Abby before? Whatever it had been, it was not there any longer.

2:45 P.M.

Robby Nichol sat beneath the old mulberry tree in Jenson's front yard. Across the street and three houses down from his own home, he had a clear view of his front door. He was watching it now, wondering if his dad was home. Robby detested himself for his cowardice, and yet—

If only the garage door had been open. Then he could easily see if his dad's car was there. But it was closed again, and he couldn't tell.

With a sigh he fell back in the grass, where he stared up through the new green leaves. He liked this tree. It was thick, and the leaves came almost to the ground, creating a sort of hiding place for him, a place of safety from which he could watch the world and remain essentially unseen. He came here often, hiding from the world while he tried to make sense of his crazy life.

And it was pretty crazy. It was as if he were two totally different people—the class clown at school and the hermit recluse at home. Robby grunted at the thought and wondered for the umpteenth time which person he really was. Of course, the kids at school who called him their friend would have been shocked that he thought of himself as a recluse. On the other hand, his dad and maybe even his mom thought of him as strange; they couldn't imagine him even having friends at all. Crazy!

His dad, Robby had long ago concluded, was a jerk who had most likely studied under Hitler. Democracy and free agency stopped at their front door, and tyranny reigned supreme. If Robby's dad told him to jump off a cliff, he would have to jump. No questions. If he argued or objected, wham! He was dead meat. And if he ever got mad, that was practically the same as committing suicide—serious pain. Then there were the inspections of his room, every day, just as if he were in the army. Every single tiny thing had to be in its place and perfect, or he was nailed. Once he had made the mistake of leaving a book out, and his dad had started yelling about how he was a disgusting pig and was going to turn out just like his mother. That had made Robby so angry that he had had to literally close down his mind for a little while and leave. Otherwise, he was certain that he probably would have been killed.

And what his dad did to his mom was even worse. He

didn't usually hit her anymore, but he had a way with his mouth that could make the most stable person in the world feel like two cents. In church he was real religious, but at home he had the foulest mouth Robby had ever heard—serious profanity and vulgarity. It was almost as if he had studied "Foul Mouth 101" in college, the way he could string those words together.

What drove Robby crazy, though, was the way his mom put up with it. She didn't have to, and Robby knew it. But try as he might to get her to see that, his mom couldn't catch the vision. "Mom," he'd plead, "just leave him. I'll get a job, and together we'll make out just fine. Come on, you deserve a better life than this."

But no, she wouldn't consider it. Worse, she would just sit there while his dad was ranting and raving, not saying a word, not even defending herself. It was the hardest thing in the world for Robby to watch.

Lately, though, Robby had been thinking of striking back. Maybe that'd shake the old man up a little. Maybe it would make him see what a total jerk he was being. Maybe it would wake his mom up, too. Even if she never defended him, that didn't mean he had to be a coward and sit by while she was being railed on. So yes, lately he'd been thinking about doing something.

Only, he thought as he stared out from under the safety of his mulberry tree, he was so doggone scared!

2:50 P.M.

Frank Greaves sat alone in his room, pondering deeply as he tidied up his desk. He had just had another visit from Mrs. O., wherein she had reminded him of the fact that she, too, had lost her mother at an early age. That, she had explained, was what made it so easy for her to see June McCrasky's problem.

Now, as Frank considered it, he felt certain that his

cousin was right. Which meant, among other things, that he needed to get June to sit down and talk with him. By talking she might just get her feelings out in the open, and then maybe he could help her deal with them.

As he sat in his empty classroom, quiet again except for the distant sounds of children boarding buses and heading homeward, Frank found himself wondering about his own childhood. Why had he been spared the pain and trauma that he saw occasionally in others? And he had been spared, he knew that. As Jeanee was so fond of saying, he had grown up with the real Brady Bunch. His home life had been happy, his parents had always supported and been there for him, he had known that they loved him, and he had been close to his brothers and sisters. In other words, he had been well-adjusted and happy. In fact, he remembered quite vividly the day, during his senior year, when he had discovered that life wasn't that way in all homes. Of course that one experience, where a girl in his class had run away from home, had been only that, an anomaly, a single event that was not normal. Until quite recently, that had been his conviction.

Of course, being bishop had shown him how crazy that idea was. Problems existed everywhere, and for some people they seemed to exist all the time. But somehow, even with all that understanding, he had not really thought of kids having problems. Now, after talking with Mrs. O., his mind had opened a little more widely, and he knew the Lord was directing him in how to be a better bishop.

He would work with June McCrasky, too, just as soon as he could find a way to visit with her.

"Bishop Greaves?"

Looking up, Frank was dumbfounded to see June once again standing in his doorway. "Hi, June," he managed to say. "I . . . I thought you would have gone home."

"I've been cleaning blackboards," she said with her metallic smile, "and I thought maybe I could clean yours while I was at it."

"Oh, sure. That'd be great. I was just . . . I . . . No, wait, June. Come on in and sit down. I've been wanting to visit with you, and now looks like a great time."

Obediently June walked forward and sat in a desk, facing him. "You wanted to talk with me?"

"That's right. I . . . uh . . . Well, are you excited to see summer here?"

"Oh, I guess so. I like school, though. Sometimes I wish it was school all year long."

Absently Frank nodded, listening and yet trying to think of some way to approach this little girl about her loneliness. Normally he had no trouble talking with children. But suddenly he was self-conscious, acutely aware of the vast differences in their backgrounds.

"Why are you cleaning the blackboards?" he finally asked, figuring that any question was better than an awkward silence.

"Well, somebody has to do it," June stated matter-of-factly. "You poor teachers are so overworked, and the custodian never has time to do it right. So I just thought I'd help out."

Adult-pleaser, Mrs. O. had called her. And suddenly Frank could see that Mrs. O. had been right. This little girl was trying to be an adult, trying desperately to get adults to accept her as one of them.

"Well," he said gently, "I'm sure the teachers appreciate your help, June. But to tell you the truth, I think you have plenty to do without taking more work on your shoulders."

June smiled brightly. "I'm used to it."

Puzzled, Frank made no comment. So June continued, "Mom always has her sick headaches when she's through working, so at home I do most of the cooking and cleaning. Then I have to help the boys with their assignments and do my own homework besides." June laughed. "Do you see what I mean, Bishop Greaves? I'm used to doing everybody else's jobs. I guess I just work best that way."

Startled by what he had heard, Frank pursued the subject of Sister McCrasky. "You say your mother has lots of sick headaches?"

June nodded. "Tons. Nearly every day. She has to work, you know, and I guess the pressure just sort of gets her down."

"That must be why she yells so much," Frank said thoughtfully, not even really speaking to the girl.

"She has a right to yell," June said defensively, once again startling Frank. "Besides, Mom doesn't yell that much, at least not any more than us kids deserve. I mean, what would you do, Bishop, if your husband was gone all the time and you had to work and still take care of a whole household of kids? You'd yell, and you'd yell loud." Frank listened carefully as the young girl justified her mother's actions. "I even have to yell at them, just to get them to sit down and do their homework," she continued emphatically. "Mom told me I'd come to it, and she was right. Why, sometimes I scream louder than she does."

Frank remained silent for a moment. Then, feeling totally uncomfortable, he rose to his feet.

"June, I feel real bad when I hear you say that, because I don't think Heavenly Father likes us to scream at each other. I just read in the scriptures today where He speaks in a still, small voice that is capable of piercing to the very center of a our beings. That doesn't sound like screaming to me. Does it to you?"

Slowly June shook her head.

"Besides," Frank continued, "I've done some dumb things in my life, and Heavenly Father has never screamed at me for them. Not once. In fact, the worse I get, the more quiet and gentle His voice becomes. June, I'll bet if you practice speaking in your home with a still, small voice, just like Heavenly Father does, you'll discover that before long your family will be paying more attention to you."

"Do you think so?" she asked hopefully.

"Absolutely."

For a moment June was silent, considering. Then she looked at Frank and with a bright smile, said, "Okay, I'll try."

For a moment after she was gone, Frank stood at the window, watching the girl skip down the sidewalk. Maybe he had helped her a little, though it was certainly hard to tell. Now if he could just figure out how to get to the issue of her mother's death . . .

5

TUESDAY, MAY 28

6:30 P.M.

Frank tossed the baseball to his son and then took off his catcher's mitt to rub his hand. "Man, kid," he groaned teasingly, "you've got to start taking it easy. Where did you get that arm?"

Erik grinned. "Too much stroganoff, huh, Dad. You just wait until my arm's really in shape."

"You get much faster, and you'll need a new catcher." Frank ignored the reference to his second helping of dinner.

"You'll do for a while." Erik teased. "Coach says I need to work a little on my control, but I've got the best speed in the school. He thinks next year, if I work at it real hard, I can make All-State. I think it'll more likely be my senior year, but I'm still going to go for it."

"How's your hitting?"

"Fair. I don't get many homers, but I'm pretty consistent at getting on base. My average is .360."

Frank scowled. "That's all?"

"Hey, Dad—"

"Relax," Frank chuckled. "My best year I only had a .275. But I can't just let you humiliate me in everything, can I? Not, at least, without giving you a hard time?"

Erik smiled widely, then wound up and burned another strike across the "plate" they'd rigged by the side of the house. Maybe a little high, Frank thought as he tossed it back, but then maybe it was in there, too. One thing though — it was certainly a fast pitch. Easily eighty miles an hour, and possibly a great deal faster. Erik had an arm, no doubt about it. Made a father proud, all right.

"Too bad we can't do this more often, huh?" Erik winked as he took his hand out of his mitt and wrapped the leather around the ball.

"We have to quit?" Frank objected. "It's not often the stake president cancels a Tuesday night meeting."

"Sorry, Dad. German . . . " Erik held his mitt under one arm and gestured helplessness with his hands.

"German can't wait?"

"Final tomorrow."

"Well, far be it from me to discourage a student who wants to study." Frank took his mitt off and walked toward his stepson. "We're both just too busy anymore. It never seems like there's enough time together." Erik stood almost eye-to-eye with him. "Why don't we plan something fun for family home evening the week after we get back from vacation?" Frank put his arm across his son's shoulders, and they began walking toward the house.

"How about swimming?" Erik suggested. "I'll cream you in a game of Marco Polo."

"You're on."

"How's he doing?" Jeanee asked as they walked in through the kitchen door. She was pouring orange juice into two tall glasses. "Not bad, not bad," Frank said as he tousled his son's hair. "You're almost getting too tall to do this to, you know that, sport?"

"You'll be looking up to me in no time," Erik teased, grabbing his orange juice and heading to his room. "Thanks, Mom." He raised the glass as he disappeared down the hall.

"I'm sorry about President Stone's mother," Frank said sympathetically. After a moment's thought he reached for a stack of mail on the counter and methodically went through it. "They were pretty close."

"I guess it was a blessing she went this quickly," Jeanee added.

"Hey," Frank said, looking at the bright side, "at least I get a night at home."

"And it's going to be wonderful!" Jeanee beamed.

"Promises, promises." Frank smiled. "How you do go on."

Sitting on one of the bar stools, he looked through the mail a second time. "The phone bill," he said finally. "Let's see what horror stories we find in here."

Jeanee winced as she turned the subject to something else. "Did you know that Erik is on the honor roll again?"

"Uh . . . really?" Frank was preoccupied.

"I overheard him talking to the Mickleson girl last night. He told her about it."

"Mmm," was the only response. Frank was marking phone numbers with his red grading pen.

"You know, the girl who just got her braces off." Jeanee started taking out the ingredients for chocolate chip cookies. "She's really turning into a pretty girl, don't you think?"

"Yeah, real pretty."

"I think he's going to ask her—"

Jeanee didn't get a chance to finish, because Frank was suddenly holding the telephone bill in front of her face. He didn't need to say anything. The red checks said it all.

"I'm sorry," Jeanee said as she scrunched her face into a little-girl pout. "It's just that, well, you know I've been worried about Megan and the baby. The doctors can't decide why this pregnancy is so difficult. And—"

"I know you're worried," Frank interrupted. "But honey, we live on a teacher's salary. Does Tony have to call collect?"

"I'm sorry. We'll do better, I promise." Jeanee almost

whined. "I can take some out of the insurance money if you want me to."

"No, no. We agreed that's for emergencies only."

"But this is—"

"No, I can cover it. Besides, Kent Bailey has some cabinet work he wants me to help with. That will mean a little extra in the budget. But really, honey, you do need to be more careful."

"It won't happen again."

Frank walked away. "We're going to be there in a week. Try to wait until then to get caught up?" Taking a handful of chocolate chips from the open package, Frank downed them, knowing he could get away with it this time.

"You always know when you have the advantage, don't you." Jeanee smiled.

"Honey, with you I've always got the advantage." Frank reached around her and took another bunch of chips.

"Only because I let you have it," Jeanee said with a laugh, slapping at the back of her husband's hand. "Now that's enough! I need some for the cookies."

"Did I hear cookies?" Angie giggled, racing around the corner in her stocking feet. "Can I help, Mommy?"

"There's always room for helping hands." Jeanee smiled, quoting the plaque that hung above the stove. "Here, Angie, you can help me crack the eggs."

Frank kissed his wife on the cheek. "I'll be in my study if you need me. I've got to unwind."

"A lot going on, huh?"

Frank shrugged his shoulders and shook his head. "It's that time of year. I just need a little music therapy." Then he grabbed the stack of bills and his planner and with a complete change of posture took on the attitude of a '50s teenager. "Nothing a little rockin' around the clock won't help." He grinned mischievously.

The harsh screams of an angry woman interrupted

Frank's exit. Through the kitchen window they all heard the shrill voice of their neighbor, Elaine McCrasky.

"Poor Elaine," Jeanee said softly, her voice filled with compassion.

"Poor kids, I say," Frank responded. "They're the ones she's screaming at."

"I don't think she means to do that," Jeanee replied, defending her neighbor.

"I'm glad you don't sound like that, Mommy," Angie declared, looking at Jeanee with wide, blue eyes.

"Who could ever scream at you?" Jeanee wiggled her nose at her daughter.

"Certainly not your mother." Frank turned to leave a second time. "She's such a softy, she can't even say no to a collect phone call." Jeanee ignored the dig, and Angie didn't understand it. "I'll be leaving you now." Frank again announced his exit.

The continual shrieks and threats from Sister McCrasky's house followed Frank into his study. Putting on his headphones he felt suddenly thankful for modern technology. If only June and her little brothers could tune their mother out as easily as he could. Of course, maybe they did, in their own way. Maybe Elaine wasn't even aware of how terrible she sounded. After all, how could she continue if she knew that every neighbor within earshot was wincing at her lack of self-control?

For a moment Frank thought again about what Mrs. O. had said about June. Was she really lonely and miserable? Could she still be grieving the death of her mother, even after four years?

Frank thought of his own time of grief—the years during which he had cared for his sweet Christine. He had done his grieving while she was still alive, though seeing her pain as she slowly slipped from this world had been almost more than he could bear. But still, his time for sorrow had ended incredibly soon, the day he had first shaken hands with Jeanee.

"Grief. Who understands it?" he muttered as he turned on the Righteous Brothers' "You've Lost That Loving Feeling." "For some people it's over so quickly, while for others it takes a lifetime. Why is that?"

" . . . and it's gone, gone, gone. And I can't go on. Wo, wo, wo." The song was ending when Angie bounced through the doorway, making the sign for telephone.

Flipping up his headset, Frank turned in his chair and picked up the phone on his desk. "Hello? . . . Yes, this is Bishop Greaves. . . . Yes . . . yes . . . "

Frank felt himself go cold inside. "I'll be there in ten minutes," he said as he pulled off his headphones. Then he turned to Angie, who was still waiting by the door.

"You gotta go, huh, Daddy?"

"I'm afraid so, Princess. Want to give Daddy a hug and a kiss goodnight?"

"Uh-huh. Want me to save you some cookies?"

"You'd better!" Frank hugged his little girl.

"Promise you won't be gone too long?"

"If it means cookies, I promise."

"Jeanee," he said as he reentered the kitchen. "There's a ward emergency. I've got to run."

"Oh, honey," she sighed. "I thought we were finally going to get to spend some time together." Then she caught herself and quickly added. "But it can wait."

"You sure?" Frank probed. He didn't have a choice, but he wanted to somehow let Jeanee know that she was more important to him than anyone else.

"Oh, I'm sure," Jeanee responded with a bright smile. "We can talk when you get back."

Frank grabbed a jacket from the hall closet, all the time watching his wife putter with the cookie dough. Something was bothering her. In spite of the teasing she'd done earlier, he could sense a melancholy in her countenance that reminded him of her insecurities the first two or three years of their marriage.

"I won't be gone any longer than I have to be," he promised, turning her around for a kiss. As he held her close for a moment, Frank again felt his wife's sadness. "If it wasn't an emergency—"

"I know," Jeanee encouraged. "It's fine, really."

Frank walked out into the evening air with an uneasy feeling in the pit of his stomach. What was it? he asked himself. What was bothering him? . . .

7:30 P.M.

Thirteen-year-old Tess Blodgett hurried through the door of her home, fearing to glance at the clock. "Hi, Mom," she said, forcing a smile.

"Don't 'Hi' me, young lady," Carol Blodgett scolded from her position before the stove. "You're four hours late from school, and I've had to hold supper for you. I want an explanation."

"Uh . . . Daddy picked me up," Tess said hesitantly, acutely aware of her sister Tish's eyes, "and we went for a ride."

"You'll have to do better than that," Carol declared as she put a casserole back in the oven. "I talked to your father earlier, and all he did was groan and moan about how much he had to do. Now, where have you really been? The truth this time!"

With a shrug of helplessness toward her older sister, Tess stepped to the stove. "Uh . . . Jackie and I got talking," she said as she took a spoon and scooped some frosting from the edge of a new cake. "And, well, I just sort of lost track of the time."

"Tess," Carol scolded again, "you've got to start paying more attention to what's going on around you. Empty-headed girls aren't attractive to anybody, and one of these days, that's going to be important to you."

"I know, Mom," Tess said humbly while Tish looked on in helpless concern. "I'll do better, I promise."

"I hope so. Besides, you should know by now that the truth always feels better than a lie. Now go get washed up, both of you. We won't be waiting for your dad tonight."

Tess walked out of the room licking the rest of the frosting from the spoon, and shortly she was joined in the bathroom by her older sister.

"Again?" Tish whispered fiercely.

Tess simply nodded her head as she ran the water and began to furiously scrub her hands.

"What are we going to do, Tess? This is getting crazy!"

"I don't know, but I hate it! I hate feeling dirty all the time! I hate knowing we're the only sluts in the school!"

"Don't *say* that word!"

"I . . . I'm sorry, Tish."

"Just don't say it again. Did you tell Daddy how you feel?"

Tess looked scornfully at her older sister. "Get real, Tish."

Tish looked out the window, feeling absolutely helpless. "I . . . I told him one time that I didn't want to play."

"What'd he do?" Tess asked, immediately interested.

"Made me feel guilty, like it was me being gross, and not him. No kidding, Tess, I really felt like a creep."

"So, did you play?"

Tish shook her head.

"Gee," Tess declared, "maybe I could do that, too. I went for a walk tonight after he dropped me off, a long walk, and that's what I kept thinking about—making him stop. Tish, I mean it! Next time he wants to play, I'm going to tell him no."

Tish looked suddenly miserable.

"What's wrong?" Tess demanded.

"What if he turns to Trace?"

"Uh-uh," Tess argued scornfully. "He wouldn't ever — "

Slowly Tish nodded affirmatively.

"How do you know?"

"Because," Tish answered, her voice low, "he started playing his games with you the same night I told him no."

Shocked, Tess could only look at her older sister.

"And Trace will be in second grade this fall. I guess that's why I'm so scared. She's too young to have to go through all this crap. Tess, are you still with me on that promise?"

"You mean about Trace?"

"Uh-huh." Tish didn't tell her sister that she had been only four when their father had started "playing games" with her.

"It's scary, Tish, really scary." Tess protested.

"I know. Are you with me?"

For a long moment Tess stared into the mirror, contemplating her first major facial blemish. "I hate zits!" she finally snarled. "They are sooo gross! A girl at school said that being a slut causes zits. Do you believe that?"

"Tess!"

Horrified at her mistake, the younger girl stared at her sister. "I . . . uh . . . I'm sorry, Tish. I didn't mean it."

"I hope not," Tish declared solemnly, "because it's wrong, and I've told you that enough times that you ought to know it."

"I know. And I really am sorry."

"Well," Tish said after a long moment, "are you with me?"

"Tish, I . . . I don't know. I think so, but I am sooo scared!"

"Girls!" Carol Blodgett yelled from the kitchen, "I'm not going to call you again. Now get in here for dinner."

"Coming, Mom," Tish called back. Then, taking her

sister's arm, she squeezed it roughly. "Tess, we'll talk about this later. And I don't blame you for being scared. So am I. But just think of little Trace . . . "

7:45 P.M.

Frank sat in the kitchen of the Nichol home, waiting for Claudia Nichol to reply to his question. It was very quiet. In the light overhead a moth circled, diving and battering itself against the fixture, attracted to the light but trying desperately to get away from it. In the corner lay the remnants of a chair, broken and tossed aside before his arrival. There were also broken plates and glasses on the floor, and the window over the sink was shattered.

"Claudia," Frank said again, speaking gently, "tell me what happened here. What happened to Robby?"

Slowly Claudia Nichol raised her tear-streaked face. "He . . . he's gone, Bishop. He ran away. He said some awful things, and then he left . . . "

"And Bob? Your husband, Claudia?"

"He's gone after him, to . . . to try to find him and bring him back before he does something awful."

"Can you tell me why Robby ran away?"

Slowly Claudia dropped her eyes, remaining silent.

"Claudia, what happened here? When you called, I could hear some sort of fight in the background."

Her face lowered so that Frank could not see her eyes, Claudia responded slowly, her voice flat and dead. "Robby . . . just broke things. He went crazy. Bob started to . . . well, he asked him a question, and Robby just went crazy. It's just that he's lonely, Bishop. He doesn't have any friends, so he doesn't know how to act. Ever since he became a teenager, Robby argues with Bob whenever they're here at the same time. I hate it!"

Frank took a deep breath. "Claudia, I've got to ask you a hard question."

"What . . . is it?"

"Outside, the police told me that Bob has been questioned two or three times about, well, beating Robby up was the way they put it. Claudia, did that happen here tonight?"

Softly Claudia sobbed. "Why . . . do you ask me things like that?" she finally asked. "You know Bob, Bishop. He's a good man. He loves us—he loves Robby. Maybe sometimes he uses stern measures to teach him. But beat him up? Who's spreading those vicious lies, Bishop?"

Frank sighed. "No one's spreading anything, Claudia." There was an uncomfortable pause. "How did Robby break his arm last year?"

"He . . . he fell."

"Claudia, look at me!"

Slowly Claudia raised her haunted, burning eyes. "Why are you doing this? He fell! Period!"

"You're certain?"

With a cry Claudia rose from the table. "He fell! I saw him, and I resent what you are trying to do to me!"

Slowly Frank rose to his feet. "I didn't mean to offend you, Sister Nichol. It's just that—"

"I . . . I'm sorry I called you. Now, please leave my home."

"Claudia," Frank pressed gently, "I need the truth."

"And you have it," Claudia said wearily, tired of fighting. "I just want you to go now. Please leave—"

The ringing of the wall phone interrupted her, and as Frank turned toward the door, Claudia answered it. For a moment she was silent, listening, and then slowly she hung up and turned toward Frank.

"There, you see?" Claudia asked bitterly. "The police have arrested Robby, and he's down at the county jail. He was walking down the street breaking out every single window he passed. Every single window!" Her voice broke with emotion. "Do you hear me, Bishop? Robby . . . broke every—"

And with that, Claudia Nichol burst into deep sobs and fled down the darkened hallway.

8:00 P.M.

Outside the bedroom window a robin was making a funny chirping sound, signaling that night would soon be closing in. Jeanee lay on her bed, looking up at the ceiling with tear-stained cheeks, listening, thinking to herself.

The day hadn't gone as she had planned. No sewing done. No packing for vacation. No time with Frank—that was the worst part. For some reason, Jeanee was feeling terribly insecure.

Turning over on her bed, she reached for her open journal and began writing.

> *Oh, Frank, why did you have to leave tonight? I needed you so badly. Couldn't you see it in my eyes? I don't know what it is, but something is dreadfully wrong. It's been churning inside me all day, and it just keeps getting worse.*
>
> *I tried my best to be cheerful and supportive tonight. Why didn't you know that I was just putting on a brave front? Don't you know, after eight years together, that I only get very cheerful when I'm really struggling?*
>
> *I don't know if it was the news about Sister Stone, or the visit from my old friend Marie (I have to talk to you about Marie). Or maybe it was the silent desperation I saw in Abby Martin's eyes. Or maybe it's a door that opened in my mind while I was swimming today, a door that has kept a silent, closed vigil for so many years. I'm afraid to tell you what's behind that door, afraid that if you knew the truth, you might not love me anymore. I don't understand why that old secret is tugging its way free. And yet, I want to open all of me to you—to know that you know me, really know me, and still love me.*
>
> *What is this aching I feel? I don't know. But something deep and destructive is tearing at my soul. And I can't find any*

*comfort except on my knees. Why aren't you here beside me? Is
another crisis more important than my own? And why do I feel
like I'm having a crisis? What has happened? I feel a numb
gray wall closing in around me, with a sadness, an emptiness
I don't understand. And it's swallowing me in its silent grip.*

Jeanee looked up from her journal. The clock read
8:10. "Maybe," she said to herself, "he'll be back soon."

From the kitchen downstairs, she could hear Angie
scolding Erik for taking too many cookies.

"Those are for Daddy!" she protested loudly.

"I'm doing him a favor," Erik teased back. "Too much
sugar isn't good for an old man."

"Erik!" Jeanee called out, getting up from the bed.
"Give it a rest. Angie promised her father —"

"Just teasing, Mom," Erik interrupted. "I already put
'em back."

"Mom," Angie called up, "can I watch *Flight of the Nav-
igator* before I go to bed?"

By then, Jeanee was standing at the head of the stairs
with a bleary look in her eyes. "That'll be fine," she responded weakly. "But get your jammies on first, and go
right to bed after it's over."

It wasn't usual for her to give in on the 9:00 bedtime,
but at that moment she had no resistance.

"Jammies on, jammies on!" Angie squealed, running
up the stairs toward her room.

Jeanee winced.

"How's the headache?" Erik asked from the foot of the
stairs. "Any better?"

"I'll be fine, honey. I just need to rest for a while."

"Need a footrub?"

Jeanee smiled at her son's thoughtfulness. "No, honey,"
she answered. "I just need some down-time."

"Yeah," Erik beamed, "that's what I'm looking forward
to, too. Good ol' summer vacation —" He made a gesture
with his hands as if he were steering a car —"and freedom."

"When does your driver's ed class start?" Jeanee asked.

"The week after we get back from Tony's. Mom, are you sure you're okay?"

"I'll be fine, Erik. Really. Would you keep an eye on Angie for me?"

"Sure, Mom. No problem. You just get some rest. I'll finish up my German, and then I'll—"

"If Dad hasn't come home by the time Angie's show is over," Jeanee interrupted, "come up for prayer. Okay? And if I'm asleep, wake me."

"You got it. I—Hey, Angie, don't bother Mom. She needs some quiet time."

"I won't bother her," Angie promised, appearing from her room in a Little Mermaid nightshirt and fuzzy slippers. "I'll be as quiet as a mouse. Night, Mommy." She hugged Jeanee around the waist and then ran down to the family room, smiling as if she were getting away with something.

"What's the matter with me?" Jeanee asked herself as she walked back into the quiet of her bedroom. "I should be the happiest woman in the world. There's so much pain around me, and here I am with a wonderful family, my health, the gospel, a good husband. How can I be depressed when I have so much?"

She picked up her journal and sat on the bed, reading through what she had written. "Wow," she silently scolded herself, "you are in pretty deep, Jeanee. You only wax this poetic when you are really hurting. But what is it?"

She picked up her pen and resumed writing:

Marie, why does your pain frighten me? How can I help you? I can't separate myself from your silent cries. They stir something so deep that I can't find my own balance. You have to find your answers in the gospel of Jesus Christ, but how do I tell you that without frightening you away? Can I tell you why I understand your pain?

And Abby, sweet, deserted Abby. I see myself in you. That desperation hidden behind your stiffened smile. I know that trick so well, Abby. I hope you know that I am here for you. I'll pray for you. I'll be your friend. You're not alone.

Oh, Father in Heaven, I don't understand this pain. I'm drowning in a vast emptiness that strangles me until I can't breathe! What is it? Is it for someone else? It feels like it's for me, but how can that be when I've already put it all behind me? Am I supposed to tell Frank about my past? Is that what it is? I think I would have told him tonight, if he'd been here. I want to tell him, to have him hold me and tell me that I'm okay—that I don't need to be afraid anymore. Only—

"Mom? Mommy?"

Angie's strident voice broke through the barrier Jeanee had mentally placed at the bedroom door, and, with a sigh, she lowered her pen. "What is it, darling?"

"I'm sorry to bother you, Mommy, but . . . is your ringer turned off?"

"Ringer?"

"Yeah, telephone ringer."

Jeanee looked toward the telephone and remembered that she had turned it off when she had first lain down. "I guess so," she replied with a shrug.

"It's Tony," Angie continued. "He wants to talk to you."

"Oh, dear." Jeanee winced, reaching for the telephone on the nightstand. "I hope he didn't call collect."

8:20 P.M.

Jeanee listened to her son's voice, her hand trembling as she gripped the receiver. "I don't think I heard you right, Tony. What did you say happened to Amber?"

"Mother," Tony spoke in a low, controlled voice, "she was molested—raped."

"That's not possible!"

"I'm only calling you now," Tony continued, "so you'll have a chance to get used to the idea before—"

"No, Tony! Not Amber! Not our little Amber!" Jeanee's

chest felt as if it were being crushed inward, and her entire being was spinning into an abyss.

"I knew how this would affect you, Mom. That's why I couldn't wait until you got here. Amber will need us to be—"

Jeanee could barely hear her son on the other end of the line. The turmoil raging in her mind was too loud. From the very depths a blackness was ripping itself open, an anger Jeanee had never allowed herself to feel.

"No! No! Tell me it isn't true! Tell me, Tony! Oh, please—"

"It's true, Mom," Tony continued calmly. "A babysitter's teenage brother did it. He's fourteen years old. His name's Benjamin Brattles."

"I can't—hear this, honey!" Jeanee began to cry. "I can't hear you saying these things—as if you were telling me about the weather. Tony, how can you be so calm? Do you realize what you're telling me? You're saying—Oh, Tony, where's your anger?"

"Mom—"

"I mean it! How's Megan taking this?"

"Mother," Tony responded in a low, controlled voice, "it's for Megan that I have to stay calm. If she doesn't get all the support she needs right now, she could lose the baby."

Deep, uncontrollable sobs began wracking Jeanee's body. She fought for control, but the anger inside was ripping her apart. "Tony," she finally whispered, "I'm sorry, honey, but I'm going to have to hang up now. I'll call you back in a little while. I just can't—"

"I understand, Mom," Tony answered. "I'm sorry I had to call and tell you this."

Jeanee dropped the receiver in its cradle and threw herself onto the bed, screaming loudly into her pillow. "It isn't true!" she cried out. "It isn't true! Not our little Amber! Not our baby! Somebody please tell me it isn't true! . . . "

6

TUESDAY, MAY 28

9:30 P.M.

"I don't know why I did it, Mister . . . I mean, Bishop Greaves."

Frank smiled. "Old habits die hard, don't they, Robby."

Ever since their year together in the sixth grade, Frank had held a soft spot in his heart for Robby. And it was difficult to see him so distant and unresponsive.

Looking around the interrogation room of the jail where they were seated, he prayed silently for inspiration. And as it became obvious that Robby was going to remain mute, Frank found himself thinking of his wife, wondering how she was getting along.

Frank had come to know her very well — well enough to realize that his leaving had bothered her. Only, what was he supposed to do about it? He couldn't just not go. There was something vital he needed to do for this poor, broken youth.

Suddenly, from another corner of his mind, the message he had written earlier, about praying for enemies, filled his mind. And almost with excitement, he wondered if the Lord had placed that principle there because he needed to teach it to Robby, as well as his parents. That made sense! If the three of them would just start praying for each other —

"Bishop?"

"Yes, Robby?" Frank was happy to have the silence broken.

"Did you see my dad?"

"I didn't. He was out looking for you when I got to your home."

"Is that what Mom said?"

"Uh-huh."

"What else did my mom say?"

Frank took a deep breath. "I asked her if there had been a fight, and she told me you had broken some things and then left."

"That's it?"

"Pretty much." Frank looked at the youth, struck by the surprise and fear in his voice.

With a strangled cry of pain Robby slammed his fist onto the table. And then, almost as if he was unaware of Frank's presence, he dissolved into long, wracking sobs that shook his entire body. And rhythmically, while he sobbed, he continued beating the table with his fist.

"Robby, are you all right?" Frank probed, feeling absolutely helpless.

"Su . . . sure," the boy lied as he wiped at his eyes.

"Then tell me what's going on. The police told me your dad has a history of hitting you."

Startled, Robby looked up. But then, quickly, he dropped his eyes again. "He . . . he doesn't hit me much — anymore."

Frank, listening to Robby's statement, noticed that, as he spoke, the youth was clasping and unclasping his hands in a very agitated manner.

"Robby," he said slowly, thinking for a moment of the irony of his earlier conversation with Kent Bailey, "I'm concerned about what I'm hearing, from you and from your mother. Can you help me with something?"

Robby looked up with vacant eyes.

"Do you think that when your father gets mad and hits

you, that he's being abusive? Would you classify it that way?"

"No," Robby was adamant. "He yells and screams a lot, and once in a while I get nailed pretty good — like any other kid. But I . . . I'm not abused."

Something about the way Robby had said the word *nailed* caused Frank to pursue Robby's definition of the word. As it turned out, Robby was "nailed" on an average of two or three times a week, usually with a belt. Nor did it take much for him to incur such a beating — a defiant word, a below-par report card, or a forgotten chore. Frank ached as he learned that any of these "crimes" was sufficient to bring down Robby's father's wrath. Neither did the man seem to care where he hit — back, legs, arms, hands, butt, once even his head. And with all this, Robby insisted he was not abused.

"Robby," Frank asked, his mind reeling with the enormity of what he was hearing, "how badly are you usually hurt?"

"I've never bled, or anything like that."

"Are you scared of your father?"

Robby winced. "Every kid's scared of his dad."

"Are you ever going to get married, Robby?"

Surprised at the change in direction, Robby looked up at Frank. "Yeah, I guess I am. Someday."

"If you have kids, do you want them to be scared of you?"

Robby dropped his eyes and went to wringing his hands again.

"Robby, if you saw a kid in school who had the same marks on his body that you have tonight, would you think that was right?"

Again Robby didn't answer. But his tears told an anguished Frank all he needed to know.

"Bishop," Robby finally whispered, "I . . . I'm really

getting a stomachache. Do you . . . do you have to ask these questions?"

9:35 P.M.

Frantically Jeanee scrubbed at the tub, expending enormous energy as she forced herself beyond the pain tearing at her soul. It was as if her body had a mind of its own, rhythmically scrubbing at the sparkling tile while deep sobs of anguish and hatred ripped her apart.

"Oh, dear God in heaven," her mind screamed, "where is Frank? Why did you take him away when I need him so badly? Isn't our family crisis as important as someone else's? How could you let our baby . . . Oh, Father, how could this have happened?"

"Mommy, are you okay?" Angie asked as she came into the bathroom to brush her teeth for bed. "Is something wrong with Megan or Tony?"

"Oh, angel," Jeanee sniffed back her tears and looked up from her scrubbing. "They're fine. But—someone has hurt Amber."

"Is she in the hospital?" Angie's eyes were wide with concern.

"No, sweetheart, she's at home."

"Then why are you crying?"

"I'll tell you about it later, honey. Okay?"

"Okay. But are we still going to Tony's for vacation?"

"Yes, darling."

Just then Erik peeked his head through the door. "I'm heading for bed," he yawned. "We going to have prayer?"

"I need to brush my teeth first," Angie announced.

Erik noticed his mother's puffy eyes. "Mom, what's wrong?" He crouched down beside her. "Did the headache get worse?"

"No, honey, it's not the headache. It's just—I can't talk about it right now. I'll tell you later. Okay?"

"It's Amber," Angie announced in a matter-of-fact tone. "But we're still going to go there for vacation."

Erik searched his mother's face. "Is there anything I can do?"

"Just say a special prayer for us. Will you do that?"

"You bet." Erik smiled as he helped Jeanee to her feet. "As soon as snaggletooth here quits foaming at the mouth."

"I don't foam at the mouth!"

"Not tonight, kids. Okay?" Jeanee sent a pleading look at her son. "I need you not to tease tonight, Erik. And after prayer, Angie, you'll need to tuck yourself in bed. I have to call Tony back."

"Oh, and Mom?" Erik remembered. "While you were lying down, Sister Martin called for Dad. Do you know if he was planning on going to see her tonight?"

"I don't even know who called him just before he left."

"Well, if it was Sister Martin," Erik continued as he walked his mother into the living room, "Dad hadn't gotten there yet. I hope he hurries, because she sounded real anxious."

10:00 P.M.

Abby Martin sat in the darkness of her living room, staring out into the street. She was numb, too tired and beaten down to turn on the overhead light. In silence she sat listening to the clock ticking and the occasional car passing in front of her window.

Where was Bishop Greaves, she wondered with each approaching headlight? He was long overdue, and Brother Blodgett had promised her that he would be by.

Subconsciously she stroked the grimy, torn fabric of her chair, one of only three chairs left in the house. In the gray-blue light that filtered in through the window sheers, she could see another hole in the carpet.

"When will I get around to that?" she murmured, remembering the day before, when she had taken a hammer and torn up some tack-strip from where the carpet had worn off the stairs. "Too many little bare feet," she yawned.

In the corner of the room she could hear movement, and she knew without looking that it would be a mouse, one of many infesting her home. Once that thought would have driven her crazy, but any more she didn't care. Caring took too much effort, and she had no energy for that.

Abby wanted to cry. With all her heart she wanted to cleanse her emotions, to set them free. But there were no tears, just hollow, burning eyes, gritty and sore from lack of sleep.

"How could he do it?" she asked herself, struggling in silence. "How could he take from his own children? Isn't it bad enough that he left them? Did he also have to take their food and furniture?"

A chill ran down her arm, and Abby pulled a cotton cardigan closer around her shoulders.

"No, it wasn't bad enough. John Martin, you coward!" She seethed inwardly. "You come when I'm at work to strip their home, right in front of their eyes! How could you be so cruel?"

In her mind she could see the helplessness of her children as they had explained to her that their daddy had even taken all the canisters of wheat.

"Where is Bishop Greaves?" she shivered. "I can't do it alone any longer!" Abby looked out at the street, now empty of any movement. Only a light mist of rain interrupted the stillness of the scene. "Bishop," her mind screamed, "please hurry!"

Abby thought back to the horror of that morning. When her neighbor had seen what was happening with the furniture, he had called the police. But their hands had been tied. With no divorce or restraining order, the property was as much John's as it was hers.

And the phone call to John earlier in the day had left

her feeling more empty and guilty than ever. In fact, it took constant effort to keep from simply admitting that the man was right, that everything was her fault.

Except that it wasn't!

Staring into the street, Abby thought of her life with John. All she had wanted was a home where family prayers were held, where the scriptures were studied daily, and where people spoke nicely to each other as they helped each other out. Was that a bad desire? Yet the mere mention of those things had been enough to drive John away.

And now — this!

Without any movement Abby mentally looked through her empty home, just as she had physically looked through it after cleaning apartments that morning. Again she felt the incredible shock of realizing that John had stripped it of almost all the furniture and bedding she and the children needed to live. John, the wonderful university professor, former campus Church leader and father of her seven children, the one who had sworn love and loyalty to her for the past eighteen years, and the one who had then cast his vows aside as so much dirt. He had learned her schedule and then sneaked in with a moving crew, and it had all been over in a couple of hours. The fact that the children had been forced to watch made it all that much worse.

That he had also cut off all her normal sources of money and was giving her only a pittance of $300 each month to care for all the needs of herself and the entire family was further evidence that he wanted nothing to do with reconciliation.

"What goes on in the mind of a man like that?" she asked herself for perhaps the thousandth time. "Doesn't he see what he's doing? His own little children having nightmares because their daddy won't come home!"

Abby thought of the muffled sounds as her eldest daughter had cried herself to sleep that very night, and anger grew within her. "I may have made a lot of mistakes," she declared fiercely, "but at least I'm here for the children — what there is left of me."

A car swerved into the driveway, and Abby sat up, considering what she would say to her bishop. But as quickly the car was gone, just someone using her driveway to turn around.

"Where is he?" she thought. "Is he like every other man that never keeps his promises?"

Abby thought of her job, a two-week apartment cleaning job she had chanced upon and eagerly accepted. The hours were hard and the pay low but desperately needed. If it had come earlier she would have been able to keep up the house payment and utilities. But now time was running out, and she didn't know what she was going to do. With next to nothing in the cupboards, Abby had swallowed her pride and called Bishop Greaves.

She thought of her embarrassment when Jeanee had brought dinner over earlier that day. She couldn't have missed the dismal picture before her: thread-bare carpet, walls washed so many times the paint was gone from the doorways, Abby's eyes swollen with tears. It was obvious to anyone who wanted to see that John had been planning his departure for a long, long time.

For perhaps the millionth time Abby searched her mind, wondering what had gone wrong in her marriage. Why had John's behavior changed so dramatically over the past few years? What had turned him so mean? More important, what had turned him so against the children? How could a man, a father, not care about whether his children were fed or dressed respectably?

She knew she had made mistakes in their marriage, so she wasn't putting all the blame for the separation on John. But the longer he was away, the more she realized that for a long time things with him had not been healthy. For instance, she knew of no other woman who was forced to pour the milk on her husband's cereal every morning. She had been. And when she hadn't done it, for whatever reason, he had silently eaten his cereal dry, staring at her the entire time he was crunching. That, she had come to realize, was not healthy behavior.

And there had been other things, so many others that it hurt her mind to remember them. Still, she and John had made eternal covenants of marriage. To discover that they had meant less than nothing to him, to discover through a note in the mail that he would not be back, had been the most devastating experience of her life. In fact, it had been so horrible that something inside her had just shut off. Her emotions had gone into a kind of limbo. Now she sat numbly, wanting nothing more than to help her family survive John's abandonment—and, at that particular moment, wanting most of all to get a little rest!

"Bishop Greaves," she whispered into the darkness, "please hurry. I am so very tired, and I have to be at my cleaning job by 4:30 in the morning."

10:30 P.M.

Jeanee hugged her coat close, shivering uncontrollably at the door inside Terri Elder's garage. She stood on one foot and then the other, waiting for Terri to answer her knock, wondering all the while if she should just get back in her car and drive away. There was an unfamiliar car parked out front—probably company. Terri likely had friends or family in. But then, just as Jeanee had almost convinced herself that no one was coming, she heard footsteps and the door opening.

"Jeanee!" Terri exclaimed as she turned on the light. "What on earth is the matter?"

Jeanee tried to answer, but the words wouldn't come.

"Jeanee, honey, what is it?" Terri grabbed her camping

parka from the peg and slipped it on, shutting the door behind her.

"Oh, Terri," Jeanee finally managed to say. "S-something terrible has happened. And I don't know where to go, or what to do."

"Where's Frank?" Terri asked, putting her arm around her friend.

"I'm not sure. He . . . he left hours ago. Some emergency."

"Wouldn't you know it. And I had to be out of town. We just got back a little while ago."

"I'm sorry," Jeanee apologized. "And you have company. I shouldn't have come."

"Oh, that's no problem. Honest. Doug's family just stopped by overnight on their way to the temple. They'll just talk and then crash in the guest room. They don't need me in order to do that. But Jeanee, you don't look well. What happened?"

Jeanee bit her lip and swallowed hard, trying to gain enough composure to tell Terri of Tony's phone call. But every time she tried to begin, the words got caught. Great sobs were welling up inside, and she fought with all her strength to hold back the tide of emotion that raged within.

"I . . . I'd ask you in, but—" Terri apologized.

"No, no! I don't want anyone to see me—like this." Jeanee buried her tear-streaked face in her hands.

"What can I do?" Terri asked.

"Just . . . tell me why it keeps happening," Jeanee wept. "What did I do? What have I done that makes it keep coming back into my life?"

"What keeps coming back?" Terri searched her friend's appearance for a clue.

Raising her grief-stricken countenance, Jeanee took a deep breath. "Tony c-called me tonight," she whimpered, fighting for control. "Amber—our little granddaughter— Oh, Terri—she . . . she's been ra . . . ra . . . raped . . . "

"Oh, Jeanee," Terri cried as she took her friend in her arms to hold her close. "I'm so sorry!"

"Why?" Jeanee sobbed. "Why does it keep happening? I can't go through this again! I've been driving around in circles, trying to understand. And there is no answer!"

Jeanee wept uncontrollably as her friend held her close, saying nothing. For several minutes Terri just let her cry, saying little more than simple phrases of comfort. Then Jeanee braced herself and wiped at her tears. "Do you know?" she asked Terri. "You've known me for years. Do you know why it keeps happening?"

Terri looked blankly at her friend as she struggled for some bit of inspiration. And then, speaking quietly and with great conviction as the words came out, she answered.

"I don't know why abuse keeps happening, Jeanee, honey. But there is a reason why you continue to experience this inner pain. And someday you will know what that reason is."

11:30 P.M.

"Bishop," Robby almost whispered, "I'm really screwed up. Nothing makes sense to me, and just when I think I'm figuring things out, I'm knocked down again. Am I going crazy?"

Nearly an hour had passed in silence, with neither Frank nor Robby speaking. Frank had been praying silently for something to happen to let him know he could go home to his wife. He had even tried to leave but had been compelled to stay, sitting in silence while this pain-filled youth worked his way toward some sort of a resolution.

"Does he still hurt you with his belt?" Frank asked.

"Not much. I think it's because I'm big enough to fight back. He . . . he's such a ——, —— coward!"

Startled at the boy's profanity, Frank remained still.

"I'm sorry for swearing," Robby said, sounding as surprised as Frank had been. "I . . . try not to do that. But sometimes I . . . well, I can't think of any better words to say how I feel. Dad says I'm a rotten kid, and I guess he's right!"

"Robby," Frank spoke directly and gently, "you and I have known each other a long time. And you're a fine young man."

Slowly Robby raised his head until he was gazing directly into Frank's eyes, the expression on his face pleading for understanding more than any words he might have said.

"Granted you have some problems," Frank continued, "but that's just part of growing up. Besides the normal challenges of being a teenager, however, your life has been complicated by your father's unrighteous anger. He must bear responsibility for that."

"You mean . . . what I do might be Dad's fault?"

Frank studied the young man carefully before he spoke. "Let me share with you something that is coming to my mind," he proceeded, "something from the sixth chapter of Ephesians. It goes like this: 'Fathers, provoke not your children to wrath: but bring them up in the nurture and admonition of the Lord.' "

"I've never heard that before."

"Here's another scripture," Frank continued as he opened up his Doctrine and Covenants to the 121st section. "Why don't you read this for me."

"Just like in school?" Robby grinned a bit uneasily.

Frank tilted his head and waited for Robby to begin.

39 We have learned by sad experience that it is the nature and disposition of almost all men, as soon as they get a little authority, as they suppose, they will immediately begin to exercise unrighteous dominion.

41 No power or influence can or ought to be main-

tained by virtue of the priesthood, only by persuasion, by long-suffering, by gentleness and meekness, and by love unfeigned;

42 By kindness, and pure knowledge, which shall greatly enlarge the soul without hypocrisy, and without guile—

43 Reproving betimes with sharpness, when moved upon by the Holy Ghost; and then showing forth afterwards an increase of love toward him whom thou hast reproved, lest he esteem thee to be his enemy.

Robby looked up from his reading. "Sounds like my dad missed both of these scriptures."

"And he'll have to be accountable for what he has done. But Robby, that does not excuse your behavior tonight!"

"Hey, I'm real sorry," Robby said slowly as a tear began moistening the corner of his eye, again revealing to Frank his tender nature. "I honestly don't know what got into me. I mean, breaking all those windows. . . . "

7

WEDNESDAY, MAY 29

12:55 A.M.

Anxiously Jeanee looked at the grandfather clock in the living room. Almost one o'clock in the morning. "What could possibly be happening," she wondered aloud, "that would keep him so late?"

After visiting with Terri Elder she had felt strangely better. Why this could be when nothing had been resolved, she didn't understand. But there was something about the way Terri had told her that someday she would know why these things kept happening that was deeply reassuring to her. And she knew, even as Terri was saying it, that it was true. But now, alone again in the quiet house and still waiting for Frank to return, she could feel her fear and anger tugging once again at her thoughts.

When Jeanee had called Tony back, she had been much more supportive and coherent. But when she learned that the abuse had been going on for several months, she had almost lost control again. How could her daughter-in-law have left Amber in a home where that kind of thing was happening, over and over again? Why hadn't she known sooner that something was wrong?

Jeanee needed to talk to her husband. More than ever she needed him there with her. And her helplessness at not knowing where he was or when he might return was churning inside her. She had busied herself around the house while she waited, picking up, dusting, doing hand-sewing. Finally, when she could think of nothing else to do, she paced the floor in front of the living room window, waiting, praying that Frank would come home soon.

"Why didn't I make some phone calls to find out where he is?" she scolded herself. "I should have done that before it got so late. Oh, Frank, please hurry home!"

A light mist was falling, diffusing the light from the street lamp out front. The night had a surreal look that was almost frightening. Jeanee grabbed a pillow from the sofa and hugged it close.

"Heavenly Father," she pleaded, "Please bring him home soon. This is too much. I know we're never given more than we can handle, but this feels like more than I can handle! This feels like hell! And it's swallowing me up! Where can I put my anguish? Oh, Father, please let me wake up and find that it's all a bad dream!"

"Bwooong!" The clock announced the hour, startling Jeanee. Silently she turned and walked up the stairs, past the family photos and the plaque she had embroidered that said "Families Are Forever." Carefully she opened Angie's bedroom door. Seeing her uncovered, she slipped in and pulled the pink comforter snug to her tiny daughter's chin.

"Little munchkin," she smiled to herself. "Your world is so innocent and beautiful. What dreams are you dreaming now?" Instantly tears filled Jeanee's eyes. "But what dreams for Amber? Our poor baby! Because of that — *boy* — her world, like mine, is forever shattered!"

Jeanee pulled the sofa pillow close to her face and fought for control. Then, moving silently out of the room, she flung the pillow down the stairs and into the entry way.

"How can this work together for good?" her mind wailed in continued prayer. "God, how can this possibly work for good? A child has been violated! Exactly like I was! A precious baby! What justice is this? And just when I needed him the most — Oh, God above, where is Frank?"

Angrily Jeanee stormed into her bedroom and threw herself down on the bed. Almost unconsciously she picked up her pen and began furiously writing in her journal.

> *Hell*
> *The pit*
> *It's swallowing*
> *Me*
> *In its utter*
> *Darkness*
> *And there is*
> *No*
> *Escape*
> *Only more*
> *Pain*
>
> *Hasn't there been*
> *Enough*
> *Suffering?*
> *Does it have to be*
> *Endless?*

And then, as wracking sobs engulfed her body, Jeanee buried her head in her pillow and wept . . .

1:30 A.M.

In the early morning darkness, Frank drove slowly toward home. A light rain was still falling, and he wondered if it would ever stop. Though he ached for his wife and the loneliness she must feel on nights like this, in reality his mind was consumed with the details of all he had experienced since leaving home.

Four hours he had spent with Robby, four hours during which he had learned with certainty that his ward was not without an abuse problem. Bob Nichol's abuse of his son was out of control, and there was no doubt of it. But what about Claudia? She had also been abused by Bob, but not only had she done nothing to stop it, neither had she tried to protect her son.

Maybe, Frank thought as he drove, this was one of those cases where a victim had to assume some of the responsibility for the abuse.

On the other hand, might Robby be making the whole thing up? Frank didn't think so, and neither did the police, who had twice been called in by the neighbors. Why hadn't he been notified of those incidents, Frank wondered? Surely someone should have thought to tell the bishop.

"The trouble is," Frank muttered aloud, "if all I heard about tonight is real, then what in merciful heaven am I to do with Bob and Claudia? I mean, that makes a sweet and active couple into child abusers, and a diligent Sunday School teacher into a wife beater. That is frightening!"

Again Frank rehearsed in his mind the scriptures he had shared with Robby, as he tried to convince him that he was not an evil young man.

The youth would be heading for a foster home in the morning. Then there would be an investigation and a hearing concerning the issue of abuse, which Frank would be involved in. And remembering Mrs. O.'s experience with Andy, he grimaced at the thought of all that would entail.

"Heavenly Father," he pleaded as he turned onto his street, "please give me the gift of discernment so that I may know how to help this dear family. I don't think I can manage this mess without Thee.

"And another thing. I feel that Thou hast given me the message today of praying for one's enemies, just so I could teach it to the Nichol family. I want to do that, Father, but I'm not certain how to go about it. I wanted to share it with Robby tonight, but I felt restrained. Wilt Thou please open up the way that I might present it to him and his parents in a way that will bless their lives?"

Pulling into his garage, Frank turned off his lights and ignition. Then he leaned back and gave a deep sigh. "And

Father, please bless Jeanee during these long hours when I am called to be away. Comfort her, O God, and help me to find a way of showing her how much she means to me, even when I can't be with her."

1:40 A.M.

Moving quietly, Frank climbed the stairs and pushed open the door of the bedroom. He was surprised to see the light still burning at the desk, but Jeanee was asleep in the bed. At least she hadn't tried waiting up for him.

Tiptoeing to the desk, Frank was reaching to turn out the light when he noticed his wife's journal, lying open before him. He had never read her journal; she had far too many volumes to entice him. But now his attention was caught by a poem, one of two, on the page of the opened journal, and quickly he read it.

> *Silence*
> *Calls me*
> *In the night*
> *Its fingers*
> *Wrap*
> *Around my mind*
> *And*
> *Hold the secret*
> *Dark*
> *Inside*
> *Till life is*
> *Numb*
> *And truth is*
> *Blind*

Always amazed at Jeanee's creativity, Frank was suddenly more puzzled than amazed. Why would she be writing poetry about truth being blind? Or about silence holding some secret inside? Did it have personal meaning? Or might it just be some creative urge that she had penned?

Probably the latter, he thought as he looked again at his sleeping wife. She was so creative, and she had such an unusual way of phrasing things—unlike his own way, which tended to be so simple and straightforward.

Smiling as he turned off the light, Frank thought about the two of them—him big and awkward, Jeanee tiny and graceful; him plain and simple, her elaborate and complex. It was hard for him to imagine that a woman such as Jeanee could actually love him. Yet she swore constantly that she did, and he was forever sending thanks heavenward for it.

Quickly Frank removed his clothing and knelt at the chair rather than at the side of the bed where Jeanee might be disturbed. "Dear Father," he prayed silently, "we've been in touch a lot tonight, and I really appreciate the help I've been given. I need to understand a lot better than I do, so again I ask for the gift of discernment. And Father, please help me to understand Jeanee. If something is troubling her, I pray that I might be able to understand what it is. More than anything, I want to be there for her when she really needs me."

2:10 A.M.

Claudia Nichol knelt beside Robby's empty bed, sobbing desperately into the blankets. What am I to do? her mind screamed over and over again. Oh, dear God above, what am I to do?

"Heavenly Father," she whispered brokenly, "all my life I have believed in you. I have tried to keep the commandments, I have tried to be active and sincere in my religious views—I have honored my covenant of eternal marriage to Bob. Only—"

Once again Claudia was aware of the excruciating pain in her stomach, a pain that for years had attacked her in the afternoon, about an hour before Bob was due home from work. It had been years before she had realized that her stomach pains were caused by his homecomings—caused simply because she was so terrified of what he might do.

What Claudia didn't understand was why she experienced an even deeper pain every time she thought of leaving him. Yet it was real, and she felt impossibly torn.

"Dear Father," she wept as she continued her prayer, "I . . . I have never wanted to leave Bob, not . . . not really. I know he's mean to me, but I'm just as certain that I deserve it. I . . . I've never been the kind of wife he needed."

More tears followed, and Claudia remained kneeling, her sobs shaking Robby's narrow bed. Then gradually, as she continued to weep, a memory began running through her mind, over and over again, like a broken record. It involved Bishop Greaves, though he had not been bishop then. He had been Robby's sixth-grade teacher at the time, and they had visited him one night at a parent-teacher meeting. She could hear his words as clearly as if he was saying them now: "Mrs. Nichol, Robby is one of the finest boys I have ever known. He is bright, quick, and anxious to learn. But best of all, he has a good, soft, gentle heart, and is one of the most thoughtful boys I have ever seen. Protect that in him, Mrs. Nichol. Don't ever let anyone destroy his tender nature."

Raising her head, Claudia stared into the darkness. "Don't ever let anyone destroy his tender nature." Claudia could not remember the rest of what Bishop Greaves had said, but suddenly, like a bolt of lightening, she had been struck with the understanding that she had allowed Robby's tenderness to be destroyed—by the one man who should have nurtured it.

"That's right," she whispered as she wiped the tears from her eyes. "I might deserve what Bob has been doing to me, but Robby doesn't! Frank Greaves knew him, and he saw in him exactly what I saw. That means those qualities were there! If they aren't there now, it means that Bob has destroyed them. And Bishop Greaves told me never to let anyone destroy them."

"Heavenly Father," she said as she began praying again in earnest, "Have I allowed Bob to destroy my son?"

Claudia paused, waiting for an answer, waiting, waiting—

"Dear God above, please tell me . . . "

Some time later, as Claudia continued to plead for a confirmation, she became aware that, in her mind's eye, she was watching a scene from ancient times, an intense drama where Christ, upon finding the temple defiled with money-changers, was overturning their tables and driving them out.

Curious, she thought, as she wondered at the Savior's controlled anger, that this particular scene should come to her mind.

"I . . . I didn't know the Lord ever got angry," she whispered in amazement. "I thought getting angry was unrighteous."

And then a question filled Claudia's mind: "Isn't Christ perfect?"

"Why . . . why, yes," she whispered in response. "Everybody knows that! But I was taught that anger is evil. I . . . I don't understand."

"Is Christ without sin?" The questions continued to formulate in her mind.

"Well, yes!"

"Then can his anger be evil?"

"No, but—"

"Why was Christ angry?"

Without a second's hesitation, Claudia replied, "Because those men were defiling his Father's temple."

"Isn't your husband defiling Robby's temple?"

"I . . . I . . . " she stammered, startled at the way the

questions came as fast as she could answer them. "Yes," she finally whispered in response. "Yes, he is!"

"Aren't you assisting him?"

Stung beyond belief by what she knew instantly as truth, Claudia could only weep as she acknowledged her own contribution to Robby's pain.

"Aren't all temples of God holy, including the bodies he created for men and women?"

Brokenhearted but filling with new understanding, Claudia slowly nodded in response to the questions forming so miraculously within her mind.

"Can you now understand Christ's anger as he beholds the defilement of these holy temples, the bodies his Father has created for his beloved children?"

"Do you . . . do you mean Jesus is angry as he watches people defiling each other?" she whispered, totally shaken by the new thought.

"If he was angered over the defilement of a temple made of wood and stone," the voice in her mind explained, "consider his wrath when holy temples of flesh and blood are defiled."

Wide-eyed, Claudia stared into the darkness, her mind churning. Robby's body was a holy temple for his spirit. The Bible declared that to be true. Therefore, when Bob did cruel things to Robby, he was being no less a defiler of God's temple than the ancient money-changers! Had Jesus been present, she suddenly knew, he would have driven Bob away from Robby just as surely.

"If you would be like Christ," the voice declared gently, kindly, "you must stop that man of wickedness from defiling your temples."

Stunned, Claudia knelt in silence. Temples? That was plural. That meant there was another temple besides Robby's—her own temple was also being defiled.

But no, she deserved what Bob did to her! She had failed him so miserably—

"Man of wickedness," the words formed in her mouth. "He called Bob a man of wickedness. But that can't be! He is so active in the Church and has such a strong testimony."

And then the reality of what she was experiencing hit Claudia. Who had been asking her those questions? Who —

"Dear God," she pleaded, the entire tone of her prayer changed, "is it Thou that I have been hearing? If this voice in my mind is from Thee, then please help me to know."

Suddenly Claudia was aware that she was once again seeing the Savior driving the money-changers from the temple. But this time, as she watched, the voice was in her mind again, no longer questioning but now issuing a commandment she suddenly knew was coming directly from God.

"Go," the voice declared softly and silently but with all the piercing authority of eternity in its tone. "Go, my daughter, and do thou likewise."

2:30 A.M.

"Tess, wake up!"

"Huh?"

"Shhh. Don't make so much noise."

Slowly Tess sat up, blinking in the brightness of the tiny flashlight her older sister was holding. "My gosh, Tish, it's the middle of the night! How come you woke me up?"

Quickly Tish turned her flashlight into the far corner of the room. "That's why," she said bitterly. "Take a look!"

"Oh. Where's Trace?"

"Where do you think?"

Tess blinked again. "In the bathroom?"

Tish shook her head in disgust. "She's with Daddy, Tess. I saw him carrying her out through the door."

"He woke you up?" Tess asked with wonder.

"Something did. All I know is that I opened my eyes just in time to see."

"Maybe she was crying or something."

"Yeah," Tish said as she switched off the flashlight. "That's what I wanted to think. I'll bet I thought of a hundred reasons why Daddy carried Trace out of here. The problem, Tess, is that I know I'm just lying to myself."

Tess shivered and then pulled the blankets back up around her.

"You know too, don't you."

It was a statement, not a question, and Tess looked up, surprised. "What makes you think that?"

"Because I heard you whispering to Trace tonight, when you thought I was asleep."

"You did not! I . . . I . . . "

"Tess," her sister scolded, "no lies between us. Remember? You were telling her to never say anything again, ever. That's true, isn't it."

Looking anguished, Tess slowly nodded.

"So she said something?"

"She was talking about playing games with Daddy." Tess's voice trailed off in pain. "Oh, Tish, you know what that means!"

Soberly the older girl nodded. "It means Daddy's . . . lost it. Something has to be done! We promised each other!"

Tess's eyes suddenly grew wide with worry and shame. "No, Tish, No! I . . . I can't do it."

"Tess, you promised!"

"I . . . I know, Tish. But think what it will mean!"

"You think I haven't thought about it? Tess, there's hardly another thing I ever think about anymore. But too many people are getting hurt, and I can't live with it any longer."

"But . . . but not tomorrow. Please, not tomorrow."

Slowly Tish drew in her breath. "No, there'll be a better day, and we'll know when it is. Now go back to sleep, Tess. I'll take care of little Trace."

2:40 A.M.

"Claudia, you awake? I couldn't find him."

Bob Nichol removed his clothing in the dark, glanced at the clock, then crawled into bed, reaching for his wife. "Hey," he said as he slapped the empty mattress, "where are you?"

Greeted by silence, Bob crawled from the bed and turned on the light. Nothing.

"Claudia," he called as he walked down the hall. "Claudia, where are you?"

As the silence continued, Bob walked into Robby's room and turned on the light there. The bed had not been slept in, and he could see no other evidence that his son had been home.

With mounting frustration he descended the stairs and turned on the lights in the living room. Empty.

"Claudia," he shouted, swearing under his breath as he headed for the kitchen, "where are you?"

"Hey," he said, laughing easily, "I'm real sorry about tonight, honey. I know things got a little rough, but it won't happen again, I promise. I've been doing a lot of thinking while I've been driving around, and I've made some changes. You'll see. Now come on, let's go to bed."

Silence continued to reign, and as Bob turned on the kitchen light and found the room empty, his temper suddenly erupted again.

"Claudia," he snarled, "—— —— it, you tell me where you are this instant, or so help me—"

It was then Bob saw the letter, lying where Claudia had left it on the kitchen table.

Sitting down, he unfolded it and began to read.

> Bob:
> I know you didn't find Robby because he is in jail tonight, driven there by your vile temper.
> I am also gone, and it will do you no good to search

for me, as I have taken steps to see that I cannot be
found. Nor will you hear from me again until you have
dealt with the evil that seems to have overcome you.

I can hear you scoffing at the word *evil,* so let me be
more specific. You're a high priest in Christ's church,
Bob. As I understand it, that means you have been called
to obey and represent the Lord Jesus Christ. What happens to your obedience to him when all that filthy profanity and vulgarity comes out of your mouth?

No answer? Well, here's another question. Maybe this
one will be easier. How does the Savior tell us to treat
our enemies? With love. Right? Love your enemies, bless
them that curse you and despitefully use you, and so
forth. No doubt you know the scriptural reference. If
Christ tells us to love our enemies, does it seem logical
to you that he would then want us to beat to a bloody
pulp the people we love?

You always tell me that the scripture says to spare the
rod and spoil the child. But I ask, what rod? The iron
rod, maybe? According to the Book of Mormon, that's
the word of God, not your fists. Perhaps what the writer
of Proverbs meant was that you were supposed to teach
your rebellious son the word of God, not beat him almost
to death.

Another scripture you love to quote says that a man
should cleave unto his wife. Bob, as far as I can tell, your
definition of the word *cleave* is to scream, swear, slap,
punch, threaten, and intimidate. Believe me, you and
Mr. Webster are not in agreement on the definition of
cleave.

Remember, I once covenanted to let you rule over me
in righteousness *as you allowed Christ to rule over you!* Since
we already know how you feel about being obedient to
Christ's commandments — since you make a daily mock-
ery of your covenants to him — you have renounced your
covenant through your actions. But I will not renounce
my covenant, Robert Nichol. I will keep it — which means
that since you have not allowed Christ to rule over you,

I will no longer allow you to rule over me in any way at all.

No longer will I support your evil with my silence. No longer will I defend you with my own lies. You are now on your own, for as long as you want it to last.

Claudia

Seething with anger, Bob crumpled the letter and threw it into the corner.

"Why," he muttered with an oath, "you miserable—"

5:10 A.M.

Jeanee sat bolt upright in bed, choking, fighting for air, ripping at her covers in a half-sleep state, suffocating from an unseen enemy.

"What am I supposed to do? What am I supposed to do?" her mind whirled, struggling to remember. "How do I make it stop?"

Her body was trembling and her heart pounding with a sudden rush of adrenalin. Yet still she couldn't breathe—

"I have to remember! What do I have to remember?" She struggled desperately. Then, as if her body had a mind of its own, it leaped into a strangely familiar knee-chest position. And only then, wet with perspiration from the struggle, did she feel her airway open and blessed oxygen enter her aching lungs.

"Finally, air!" she gasped, inhaling and exhaling in one exultant rhythm of relief. "I'm alive! At least I'm alive! But where—and when—?"

Absolute confusion filled Jeanee's mind. Not only did she not know where she was, but she had no comprehension of how old she was or of what year in time she was living. She was lost in a terrifying hole, her mind reeling in a frightening darkness that ripped away every reference point, every security. At once she was falling, and cold, and lost, and all alone! And there was no "now"—only terror and pain.

Another deep breath as she fought for awareness, and then another. Then, struggling somewhere between the moment and the terrifying hole that was closing in her mind, her senses began to return. Gradually she could feel the weight of the covers around her and the warmth of the bed she had been sleeping in. Cautiously, in the half-light of early morning, she allowed her eyes to drink in the security of her bedroom.

"I'm here," she thought, still heaving against the burning in her chest. "I'm here, and I'm safe!" Then, pulling herself further awake, she realized that her husband was sleeping beside her.

"Oh, Frank," she thought, tears in her eyes. "You're finally here. Thank God, you're here!"

For a moment Jeanee just sat in the half-darkness, breathing deeply, fighting against the tears that were now spilling down her cheeks.

"Frank, where have you been?" she pleaded silently. "I waited. I needed you so badly! And now, here you are sleeping soundly beside me as if nothing had happened, as if all the world is right—and it isn't!"

Carefully Jeanee reached for the lamp on the nightstand and turned it on to the lowest setting. Grabbing a tissue and drying at her tears, she allowed her eyes to fully focus on the security of her surroundings. Yes, she was in her own room. And as sleep continued to fall from her mind, she realized that her unseen enemy was gone.

"I'm safe," she thought to herself. "I'm in my own room, and I'm safe!"

Breathing deeply to calm herself, Jeanee continued her survey of the room. On the nightstand next to the lamp were the little Fenton glass figures of a boy and a girl, praying. Frank had given them to her the first year of their marriage, along with a card, now framed, that read, 'Don't be afraid to love someone totally and completely—' The message continued, but for Jeanee, the first line had been the most important. Had it been that obvious, she wondered, that it was difficult for her to love? Frank had once told her that all she needed was to be loved right and she would be happy.

And he had been right. After eight years together, their lives had grown so close that she couldn't imagine herself without him.

On the dresser next to the mirror was a collage of family pictures—Frank stuffing a huge piece of frosted cake into Jeanee's mouth on their fifth anniversary, Erik with his racing bike, Tony and Megan with their children, and Angie on her sixth birthday. Beyond that were Frank's scriptures, with his blue highlighter pen neatly capped in the margin.

Just then the clock flipped to 5:15. Adjusting her covers, Jeanee slipped back down beside Frank, watching the effortless rhythm of his sleep. He was beautiful to her, even now, with his face all scrunched up against the pillow like a little boy. There was something so innocent about him. In his large, rugged frame beat a heart that was still untouched by the world.

"I could almost believe the world was all right," Jeanee thought to herself, "lying here, looking at this man I love."

A shock of silver wove its way through Frank's thinning hair. Yet his expression, the pouty fullness of his mouth, the set of his jaw, the direct clarity of his hazel-gray eyes— they all spoke of an honesty enjoyed only by the very young or the very pure.

"How do I tell him?" Jeanee wondered to herself. "He looks so peaceful lying there. How do I wake him up and tell him something like this?"

A funny squeak escaped Frank's lips as he turned more on his side, facing Jeanee. "You're such a little boy," she thought with a smile. "How can you comprehend what I'm going to tell you? Oh, Frank, what a paradox! I look to you for strength and protection, and yet I feel that I should protect you. I feel so safe with you, and yet — Oh, Frank, is there really any safety?"

The golden pink of early morning began creeping in the east window of their bedroom. Just a few more minutes and the alarm would go off. Another busy day lay ahead. And it would probably be a very difficult day.

Reluctantly Jeanee began nudging her husband awake. "Frank," she whispered as she gently shook him. "Frank, its nearly time for prayer and scriptures, and we need to talk. . . . "

PART TWO

GATHERING DARKNESS

This darkness
Where did it
Come from?

I was washed clean
I thought
But still it
Remains

Gathering
New darkness

8

SATURDAY, JULY 13

6:00 A.M.

Early morning dew was on the grass, and here and there sparkling glints of sunshine were turning it into myriad tiny diamonds of light. Jeanee looked ahead at the pacing form of her dear friend Terry Elder. In her summer sweats and dirty Reeboks, Terri moved effortlessly through the morning mist, and Jeanee felt hard pressed just keeping up.

"Do you do this every morning?" she gasped.

"Every morning but Sunday," her friend replied, smiling back at her.

"No wonder your calves are so well-defined."

"What your swimming pool is for you, my striding is for me," Terri explained.

"But this pace?"

"Hey, I thought you were in shape!"

Jeanee laughed. "That's precisely why I called you to meet me. I'm not in shape. Not physically, not spiritually, and especially not emotionally."

Terri slowed her pace to let Jeanee catch up. "Having a rough time?" she sympathized.

"Terri," Jeanee panted, "ever since this past May when Tony called about Amber I've been a basket case. I keep doing the same things that pulled me out of it before, but nothing is working! I . . . I feel so much anger inside! I know that's wrong, but—"

"Wait a minute," Terri interrupted. "Who said it's wrong to get angry?"

"But what I'm feeling, Terri, it's . . . it's black and ugly and hateful."

"Then you're talking about more than honest anger. Let's take a breather up here on the church lawn." Terri motioned to a place a few yards ahead. "I need to switch focuses."

Both women walked briskly to the front lawn of the chapel where they each attended church. Neither spoke, and the hush of the early July morning was all around them.

"Do you mind a little moisture?" Terri finally asked as she swished her foot through the dew on the grass.

"How about the steps over there?"

"Good idea."

As they moved toward the steps, they could hear the crowing of a rooster in the distance.

"It's surprising what you see and hear when you're up early enough." Terri smiled and seated herself on the top of the two steps.

As Jeanee sat one step down from her friend, she began to shiver.

"Jeanee," Terri almost whispered, "are you okay?"

"Who knows?" Jeanee grimaced. "Who knows what's going on with me nowadays?"

"It's been hard, hasn't it," Terri acknowledged, her voice filled with sympathy.

"Harder than anything I've ever experienced," Jeanee declared. I can't sleep. I can't sit still. And worst of all, I can't get close to my husband."

Terri looked at her friend. "Jeanee, have you told Frank about your past?"

"I almost did, a few weeks ago," Jeanee responded miserably. "And then all this with Amber happened, plus a bunch of other stuff! Tell me, how were you able to be there for me when I was going through it before?"

"I don't understand." Terry breathed deeply as she spoke.

"Well, I have this friend, someone I knew years ago, who came to me because she was remembering being molested by her father, and—"

"When did she come to you?" Terri interrupted.

"The same day I learned about Amber. The same day that Frank was gone half the night with the Nichol family. Remember? That was the night we talked in your garage?"

"I remember," Terri answered quietly. "How could I forget?"

"Well, that's when it all started."

"I don't wonder." Terri leaned her head back and began rolling it from side to side. "You realize that you're dealing with some pretty strong triggers, don't you?"

"Triggers?"

"Yes, like the ones that go 'bang, bang.' Only these go 'bang, bang' in your head."

"I . . . I don't know what I'm dealing with anymore," Jeanee admitted. "I thought that once I had forgiven my dad, it would all be behind me. You were there, Terri. You know what it was like."

"Yes, I know."

"Well then, why am I going through this? When you forgive someone, aren't you supposed to be able to forget?"

Jeanee didn't wait for her friend to answer. She just went on, in frustration.

"Do you know I lay awake for hours every night, twitching and fighting to go to sleep, and afraid at the same time that I might—because then I'll have to deal with the dreams? I have to keep busy all the time I'm awake, or the grief is unbearable. And all the time I'm struggling to let this go, I keep aching. Right now I feel like I have the flu in every muscle in my body."

"Are you still swimming?"

"It's not the same. I get anxious when I'm in the pool."

"How about your prayers?"

"They're bouncing off the ceiling. I struggle to put myself in the right frame of mind, but it's just words."

"And reading the scriptures? The same?"

"A major effort." Jeanee nodded her head.

"How's Frank taking this?" Terri moved down to the step Jeanee was sitting on.

"I'm afraid to tell Frank what I'm going through, afraid he'll tell me I haven't forgiven my dad.

"But worse," Jeanee could barely get the words out, "what if he—Oh Terri, how could he possibly love me?"

Terri wiped a bead of perspiration from her temple. "How can you question his love, Jeanee, after all he's been for you?"

Jeanee looked down on the sidewalk, where a spider had left a silvery web against the bottom step.

"You don't trust his love," Terri stated softly.

Jeanee continued to stare at the web, gathering her thoughts. Then, hugging her arms tightly around herself, she began to rock softly back and forth.

"How can I trust him when I can't even trust myself?" she finally admitted. "Terri, I thought I had this thing licked. I really did. And now I'm right back where I started. I don't want Frank to know how unstable I am. He needs me to be strong."

"He needs you to be honest." Terri gently urged.

Jeanee kicked at the spider web. "If I can talk my friend Marie into visiting with you," she said, changing the subject, "would you be willing to help her? The way you helped me?"

A pickup truck pulled into the parking lot of the chapel and parked, and the custodian got out. "Morning, ladies." He smiled in greeting. "Looks like it's going to be a scorcher today. Sure hope we can get the air-conditioning working before Church tomorrow."

"Fred, we have all the faith in the world in you." Terri smiled.

"It's going to take more than faith, I'm afraid," came the reply. "Well, Terri, you and Jeanee have a nice morning."

"Now, where were we?" Terri wondered aloud after the man had gone inside. "Oh, yes, about your friend. Of course I'd be willing to talk with her. But something even better than that might be in the future for us."

"What do you mean?" Jeanee began massaging her aching muscles.

"AMAC," Terri answered. "A program the Church Social Services is piloting in some areas. It stands for 'Adults Molested As Children.' It's a support group for women like us, and men too, who have survived sexual abuse. An area I visited last month has a group going, and it's pretty good."

"How long will it take to get one started here?" Jeanee sat back down.

"Depends. I talked to Brother Wixom of Social Services about it last week, and he said that if enough people show a need for it, he'll see what can be done about getting one started here." Terri stood up. "Want to walk some more? Slowly—I promise."

Jeanee climbed to her feet, her mind a blur. Everything was becoming so confusing to her. The darkness in her mind was so relentless, she was afraid she was getting lost in it.

"Is that therapist still in the Professional Building?" she asked, knowing that Terri would have the answer.

"Peggy? Yes, she's still there. Are you going to call her?"

Jeanee was quiet as they began walking back the way they had come. A car hurried past them, its windshield glinting in the sun.

"Are you going to call her?" Terri repeated.

"I'm going to think about it," Jeanee finally answered, her eyes seeing only distance. "At least I'm going to do that."

9:15 A.M.

"Man," Frank said as he paused from his weeding to wipe his brow, "is it hot enough, or what?"

Looking up from where he was kneeling in the young corn, Erik grinned. "They say the heat really gets to folks when they get old," he teased.

"Not as bad as this hoe's going to get you," Frank countered, "if you don't let up on me and get back to work."

"Hey, I've been weeding two rows to your one all morning."

"Yeah, and they're a third as long, too."

Frank frowned fiercely at his son and raised his hoe menacingly. "Now get back to work!"

Showing mock fear, Erik turned and began scattering weeds behind him, the bulk of them seeming to end up right where Frank was standing. "That better?" he asked.

"Much," Frank said as he ducked a huge redroot. "But be sure and leave a little corn—"

Intentionally Erik pulled a green corn stalk and tossed it backward. "Oh," he said teasingly as he turned to see Frank's expression, "I'm sorry, Dad."

"Yeah, I'll bet. Tell you what, sport. I'll race you and even give you the head-start you already have. First one to the end of his row, with a clean job, buys milkshakes."

"You're on!" Erik agreed, and then suddenly realized what he had agreed to.

"Hey, wait a minute! Last one finished buys, not first."

Frank smiled widely. "Well, it was worth a try."

"I can't believe it. The bishop, trying to cheat me. Wait'll the ward hears about this."

"Who's trying to cheat? I figured you'd win, and I just wanted a free shake. What's to cheat about that?"

Erik shook his head. "You're like Brother Blodgett. You always have to watch that guy."

"Is that right?"

"Yeah. Every time we're on a Scouting activity, he tries to pull something or other on us. He's really funny."

For a moment Frank thought of Mel. Without exception, everyone in the ward loved the man, and Frank knew it. Mel seemed to have it all together in a way Frank only wished for.

"Is Mel working with you on your Eagle project?" Frank asked, forcing his mind to change direction.

"Uh-huh," Erik grunted. "Next Saturday is the big day. Painting benches at the city park. You going to be there?"

"Next Saturday? What's happening next Saturday?" Frank paused. "That's right. It's the 24th of July picnic."

"But that's in the afternoon," Erik reminded his father. "We'll be done by then."

"Do I have to help?" Frank asked teasingly. "Or can I supervise?"

"Sorry, Dad. That's my job. Next week I get to boss you around. And you'd better be in shape by then, because I'm really going to lay it on."

"Like I am today?" Frank asked, mimicking with his hands and arms the fact that Erik was sprawled on his elbow in one of the furrows.

"Hey, I'm still ahead of you."

"Not for long."

Both weeded for a moment, and then, without pausing in his work, Erik spoke again. "Dad, what's wrong with Mom?"

"What do you mean?"

"Oh, you know, she's just acting different. I mean, it's like she's in high gear all the time. What happened over at Megan and Tony's?"

"What happened?" Frank repeated, not knowing exactly how to respond.

"Yeah. Ever since we went there on vacation, Mom's been acting weird, on the go, like she's in a race or something and can't ever cross the finish line. I figure something had to have happened there. Did Megan or Tony do something wrong?"

"No, of course not, Erik. But you're right—Mom is really struggling. A situation developed with Megan and Tony, a real sad situation, and your mom isn't handling it very well. That's all."

"It was Amber, wasn't it."

"It was, but how do you know?"

"Oh, Angie overheard something or other and told me. Can I know about it?"

"Right now I think it's better that you don't. Is that okay?"

Erik nodded. "Sure. Can I help?"

"You are helping. Just keep being the great kid you are."

"Dad, I mean seriously."

"I am being serious," Frank stated soberly. "But another thing might be showing a little extra tenderness toward your mother. If you see that she's struggling, then just be super thoughtful."

"Oh, I get it. Like, no arguing with Angie."

Frank chuckled. "Exactly."

"No sweat, Dad. I just like to get Angie running, is all."

"I know. But it does get on your mother's nerves, especially when Angie doesn't handle it well. You know that."

Erik sighed. "Yeah, I know. And I'll do better, Dad. I promise. Is . . . is Amber . . . okay?"

"She'll be fine," Frank assured him. "It'll probably take a little time, but yes, she'll be just fine." The assurance was as much for himself, Frank realized, as it was for Erik.

"Good," Erik declared, sounding relieved. "I was really worried."

"Hi, Bishop," a child's voice giggled from the top of the fence behind them. "Hi, Erik. Whatcha doing?"

Looking up, Frank saw the McCrasky boys, Jimmy and Willy. Aged eight and nine, they rarely failed to appear when he was working in the garden, always offering to help. And under his direction they had become pretty good little gardeners, too.

"Top o' the morning, boys," he said with a smile.

"What're you guys doing on top of that fence?" Erik growled with mock severity. "Get on down here and get to work! Dad's buying extra-large, double-thick, chocolate milkshakes when we're finished."

With a squeal of delight the boys scrambled over the top of the fence, and seconds later they were on their knees beside Erik, all three of them weeding with a frenzy.

"Hey," Frank said as he began hoeing, "not so darn fast. I don't have to be at the church for my interviews until five o'clock tonight."

"But we have to have those shakes earlier than that," Erik teased, and as a chorus the McCrasky boys agreed.

Frank smiled as he watched the three working. "Now if only Sister McCrasky doesn't start screaming for them to get home this instant," he muttered to himself as he lifted his hoe and returned to work.

10:56 P.M.

"You ready?"

Tish Blodgett looked at her younger sister, as aware of her nervousness and fear as she was of her own. It was nearly eleven o'clock on Saturday night, and with their early Sunday meeting schedule, normally both girls would have been in bed. But this night they were still dressed,

still nervously trying to build the courage to do what they
had to do.

"I . . . guess so. Are you sure that Daddy isn't going to
be coming home?"

"He called Mom and told her, Tess. I was listening. He
said it would be at least two in the morning, because I
heard her repeat it back to him. Now, stop worrying."

"But what's Mom going to do, Tish? What if she doesn't
believe us?"

"I . . . I guess we just have to tell her in a way that she'll
believe. Besides, that's why we had prayer together. Remember? We asked Heavenly Father to help us convince
Mom, and he will. But Tess, we have to do it tonight. For
Trace's sake!"

Tess sighed deeply. "For Trace's sake," she repeated.
For a moment the two sisters touched hands, gaining
strength from each other. And then, silently, they opened
the door of their bedroom and walked down the hall and
into the kitchen, where their mother was working on her
Relief Society lesson for the next morning.

"Mom," Tish said quietly, "I know you're busy, but Tess
and I have to talk to you. Right now."

11:15 P.M.

The clock in the living room chimed 11:15, past time
to be in bed. From in front of her sewing center in the
family room, Jeanee raced against the hour. By 11:30 she
would have the white eyelet lace attached to the collar.
Smiling, she thought of how darling little Amber would
look in delicate pink little hearts with white lace framing
her little pixie face.

Off in the corner a television newscast was on mute.
Jeanee kept the picture on for "company." But she was in
her own world, separate from harsh realities, her head
down and her surger pushed to the maximum. Beautiful

little dresses and nighties and summer jams and T-shirts filled her mind, and nothing else. In another corner the paint on a little clown face was drying for the T-shirt that would be her next project.

"She's going to be the best-dressed little two-year-old in her ward."

Startled by Frank's voice, Jeanee spun around. "You frightened me," she gasped. "I didn't even know you were home from the church."

"I've been standing here for the past two or three minutes, Jeanee. But I don't wonder that you didn't hear me. I . . . I don't know how to get your attention anymore."

"I'm sorry," Jeanee said, avoiding the unspoken plea for communication. "I just have a couple more things I want to get done."

"Tonight?" Frank protested.

"You know how it is, honey. I'm on a creative roll."

"Don't you want to create a little sleep?" Frank persisted, attempting humor.

Jeanee squinted her eyes and tilted her head to one side. She couldn't explain to Frank how afraid she had become of bedtime. She herself did not understand. Giving Frank her "poor-picked-on-little-girl" look, she pleaded. "Oh, honey, I'm sorry. I really need to do this. Please try to understand."

"I'm trying," Frank said with a shrug, "but the next time I try to pull myself away from my music, Jeanee . . . "

"I know," she said as she finished his sentence, "I'll understand."

Frank looked around the family room as he walked away. A week's worth of laundry was waiting to be folded, and several newspapers were piled by the end table. It wasn't like Jeanee to leave things undone, but for the last month her behavior had grown increasingly compulsive. She'd leave something undone for too long, then feverishly catch it up to perfection. There was no slowing her down, whatever she did.

And her refusal to go to bed with him at night was beginning to be a real problem. Frank liked to believe that he was an understanding husband, but this was beyond reason. He knew his wife was hurting, and he wanted to be supportive. But the fact was that Jeanee was shutting him out of her life. And right now, with what was happening in the ward, he needed her to be there for him.

"Jeanee," he said, grabbing a chair and sitting down beside her, "I know you're upset about Amber, and it's going to take time for all of us to get over it. But you've got to understand that they're doing everything they can for her."

Jeanee continued to rip out a row of lace with the seam ripper. There was no expression on her face.

"Jeanee," he pleaded, reaching out and taking her hand, "please. It might help to talk about it."

Jeanee swallowed hard, not wanting to approach the subject of Amber's abuse.

"Frank," she finally responded, "I know you believe they're doing everything they can. But tonight, when you were at the church, Megan called. They're not going to be pressing charges against that boy."

"*What?*"

"I said, they're not going to be pressing charges." There was no feeling in Jeanee's voice.

"That doesn't make sense. How can they *not* press charges?"

"Amber's too young to testify."

"But they have the hospital records!"

"That doesn't prove he did it."

"Well, Amber pointed him out! She said his name. What can they say to that?"

"They can't say anything. Amber is too young to testify in court, so he goes free. Benjamin Brattles has committed the perfect crime." Jeanee's voice was still without expression.

Frank dropped his head into his hands. Ever since they had returned from vacation, a distance had been growing between him and Jeanee. He didn't understand why, but it was there.

During the entire time they had been with Tony and Megan, Jeanee had gone around the house picking up, cleaning the bathroom, cleaning the refrigerator, and making meals for the freezer, refusing to offer comfort and tenderness. It was unlike his wife to be so distant. And it concerned him then.

But now—this new information.

"Jeanee, honey, we just have to trust that Heavenly Father will work all this out—for good."

Jeanee didn't respond, and Frank, looking at her expressionless face, felt a sudden chill. "What are you feeling?" he coaxed.

"Feeling?" Jeanee responded. "I don't feel anything. Nothing. That's what I feel."

Jeanee's emotions had gone into hiding the moment Frank mentioned Amber. And her only hope to maintain some semblance of strength was to keep them safely sealed in that darkness.

"Honey," Frank said softly, "I'm sorry. I wish I could have been here with you and helped you with the call."

"I know," Jeanee returned. "I know you're doing what you're supposed to do. You can't be here all the time, and I know that. So I have to be strong and—" Jeanee's lip quivered but she fought against it.

"I'm here now, Jeanee," Frank stated hopefully. "I'm here. What can I do to make it better?"

"I don't know that anybody can make it better." Jeanee's voice was flat.

"But let me try, honey," Frank pleaded. "Let me try."

Woodenly, Jeanee dropped her sewing in her lap and

turned to search her husband's face. And that was all it took to overtake her stony resistance. She could hold the flood of emotions no longer.

"Make the bad things stop happening," she cried, breaking into sobs. "Somebody *has* to make the bad things stop happening." And as Frank held her close, breathing all the love he could into her trembling body, he was amazed at how much like a little girl his wife suddenly sounded.

9

SUNDAY, JULY 14

10:05 A.M.

The side doors of the chapel were opened to the outside, letting in the slightest morning breeze — a welcome relief for those sitting close to the doors. The rest of the congregation sat either dozing uncomfortably or fanning themselves with paper programs.

"It's a good thing this is the last speaker," Mel Blodgett whispered as he leaned toward Frank. "The natives are restless today. Too bad they didn't get that air-conditioning fixed."

From the stand Frank looked over his congregation. The noise level was too high, with little children fidgeting after nearly an hour's worth of sacrament meeting. Brother Wally Bradshaw was just starting his talk on the Mormon pioneers.

"Think of what Primary is going to be like," Mel whispered out of the side of his mouth. "Especially with those McCrasky boys."

"And as we sit here," Brother Bradshaw was saying from the pulpit, "in our comfortable chapel" — the congregation chuckled as he flapped his arms for ventilation — "we need to think of our forefathers and their trek over a dusty, hot, snake- and insect-ridden wilderness to find the place they could finally call their own.

"They willingly paid such a price so that we could enjoy the freedom to worship, free from persecution, free from intolerance, free from outside interference and mob rule. Thus we commemorate their legacy to us this coming week, as we celebrate the 24th of July—"

Frank scanned his program. The picnic was scheduled at Lincoln Rock Park, north of town, and would take most of the following Saturday afternoon.

A scuffle on the front row caused Frank to look down. Jimmy and Willy McCrasky were at it again, fighting a perpetual battle that never seemed to end, except in his garden.

"I'll be hearing from the Primary president today for sure," Frank said to himself, wincing. "Oh, those boys! And they're such good kids, too. All they need is some gentle encouragement and understanding."

On the other side of the boys sat June, bright, articulate, adult-pleasing June, now doing her best to calm her brothers down. Despite what Mrs. O. had said, Frank was hoping she would be assigned to his class in school. Next to June sat her mother, Elaine McCrasky, silent now in meeting but looking harried and frustrated nonetheless. As he studied Elaine, Frank knew that something was going to need to be said or she would never stop her verbal abuse of the children. Of course, Frank would also need to visit with Brother Ralph McCrasky the next time he was in town.

Behind the McCrasky family sat the Nelsons, real stalwarts in the ward. Lowell was a Scouter's Scouter, and Rita was one of the most tenderhearted women he had ever known. They had a family of fantastic children, too—great people! Near them were the Lamberts, Richard and Sharon, and two rows back were Craig and LaDawn Godwin and their lovely daughter Jillyne. Those as well as Susan and Luke Savage, and, before her mission call, Christine Dees, were currently assisting an elderly couple from another ward in caring for their severely handicapped daughter. They did this not with money but with their precious time, tending the child over and over again so the parents could attend church together and get an occasional evening out. Frank's heart swelled with love as he considered them, for this was done quietly, with no fanfare whatsoever. Continually he found himself thanking God that he could be associated with such wonderful, giving people.

A few rows behind the Godwins, Jeanee sat quietly next to her friend Marie, with her arm around Angie. She looked beautiful in her early summer tan, even though it was obvious to Frank that she was too tired.

"I wish," Frank said to himself, "that she could just let go of this thing with Amber. As terrible as it is, she can't make it better by falling apart. If she would just realize that in time Amber will forget."

Frank was proud of Jeanee's fellowshipping efforts with Marie the past few weeks, however, especially in the face of her own personal struggles. His wife seemed to force herself to rise above her own problems whenever Marie called or came for a visit. In fact, she pushed herself too hard. It was just as Erik had said—she acted as if she were in a race that had no finish line. And that concerned Frank.

"Well," he said to himself as his heart swelled with benevolence, "after my interview with Marie this afternoon, she won't be leaning on Jeanee so much. Marie needs to stop letting scars from her past rob her of the happiness she deserves today."

Frank had already interviewed Marie twice in the past few weeks, letting her do most of the talking. And that had seemed good, despite the fact that her monologue had been such a rehash of old problems.

"It's time," he thought, "that I reassure Marie that she doesn't have to hold onto them any longer." Frank almost smiled as he thought of how relieved Marie would feel when he explained that none of the terrible things she remembered had been her fault, so she could get on with her life.

Across the aisle from Marie, Abby Martin was taking a paper airplane away from her youngest son. "The poor woman," he thought to himself, "If only she had been more understanding with her husband, he would be with her right now."

Frank thought back to his last interview with John Martin. Speaking softly and yet earnestly, John had convinced him that if Abby hadn't been such a nag, they would still be together.

Of course Abby and the children did have physical needs that had to be met — needs that for some reason John was neglecting. That had to be because John didn't have things worked out yet, and so Frank was willing to offer assistance until he did. Meanwhile, somehow he needed to get Abby into his office to talk. There, he felt certain, he could make her understand that if she would only be more tolerant, her marriage would be fine.

Mel Blodgett didn't share Frank's opinion. To Mel, John Martin was a first-class jerk, and he wasn't the least bit hesitant in saying so. But then, there were times when Frank had some uneasy feelings about Mel.

Abruptly Frank stopped, chagrined. All that he had against the man, he convinced himself, was the fact that he seemed so many of the things Frank himself wished to be. It went beyond admiration to envy sometimes. And scolding himself for his own unrighteousness, Frank forced his thoughts back to the people before him.

For a moment, he thought about Claudia and Robby Nichol and wondered how they were doing now that they had moved out of the ward. He was also missing Bob Nichol, who definitely should have been in attendance.

Whereas Frank felt critical of Abby Martin for the failure of her marriage, he felt that Claudia Nichol was perfectly justified in leaving her husband. Until Bob could learn to control his temper, Frank felt, he was an absolute menace.

"So as we fill our picnic plates, and enjoy the games of our celebration this coming Saturday," Brother Bradshaw's booming voice declared, interrupting Frank's thoughts, "let's remember the reason behind our celebration. These great pioneers that have gone before us deserve both our memories and our respect. They sacrificed so much for our freedom. They suffered, chose to suffer, actually, in order that we might have this great heritage."

"Choosing to suffer," Frank said to himself. "Interesting concept. It's certainly different from suffering because of someone else's choices." Again Frank surveyed the congregation, feeling his heart swelling with emotion and his eyes moistening. How he loved these people! Of course he would have preferred being a little less weepy about it. But tenderness was a part of Frank's nature. And he was ever thankful that Heavenly Father had given him the capacity to love his ward members as he did.

"How many of these people are suffering because of someone else's choices?" he pondered. "After all, abuse is an unrighteous attack on another's freedom, and whether I wanted to admit it or not, my ward is not immune to it."

Actually, he thought with startling clarity, the several different and unique problems a few of his ward members were experiencing really were abuse. Marie had been abused, Jeanee was convinced that Abby Martin had been abused—though Frank was concerned it was the other way around—Claudia and Robby Nichol had been abused by Bob, and Elaine McCrasky was verbally abusing her children. Frank's eyes again fell on his wife, and for the first time he realized that she was also dealing with abuse. "But why is she struggling so with it?" he wondered. "Why can't she accept what has happened and put it behind her?

"Maybe I need to remind her of what she taught me, about praying for our enemies. Jeanee needs to be praying for that Brattles boy, not hating him. I can't blame her under the circumstances. But the poor kid needs her prayers, not her anger."

Abruptly, Frank realized that Mel Blodgett was back at the pulpit, and, as always, everyone in the congregation was riveted by the man's charisma.

"It has been requested by our lovely chorister that we change the final hymn to number 143. And of course I give in to my better half." Mel grinned back at his wife, Carol, who stood unsmiling behind the music stand next to the organ. He winked broadly at the approving congregation and sat down. There was a rustling of pages and a combined sigh of relief from all of them.

Then, as everyone joined in singing, "Let the Holy Spirit Guide," Frank fought once more against some troubled thoughts concerning his counselor.

12:02 P.M.

As they walked out of the Relief Society room, Marie's anger was obvious even to Jeanee.

"I'm sorry," Marie apologized, "for being so upset."

"Well, Marie, some of the comments people made during Carol's lesson were a little strange, especially those made by Sister Byston."

"I can't believe how myopic that woman is."

"She was kind of strange," Jeanee agreed. "Did you see her expression when that young mother said her husband was in counseling?"

Marie grimaced. "She didn't have a clue, did she?"

"She definitely didn't agree that counseling might occasionally be necessary."

"I'll say! I thought for a moment they were going to get into it right there in front of everyone." Marie smiled thinly.

"Carol usually has better control of her classes than

that," Jeanee said. "I don't understand what was wrong today."

"Oh, don't worry about it," Marie answered. "With all that woman does, who wouldn't be flustered? I mean, leading the singing, three children, PTA president, and a husband in the bishopric? And her husband — isn't there something odd about him? He seems too good to be true. You know what I mean?"

Jeanee was surprised by Marie's comment, and embarrassed. "Yes, I guess he comes across that way. But he's Frank's right-hand man, and Frank swears by him." Jeanee couldn't tell Marie that she, too, had never felt comfortable around Mel Blodgett.

"Jeanee," a smiling, round woman interrupted, "I want to meet your friend." She reached her hand out to Marie. "I'm Blanche Byston. It was wonderful of you to come today. Has Jeanee told you that we can use your lovely voice in our ward choir?"

"Blanche is the choir organist," Jeanee explained.

"Jeanee hasn't said anything about the choir yet." Marie looked to Jeanee for support. "But she probably will."

"I'd like to meet this lady, too," another voice called from the stream of sisters filing from the Relief Society room.

"Oh, Terri," Jeanee responded, "and I want you to meet her. Marie, this is Terri Elder, our Relief Society president and a very dear friend. Terri, Marie Spencer."

"What a brave soul, to come on the one day when the air-conditioning isn't working," Terri joked, fanning herself. "Are you visiting from out of town, or are you new in our ward?"

"I hope she's new in the ward." Sister Byston nudged Terri with her elbow. "Her voice would sound wonderful in our choir, don't you think?"

"I do think so." Terri smiled. "Oh, and by the way,

here's that piece I wanted you to put in the ward news-letter, Blanche. Can you get it in for August?" Terri handed Sister Byston a slip of paper.

"One thing about me," the woman nodded. "When you ask me to do something, you know it will get done."

Terri smiled. "You do keep things going."

"Speaking of going," Sister Byston said, looking around, "I'm having the Bailey family over for dinner. I really need to run."

"She has enough energy for two people," Marie observed as the woman hurried away.

"She's right about the ward choir," Terri said to Marie. "Your voice would be a nice addition." Then, turning to Jeanee, she asked, "You okay today?"

"I'm fine," Jeanee assured her. "Just a little tired, is all."

"And this heat doesn't help," Terri agreed, smiling at Marie. "I feel sorry for the next ward."

Terri squeezed Jeanee's hand. "If you need to talk," she whispered in her ear, "I'm here."

Jeanee bit her lip and swallowed hard. "I know," she whispered back. "And thanks—a lot."

As Terri was turning to leave, Jeanee noticed Tish Blodgett. "There's someone I want you to meet." Jeanee guided Marie toward the foyer.

Tish turned from her search of the Primary children filing into the foyer. "Oh, hi, Jeanee," she smiled, "I was just looking for Trace."

"Trace is her little sister," Jeanee explained to Marie. "This is Carol Blodgett's daughter, Tish. If you ever need a super babysitter, Marie, Tish is it."

"That's good to know." Marie laughed.

"Nice to meet you." Tish smiled rather weakly. "There's Trace. I guess I need to be going." She excused herself, leaving Jeanee puzzled at the distance in her behavior.

Just then Trace came bouncing up to her sister, along

with a large group of children who were all searching for their parents. The foyer was bustling with crowds all look-ing for family members so they could escape the heat into their air-conditioned cars. Jeanee felt suddenly drained.

"Can you imagine what it's going to be like for the next ward?" Erik laughed as he caught up with his mother and Marie. "I really feel sorry for them."

"Feel sorry for your father," Jeanee countered weakly. "He's got interviews all afternoon."

"Oh, that reminds me," Marie interjected. "I'm one of them. I need to let Dave know that I'll be home later than I thought."

She was dialing the phone on the wall when Frank opened the door to his office. "Whew!" he said, fanning himself as his two counselors followed out behind him. "If this is a preview of hades, brethren, I'm going to start repenting immediately."

Jeanee smiled across the foyer at him as Angie appeared with a group of searching little children. She was carrying a smiley face on a stick. "See, Mommy," she said, beaming. "It has a happy face on one side and a sad face on the other. Teacher says we get to decide—"

"Well, let's decide to be cool," Erik interrupted. "I'm ready for some air-conditioning." With that, he headed for the door.

Jeanee looked over at Frank. "Will you be long?" she asked.

"Only long enough to soak a perfectly clean suit," he teased, winking. Then, seeing that his joke hadn't been funny to Jeanee, he asked, "Are you okay?"

Jeanee shrugged. "Hot and tired," she responded. "I need to get home."

"And you need to get some rest," Frank encouraged, speaking above the confusion around them. "Remember, this *is* a day of rest."

Jeanee caught the strong message her husband was

sending. "I hear you," she replied, forcing another weak smile. "I'll get some rest."

Then, while Marie followed Frank into his office, Jeanee and Angie walked out through the door, Angie loudly singing, "No one likes a frowny face. Change it for a smile. Make the world a better place, by smiling all the while."

2:15 P.M.

"Mom." Erik walked up behind his mother in the kitchen. "What're you doing?"

Jeanee was at the counter, feverishly organizing a stack of file cards.

"Just getting some things in order," she said with a sigh.

"What're all those cards?"

"All the sisters in the ward. I'm organizing them according to their needs so I can make certain they're all being taken care of."

She took out the card with Abby Martin's name on it and made a note to drop off a couple of encouraging tapes for Abby to listen to.

"Is that restful for you?" Erik probed.

"Uh . . . yes, I guess so," was the only reply.

"That's good," Erik said, sounding unconvinced. "Because I wouldn't want you to ignore Dad's advice."

"What advice?"

"Angie told me. He told you to rest this afternoon."

"Oh, yes," Jeanee replied, sounding preoccupied. "He did, didn't he."

"And a ten-minute nap probably isn't what he had in mind — do you think?"

Jeanee looked up at her son and took a deep breath. "No, it probably isn't."

"Mom?" Erik straddled a stool and sat next to his

mother. "Dad told me I didn't need to know about this, but I've been thinking a lot. I'd like to know what happened to Amber. That's why you can't sleep, isn't it? I've been watching you lately, and you're not looking so good."

Tears sprang instantly to Jeanee's eyes. She made a strange little laugh/sigh and turned to face her son. "Erik, I . . ."

"Mom, if you don't want to, you don't have to tell me."

Smiling through tears, Jeanee reached out and touched Erik's cheek. "Yes, Amber was hurt — and no, it isn't why I can't sleep, at least not altogether. It's just so many things —"

Jeanee paused for a moment and then looked beyond her son.

"I guess you have a right to know what's going on." Jeanee swallowed hard and bit her lips together. She didn't want to wound her son with the information he was asking for. And yet her silence was probably more painful for him than the truth she was hiding. Strange, that in this situation it was clear she needed to tell.

"Erik," she finally admitted, "little Amber was molested."

Erik almost gasped. "That explains it," he managed to say. "Mom, I'm so sorry." There was deep empathy in his voice and in his eyes. "Is there anything I can do — to help you feel better?"

"I . . . I'm not sure what that would take, son." Jeanee shook her head and sniffed back her tears. "I don't . . . understand what I'm feeling. It seems my world is tumbling down around me, and yet when I look at it, all is intact. You're here," Jeanee reached out and patted Erik's hand, "and Angie, and your dad — and all I can do is keep pushing ahead, trying not to feel —"

The ring of the telephone startled Jeanee, but Erik picked it up before she could respond.

"Yes, this is the Greaves residence . . . No, he's at the

church. Would you like the number?" Erik rattled off the number at his father's office, said good-bye, and then turned back to his mother.

"Would you like a foot-rub?" he asked. "You know that helps."

"I just want to keep busy," Jeanee countered. "When I stop moving or sit for too long or lie down, I feel like my nerves are going to crawl right out of my body."

"Weird, Mom."

"I . . . know," she replied, forcing a laugh. "But I'll be okay, really."

The telephone rang again, and this time, as Erik handed it to Jeanee, he whispered, "we should take that thing off the hook. Either that or get Dad to hook up his new answering machine."

Jeanee sat up straight and forced a cheery voice. "Hello? Oh, yes, Tish." There was a long pause, and then Jeanee became concerned. "Of course you can come over. . . . Right away would be fine. . . . No, the bishop isn't here. I don't expect him for another hour or so. I took his lunch to him at the church, so he may even be longer than that. . . . You bet, Tish. I'll see you in a few minutes."

As Jeanee hung up the phone, Erik looked concerned. "Mom," he pleaded, "please don't overdo it."

"For a sixteen-year-old kid, you sure worry a lot."

"Just promise me," he persisted.

"All right, I promise. In fact, I think I'll go to my room and read the scriptures for a few minutes while I wait for Tish."

Leaning down, Erik kissed Jeanee on the nose. "Love ya, Mom. We'll let you know when Tish arrives."

2:40 P.M.

"Mom, Tish is here."

"Thanks, punkin," Jeanee answered her daughter. "What're you doing now?"

"I'm just listening to the *Scripture Scouts* and coloring."

"Good for you," Jeanee replied, getting up from the bed and straightening her hair in the mirror. "Will you be okay for another hour if I take Tish into Daddy's office?"

"Isn't Tish going to play with me?" Angie asked, sounding disappointed.

"Not this time, honey. Will you be okay?"

"Is it okay if I call Trace?" Angie asked. "And can she spend the night?"

"If you'd like. Now don't bother me anymore. Okay?"

Jeanee could hear Angie's excited voice on the phone as she walked to meet Tish at the door. Tish, a very pretty girl with huge brown eyes, was the oldest of the Blodgett girls.

"Come in out of that heat!" Jeanee invited.

"Days like today," Tish said sheepishly, "I wish it was okay to swim on Sunday."

"I know what you mean," Jeanee replied, making conversation. "Can I get you something to drink? Juice? Ice water?"

"No, thank you," Tish answered a bit uneasily. "Can we talk, Jeanee? In private?"

Jeanee had known when she saw Tish at church that something had been bothering her. But she wasn't prepared to hear the story Tish began pouring out once they were in Frank's office.

It was a horrible story. Between tears and angry outbursts, Tish went on about years of desperation and shame. And Jeanee just listened, fighting back her own tears.

Why hadn't she noticed that something was wrong? All these years and she had never suspected. Jeanee was suddenly angry at herself. And yet, even if she had known, what could she have done?

"What about your mother, Tish?" Jeanee finally asked. "Has she known?"

"That's the crazy part," Tish replied. "I really think

she has. But she wouldn't admit it. Tess and I tried to tell
her once—in fact, one time she walked in on Dad and me
in the bathroom. But she wouldn't believe what she saw."

"And now she knows?"

"Tess and I told her last night, late, while Dad was still
at work." Fresh tears sprang to the young girl's eyes. "Then
we told the police. All three of us talked to Jerry Crandal."

"Oh, Tish, honey. That must have scared you to death!"

Again Tish broke down and cried. "But we had to,
Jeanee! He started in on Trace!"

"Oh, no!" Jeanee cried out.

Abruptly there was a knock at the door.

"Mom," Angie's voice called, sounding worried, "are
you okay in there?"

"Honey, we're okay. We won't be much longer."

"I'm scared, Mommy. I have a funny feeling. Please
come out."

Jeanee opened the door and knelt to hug her little
daughter. "Would you do me a favor?" she asked. "Would
you go turn *Scripture Scouts* on one more time. Then I'll
be finished before you're through listening to it. Would
you do that for Mommy?"

Angie reluctantly agreed and went back up to her bedroom.

"I really do need to get home," Tish said, clearing her
throat. "I don't want to leave my sisters alone for too long."

"I understand," Jeanee said softly.

"Just pray for us," Tish said as she squeezed Jeanee's
hand. "I don't want anything bad to happen to Daddy, or
us either, and I'm scared maybe it will."

"I'll pray for you," Jeanee assured her, tears starting
once again in her eyes. "Honey, I'm so sorry this happened."

"I just had to tell you, even though we weren't supposed to tell anyone until after the police decide what to
do. Mom says we have to go in to visit with some people

at the State Social Services tomorrow, and I'm really scared about that. What if they don't believe us? What if Daddy finds out and tells them it's all a big lie? *Please* don't tell anybody, Jeanee. Not yet."

"I won't," Jeanee promised as she hugged Tish close to her. "Not even my husband."

As Jeanee watched Tish walk down the street in the afternoon heat, she shuddered to think of what lay ahead for the girl. How could this have happened? How could something like this go on, with nobody knowing? Remembering her promise to Tish, however, she knew that she had the answer.

"It's a secret," she whispered softly, fiercely. "Everyone is sworn not to tell. It's the deep, dark secret that you hold inside because to tell it would mean to destroy the perverted balance of things."

Even she, who should have known better, had agreed to remain silent. But this time something was going to be done, she consoled herself. She wouldn't have to remain silent too long. This time, something was going to be done.

10

MONDAY, JULY 15

6:30 P.M.

With a "whoosh" Frank came to the surface of the pool, shaking his head to clear the water from his ears. Angie squealed with delight as he looked in her direction and then began frantically swimming toward the corner where Jeanee waited. Leisurely Frank stroked in that direction, forgetting for the moment that Erik was somewhere behind or beneath him. The break being all he needed, Erik slipped silently beneath the water where he kicked himself forward, and the next thing Frank knew, he had been grabbed forcefully by the ankles and yanked violently toward the bottom of the pool.

Sputtering as he finally broke the surface again, Frank found himself beset by two attackers who were both bent on splashing him into oblivion. Fighting back valiantly, he again drove Angie toward her mother's corner, and then, after a fierce battle with Erik, drove him at last to dive and get away.

"Whew!" he gasped as he dog-paddled to the corner where Jeanee waited quietly. "That gets harder every time!"

As Frank caught his breath, Angie once again launched an attack, which he quickly ended by grabbing his daughter and pinioning her arms to her sides.

"Daddy!" she shrieked, holding her nose in preparation. "Don't put me under! Please don't—"

With a wild yell Frank did just that, then laughed with his little daughter as he helped her break the surface of the pool a few seconds later.

"Do it again, Daddy! Do it again!"

Laughing, Frank gave Angie a bear hug. "Not now, punkin. Daddy's nearly drowned as it is. I think it's about time to get out."

"What's the matter, Dad?" Erik growled in his newly acquired deep voice. "Chicken?"

Animatedly Frank nodded. "I'll say, at least when you're around. Personally, I've had enough of this particular family home evening activity. I've got so much water in me that I'll never have room for those chocolate éclairs I picked up earlier."

"Chocolate éclairs!" Angie shrieked. "Yay for Daddy! Yay for Daddy!"

"Erik," Frank said, "why don't you and Angie take charge of getting them for us. I left them in the trunk of the car."

"In the trunk of the car? In this heat?" Erik was surprised.

"Oops! Guess that wasn't such a good idea," Frank admitted. "Looks like we'll have hot éclairs for desert."

"We'll just stick 'em in the freezer for a couple of minutes," Erik suggested. "Come on, Angie-pangie."

"I'm not Angie-pangie!"

"You are so," Erik teased. "Now get my legs in gear, and let's get moving!"

"They're not your legs!" Angie retorted. "They're mine!"

"You're my sister, aren't you?"

"Well, yes. But—"

Erik grinned. "Then they're my legs. Now come on, let's move them!"

"Get some milk, too!" Frank called as the two disappeared into the house, still arguing good-naturedly. Then he turned toward his wife. "Boy, those kids can sure give you a workout!"

Jeanee floated in the corner of the pool without moving, no expression on her face. Frank moved silently toward her, pulled her up close to him in the water, and kissed her tenderly.

"Hey, I noticed that you weren't in on the attack."

Saying nothing, Jeanee simply looked at her husband with empty eyes.

"Jeanee," Frank said, pulling back a little. "what's wrong?"

"Wrong?" she repeated, finally breaking her silence. "Why . . . do you think something has to be wrong?"

Frank laughed with good-natured sarcasm. "Why? My darling, let me count the ways. First, I don't think you've given me a real smile since our vacation. I know it's a difficult situation, honey, but I just wish you could look beyond your own pain and start reaching out a little to those who love you."

Jeanee tensed in Frank's arms, but he pretended not to notice.

"Tony even asked me, when we were visiting," he continued, "if he'd done something to offend you. Everybody's concerned about you. Terri Elder asked me how you were doing yesterday after sacrament meeting. I guess you already told her about Amber?"

Jeanee nodded as she stared into the water.

"Anyway, she's obviously worried too."

"There's no reason for you to be worried," Jeanee stated flatly.

"Oh, right. 'Don't worry, Frank. My behavior is totally altered, and I look like a walking depression factory, but don't worry about me. I won't be fine.' Come on, Jeanee. What do you want of me? To stop loving you, or caring about you? I'm sorry, but I can't do that."

"You can't understand, either!"

"What?"

"It just isn't possible."

A new edge was growing between them. And Frank was caught completely at a disadvantage.

"What are you telling me, Jeanee?" he asked, shaking the water from his ears.

"You don't know the language." Jeanee turned quietly to climb out of the pool.

"Heavenly Father," Frank prayed silently, "this makes no sense to me. Please help me to understand what she's talking about . . . " He left the prayer open.

"Is this some kind of riddle?" he asked in a matter-of-fact tone as he followed her to the towels on the chaise lounge.

Jeanee was silent. The only sounds were the pool pump and the air conditioner.

"Jeanee" — Frank walked closer, taking one of the towels and beginning to dry himself — "if you don't want to talk about it, I'll try to understand. But this has been going on for too long now, honey. We need to get some dialogue going here."

Jeanee clutched her towel neatly in front of her and looked directly into her husband's eyes and then quickly away.

"You can't understand, Frank. You just *can't.*"

"Try me."

"I have been."

"What?"

"I sent a dear friend to see you, someone who needs desperately to find some hope in the gospel of Jesus Christ. And you — "

"I what?"

"You told her to stop feeling sorry for herself and to get on with her life."

"I don't recall saying that to anyone. Who are you talking about? Not Marie, surely?"

Jeanee looked at Frank with a expression of despair. "*Yes*, Marie. She called me this afternoon, and—"

"Honey, I did not tell Marie to stop feeling sorry for herself. I did nothing but encourage her. In fact, I told her that as her bishop, I felt impressed to tell her that she was free to go on with her life."

Jeanee cringed. "You *wounded* her! You *minimized* her pain! You made her feel that the gospel has *no* place for people who are hurting!"

"Whoa, whoa, whoa!" Frank put a finger to his wife's lips. "Settle down, honey. You're giving Sister McCrasky a run for her money."

"It's serious, Frank! And you don't even seem to have a clue what it's all about!" With that, Jeanee turned to leave.

"Eclairs and milk!" Erik and Angie appeared from the kitchen with paper plates, cups, and napkins. "One more trip and we'll see how the éclairs fared their harrowing experience in the trunk of the Greaves family limousine."

Jeanee hurried past her children and into the house. "Don't you *dare* eat those éclairs," she ordered brusquely.

"They won't be that bad," Erik defended, looking after her.

"I said don't eat them, Erik, and I meant it!"

"Is Mommy okay?" Angie asked Frank. "She sounds upset."

"Did I say something wrong?" Erik pressed.

"You kids are fine," Frank assured them, watching his wife disappear behind the french doors. "The éclairs are probably spoiled, all right, so why don't you get some ice cream or frozen yogurt out of the freezer and get started on dessert. Mom and I will be out in a minute or two."

The door to the bedroom was shut when Frank reached the top of the stairs, but he could hear Jeanee sobbing quietly behind it. Reaching down, he discovered that it was also locked. For a moment he waited, listening. Then, knowing that the confrontation had to be made, he began gently knocking.

"Jeanee," he spoke loud enough for her to hear clearly. "I know you're upset, but you need to let me in."

There was no response.

"I can get the key and open the door myself," Frank persisted.

Still no response.

"Okay, I'm leaving now," he called to his wife. "I'll be back in a minute with the key, and we can talk then."

The door opened as he was turning to walk downstairs. Jeanee's wet hair was tousled down to her shoulders. She was wearing a robe, and her eyes were wet with tears.

"You can come in. I'm sorry." Jeanee sniffled. "But there's too much happening and too many people getting hurt!"

"Okay," Frank conceded, "a lot is going on." He walked into the room, wrapping his towel around him. "And I know you're upset. So let's take it one thing at a time, okay?"

"Okay."

"Where do you want to sit?"

"Can we sit on the floor?"

"Floor's fine," Frank agreed as he tried to sit at the foot of the bed, Indian style. "Well, it would have been fine a few years ago." He smiled as he climbed back up. "How about you take the bed and I'll take the chair?"

Jeanee agreed, handing him a dry towel to sit on.

Once they were seated and facing each other, Frank began. "Okay, one thing at a time. What's bothering you the most?"

"I . . . don't know."

"All right, when did it start?"

There was a long pause, the only sounds being cars that were passing outside the window. Frank waited and silently continued praying.

"It . . . it started with Amber — no, with Marie — no, with President Stone's mother dying — no, I don't remember. It was the time you were gone most of the night with Robby Nichol."

Jeanee's eyes were on her hands in her lap. Frank waited and listened.

"I thought it was going to be such a wonderful summer — the vacation to see Tony and Megan, and you were going to be home more, and — well — everything was going to be so perfect. And then everything went wrong!"

Jeanee looked at her husband and sniffled again. "You know all that's been going wrong since then."

Frank reached out and gently covered his wife's hand with his. "I know what's been going wrong, honey. It's how it has been affecting you that I don't understand."

"I know." Jeanee wiped a tear with her free hand. "That's what I'm trying to explain."

"I'm listening."

"But will you hear?"

"I'll do my best."

"Okay, it's like, I know men don't see things the way women do." Jeanee looked intently into her husband's eyes.

"True." Frank smiled.

"Women have needs that men don't understand."

"And vise versa." Frank ignored a chill hitting his back.

"Okay. One of the needs that women have is that when bad things happen to them, they need to talk about it. They need someone they can trust to help them through it, to listen, like you're doing now."

"Makes sense so far."

"Well, when it's men that hurt women, women need to find out and understand that all men aren't like the ones who hurt them."

Jeanee reached for the afghan at the foot of the bed and handed it to her shivering husband.

"Let's start with Marie. She's been hurt a lot—by men, many of them, in fact."

"She's been hurt far too much," Frank agreed. "And I don't want to see her hurt anymore."

"That's it!" Jeanee finally let her anger out. "*You* don't want to *see* her hurt. But she'll keep on hurting whether you want to *see* it or not. The pain is there, Frank. And until it's fully resolved, it has to be accepted—by you—by whomever she goes to for help. Until someone cares enough to let her talk about it until she thinks she's finished talking about it, she's going to hurt more than you will ever know! In fact, she's hurting so bad that she's turning completely away from the gospel that was sent by Christ to save her!"

"Jeanee, I think you're being dramatic," Frank declared by way of disagreement. "She's an intelligent woman. She'll do just fine."

"No, Frank, she won't! Because inside that intelligent woman is the soul of a wounded, immature child. And that child is terrified of trusting a man. Yet you, a man, told her not to talk about it ever again—just like her father did every time he molested her!"

Frank was silent.

"Marie called me this afternoon. She's written you a letter. She'll be dropping it by either tonight or tomorrow morning."

"I'm sorry if I upset her," Frank said sincerely. "I . . . I only wanted to make her life happier."

"I know," Jeanee sighed, knowing her husband's heart. "But you hurt her."

"Well, I'll read the letter and see what I can do after that."

"Tread softly, Frank," Jeanee urged. "You have no idea the depth of pain she's feeling."

"I'll tread softly," Frank promised, squeezing his wife's hand. "Is there something more you wanted to talk about?"

Jeanee hesitated a moment and then took a deep breath. "I don't understand at all what you're doing about Abby—"

"Sister Martin is another story," Frank interrupted. "I've talked with John. Abby has brought her problems upon herself. I'm trying to help her see that."

"But Frank—"

"Jeanee," Frank said, holding up his hand, "believe me. Abby is taking advantage here if she's telling you otherwise. John told me that she was manipulative, and this just proves it."

Jeanee dropped her head in sorrow. "Frank, you've always been so loving, to me and the children as well as to the ward members. I can't believe I'm hearing what you're saying."

"Sweetheart," Frank said, patting his wife's hand, "you just can't stand to see anyone suffer, even if they deserve it."

"Frank, Abby *doesn't* deserve it!"

Frank sighed. "Okay, I'll talk with her again. Will that make you happy?"

Jeanee nodded. "But Frank, promise me that you'll pray about her before you do. Please?"

With a start, Frank realized that he had not prayed about John and Abby. Oh, he had prayed for them, but he had never prayed *about* them. Only the situation was so obvious there that he had seen no need. Even now—

"Please, Frank?"

"Okay," he sighed, "I'll pray about it. What's next?"

"I don't like the way Erik called Angie's legs his legs."

Frank stifled a laugh. "Are you kidding? That's just a tease, and you know it! Jeanee, I think you're carrying this thing too far."

"But it's not a good tease!" Jeanee was emphatic. "They're Angie's legs and no one else's! They're her legs!"

"Come on, Jeanee, lighten up."

"I mean it, Frank. That needs to stop."

"Okay, whatever you say." Frank, finally irritated, rolled his eyes and tilted his head to one side.

"I hate it when you do that," Jeanee's tone was accusing. "You don't mean what you just promised. You're patronizing me!"

"Okay, Jeanee," Frank countered, his patience almost at an end. "We won't talk about that anymore. Okay?"

There was a long pause, and Jeanee's irritation with Frank was obvious.

"Now let's talk about what's really bothering you," Frank continued. "Okay? Let's talk about Amber. Isn't that what all this is really about?"

There was no response.

"Jeanee."

"I can't talk about that," Jeanee stated flatly.

"What's the difference between me not talking and you not talking?"

"There's a big difference," Jeanee said with a sigh.

"That's nonsense. Besides, if we don't talk about Amber, how can we ever work it out?"

"I don't know if we ever can. Besides, isn't this how you avoid conflicts?"

"Not conflicts that have been continuing for months. Jeanne, we do need to open up about this—"

There was a knock at the door.

"Erik's going to eat all the ice cream, Mommy," Angie whined from outside. "He says I can't have any more. Can I have another scoop?"

"We'd better go out and finish our home evening," Jeanee whispered, grateful for the reprieve.

Frank shrugged his shoulders in frustration.

"Yes, Angie," Jeanee called to her daughter, "you can have some more. We'll be right down."

11

TUESDAY, JULY 16

9:10 A.M.

"Hey, get that tractor over here!" Mel Blodgett yelled. "No, not that way—"

In total frustration he watched as the man on the tractor maneuvered directly onto the spot where the next soil sample was to come from. "All right," he shouted sarcastically as the man looked back to him for instructions. "Now back up, and let's try it *my* way!"

The driver shrugged, shouted an apology that couldn't be heard above the noise of the heavy equipment, and began maneuvering again.

Mel nodded, waved, and turned back toward his pickup. "Boy," he muttered, "if people would just listen, things would be done right the first time. Wouldn't that be an amazing thing!"

Moments later, frustrated and angry, he left the site and headed down into the valley. Fighting traffic, he continued making necessary calls with his mobile phone, doing everything he could to keep his various projects up and running on schedule. As he did, he discovered that two of his engineers were having a major problem at the location of a new supermarket, another engineer had chosen this week for his vacation, and a firm Mel had done a huge project for earlier in the year had filed a bankruptcy petition that morning. He had been counting on the money, really counting on it. In fact, he had written checks on it.

146

Now he shook his head in disgust. People! You could never depend on them.

Waiting at a traffic light, he thumped his fingers on the steering wheel, and suddenly, as if something had hit him in the stomach, he realized he was supposed to take care of some new Primary callings. They had to be ready for a sustaining vote the following weekend. Such things were not normally his responsibility, but Mel had agreed to take care of the assignment when the counselor who was over the Primary had been called out of town on a business trip. And then he forgot!

"If it isn't one thing it's another!" he stormed, hitting the wheel with his open palm. Those calls had to be made immediately, and for the life of him he couldn't imagine when it would all get done.

As he pulled into his reserved parking stall at Blodgett Engineering, Mel noticed that several cars were parked in the lot.

"Well, good," he thought as he gathered his papers together. "We need some more customers."

"Melburn Blodgett?"

Looking up, Mel was surprised to see a man standing beside his pickup. "Hi," he said as he reached for the door handle. "What can I do for you?"

"Are you Melburn Blodgett?"

"That's right. I—"

"Mister Blodgett, I am placing you under arrest."

For an instant Mel's heart seemed to stop. But then, realizing that it must be a joke some of his men was playing on him, he started to laugh. "Hey, you guys had me going there!"

"Mister Blodgett, would you step out of the truck, please?"

"Sure." Mel grinned as he complied. "But enough is enough."

"Face the truck, Mister Blodgett. Place your hands here and here, and spread your legs wide apart. That's good."

As the man expertly frisked him for weapons — a crazy idea, but very effective in making this joke seem real — Mel became aware that he was surrounded by several men. One of them, Jerry Crandal, was in the bishopric of one of the other wards in his building, and they were pretty good friends. In fact, they —

"Jerry Crandal!" Mel's mind was suddenly screaming. He was an investigator with the police department! This was *real!* This was not a joke!

Only, why? He was no criminal! So why —

"Jerry," he managed to ask with a trembling voice, turning his head toward the other man, "what . . . what's going on?"

"Your daughters, Mel. They came to see us."

"My daughters? What about my daughters?"

"Mister Blodgett," the arresting officer said as he snapped handcuffs onto Mel's wrists, "you have the right to remain silent. Anything you say . . . "

1:15 P.M.

Frank sat slumped in the overstuffed chair in the lounge of the university library, staring at the letter on his lap. He should have been upstairs working on his project paper, but he couldn't bring himself to think about it. Instead, his mind continued to return to the letter, a letter he had first opened early that morning. In him was a hollow feeling, a terrible emptiness that he felt certain was the herald of some impending doom.

Lifting the letter Marie had delivered to his home earlier that morning, he began reading again, considering for maybe the tenth time her words.

Dear Mr. Greaves:

It has been such a long time since I attended church, but when I found out that I lived in your ward, I thought that maybe now I could come back. I actually thought that someone would want to help me lift this hellacious burden from the center of my soul.

I can't believe that I was such a fool! I actually believed that you, of all people, would at least want to understand. But no, you're just like all the rest of your abusive Band-Aid passer-outers.

All you can say is, "Okay, Marie! It's over! It happened a long time ago, so you don't need to talk about it any-more. It was bad, it might even have been most of the things you say you remember. But now you must put aside your self-pity and get on with life as it is today."

I should have known! The one thing I feared most was rejection and nothingness. And my fears have been transformed into a reality of emptiness I can never en-dure.

Why can't I get it through my stupid head that you and your churchy colleagues have only so deep a res-ervoir when it comes to empathy and caring? Nobody really wants to know who I am or what actually happened that destroyed me. I will only be accepted for who they want me to be. When I am foolish enough to trust in anyone besides myself, I'll pay a very dear price indeed.

I actually *believed* in such things as unconditional love, forgiveness, and mercy! Why can't I remember the rules that govern abuse? You know—the ones that say I must never recognize or tell the truth. No one wants to feel or know anything that doesn't suit them or make them feel more comfortable with their own private lies.

I have forced a focus that is not only uncomfortable because of its unsightly and stenchy nature, but because it hits too closely to the old nerve of lust that causes shame and guilt in most men! And we can't allow that to happen now, can we, Bishop? *No way!*

So with a torrent of priestly platitudes you tell me to either stuff it back inside or go someplace else to suffer.

You say, "I don't want to be troubled by your nasty little messes or your endless tears."

Well, Bishop G., you can go to ———, right along with the rest of your closed-minded religious quacks. I don't need your witless commentary on my woeful lack of spirituality! I've got enough garbage to shovel off my soul without you adding to the burden.

I trust no one! I hate instantly. I choose to stay closed. You can call it snooty or inactive or less active or apostate or whatever else you want, but I'll survive, and you don't ever need to know anything. You can believe any fairy tale that suits you. Never more will I need to talk with you or anyone else. You are pain. I refuse to feel that kind of pain ever again!

Thank you, Bishop, thanks Dad, Mom, Bill—thank you, everyone!

Go to ———! Go to ———, all of you!

Marie

Slowly Frank lowered the letter, thinking of the fact that Marie's signature was scrawled in large, bold, angry letters across the entire bottom of the letter. To him that meant as much as her words, which he found as troubling as they were offensive. This woman was hurt far more deeply than he had imagined, maybe even more than Jeanee had thought.

But why? By her own admission, what Marie's father had done to her—which she couldn't even really remember—had been more than thirty years before! For crying out loud, wasn't that enough time to get over something? To heal?

Her rape had been terrible, she had a case against her father, and maybe even against a priesthood leader or two. If her father was unrepentant, and that must be the case since he had never apologized to her or even acknowledged his unrighteousness, then he had no right attending the temple, either.

Frank shook his head as he thought of his own anger at Marie's letter. The woman obviously hadn't understood what Frank had tried to tell her. Had she understood, she wouldn't have been so upset. He had tried to lift her burden by opening the scriptures and teaching her of Christ's atonement and its effect on her, and in return she had struck out at him. Thankfully, as he had prayed that morning to understand her feelings, his own anger had diminished, and now he just felt sorrow for the depth of her pain.

But now the question arose: what to do? Jeanee was already upset about it, and he could think of no earthly way that he could ever get Marie's attention again — even if he wanted it. And to be truthful, he wasn't certain that he did. But, he admitted a little sadly, he knew that he had to make the effort.

1:35 P.M.

"Hi, Frank."

Looking up, Frank was surprised to see Mrs. O. beaming down at him. "Hello, Cousin. What brings you to the library this lovely summer day?"

"Same old thing," Mrs. O. exclaimed as she waved her bag of research at him. "Get this dissertation, one or two more classes, and my orals finished, and I will be Dr. O. instead of Mrs. O."

"Good on you!" Frank declared.

"How's your project coming?"

"Today, not so hot. Too many distractions, I guess."

"I've noticed I haven't seen you up in our room lately," Mrs. O. said as she took a seat beside him. "Anything I can do to help?"

"Not really," Frank replied. "It's just a little bit of everything. Of course this letter I got today hasn't helped a whole lot."

"Let's not talk here," Mrs. O. said, jumping up. "Let's go upstairs, where we can have a little privacy. I've been wanting to ask you a question anyway, so this should be perfect."

Quickly Frank agreed, and soon the two were seated across the table from each other in the tiny study room of the university library.

"So," Frank pressed, "what great question can I elucidate for you today?"

"I'm not certain how to put it into words," Mrs. O. replied.

"Just give it your best shot."

Mrs. O. sighed. "All right, I will. Now understand, Frank, that I'm not attacking anything. I have a very solid testimony of the truthfulness of the gospel. But why does it seem like Church leaders, at least some of them, demand silence on the issue of abuse?"

"That's an interesting question," Frank stated thoughtfully. "What made you ask it?"

"Oh, I got a letter the other day from a friend of mine, an adult survivor of childhood abuse. She seems to be in the middle of some difficult memories, and the powers that be in her ward have ordered her to be silent about her past."

"Are you sure that's what she was told?"

Mrs. O. looked surprised. "What do you mean?"

"I mean this woman may have misunderstood. We do have some current Church counsel about discussing abuse. Do you recall it?"

"Refresh my memory."

"In one of the recent General Conference addresses, victims were counseled to accomplish their healing privately, confidentially, with a trusted priesthood leader and, if needed, professional help. Beyond that, such memories should be shared very, very carefully, if at all."

Mrs. O. nodded. "I understand what you're saying,

Frank. But for most people, the memories do have to come out. If a Church leader won't listen, then someone else must be found who will."

Frank sighed. "Cousin, I think we're dealing with a communication gap. Take a minute and read this letter, will you?" Frank folded Marie's signature under to protect her anonymity, and then he handed it to Mrs. O.

Quickly the woman scanned down the page.

"Wow."

Frank nodded. " 'Wow' is right. This woman had some terrible things done to her, things I can't even comprehend. Now she's thinking about abandoning a perfectly good marriage just because these memories keep telling her how awful and unworthy she is. So this past Sunday I opened the scriptures to her and taught her Jacob's words about the Lord seeing the sorrow and mourning of His daughters because the men had broken their wives' tender hearts and destroyed the confidence of their children. We then discussed the full range of Christ's atonement. She opened up and shared some things she needed to repent of. And, knowing she had suffered for years, I told her I felt that as far as my authority as her bishop was concerned, she was clean before the Lord."

"Not exactly what she wanted to hear."

"Obviously not. But after reading her perception of what I told her, can you see the communication gap I was talking about?"

"I can. I also see the depth of her anger."

Frank nodded his head. "So do I. I just can't understand why she hasn't rid herself of it."

For a moment Mrs. O. was silent. "Frank," she finally said, "in my family I was taught that anger was wrong. Were you?"

Smiling at the memories, Frank nodded.

"Why?" she asked.

"Well, it started with temper tantrums, I suppose. Dad and Mom were always telling us to control ourselves."

"But did that make anger wrong?"

Frank looked quizzically at his cousin. "What do you mean?"

"Okay." Mrs. O. smiled. "This is from the Book of Mrs. O., chapter 1, verses 1 through whatever."

"Sounds ominous."

"Maybe. Say two boys are camping and one chops the foot off the other. Is the boy who has lost the foot at fault?"

"No."

"Does he have a right to be angry because he is now maimed for life through no fault of his own?"

"Well, I'd be angry if it happened to me."

"Is anger a healthy emotion, then, or is it evil?"

"Hmmm. In that sense —"

Mrs. O. smiled. "Gets sort of squirrely here, doesn't it. We say we have a right to be angry in these sorts of situations, and yet we are taught that we shouldn't be angry."

"So what's your answer from the Book of Mrs. O.?" Frank grinned. "Is anger evil, or isn't it?"

"Good question. I think the answer is, it depends on what we do with the anger. And this brings us back to your letter writer. When the boy's foot is cut off, I believe he has a right to be angry and to deal fully with all the emotions relevant to his losing his foot. If he does so, his anger has not been evil.

"On the other hand, if for one reason or another the boy is not allowed to deal with the emotional issues resulting from the loss of his foot, he will stuff those emotions inside himself and pretend they're not there. His anger will then turn to bitterness, and that, I believe, is evil."

"Wait a minute," Frank questioned. "You mean to tell me you believe that if we don't feel anger honestly when our emotional circumstances demand it, that it becomes sin?"

Mrs. O. shook her head. "No, it becomes bitterness. And since bitterness is an unrighteous emotion, harboring it is a sin. Remember Andy Bartelli?"

Frank nodded.

"This was one of the big obstacles in his healing — not being allowed to deal honestly with his anger when it was provoked. Even when his anger all came out in therapy, he didn't understand it."

Frank looked perplexed.

"Have you ever noticed Ephesians, chapter 4, verses 26 and 27, where it says, 'Be ye angry, and sin not: let not the sun go down on your wrath: neither give place to the devil'? Frank, I believe that when we don't honestly deal with our feelings and emotions, when we let the sun go down on them, then those feelings turn to bitterness and become sin. And that gives place to the devil."

"Interesting," Frank mused. "And from what little I've seen, this woman wasn't allowed to deal honestly with her feelings when she was abused. Do you think that's why — "

"Again," Mrs. O. interrupted, "that's what we learned with poor little Andy. By the time his story all came out in the open, he was a very bitter child. In my opinion, this scripture applies directly to him and other silenced victims.

"We can't know what being forced to be silent means to a child. But it must be hell. Which brings us back to your letter writer."

Frank nodded. "No wonder she's so full of bitterness. That's probably why she couldn't hear what I was saying. You know, Cousin, I'm having some interesting thoughts right now. Let me say them, and you tell me what you think."

"Go ahead." Mrs. O. smiled.

"All right. When someone abuses someone else, physically, emotionally, or whatever, it is actually further abuse when they demand silence from them concerning the abuse."

"The literature discusses that," Mrs. O. agreed.

"This woman's father," Frank continued, "threatened that if she told, it would make her mother go crazy. So not only was she abused sexually, she was also frightened into thinking that if she ever went to anyone for help, she would be responsible for her mother going insane."

"Sad," Mrs. O. responded. "But typical. Abusers tend to threaten their victims. 'You tell anybody what we did,' a parent will say to a little child who has just been molested, 'and I'll hurt your mother.' Or, 'Your father won't love us anymore,' or something like that."

"So this really is abuse heaped upon abuse," Frank stated.

"Yes," Mrs. O. agreed. "Sexual and emotional."

"And both kinds—wouldn't they both have to be dealt with for healing to occur?"

Mrs. O. nodded. "Of course they would."

Quiet for a moment, Mrs. O. carried it a step further. "You know, as I think of it, that has another application. This demanding secrecy, when it's done unrighteously, can do harm in other settings besides that of sexual or physical abuse. What about in the case of gossip, or of dumping some other sort of verbal vomit on a person?"

"Like confessing sins to your neighbor?"

"That's right. Or divulging wounds caused by other people, tragic secrets, or whatever. If we then demand silence about what we've shared, isn't that emotional abuse too? It's taking away the second person's agency to be free of such information, or to free themselves from it once it's been dumped on them."

Frank grinned. "Right, and you just answered the question you first asked me today about priesthood leaders and confidentiality. It's also why victims of abuse are counseled to deal with their healing privately, with a trusted priesthood leader and appropriate professional help."

"So by sharing their secrets with others and then demanding silence, you feel victims are turning into perpetrators?" Mrs. O. asked.

"It seems to me the only place where silence can legitimately be demanded is in an ecclesiastical setting where someone tells a Church leader something in confidence."

"But it isn't the Church leader who has the right to demand silence," Mrs. O. stated. "Instead it's the member who has gone to him in confidence, confessing sins or trying to clear up other problems. The Church leader agrees to silence because that's his calling, and the Lord helps and sustains him in it. Members certainly aren't called to be silent."

Frank considered how many times he had sat in counsel with members of his ward about serious matters only to have the memory taken from him after he was through counseling with them. Yes, the blessings of being a bishop did make it possible to keep those confidences.

"So it goes both ways," Frank acknowledged, "making the issue one of agency and accountability. For instance, I'm having a busy afternoon as a bishop when along comes this sister, and without proper understanding I say to her, 'There's no need to discuss this further, because it's over.' But since she has never been able to fully heal from the emotional devastation of her abuse, I am simply giving the same sort of message to her that her father once gave—"

"That's a sobering thought," Mrs. O. stated quietly. "How do you feel, in light of that realization?"

"Like I've got some work to do," Frank acknowledged. "This sister needs to have a chance to do the healing that she didn't do when she was wounded."

Mrs. O. smiled at Frank's commitment. But her thoughts were going somewhere else. Finally, after a moment of silence, she added another dimension to their conversation.

"Frank," she mused, "I don't know if I agree that the only people a victim should talk to are Church leaders and therapists. For instance, I have been happy to be here for my friend, the one I told you about earlier. It isn't a burden for me to be a support to her. In fact, I want to be here for her. And I don't mind being silent."

"She's lucky to have you for a friend. But here again," Frank added, "you *choose* to be there for her. If she were dumping something on you that you couldn't deal with—"

"Ahh." Mrs. O. finished the sentence: "it would be a different picture. That's why we need to be very private about whom we counsel with."

"Still," Frank continued, "I don't understand why, after thirty years, the woman who wrote this terrible letter hasn't had time to heal."

"Maybe because she was never allowed to begin the healing process until recently. One of my professors told me that children who are abused are simply too young to understand what's happening to them. The abuse is beyond their comprehension. And many of them will be seasoned adults before those memories start to make themselves known."

"I have heard that excessive probing of these memories is dangerous, though."

Mrs. O. smiled. "My professor told me the same thing. Too much probing, or too much asking of leading questions, can even lead to false memories. The mind, when it is wounded, searches to make sense of what little pieces of the past it may have. And sometimes, when guided unwisely, the victim, or survivor, which is what my friend calls herself, may attribute abuse to an innocent person. Though abuse may well be an issue for the person, the integrity of the person's memories, when prodded and embellished, may actually point an accusing finger at someone who is totally without fault."

"A scary thought. So what should a person do?"

"Not probe, and *not* submit to one who asks leading

questions. Frank, I believe it is the Holy Ghost who orchestrates proper, true memories, bringing them forth in birth just as fast as a person can, and should, deal with them. And that takes time, because some memories are excruciatingly painful and buried very deep. That's probably another reason why your letter-writing friend got so angry. Her memories could well be ready to be born, and they will be horrendous. And though she's dealing with flying, fire-breathing dragons, you told her to swat them like houseflies and get on with it. My professor said that's like applying Band-Aids to cancer."

Frank nodded miserably.

"You know," Mrs. O. concluded, "until Andy's problem surfaced, I didn't think I had much to do with abuse. I had been neither a victim nor an abuser. But the truth, Frank, is that all of us are involved. The most destructive player in the abuse cycle is probably what they call the 'enabler.' That's the person who sits idly by and ignores the abuse that is happening around them. If people would just get their blinders off and get educated!

"Oh, by the way, did you hear the news this morning?"

Intrigued, Frank looked at his cousin. "No. What?"

"Isn't Melburn Blodgett your counselor?"

"That's right?"

"Well, it may not be the same person. In fact, it probably isn't. But as I was driving down here earlier, there was a news item on the radio about a Melburn Blodgett being arrested for sexual abuse of children. I thought you would want to know."

3:10 P.M.

"My hours are on the calendar, Mom." Erik smiled at his mother as he grabbed a couple of oatmeal cookies and headed for the pool. "Oh, and I have some new merit badges to go on my sash for the Court of Honor this week."

"Aren't you about through earning merit badges?"

Erik grinned. "About five more, Mom, and I'll have 'em all. Gotta go!"

"Do you have your bike fixed?" Jeanee called after him as she peeled baby carrots from the garden into the kitchen sink.

"I need a new tube," Erik called from the patio. "Can I take the car this afternoon?"

"Erik—"

"But Mom, I'm sixteen."

"And you don't have your license yet, either," she responded, doing her best to sound normal.

"Yeah, stupid driver's ed schedule. Okay, can I at least get a ride?"

Jeanee wiped her hands on her oversized shirt and checked the calendar. "You have to be there by 4:30?"

"Yeah. I'll just be in the pool for an hour. Can you iron my shirt?"

"Just spray it wet and throw it in the dryer, Erik. It's permanent press." Jeanee's tone was stern, which was not normal.

"Okay, Mom," Erik agreed as he headed toward the pool. "You have too much on your mind anyway."

"It's not that," Jeanee protested, raising her voice so he could hear her. "You can do it yourself, and you need to learn before your mission— "

"Mom," Angie interrupted from the deck. "Is my swimming party off?"

"Swimming party? Uh . . . no, honey. That's still okay. We just have to— "

Suddenly something within Jeanee clicked off. The sunny kitchen began spinning around her, and she felt a falling sensation. She shook her head and blinked hard, drawing in a deep breath for control. But she was losing it.

"Uh . . . just a minute, Angie." Jeanee dropped the carrot peeler and stumbled. "I . . . need to sit down . . . "

Angie followed as Jeanee shuffled into the living room. "Mom," she asked anxiously, "are you okay?"

"I . . . I'm ffffine . . . honey—" Jeanee's words were starting to slur. "I . . . jusssst need a little ressst . . . "

She slumped down into the sofa, energy draining from her body as if an invisible magnet was drawing it downward. Angie stood horrified as the expression on her mother's face turned lifeless.

"Mommy, are you okay?"

"Uh huuuh," Jeanee mumbled.

"What do I do?" Angie blurted fearfully.

Jeanee struggled to reassure her daughter but ended up just scaring her even more.

"Oh, yeah." Angie suddenly beamed. "I know what to do. I'll take care of you, Mom."

Running to the kitchen, she filled a glass with water. Then popping in a straw, she took it to her mother. "Here," she offered, "this can make you feel better."

Jeanee managed a smile.

"Do you need me to get Erik?" Angie pressed, concern still in her voice.

"Nnnooo, I'll beee ffffiiiine." It was difficult to move, but Jeanee forced herself to take a couple of swallows of water to make her little daughter feel as though she were helping.

"Mom," she whimpered, "I'm sorry. It was me, wasn't it. I should be helping you more."

"Errrik . . . g-get rrride," Jeanee said, struggling.

"Erik? Oh, yeah, he needs a ride to work! I'll tell him."

As Angie disappeared onto the patio, Jeanee began shaking uncontrollably. Tears ran down the sides of her face as she sobbed in helplessness. "This can't be happening," she thought angrily. "This can't be happening again!

After all these years, why is it all coming back? I don't understand!!"

"Mom!" Erik called as he bounded into the house. "Are you all right?"

Angie followed him, worry on her face. "She was just peeling carrots, Erik, and all of a sudden she got real tired!"

"What. do you need, Mom? Do you need me to do anything?"

"Rrrride . . . worrrk." Words were difficult for Jeanee to get out.

"Ride to work?" Erik understood. "I'll be fine. I'll get a ride, or I'll walk. But Mom," Erik sat his wet body on the floor next to Jeanee, "should I stay home? Are you going to be okay? Should I call Dad at the university?"

Jeanee raised her head slightly, fighting for control. "Caaalll Daaad . . . number by phooone . . . "

"You stay with her, Angie," Erik said, giving orders. "I'll see if I can get Dad on the phone. Rub her feet. That helps."

As he headed for the phone, Erik took the towel from around his waist and dried his hair. Searching through his mother's scratch pad, he found the number she had written earlier. Then he picked up the phone and dialed.

"H-hello," he stammered. "I'm looking for Mister Frank Greaves. Is there some way of getting in touch with him. It's a family emergency. . . . Yeah, that's right, a family emergency."

"Emergency?" Jeanee thought, fighting to hold back the flood of tears forcing their way to the surface. "Family embarrassment is more like it!"

Angie was rubbing Jeanee's left heel over and over. "Do you want me to hum you a song, Mommy?"

Jeanee jerked her head in agreement and then lay perfectly still, surprised at the strength in her children.

"Yeah, Dad," Erik was speaking softly from the kitchen. "It's Mom. I think you'd better come home. She's having

a real rough time. . . . Yeah, I think so. . . . No, we're okay.
Angie and I can take care of her until you get here. . . .
Yeah, I'll call Jim for a ride. I'll be okay. How long do you
think you'll be? . . . Oh, is that all? That'll be fine. We can
handle it. . . . Okay. Bye."

Except for Angie's humming, there was silence. Jeanee
waited to hear what her son had learned, but for two or
three minutes he didn't appear. Then he came into the
room, smiling calmly.

"You're going to be fine, Mom," he said reassuringly.
"I just had a prayer."

Again Jeanee's tears started flowing. "Thaaank youuu,"
she slurred.

"I'm going to get into some dry clothes and put my
shirt in the dryer, but I'll be right back." Erik disappeared
up the stairs into his room.

"Would you like me to read to you, Mommy?" Angie
offered. "Daddy got me a new book."

"Rrrrread," Jeanee agreed.

Jeanee closed her eyes as Angie walked out of the room
to get her book. With all her strength she fought to regain
control of her body. And focusing all her mental determination, she tried to move her hand, only to feel it jerking
helplessly out of control. She couldn't rise above the paralysis. So, taking a deep breath, she tried to relax and
accept the inevitable.

"How long this time?" she wondered. "Hours? Days?"

She thought back to the first time this had happened,
nearly sixteen years ago, just shortly after Erik's birth. No
one had known what was wrong. Her body had gone into
thrashing convulsions and had been left helplessly paralyzed for hours, then nonfunctional for days afterward.
She had been in the hospital for nearly two weeks. And all
the doctors could come up with was that she was having
some kind of breakdown.

It was years later, after Angie's birth, that they finally

diagnosed catalepsy—not life-threatening, but frightening if you didn't know what to expect. The attacks, or "spells," as Jeanee called them, came and went with little or no warning. And she would never know how long she might be incapacitated afterward.

"This can't be happening!" her mind screamed. "This is no time for me to be having a trauma! It's been five years! Why is it happening now?"

Again Jeanee closed her eyes. Then silently she began to pray for the strength to rise above her old weakness. This was no time for her to fall apart. Her family and her friends needed her to be strong, and she couldn't let them down.

12

TUESDAY, JULY 16

4:30 P.M.

"Honey, what is it? What's happened?"

Frank knelt beside the couch, Jeanee's hand in his.

"Ohhhh, Fraaank," Jeanee slurred as she dissolved into tears.

"Hey, Jeanee," Frank soothed while Erik and Angie looked anxiously on, "it will be all right."

"But . . . but I thooought I was ovvver thisss. I . . . sooo sorrry."

"Is Mom going to be okay, Dad?"

Frank looked up. "She'll be fine, Erik. But I surely appreciate you and Angie taking care of her until I got here."

"I read to Mommy," Angie declared brightly.

"That's my good little angel." Frank smiled.

"Dad, is it serious?"

Frank caressed Jeanee's hand. "It looks like the same old thing. You may not remember this, but we've been here before." Erik nodded understanding, but Angie had been a baby the last time Jeanee had experienced one of these spells, and she did not understand.

"Angie, honey," Frank said as he turned to his daughter, "what your mom has is called catalepsy. It's not dangerous. It's just real scary if you don't understand it."

"But why can't Mommy move?"

"Her body is just very tired, honey. The doctors don't

165

know why it does this, but when she gets very, very tired, her body just turns itself off."

"But Daddy, she can't talk right."

"I know, punkin, but it will get better."

"Will it take long?"

Frank looked at his wife, who was fighting to hold back tears of frustration. "I don't know, sweetie. I hope not. Daddy's going to give her a blessing, so I'm sure she'll be okay soon."

"I had a good feeling about her in my prayer," Erik stated simply.

"Annnd I thaaank youuu fooor thaaat," Jeanee murmured, trying to smile at her son.

Frank nodded at Erik. "I'll give her a blessing now, and she'll be fine."

Erik smiled sadly. "Wish I could help you."

"You already have, both you and Angie. And your faith will help the blessing work."

"Thanks, Dad. Listen, I can stay home from work if you think I'll be needed."

Shaking his head, Frank smiled. "No thanks, Erik. I'll be here for a while, and I'll find someone to help later on. You go on to work.

"Angie," he said, turning to his daughter, "would you like to stay for Mommy's blessing?"

Angie frowned briefly. "Can I watch TV instead?"

Smiling at the sweet simplicity of his daughter, Frank agreed. "But be sure not to spend more than an hour in front of the TV."

"Promise, Daddy." She beamed and skipped out of the room.

"I'll see you after work, Dad," Erik stated. "I need to get ready if I'm going to go."

And with that, Frank was alone with his helpless wife.

"I sorrry." She began to cry softly.

"Did you see this coming, Jeanee?"

Recognizing that Frank was really upset, Jeanee just nodded.

"So did I, honey, and I tried to warn you."

"I . . . I knooow . . ."

"I don't understand why you won't slow down! You know what you're like."

Tears of fatigue and frustration fell from Jeanee's eyes, but still she said nothing.

"Don't cry," Frank pleaded soothingly. "I'm not angry. It's just that, well, I've seen you carrying burdens that you don't need to carry. And it's not fair to you or the people you're trying to help."

Slowly Jeanee nodded her head.

"And no sewing project in the world is worth making yourself sick over. You should know that by now."

A gray wall climbed up around her mind as Jeanee continued to listen to her husband tenderly scolding her. He did not have the capacity to see what she was really going through, or that she wasn't choosing to drive herself to exhaustion. Her *pain* was driving her. The only way she could turn it off was to keep pushing beyond her strength.

"And this thing with Amber," Frank continued. "I know that's when all this started. Honey, you just have to be able to let it go. Your worrying can't change one thing that happened. Do you understand what I'm saying?"

"I . . . unnnderstaaand . . ."

"Good." Leaning down, Frank held his trembling wife close. "I just can't stand to see you suffering. If I could do anything at all to take this pain from you, you know I'd do it. For weeks I've pleaded that you would somehow let this go. And for weeks —"

"I knooow," Jeanee cried. "I tryyy."

"I know you do, sweetie. Listen, I should have given you a blessing a long time ago. I don't know why I didn't. Maybe we could have saved some of this grief."

Jeanee sighed deeply, anticipating the strength she

would receive from the blessing. She had needed one for such a long time, and after all she had been holding in, it was comforting to know that help was on its way.

4:50 P.M.

"Know that the Lord's hand is in your life and that your Father in Heaven loves you. Be patient in this tribulation and trust the healing power of the Savior." The words of the blessing repeated in Jeanee's mind as she lay unmoving on the sofa, and the regenerating power of the priesthood wrapped her in its peaceful, healing glow.

Frank sat half on the sofa beside her, his head in his hands, and he looked up only when the clock chimed 4:30.

"Jeanee, honey," he finally spoke. "I feel so helpless."

Jeanee smiled and sent a look to this man who had been her hero for so long.

"I don't understand any of this . . . this stuff that is going on. I know the Lord does, and I felt His Spirit very strongly when I gave you the blessing." Tears welled up in Frank's eyes. "I don't know how he's going to work all this out, Jeanee, but I know he has a plan. If I can just stay out of his way long enough for him to get it working."

"Oooh," was all Jeanee could say. She wanted to sit up and hold her husband and tell him what a wonderful man he was, and how sorry she was for the grief she was putting him through. But movement was impossible. Words were impossible. "Dear God," she prayed in her mind, "please let Frank know how much I love him. Please make him able—"

"I don't know what to do about Marie," Frank agonized. "I don't understand her grief. I know it's real, but I don't understand it. And that *letter*—" He paused, and one deep sob escaped from the very center of his soul. "Wh-what do I do about that letter?"

"Telephone, Daddy," Angie announced as she walked into the room.

Surprised that he hadn't heard the ring, Frank stood and walked to the wall phone that hung just inside the kitchen door. Clearing his throat, he answered.

"Hello? Oh, hi, President Stone."

For a moment Frank listened as his stake president spoke, and Jeanee, listening from her position on the couch, knew instantly what was coming. Thank goodness Frank had found time to give her the blessing.

"You're sure?" Frank questioned, his face showing total dismay. "I heard this afternoon, President, but I didn't believe it. I was hoping it was some other Mel Blodgett. Then, before I could check it out for myself—"

Frank paused as President Stone continued on the other end of the line. "All right, I'll do it right away. . . . Uh-huh. I'll give you a call as soon as I learn something. . . . Tonight? Well, I do have several temple recommend interviews set up—"

Frank looked around the corner at his helpless wife, wondering how he could possibly be everywhere he was suddenly needed.

"You bet." he responded to his Church leader, "To-morrow night at 7:00 at the stake offices would be fine.

"And President, I'm real sorry about this. I just had no idea—"

Hanging up, Frank walked back and sat on the edge of the couch. "I guess you heard?"

Jeanee managed a nod.

"Honey, I hate to leave you like this"—Frank looked longingly at his wife—"but, there's a situation with Mel. I really hoped it was some kind of a mistake, but the president confirmed that he's been arrested. Jerry Crandal also called him and told him it looked like a pretty tight case. So the president wants me to go see Mel and find out what's going on."

"Mmmm," Jeanee moaned softly.

"I have to do it, honey. It's my stewardship. I just wish I knew what to do about you and Angie."

Angie poked her head around the corner and smiled. "I can take care of Mommy, Daddy. You go take care of your work."

"You're quite a helper, aren't you." Frank smiled at his daughter.

"I can fix soup, Daddy," Angie assured him.

"How about pizza, munchkin?"

"Yay! Pizza!"

"If Terri weren't out of town," Frank added, turning back to his wife, "I'd ask her to come over."

Jeanee was wrapped in a numb cocoon, unable to even suggest someone.

"Wait a minute!" Frank declared with a sudden stroke of inspiration. "What about Marie Spencer? That's perfect! She's part of the reason you're like this."

Jeanee was helpless to defend her friend, but she was thankful that Frank would be calling her. If anyone besides Terri would be able to understand, it would be Marie.

"Mmmm huh," she moaned softly.

"It'll be good for her," Frank said as he stood again and walked to the telephone. "Service always is. Oh, I'll order a pizza, too. And I'm going to get that answering machine connected. That way you won't have to worry about the phone."

Taking Marie's card from where Jeanee had tacked it to the wall, Frank dialed the number and then waited. "Hello, Marie Spencer?" he finally said, "Frank Greaves here. . . . Yes, but that isn't why I'm calling. I . . . wait just a minute, Marie! Give me a chance to say something. I'm calling about Jeanee."

Jeanee listened, wondering what Marie might be saying on the other end. Frank quickly explained the problem and his own quandary. "Anyway, Marie," he continued, "since I know that you're her friend, I thought maybe you'd be able to be with her for a while this afternoon and evening."

There was a long pause, and Frank let out a deep sigh. "Yes. That would be just fine. Thirty minutes is great. I'll carry Jeanee up to the bedroom and make sure everything is okay. I'll try to stick around until you get here, but if I'm gone, just come in and make yourself at home. . . . No, that won't be necessary, Marie. I'm ordering pizza. But thanks for the offer. And Angie will be a good help to you. Just let her know if you need anything. Also, I'll see if Erik can come home from work a little early tonight. . . . Thanks, Marie. I really appreciate it, and I know Jeanee appreciates it, too."

Hanging up the phone, Frank sent thanks heavenward. Then he returned to care briefly for his helpless wife.

5:00 P.M.

Jeanee fumbled to reach the lamp as Angie led Marie into her darkened bedroom. The shades were down, and late afternoon sun shown around the edges of the window.

"You okay, Mommy?" Angie whispered as she turned on the light.

"Much . . . better . . . punkin." Jeanee squinted and wiped at the last of her tears. "Thank you — for taking care of my friend."

"Can I get you another drink?" Angie asked, walking over to the bed.

"I'm fine, honey," Jeanee assured the small girl. "See, I can even talk right again." Jeanee was amazed herself that in such a few short minutes her strength was beginning to return.

Angie smiled and stroked her mother's hair as Marie came slowly into the room, carrying a small package. "It scared me when you couldn't talk," Angie continued, her blue eyes wide with concern.

"I'm feeling lots better," Jeanee reassured her daughter. "I just need to keep resting."

"And then you'll be okay?"

"Then I'll be okay. Here, give me a hug. Then I'll visit with Marie. Okay?"

Angie hugged her mother gently and then turned slowly toward the door. "Are you sure you'll be fine?" she probed with her toothless smile.

"I'm feeling better every minute. Really, you can go." Jeanee smiled as Angie walked out of the room.

"I'll be in my room playing with my Legos. Okay?"

"That's fine, punkin."

"She's quite the little nurse," Marie observed. Then, turning to Jeanee with a look of concern on her face, she asked, "How are you feeling, really?"

Jeanee looked up at her friend. "I feel like I'm in a tunnel, and everything around me is fuzzy."

"Pretty out of it, huh?"

"I'm sorry to put you out, Marie."

"It's not a problem. I want to be here for you."

"Well, I don't want to be here—not like this!" Jeanee struggled to sit up. "I feel so helpless! If I could just get my legs to move."

"Does this last long?" Marie asked, moving a chair to the bed and sitting down.

"I never know how long," Jeanee conceded, finally giving up and accepting her prone position. "And it hasn't happened in years! Poor Frank. He doesn't know what to do with me. He's got so much on his mind lately. And—" Jeanee paused. "Oh, Marie, what did you say to him in that letter?"

"Jeanee, what I said to your husband has nothing to do with my relationship with you. I hope you know that."

"Yes, but—"

"It's just that I can't take any more from these noble and godly men of the priesthood."

"I . . . think you're being a bit unfair," Jeanee said slowly.

"You didn't hear what he said to me—how he dismissed me."

"And perhaps you didn't hear Frank, Marie. In all the years I've known him, he's never intentionally hurt another human being. Are you sure you didn't misunderstand him?"

A silent wall instantly went up in Marie's countenance. Seeing her reaction, Jeanee began to tremble.

"Oh—I'm sorry," Marie apologized. "I have no right to upset you with my problems."

"It's okay. It just comes and goes," Jeanee explained with a shiver. "It's the craziest thing. One minute I'm fine, and the next minute my body shuts off."

"Well, I just want you to understand that I went to a man like Frank a few years ago. Not only did he not help me, but it turned out he was as evil as my father had been."

"I'm sorry about that, Marie." Jeanee was saddened to hear that Marie had been further wounded by a priesthood leader. And yet, struggling for a way to defend her husband's innocent though ineffective efforts, she countered, "I believe it's important to remember that just because a Church leader might give bad counsel, or even make a serious spiritual or even moral error, that doesn't mean every Church leader is suspect. There are some wonderful priesthood leaders in the Church."

"Well, obviously we have a difference of opinion on that score." Marie dismissed Jeanee's efforts at persuasion. "Can I get you something?"

Jeanee smiled, recognizing Marie's tactics. "If you could just turn off that overhead light and help me with this lamp."

Marie set her package on the nightstand and softened

the lights, looking around the room as she did. "What a lovely room," she observed, looking at the pictures and figures on the dresser beside them. "There is such a peaceful feeling here."

Jeanee smiled, thankful that in spite of the conflict between her and her friend, Marie could still feel the Spirit in her home.

"Tell me," Jeanee spoke softly, "about your package."

"Oh, this," Marie said. "It's a book I picked up for you. It's about a woman who starts remembering her abuse from childhood, and, well, she splits into several personalities. I'm not sure what to think about it. But, well, check it out when you have the chance."

Jeanee thanked her and then became silent.

"You don't have to like it," Marie joked. "I just—"

"It's not that," Jeanee explained. "It's just that—I wish I could help you see how badly Frank wanted to help you."

"I told you, it's not your problem," Marie reassured her. "I should have known not to open up to any man!"

There was a moment of silence as Jeanee gathered strength to ask her next question, a question that had repeatedly come to her mind since the previous Sunday. "Marie," she finally asked softly, "can you tell me about your father?"

"My father?" Marie looked surprised.

"Do you know where he is now? Is he alive?"

There was a moment of silence, and then Marie answered, her tone distant. "Oh, yeah, Dad's still alive. He and Mom joined the Church. They're real active."

Jeanee could feel Marie's turmoil and wondered why it seemed so important to ask questions that she knew were making her friend uncomfortable. Yet in spite of her concern, she felt compelled to continue. "Have you ever been able to talk to your parents about what happened?"

"Talk to them? No way!"

"Does your mother know about it?"

Marie sighed, almost irritated. "I think my mom knew. But I think my mom thinks like everyone else—'Ignore it and it will go away.' "

"And it doesn't."

"No." There was a bitter edge to Marie's voice. "It doesn't."

Jeanee continued probing. "Is it difficult for you, knowing that your father is active in the Church?"

"Hey, what is this?" Marie laughed to cover her uneasiness. "I thought I was coming over to help you this time."

"I'm sorry," Jeanee apologized. "It's just that these questions have been going through my mind, and—"

"Okay," Marie said with a faint smile, "I'll answer. But someday I get to ask the questions. Fair?"

"Fair," Jeanee reluctantly agreed.

"Okay, about my dad," Marie began. "Yes, it's hard to know he's an active Church man. But it's harder knowing that everybody else thinks he's this wonderful, saintly fellow who gives wonderful talks and distributes candy to all the little children in Church. Everybody loves him and thinks he's nearly perfect, and it all makes me gag!"

"He's never asked you to forgive him?"

"No. It's just like it didn't happen." Marie sighed. "But how can I fault him for finding his peace in life and for doing things that give him fulfillment?"

"That's a hard one," Jeanee agreed.

"Besides, he's old. Both my parents are. They have so little time left in life—ten years, maybe? How do I shatter that?"

"So you'll just carry it all around inside you—"

"Until they're dead!"

There was that word again. Death. Jeanee knew only too well that death didn't end conflicts.

"Are you okay?" Marie asked. "You look pale."

"I'm fine." Jeanee squirmed. "Just a bit tired."

"Maybe I should let you get some rest."

"No. If you don't mind, I want to talk."

"Whatever you say." Marie smiled. "I'm here to serve."

"Do you mind if I ask about Sunday?"

"About Sunday?"

"About the interview—with Frank. I don't want to pry, but I'm really concerned."

"To put it bluntly, your husband bulldozed right through my most tender and frightening secrets as if they were wisps of vapor from an easily forgettable past. I tried to help him understand. I really did. But he never even heard me. Before I knew it, we were through and he was heading for the door!"

Jeanee remained silent, her energy seeming to drain out of her as Marie continued.

"There was a part of me that wanted to say, 'Good. It's over! It's finished!' But there was a bigger part of me that said, 'It's still here. This terrible black spot won't go away!' "

Tears were filling Jeanee's eyes. Physically she was too weak to do much more than listen. But she knew that more than anything Marie needed someone to listen to her without trying to silence her pain.

"I understand the anger," she whispered, fighting back her emotions. "I have problems myself with the myopic vision some people in the Church seem to have. But it's just because they haven't experienced the things you have. Marie, it's okay to be angry. Jesus himself was angry when he cleansed the temple. He was even more angry, Marie, when you were violated!"

There was silence for a minute, and then Jeanee spoke again, pointing toward her desk. "You gave me a book to read. I want to share one with you."

Marie walked to the rolltop desk and turned on the desk light.

"It's the one with the red spine. Yes, that's it. *The Miracle of Forgiveness*, by Spencer W. Kimball. Will you bring it here?"

"Jeanee, you don't have to—"

"Marie, I've wanted to share this with you." She opened the book. "See, it has my yellow marks all over it."

"But it's your personal copy," Marie protested.

"Marie," Jeanee said, her eyes misting over, "this book changed my life. I don't know how it will affect you, but it was a beginning for me. Quite literally it brought me— to the only One who can resolve all this. Please take it. And pray about it."

"I'll take it," Marie assured her. Then, looking tenderly at her friend, she added, "But I think its time for you to get some rest. If I go in and visit with Angie, will you do that?"

Jeanee was too exhausted not to agree. So, pulling a fuzzy blue afghan up around her shoulders, she lay back down.

"You're probably right," she said with a sigh. "That pizza should be coming any minute now. Eat all you want . . . "

5:10 P.M.

"Mel Blodgett," Frank thought as he drummed his fingers on the table in the interrogation room of the county jail. "Mel, Mel, Mel. What have you gotten yourself into? Can it possibly be true? Have you really been sexually abusing children?"

For a moment Frank thought of Mel, of his rugged looks and commanding presence. Besides being such an outstanding counselor, Mel was a force to be reckoned with in Scouting. He had done incredible good, not only in the district but one-on-one in helping numerous young men along the trail to Eagle. In fact, when he accompanied the boys to their annual summer camp, the merit badge earning rate usually tripled.

Suddenly Frank's mind seemed to freeze. Was that it? Had Mel been molesting those young boys?

Abruptly the door opened, and Mel Blodgett stood in the doorway, a uniformed officer beside him. With a slight nudge Mel was urged into the room, the door closed behind him, and Frank sat facing his first counselor.

"Hi, Mel."

"H-hello, Frank."

There was an awkward pause as Mel stood with his hands opening and closing nervously at his sides, his eyes directed toward the floor.

"Have a chair," Frank finally said for want of something better to say.

Slowly Mel took the other chair and sat in it. "I . . . I'm sorry," he said, his words hardly above a whisper. "I wish you hadn't come. I hate to have you see me in here like this."

"It's hard on me, too," Frank agreed.

"Yeah, I'll bet it is."

"Talk to me, Mel."

"What do you want me to say?" Mel answered without lifting his eyes.

"Whatever you want to," Frank replied. "But I think you know I need some questions answered."

Silently Mel nodded, and then the silence began to stretch out. Praying steadily for inspiration, Frank watched the man who, until this morning, had been his closest confident in things pertaining to the ward. Somehow now he seemed smaller, older, and much less charismatic.

"I hate this place!" Mel suddenly declared, deep anger in his voice. "Have you seen the people in here, Frank? Losers and misfits, every one of them. They're dirty, unshaven, drunk—I'm telling you, I don't belong here!"

"There has to be a reason, Mel."

"Not for this! I mean, look at me, and tell me what you see. A criminal? Hardly! I'm an upstanding citizen. I'm educated—well-educated, one of the best engineers in my field. I'm a leader in the Church and in the community—I'm telling you, Frank, I don't belong here!"

"So why did they arrest you, Mel? Are you guilty?"

Slowly the man dropped his eyes again. "I . . . I guess so."

"You guess?"

"All right," Mel Blodgett fumed, sounding desperate. "I'm guilty."

"What are you guilty of, Mel? I don't even know specifically what charges have been filed against you."

"Sexual abuse of a child," Mel stated quietly. "Three counts. There are some more things, lesser charges, but I can't remember them right now."

"And you're guilty of all of it?"

"Well, if you interpret the law the way they do."

"Who, Mel? Who were the children? The boys at Scout camp?"

Mel's eyes widened with shock and disbelief. "The boys? Who told you that?"

"Nobody. I just assumed—"

"Well, stop assuming, Frank. Nothing could be further from the truth."

"So, who were the children?"

"My . . . daughters."

"What?" Frank couldn't believe what he was hearing. "You mean Tish and Tess?"

"Yeah," Mel snarled, his eyes defiant again. "And Trace."

Frank could only sit in silence, numbly shaking his head. The enormity of what the man was telling him was overwhelming.

"Frank," Mel said, his voice pleading for understanding, "I . . . I didn't think I was doing anything wrong. I mean, I love my girls, and they love me. We . . . we're family!"

"But Mel, they're just little girls, for crying out loud!" The thought of what those little girls had been suffering was suddenly causing Frank to feel nauseated. It was unbelievable, too gross to even begin to fathom!

"Listen to me," Mel continued, "and maybe you'll understand. Carol and I haven't seen eye-to-eye for a long time. There's this incredible gulf between us, physically as well as emotionally. She just isn't meeting my needs, and hasn't done for years."

Frank was stunned. "And that's why you forced yourself on your daughters?" he asked in disbelief.

"Who else should I turn to? Good gosh, Frank. They're my own flesh and blood. What was I to do?"

"But . . . but they're innocent little children!"

"Frank, they're a lot smarter than you might think. This hasn't just been for me, you know. Those girls deserve some pleasure in their lives, and I've given it to them. We've enjoyed each other in very tender ways, and in the process they've gained some education that will help them in their own marital relationships when that time comes."

Bewildered, Frank shook his head. "Oh, Mel, you poor, sorry fool. You have no idea what you've done."

"Sure I do. I've taught them better than to be like their prissy mother, and I've become real close to them, just like parents are supposed to be with their kids. I know just what I've done."

"If you're so close, Mel, then why did your daughters turn you in?"

"Who said they did?"

"Come on, Mel," Frank said disgustedly, "You know they turned you in. Do you think they did that because they felt close to you? Imagine what it would be like, Mel, for a daughter to turn her own father over to the police. Just imagine how embarrassing that must have been for Tish and Tess, not to mention how it tore at their hearts."

Silently Mel stared at Frank, his countenance hard and unchanging.

"I met the other day with a member of the ward, a mature woman, who has considered suicide and at this very moment is living in agony because she can't get over what her father did to her when she was a little girl."

"What'd he do?" Mel asked sullenly.

"Exactly what you did, Mel. He sexually abused her."

"He probably *hurt* her," Mel said defensively. "That's one thing I never did, Frank. I never hurt any of them!"

"You didn't *hurt* them?" Frank questioned in disbelief. "You don't think you damaged your girls?"

Firmly Mel shook his head. "I know I didn't. I'm telling you, there is real tenderness between my girls and me. I don't abuse them, I don't hurt them, and I *never* have. We love each other, and that's how it has always been!"

"And that," Frank said quietly, "is why I called you a poor, sorry fool. You filled those innocent little children of yours so full of darkness and confusion that they may never get over it."

"You don't understand," Mel stated defiantly.

"Let me ask you about something else," Frank continued boldly. "What about the covenant of sexual purity and fidelity to Carol you made in the temple? And how could you defile the temple by your attendance, when you knew all along what you were doing?"

"Huh?"

"You heard me, Mel. How do you rationalize your way out of that?"

For an instant Mel stared at Frank, an expression of stone on his face. Then, slowly, his eyes dropped. "I . . . I don't know. That pertained to being immoral with other women, I guess. I mean, it says that quite clearly, doesn't it? My girls aren't other women, Frank. Can't you see that? I've never in my life stepped out on Carol. I don't think

I could cheat on her if I had to. I'm just not that kind of man."

"And sexually abusing your daughters doesn't count?"

Slowly Mel Blodgett shook his head.

For a moment Frank stared at his friend, wondering what to say next. To say that he was dumbfounded was such an understatement as to seem almost ridiculous. Yet he was! Here was this man, this religious counselor who considered himself completely moral, defending his persistent defiling of three innocent little children as a good, beneficial thing to do. There had to be some form of mental illness here, he finally concluded. There had to be!

"When I came in here, Mel," Frank finally continued, "you said right off that you were guilty. Yet our entire conversation has been you justifying your perversion and attempting to make it seem natural. Tell me—just what do you think you are guilty of?"

"I . . . I don't know," Mel responded quietly. "I mean, I must be guilty of something, or they wouldn't have arrested me."

"That's it? You really don't know more than that?"

In anguish Mel looked at his bishop. "How can I explain this, Frank? Deep down I have this . . . this feeling like I've been doing something terrible. I feel it most when I have to look at Carol. She makes me feel so . . . so dirty! Tish, Tess, even little Trace, they don't make me feel that way. They accept me and love me. But not Carol. Around her I just get this awful feeling of dirty inferiority—

"On the other hand, when I think about what I do, when I analyze it in my mind, it all seems so logical, so helpful. I mean, how can it be bad to feel so good?

"So, I guess my answer is, I feel guilty, but I don't think I am. The heart versus the mind, I suppose. You tell me which is right, Frank."

Feeling absolutely helpless, Frank slowly rose to his feet, stepped to the door, and gave a couple of taps with his knuckle. Then he turned back to his friend. "I don't need to tell you anything, Mel. You already know, because the Holy Ghost told you when this all started. I just wish, for your sake, but especially for your family's sake, that you had had sense enough to listen."

6:30 P.M.

"How is she feeling, Marie?"

Frank, home from visiting with Mel Blodgett, had found Marie sitting in the bedroom beside his wife.

"She's just waking up," Marie responded as she looked up.

"Mmmm. Hi, honey." Jeanee smiled. "Still numb, but I'm talking again."

Frank walked over and caressed his wife's foot. "I'm glad to hear that." He sighed. "Of all the nights not to be able to cancel something. I tell you, this is one for the old journal!"

"How did things go with Mel?" Jeanee asked.

"Actually, not too well," Frank declared, shaking his head. "I really can't figure the man out."

"I heard on the radio that he admits what he did but acknowledges no guilt," Marie stated.

"You mean, he thinks he has a right to violate his daughters?" Jeanee questioned.

"Don't they all?" Marie gave Jeanee a knowing glance.

"Yes, and I can't understand it," Frank continued. "It just makes no sense to me."

"I think I should be going now," Marie whispered as she reached for Jeanee's hand. "You get some rest, okay? I'll be calling tomorrow. And thank you," she added as she turned to Frank, "for calling me. Your wife and I had a good talk."

"We appreciate your coming. I'll walk with you to the door."

Once they were in the entryway, Frank turned to Marie. "Thank you for your letter," he offered sincerely.

"What?" Marie asked, surprised.

"I'm afraid you were right when you said I wasn't listening. Very honestly, Marie, I owe you an apology."

Marie stared at the floor, suddenly uncomfortable. "You don't owe me anything."

"But I do. As a counselor, I was insensitive to your needs. As your bishop, I have not adequately represented the Savior. For both these things, I am deeply sorry."

Marie looked up at Frank with a bitter smile. "Well," she said, "it's over. What's done is done. Besides, I'm the fool here, not you."

"Why do you say that?" Frank asked.

"It's not important." Marie turned toward the door.

"Marie?"

"Yes?" she replied, turning back around.

"How old were you when you joined the church?"

"Thirteen. Why?"

"Did you have a testimony that it was truly Christ's church?"

Obviously uncomfortable, Marie nodded. "I thought it was true, if that's what you mean."

"Do you still believe that?"

Marie looked out the window.

"It is true, Marie," Frank declared softly. "Jesus Christ is at the head of this Church. He lives now as surely as he lived anciently, and through his suffering he offered himself that your pain and sorrow could be taken away."

"You could never comprehend what I'm dealing with," Marie stormed, more irritated than ever, "you and your chosen generation! Have you ever thought that people like me have been chosen, too? Chosen to be raped, tortured, beaten, and abandoned, and then forced to endure the process over and over again?"

Frank hadn't expected such venom. And yet, Marie's pain demanded an audience.

"And when I cry out," she continued angrily, "who is there to hear? Not you, not with your busy world of pretense and pious platitudes. The only hope you offer is my quick dismissal."

"I've apologized about that, Marie."

"And that *helps*? That *ends* it? Who is this Jesus of whom you speak? How could this God, who professes to love us unconditionally and equally, allow all those other girls to grow up blissfully, blessedly ignorant, while I was forced to grow up with shame? They flitted happily about while I was ground through the muck and made prey to those who would use me for their own selfish lusts.

"I was a *child*! I had *no* defenses! Jesus didn't protect me, and now you tell me he is ready to take away my *pain*?"

"Marie," Frank gently protested, "Jesus does love you—"

"Love? I don't know anything about that. Love is just a four-letter word in my book!

"But truth? Talk to me about *truth*, Frank. I don't want any more lies! I don't want any more cover-up! I want to get this stuff out! But maybe truth doesn't fit into this gospel of yours! You don't want to hear it! Jeanee tells me the truth will set me free. Well, maybe, but I don't know if I'm going to find it in this church! I haven't yet met a priesthood leader who had the courage to face it, let alone hear it!"

"Daddy." Angie came around the corner in her pajamas. "Can we have family prayer before you go to the church?"

Suddenly embarrassed at her outburst, Marie clutched tighter at the book Jeanee had loaned her. "I . . . I'm sorry," she gasped. "I just have so much anger."

"It was nice to meet you." Angie smiled up at Marie. "You're a nice lady."

Tears instantly filled Marie's eyes, and she turned as if to leave. Then, slowly, she turned back. "And you have a very nice family, Angie. Tell your Mommy goodnight for me. Okay?"

"Okay," Angie beamed.

"And Frank," Marie said as she regained her composure, "for whatever it's worth, your apology is accepted."

TUESDAY, JULY 16

7:30 P.M.

The silence of the bishop's office was deafening. There was no sound in the empty building, none except Frank's own breathing and the occasional squeak of his chair. Numbly he sat at the desk, his fingers tapping softly against each other. He couldn't believe it! He just couldn't believe it! What was happening? What was going on in his ward? It seemed that in every direction he turned, he was running into problems, serious problems that to him seemed incomprehensible.

Even at home he couldn't understand what was happening. Jeanee's behavior baffled him. After all, they had discovered years earlier that it was stress that put her over the edge and triggered her illness. So why was she driving herself as she was? Frank shook his head in frustration. What was it in his wife that caused her to be this way?

For a moment his thoughts shifted, and he found himself thinking again of his ward. In homes such as the Nichol's, the McCrasky's, and the Martin's, as well as with Marie, there was more pain than he could even comprehend. But this thing with Mel Blodgett and his family was so incredibly foreign to Frank's thinking that he still couldn't come to grips with it.

"Heavenly Father," Frank prayed as he bowed his head, "wilt Thou please help me to understand what is happening with these people I love?"

187

Instantly Frank's soul filled with emotion, and as he wept before the Lord it seemed to him that he was actually feeling all the pain his ward members were experiencing. It was excruciating, and for a moment or so he could not even pray.

"Thou hast given me a bishop's stewardship," he finally continued, striving to control his tears, "and now things are happening to some of these people that I can't even begin to understand. Father, if I am to be a common judge over them, then fill my mind with inspiration. Please, Heavenly Father, I must have help, I must have understanding. This can't come from within me, for I have no experience that would prepare me for it. Even Jeanee tells me I've lived a sheltered life, and it's true. Most of my memories are happy ones, and I can't comprehend what these people are dealing with. What Mel Blodgett has done to his daughters—and his wife—is *beyond* me, as is what Bob Nichol did to Claudia and Robby. I think June McCrasky is out of line, but I don't know what to say to her. And what happened with Marie Spencer—well, I feel terrible about offending her. I was just trying to help, and she twisted it all around in a way I never even thought, let alone meant. Bless her Father, that her heart will be softened, that perhaps I might be able to do some good in her life.

"Help me to understand Abby Martin, Heavenly Father. I have always had such admiration and respect for John. Yet he did leave them, he is not supporting them, and I don't understand why he would ever strip their home of furniture the way he did. Something is not right there, Father, and I ask Thee to make known to me the truth, that I might be able to help them all.

"Then there is Jeanee. Dear Father, I don't know what is wrong with her, but I know that Thou knowest. Please tell me what I must do to help her get beyond what is bothering her so terribly—"

Frank was still overcome with emotion when the first knock came at his door. Sighing, he thought how thankful he was to finally be able to get his mind onto something other than the trauma in his own life.

"Come in," he called out as he wiped his eyes one more time.

8:15 P.M.

"Mommy, is it okay if I play paper dolls in your bedroom and keep you company?"

Angie was dressed in her pajamas and ready for bed, but she was feeling a little insecure about all the excitement in the house.

"That's fine, sweetie," Jeanee yawned. "I'll just lie here and rest while you play, okay?"

"Okay. Are you going to be better tomorrow?" Angie set a pile of paper doll clothes on the floor.

"I hope so, punkin. If I get enough rest I will be."

"You've been working really hard, huh."

"I guess so."

"Daddy's been worried about you."

"I know he has, honey."

"I've been worried, too."

"Come up here." Jeanee motioned for Angie to join her on the bed.

"Do you want me to bring my paper dolls?"

"You can leave them there, if you want."

"Okay," Angie agreed, stacking them neatly next to the dresser. Then she happily climbed onto the bed next to her mother.

"It's been a long time since we took a nap together, hasn't it, punkin."

"I can remember when I was a really little girl, we took lots of naps together. Mommy, you get tired a lot, don't you."

"Does it seem that way to you?"

"Uh-huh."

"Well, I guess it must be true."

"Erik says you have two speeds—fast forward and stop."

"Oh, he does, does he?" Jeanee smiled and snuggled her little girl close.

"Yeah," Angie giggled. "Erik's funny, isn't he."

"You like your big brother, don't you."

"I like him. But sometimes he teases me too much."

"I know."

"But he's a good brother. Am I ever going to have a little sister?"

Jeanee was silent.

"Mommy, did you hear me?"

"Yes, honey, I heard you."

"Well, am I?"

"You have two brothers. Isn't that enough?"

"Uh-uh." Angie shook her head. "I think it would be nice to have a little sister. Then I wouldn't be the youngest. I'd get to be the big sister."

"Oh, angel," Jeanee sighed, "I wish I could get you a little sister. But the doctor says that's probably not going to happen. But I'll tell you what—maybe someday we can talk Tony and Megan into letting Amber or Nicole come stay for a couple of weeks—"

"That would be wonderful! And we could pretend they were my little sisters. And I could be the big sister!"

"That's right."

"Mommy?" Angie looked up at the ceiling. "Do you ever wish that Daddy wasn't the bishop?"

"Why do you ask that?" Jeanee avoided answering.

"Because if he wasn't the bishop, he would be home with you tonight. And I wouldn't be so worried."

"As long as Heavenly Father wants Daddy to be the bishop," Jeanee whispered, "so do I." She held her little girl close and began softly humming for a moment and then—

"I'll tell you what—when I get all better, you and I will go down to the fabric store and pick out some fabric for a new swimming suit for your party."

"I don't think I want a swimming party," Angie said with a yawn.

Jeanee was surprised. "You don't?"

"No, Mommy," Angie declared, snuggling closer. "I think I just want to spend some time with you."

8:45 P.M.

Terri Elder was Frank's last temple recommend interview of the evening, and he was pleased about that. Terri was one of the best Relief Society presidents in the stake. Even with her out-of-town involvement with her husband's business trips, she seemed more aware of what was going on in the ward than anyone else he knew. And her interest was more than the surface fulfilling of a calling. She deeply cared for the women she worked with. For years she and Jeanee had shared a friendship more closely knit than any other Frank had seen between two women. Every year they were both wrapped up in roadshow together, Jeanee working on costumes, Terri using her acting talent.

"Hello, Sister Terri," Frank smiled as he shook her hand. "You and Doug got back from 'Elder's Haven' all right?"

"We did," Terri replied in her usual forthright manner. "That cabin is the most relaxing place on earth. But you look like you could handle a two-day vacation yourself."

Frank grinned sheepishly. "Too many emotions, Terri."

Terri's countenance immediately softened, as if she could actually feel what Frank was experiencing. "Or too much pain, maybe?"

"That, too," Frank admitted. "I don't understand what's going on with some of our ward families."

Terri nodded empathetically. "This disaster with the Blodgetts is such a tragedy, such a terrible, terrible tragedy!"

"You heard?"

"On our way into town. It was on the radio. What all this publicity is going to do to that poor family—"

"I went to see Mel earlier."

"I thought you would. But what about Carol and the girls? Have you been to see them?"

Taken aback, Frank suddenly felt guilty. "I . . . well, no, I haven't. To tell you the truth, Terri, I'm sort of at a loss about what to say. Besides, I imagine they want a little privacy—"

"Frank," Terri cut in, "may I speak candidly? I don't mean to seem overbearing. But there are some serious issues of concern here."

"That's fine." Frank agreed. "I welcome your input."

"First, Carol and the girls—Frank, right now your acceptance and support is tremendously important. They're experiencing an incredible sense of loss, and no matter how this turns out, their lives will never be the same. As bishop, you're in a position to be of great comfort to them."

Frank nodded his comprehension.

"They'll also require professional therapy," Terri continued, "the sooner the better. Have you contacted Social Services?"

"No, I haven't."

"Well, it's too late tonight, but first thing in the morning you'll need to call and—" Suddenly Terri laughed. "Oops! I just slipped into my 'president' mode. Sorry about that. Of course what I've said are only suggestions, Bishop. Strongly felt, but suggestions nonetheless."

Frank smiled. "Understood, Terri. I'm glad you said what you did. I'll make it a priority to visit with Carol and the girls, and therapy probably wouldn't have occurred to me until much later. I'll call LDS Social Services in the morning."

Terri smiled. "Good. What about Brother Blodgett? Are there any signs that he understands the enormity of what he's done?"

"Not from what I saw today. All I heard from him were excuses."

"That's sadly typical." Terri leaned forward slightly, and with great tenderness in her voice, she continued. "He's stolen his daughters' childhood and destroyed their trust, he's violated their innocence and sense of purity and self-worth. He can't begin to know the scars he's left on their souls."

Frank listened, remembering Mel's comments earlier in the day. "Tell me about Jeanee," Terri continued. "I haven't been able to get her out of my mind the whole time we were out of town."

"There's probably a good reason for that," Frank admitted. "She's not doing well at all. Just this afternoon I had to get someone to take care of her while I went to the jail."

"Frank, what's wrong?" Terri was suddenly sitting straight up in her chair.

"Remember those spells she took after Angie was born?"

"The paralysis?"

"Yeah." Frank shrugged. "It's the darndest thing! If I'd had any suspicion that she hadn't been completely over that, I don't think I could have accepted this calling. I tell you, Terri, it's ripping me apart to know I can't be there for her. When I think that I have to take care of the other emergencies in the ward while I leave my own wife alone in the house and so sick—"

"That's what I saw on your face when I came in," Terri realized out loud.

"She just pushes herself too hard," Frank continued. "Ever since we heard about Amber's abuse this past spring, she's been like a crazy woman."

Terri's mind raced, trying to find a way of saying things Frank needed to know without breaking Jeanee's confidence. But he had to be aware, or he would never be able to help his wife through what seemed to be destroying her.

"Do you suppose Jeanee's illness and your granddaughter's abuse might be related?"

"Well, they both happened at the same time, so they're probably related. But the way she keeps throwing herself into other peoples' problems, taking responsibility that isn't hers, only compounds the problem."

"That doesn't make sense to you?"

"Does it to you?" Frank shot a look of desperation at Terri.

"Frank," Terri responded thoughtfully, moving very gingerly forward, "you need to get Jeanee to talk."

"Frank shrugged helplessly. "That's what I've been trying to do for weeks now. She just won't."

"Maybe," Terri suggested, "you need to think about a different approach. In fact"—Terri took a deep breath— "it sounds to me like Jeanee's body is sending out distress signals that her conscious mind is denying."

Frank laughed. "I'm sorry, Terri, but you lost me on that one."

"Well," Terri adjusted herself on her chair, "if I explain myself much further, you might be in for a bit of a shock."

Saying nothing, Frank simply waited.

"First," Terri finally began, "you should know that I almost didn't come in to see you tonight. The reason is because . . . my voices told me I wouldn't pass the interview, and that I wasn't deserving of going to the temple."

"Voices?" Frank asked, now totally puzzled.

"Yes, voices. I think they are the voices of my body, screaming in anguish. At times they are the hardest part of my day-to-day living. When I am spiritually weak, they can be very oppressive —"

"You actually hear voices?" Frank interrupted, furrowing his brow.

"Yes, Frank, I do. I've come to the conclusion that they're internally generated because they don't respond to being cast out. In other words, the voices come from my own body, sending out distress signals."

"Don't tell me," Frank said with a sigh of understanding. "You were abused as a child."

"I was," Terri admitted, looking Frank right in the eye.

"But . . . compared to this other sister I've been seeing, you seem so normal." Frank was referring to Marie.

"Remember, Frank. I'm an actress."

"And the voices?"

"They may be with me for the rest of my life."

"But how do you live with them?"

Terri smiled patiently. "Frank, before we moved here, I was in an incest survivor's group. They helped me learn how."

"Incest survivors?"

"That's what we call ourselves — those of us who have survived it and are in recovery."

"There's actually enough incest going on to have a group?"

"Oh, Frank, you *have* led a sheltered life." Terri smiled again. "The other night I heard on public television the current estimate that one of every six American men and women has been sexually abused."

"You don't think it's that high among members of the Church, do you?" Frank questioned.

"Who knows? But even one out of a hundred is too many.

"Let me tell you," Terri continued, "about one particular friend of mine in our survivor's group. She was a member of the Church. She couldn't attend church regularly because she spent most of her time in the state hospital. Her father, while serving in a responsible Church position, began violating her when she was twelve. Every Thursday when her mother and the younger children left for Primary, she knew what was ahead for her."

Frank couldn't believe what he was hearing. "She should have said something to her mother — or her bishop."

"She finally did," Terri replied quietly. "No one believed her, and she had trouble staying sane after that."

"Unbelievable. Her bishop didn't believe her?"

Terri shook her head. "It has been my sad experience that some of the deepest wounds have been given their sisters by a few of my brothers who wield priesthood authority without charity, compassion, or inspiration."

Frank remained silent, struggling with this information.

"Now about those distress signals."

"Oh, yes," Frank nodded, "your voices."

"When someone has been hurt but has not been allowed to honestly deal with the pain, their body finds a way of reminding them that the pain is there and needs to be dealt with."

"Distress signals?"

"That's right."

"Hmmm. If your voices are your distress signals, Terri, then might Jeanee's paralysis also be a distress signal?"

Terri held her gaze on Frank while she carefully formulated her next statement. "It seems possible," she finally said.

"So what might have caused it?" Frank wondered aloud.

"Most likely," Terri responded carefully, "some wound from her past, a wound re-opened by the news of your granddaughter's violation."

Reaching up, Frank scratched at the back of his head.

"Interesting," he finally said. "You'd think, though, that in the last eight years I would have seen some sort of evidence of a wound like that. But there's been nothing—"

"Except the screams of her body," Terri interrupted as tenderly as she could. "But maybe you can't hear that particular sort of screaming because you're not used to listening to it."

"Maybe," Frank agreed thoughtfully.

"Let me explain distress signals this way," Terri said, sitting back in her chair. "Say you accidentally cut your finger off. What would happen if you did that?"

"It would hurt," Frank responded easily.

"And would it bleed?"

"Yes, that, too."

"What if, for some reason, you couldn't or wouldn't admit that your finger had been cut off? Would the bleeding stop then? Or the pain?"

Frank smiled. "I don't think so."

"You're right. Whether or not the mind admits the wound, the body is going to do what it has to do to deal with it."

Frank's office became silent as he considered what Terri was saying. The thought of Jeanee's paralysis being some sort of a signal of a wound from the past seemed totally foreign to him. And yet he also had the feeling that Terri's words were true.

"Terri," he finally responded, "if Jeanee is really screaming for help, I want to be able to help her. Only I can't for the life of me imagine why it would be happening. Another thing—how is it that you can see and hear so clearly when I can't?"

"Maybe," Terri answered quietly, "because you've never screamed in distress yourself, Frank. Remember, I have, and I know the sound!"

Thoughtfully Frank looked at her. "How is it that you seem so well now? This other woman I have been seeing is so bitter about her father's abuse of her that she's actually afraid she's becoming a multiple personality."

"That sometimes happens," Terri acknowledged, "when the abuse is damaging enough and the childhood trauma isn't allowed to heal."

"Again, Terri, what happened to you that makes you seem so well? And don't tell me it's all acting. I know better."

"You're right, Frank," Terri stated simply and humbly. "And you said it earlier. The real healer is the power of Christ. I'd love to tell you about his healing in my life — which, by the way, is not yet finished — but it's getting late, and I have a family at home that hasn't seen me for two days."

Frank nodded. "And I need to be getting back to Jeanee, too."

Terri smiled warmly. "Before we get to that temple recommend, Frank, let me assure you of one other thing. Despite my voices, the only Twilight Zone I'm an escapee from is the one in my own past. I guess what I want to say is that those of us who have been victimized find our own way of surviving, carry our own hidden scars, and send out distress signals in our own unique way while we are coming to a knowledge of the truth. Poor health may be Jeanee's distress signal; the voices are mine. Maybe some-day they'll be silenced. I hope so. Until then, I've come to the realization that I can only do my best, and my best is different from day to day. For now, knowing I'm a daugh-ter of Christ, one he loves, is enough."

Again the room was quiet, and Frank found himself looking at his friend with a new appreciation. "Sister Elder," he finally said, his tender emotions close to the surface, "thank you very much for sharing. I had no idea."

9:40 P.M.

The Blodgett living room seemed unnaturally quiet. Frank sat uncomfortably across from Carol on one of her matching loveseats, praying for the right words to comfort his friend's wife.

Carol had always seemed so competent and able to meet all her challenges. Along with her husband, they made an awesome pair. Yet, sitting across the coffee table from Frank, her head in her hands, Carol looked more like a lost soul than a commanding presence. Small wonder. How she was enduring the pain Frank could not imagine. Not only had her husband violated both her and her daughters, but already the publicity had been horrendous.

"Carol," Frank said softly, "how are you handling this?"

Looking up, Carol answered. "More than anything, Bishop, I feel stupid. There were so many signs I should have seen—"

Frank nodded. "I keep asking myself why I didn't see anything amiss."

Carol dropped her eyes to the floor again.

"Can you tell me what happened?"

"I . . . I don't know, Bishop. All I really know is that I feel like a fool."

Silence punctuated her helplessness as Frank waited for her to continue.

"All summer long," Carol continued at length, "Mel has been getting worse about spending time with me. He was putting more and more time into his work and yet complaining because he couldn't pay himself overtime. We have hardly talked since spring."

Carol paused again, then added quietly, "And we haven't been sleeping together. I should have seen that as a sign, too."

Carol's eyes were dry, as if she wasn't fully feeling the impact of what she was saying.

"It was about 11:00 last Saturday night," she continued. "Mel hadn't come home yet, and the girls said they had to tell me something. I was working on my Relief Society lesson, 'Making a Joyful Noise unto the Lord.' Can you believe the irony?" One side of Carol's mouth lifted in a mock smile. "Tish and Tess came into the kitchen—they said it had been happening for ten years. *Ten years,* Bishop!"

Frank winced and shook his head, wondering how that could have been possible.

"I wanted to scream at them to stop," Carol continued, too calmly. "But inside I knew that what they were saying was true. For some reason it had been snowballing these past few months, getting worse. The girls told me that when Mel started involving little Trace, they just couldn't handle it anymore."

"It must have been a terrible moment for you," Frank said softly.

Carol nodded. "But it was like a power came in and took over. I went to the phone and called Jerry Crandal at the police station—you know Brother Crandal, don't you?"

"I do."

"We were in the same ward once and were pretty good friends. Anyway, I called Jerry and told him we needed to talk—right away. If I'd had time to stop and think and wait until morning, I don't know if I would have had the courage to go through with it."

"May I ask why you didn't call me?" Frank asked miserably.

Carol paused for a moment, embarrassed. "Actually, Bishop, I was still hoping I was wrong, and I didn't want to hurt the wonderful relationship Mel had with you."

"I appreciate that."

"After the girls told Jerry what had happened, he told

us not to tell a soul until the police had made their move, whatever that was going to be. So I didn't call you."

"And this all happened Saturday night?" Frank was only beginning to realize that three days had passed since Carol had called Jerry Crandal.

"The longest three days of my life," Carol said miserably. "I took the girls into State Social Services on Monday, and they had to tell their story all over again. It was pretty hard for them."

"It must have been terrible," Frank agreed. "But what about you? How are you able to handle this?"

"I don't know how to explain it, Bishop. I have so much that I can't feel—not yet. It's like a protective shield is holding me from the fury of my emotions. And I'm on 'automatic pilot,' trying to be there for the girls, trying to see that everything gets handled. By the way, Jerry told me Mel wants to see you again."

Frank looked at his watch. "It'll have to be tomorrow," he responded. "Have you been in to see him yet?"

Carol let out a sigh. "It's not the right time. Jerry tells me Mel is blaming me for all this and is very bitter."

"Though I don't understand it, Claudia, he said almost the same thing to me," Frank said.

"Well, at least he's admitted to everything."

"He has?"

"Well, almost. Now he is saying he didn't even touch Trace—" Carol's voice seemed to lose strength.

"But he told me—" Frank stopped abruptly, aware that he was divulging confidential information.

"I know," Carol said understandingly. "He told Jerry the same thing. But I guess he's changed his mind, either that or grown afraid."

For a moment there was silence, and Frank found himself wishing that Mel could be there beside him, observing the misery his wife was experiencing.

"But the worst part right now," Carol went on, "is what

the publicity is doing to the girls. It's killing them, Bishop!"
Carol's eyes became intense. "Those poor girls are beginning to look like the bad guys in all this. Tish is really upset
because she doesn't think Mel has to live through the hate
of the people like she does. Already today kids have said
to the girls, 'We know why your dad's in jail.' Worse, Tess
has been called some horrible names today, just because
she and Tish waited so long to turn him in."

Frank didn't want to add to Carol's burden, but his
mind demanded an explanation to that very question.
Praying that he wouldn't offend, he asked, "Why didn't
they do it sooner, Carol?"

"Because of exactly what's happened today. Bishop, *you
just don't know what it's like!* Their biggest fear was that they
would destroy the family—cause it to break up. Well, with
Mel in jail, that's already happening."

Frank nodded in understanding.

"And the girls *love* their father, Bishop. You know they
do. They love him and they love me. And yet—" Carol's
voice broke with emotion. "How do you choose which parent you are going to hurt? The more I think about the
pressures they've lived under—"

"How will you deal with the publicity of the trial?"
Frank asked when Carol didn't finish her sentence. "What
can we do to help you make it through that?"

Carol shook her head. "Jerry says there won't be one.
Mel has admitted so much that apparently it will go right
to sentencing—thank goodness."

Frank nodded. "Are you going to go see him?"

Carol hesitated, then answered. "In a few days. He
doesn't expect me to, though. He told Jerry that he expects
that I'll divorce him."

"Will you?"

Carol looked at Frank, the agony of her decision written
unmistakably across her face. "I . . . I don't think so." A

single tear escaped down her cheek. "I still . . . love him, Bishop.

"The woman at Social Services said I should look at what he has done as an illness. If he had cancer I wouldn't divorce him, and I have to look at it like that. I want the girls to think of it that way, too. It's not their fault. I keep telling them that."

"Your girls are lucky to have your support."

"What else could I do? I'm their mother?"

"Believe me," Frank restated his encouragement. "They're very lucky."

"Isn't it strange," Carol continued, not comprehending Frank's insight, "that a man can be so many things at the same time?"

Soberly Frank nodded.

"He has so much that's good in him. He's always been a complete gentleman, so unselfish — " Suddenly realizing that Mel's treatment of her daughters was anything but unselfish, Carol stopped and changed direction.

"Will there be a Church trial?" she asked.

"There will have to be," Frank replied. "Incest has to be dealt with, Carol, for Mel's sake as well as for yours."

"I . . . thought so. Can . . . can he ever come back, do you think?"

Frank shrugged. "There is no simple answer to that question. A better question would likely be, 'Will he?' I'm sure he can, but whether or not he will is up to him.

"Carol," Frank said softly, looking her directly in the eyes, "you know as well as I do that Mel has a personal Savior." Frank paused as emotion began shaking his voice. "Christ's love for Mel is beyond anything you or I have ever comprehended, and certainly beyond anything Mel has comprehended."

Carol looked into Frank's clear, honest eyes, searching for strength to bolster her determination.

"His sacrifice in Gethsemane was for this very day,"

Frank continued. "Christ knows your daughters and in time will heal them. He also knows Mel, and He has suffered for Mel's sins already. But will Mel humble himself so that Christ's sacrifice won't be in vain?" Frank looked down at his hands, realizing how deeply he felt about this man who had done such evil.

"Carol, there's only one answer to your question. *Yes!* Yes, Mel can come back. There's no question about it. But will he? Will he?"

Tears welled up in Carol's eyes as she began realizing, for the first time, that even in this there was hope. As impossible as the challenge seemed, through the Savior there was still hope for her family.

"Dear God," she whispered, shaking her head back and forth. "He has to! He just has to!"

14

WEDNESDAY, JULY 17

4:00 A.M.

It was early morning, still dark, though a twinge of light was creeping into the eastern sky. Jeanee sighed as the grandfather clock in the living room announced 4:00 A.M. She hadn't slept in hours.

After Frank had returned home and had awakened her to see how she was doing, he had drifted off to sleep. But once awake, Jeanee had tossed and turned restlessly.

Now, after hours of fighting to get back to sleep, she opened her eyes and looked around the room. Pre-dawn light cast an eerie shadow beyond the foot of the bed. Jeanee had the uneasy feeling that something evil was in the room with her, something she could not identify. Closing her eyes, she tried to shake the feeling. But it would not leave.

"Come on, Jeanee," she scolded herself silently. "You're a big girl now. There are no monsters in your closet."

Suddenly there was a creaking sound just outside the door. "No one's there," she coaxed her courage. "The house is just settling. You're safe beside your husband. Now go to sleep!"

But sleep would not come.

"Okay, if you won't go to sleep," she continued, "let's try to do something constructive. Okay? How about figuring out why this is happening?"

Again and again Jeanee searched through the cata-
combs of her mind, seeking a sealed door, a room where
secrets were hidden, some clue as to the reason for this
anxiety—and the uncomfortable feelings she was experiencing. Such a room had to be there! And the secrets must
be very dark and evil or they could never do so much
damage.

Jeanee had discarded the thought that healing could
be as simple as telling Frank about her past. She was sure
there was more to this experience than opening up to her
husband. In spite of Terri's encouragement to the contrary, she fully believed that she had made the right decision. Frank couldn't handle the kind of information she
had to share, especially on top of everything else he was
dealing with.

No, Terri was wrong.

"What else could it be?" she wondered. Thoughts and
memories flooded her mind, bits and snatches of things
that seemed unrelated to each other, unrelated even to
her. A myriad of overwhelming and confusing pictures
competed for her attention until her entire consciousness
seemed to be slipping. She was falling into a darkness
where the only light her mind allowed was focused on a
kaleidoscope of disjointed and oppressive experiences.
Too much to sort through. Too much to comprehend.

Jeanee thought back to when her present confusion
had started. After Frank had given her a blessing she had
felt peaceful and serene, and even after talking with Marie
the Lord's strength had been with her. Alone with Angie,
there had been a special time of sharing for them both. So
what was this darkness that was tormenting her?

Then her mind went back to a few hours earlier, and
she knew.

Lying beside Frank, unable to sleep, Jeanee had finally
picked up and begun to read the book Marie had left. The
story was an account of a woman who started remembering

horrendous abuse from her childhood. As the flashes of memory surfaced, it became obvious that her mind had fragmented during childhood from the abuse, leaving her with what the text called multiple personalities.

At once Jeanee had been intrigued by the similarities of this woman's story with her own. It was fascinating to read how the woman's mind recalled the abuse and how she dealt with it. But gradually, as one chapter led to another, Jeanee became aware that the woman was losing the battle for her own sanity. She was doing what abuse victims had been warned against, probing and probing as she moved from hell into an even deeper abyss, doomed forever to live with the damage that had been done to her.

Jeanee thumbed ahead through the chapters, looking for a message of hope, a message of recovery for the woman. But each page seemed to unleash a newer and more terrifying message of endless torment. Jeanee raced ahead to the final chapter, only to find that the woman was finally left hopelessly insane.

"No!" her mind screamed. "That's *not* the message! That's *not* the way it is! *I know!*"

Unable to move from the bed, Jeanee had set the book on the nightstand and turned over to go to sleep. But sleep hadn't come. A presence had entered the room as Jeanee had been reading, and it seemed to be hovering over the book.

"It's your imagination," she had tried to tell herself. "There is nothing there! Just go to sleep and don't let it get the best of you."

But as the night had slowly dragged on, and one hour had moved into another, her uneasiness had grown. Now, as she lay wide-eyed in the darkness, she was beginning to wonder about her first suspicions. "Could it be that the book is really evil and can torment those who read it?" She shuddered at the thought. The book did oppose what she knew to be true, teaching instead that there was no hope and no Savior — only endless despair and endless torment. That certainly wasn't a good message.

But could a simple message, written on the pages of a book, carry with it such evil as she was feeling? Jeanee opened her eyes and looked at the nightstand where the book lay open. The glass figure of the little girl praying had fallen to its side next to it.

A shiver caught the back of Jeanee's neck. In the near darkness she looked again around her bedroom. Even in the stillness she could feel laughter. What was it? Was she dreaming? Was she caught in a half-sleep state that wouldn't let her return fully to reality?

Suddenly struck with the surety of what she was dealing with, Jeanee's body trembled. "It *is* the book!" her mind recoiled. "Without a doubt these feelings are coming from that book! Or because that book is here. That's it! Because it teaches evil, Satan is using it to get at me, or anyone else who reads it!"

The confusion that had entered Jeanee's mind from the first moment she had become interested in what she was reading was now explained. It was as if the evil one had spun a web of darkness as she read. And it had remained with her as she fought to go back to sleep.

Whatever the merits of other books dealing with abuse, this one was evil! No doubt about it. The author had spawned a message so completely denying the healing power of Christ that suddenly Jeanee wanted it as far from her as possible.

"Frank," she said, rousing her husband from his deep sleep. "I'm . . . not doing so well."

Frank reached over and hugged Jeanee to his chest. "A bad time, honey?" he asked, clearing the sleep from his voice.

"I'm going to throw that book away," she stated firmly.

"Book? What book?"

"The one Marie gave me yesterday. The one about the woman with all those personalities."

"Mmm," was all he answered.

Jeanee pulled herself up on the bed, but Frank gave no response. Inside, her nerves were crawling, and her mind was screaming with the urgency to get rid of the book. Fighting for control of her body, she reached first one foot and then the other off the side of the bed. Shakily, she got up.

"Ahh." She smiled to herself. "I can do it! I can move again! I feel as though I weigh two tons, but I can move!"

Despite her difficulty in maneuvering, Jeanee was able to force one strained step after another until she stood trembling at the bedroom door, facing the dark stairwell. Everything was shrouded in darkness. Jeanee moved slowly forward, feeling nervous about being alone, half-expecting someone to appear before her.

"You can do this," she coaxed herself. "It's just a few more steps. You can do this!"

The book made a thudding sound as it hit the bottom of the kitchen garbage. And though Jeanee didn't understand it fully, now that it was gone she felt better.

"Now," she muttered as she turned slowly back toward the stairs and her bedroom, "maybe I can get a little sleep."

Frank was sitting on the side of the bed when she returned, the light on the nightstand turned low. "Would you like to have a prayer?" he asked, rubbing his head.

Jeanee nodded and knelt in a crumpled heap beside him. Frank's prayer was short but fervent, and she felt even better when he had finished, " . . . in the name of Jesus Christ we pray. Amen."

"Do you want to talk about it?" Frank whispered after they got back into bed.

"Not . . . really," Jeanee answered slowly. "Right now I've got to get some sleep."

"I understand. Are you going to be okay?"

"I'll be fine," Jeanee answered, hoping against hope that she was telling the truth. Then, closing her eyes, she began searching mentally for the peace and serenity she had known only a few short weeks before.

Suddenly a scripture came into her mind, a verse from the 26th chapter of Isaiah that she had memorized long years before. "Thou wilt keep him in perfect peace, whose mind is stayed on thee, because he trusteth in thee."

"That's perfect peace, Jeanee," her thoughts assured her. "Perfect peace—and you know you can trust Him. You know you can." She could hear the chirping of a bird outside the window, heralding the dawn. A new day was beginning, and the battle with darkness was passing. Snuggling safely next to her husband, Jeanee finally began to relax—and to drift off to sleep.

6:20 A.M.

"Hello. Mrs O.?" It was early morning, and Frank was already late for a meeting with one of his committee members at the university, a meeting he wouldn't be making. After his prayer with Jeanee a couple of hours earlier, he had been overcome with the need to understand her unusual behavior.

"Well, hello, sweet cousin," Mrs. O. replied through the telephone. "How are you?"

"A little harassed. I hope you don't mind me calling you this early."

Mrs. O. yawned. "I'm glad you called, Frank. It's time I was up and at it. My goodness, it's almost 6:30!"

"Do I detect a note of sarcasm?" Frank winced.

Mrs. O. laughed. "More than a note. Probably a whole bar. But seriously, Frank, what can I do for you?"

"Do you have time to talk? This early, I mean?"

"Give me half a minute. I'll get on my kitchen phone and get breakfast started while we visit. Okay?"

Frank looked miserably around his own kitchen. An empty pizza box sat on the counter top. By the sink the carrot peeler lay next to some shriveled peelings and limp baby carrots. Ignoring the carrots, Frank checked the refrigerator. One piece of pepperoni pizza, wrapped in foil. Quickly he opened the foil and took a bite.

"Frank, are you there?" Mrs. O. sounded too bright.

"Yup," he answered, gulping the bite of pizza down almost whole.

"Before we start, what did you learn about Mel Blodgett?"

Frank swallowed again. "He's in jail, Mrs. O. My first counselor is in jail for molesting his three daughters." Frank poured himself a glass of milk to wash the pizza down.

"I'm so sorry to hear that, Frank."

"Well, I never in a million years would have thought— Anyway, I have so many mixed emotions, it's pathetic."

"Is that why you called?"

"Not really." Frank looked around the corner to make sure he was the only one in the house that was awake. Then he took a deep breath. "Actually, I'm calling because I don't know who else might have some insights into what I'm dealing with in my marriage."

"What's happening, Frank?"

"Jeanee took a turn for the worse yesterday."

"I'm sorry."

"We've been through this before, at least part of it, and it isn't all that terrible, unless of course you're experiencing it. She has this paralysis that hits when she's overstressed."

"Oh, my." Mrs. O. sounded concerned.

"But what really puzzles me is what she's been doing these past few weeks leading up to it. Her behavior is so— unpredictable. It's like she's a crazy woman, pushing herself beyond where she has the strength to go. She won't tell me what's bothering her. And when I do get her to open up, she's almost like a — I don't know how else to say it — but there are times she sounds like a little girl."

"What can I do to help?" Mrs O. asked gently.

"I think . . . just teach me what you can about abuse. Last night I interviewed a woman who said some things that made me think maybe Jeanee is dealing with some form of abuse. I guess I'm blind, but I've never even had an inkling that Jeanee might have come from an abusive background."

"Do you know much about her past?"

Frank chuckled. "Not much, actually. Might that be an indication?"

"It could well be. Does Jeanee trust you?"

"I used to think so."

"Let me share something with you, Frank. It may or may not apply to Jeanee. But I found it most interesting when I read it. And if indeed she is dealing with abuse, it might explain her behavior."

"I'm listening." Frank responded.

"According to some theorists, inside every adult survivor of abuse lives what is being called a child victim. According to these theorists, that child victim, in some instances, dictates how the adult will respond to circumstances pertaining to the abuse."

"That's not clear to me at all."

Mrs. O. chuckled. "I don't know exactly how it works, either. But let me explain it the way I think it does. A person is made up of several aspects — the physical, mental, spiritual, and emotional self, and so on. The article explains it this way — while a victim of abuse may grow older physically, mentally and spiritually, his or her emotional self will remain undeveloped and immature, like a small child hidden within the adult person."

"I don't know if that computes, cousin. How is it possible for a child to exist within an adult?"

"Well, it isn't literally possible, of course. But for the

purpose of explaining this avenue of healing, bear with me, okay?"

Frank agreed and continued listening.

"When adult survivors experience something that re-minds them of something painful from their past, no mat-ter how mature they may seem at other times, when this trigger experience happens they will revert back to childish ways of solving or hiding from their problems.

"For instance, the adult Jeanee may know very well, mentally and spiritually, that she can trust you. However, the little girl inside her, which in reality is her emotional immaturity, knows no such thing. If she truly does come from an abusive past, if she was abused by a man, for instance, that wounded little girl inside your wife may see you as being just like him. So how can she possibly trust you?"

"You know," Frank said thoughtfully, "ever since we've been married, but especially early on, little things I did, dumb things like putting on my tie before my trousers, have caused Jeanee some real problems. I know in some ways I remind her of someone that she didn't like. To tell you the truth, I have always thought it was Earl, her former husband. Might that be it?"

"Your guess is as good as mine. But if Jeanee is hiding something, or if in fact she can't remember something that was truly horrible, that could account for her unpredict-able behavior."

"So what do you suggest I do? I'm really concerned."

"Well, the only thing I can offer is that you make every effort to convince your wife she is safe with you and can trust you. Then time will take care of the rest."

"How much time?" Frank was unencouraged.

"As much time as it takes," Mrs. O. answered firmly. "I mean that, Frank. It takes as long as it takes. And you can't force it. That's important.

"Let's say your wife was abused and she doesn't remember it. Or she doesn't remember all of it. But her behavior keeps pointing to the possibility that she was. You just have to be gentle and kind and—Remember what it says in D&C 121:41–45 about gentleness, meekness, and love unfeigned? That especially applies in this situation. Healing from abuse is a very painful process and needs the kind of gentle, firm strength that scripture teaches."

With chagrin, Frank remembered using that same scripture to help Robby understand his father.

"And if she does have things she needs to remember?" Frank pressed. "What can I do to help that happen?"

"Same answer. Be patient. We can't expect it all to come flooding out just because we want it to. It won't do that even if *she* wants it to. But be prepared, Frank. If memories of abuse are there to be dealt with, no matter that thirty or forty years have passed, you need to be prepared to help Jeanee through some real pain."

7:30 A.M.

"Daddy." Angie giggled as Frank handed her a waffle. "You look funny."

"What? You've never seen me in my chef's hat?"

"You look like a big mushroom." Angie smiled. "Can I try it on?"

Frank slid the white oversized hat over Angie's ears. "Now who looks like a mushroom?"

"And who looks like a mess?" Erik teased Frank as he poured orange juice. "Guess we know who's going to clean up, huh, Dad?"

Frank smiled, acknowledging the batter all over the waffle maker.

"I found squirt there in bed with Mom when I checked on her last night," Erik continued as he handed a glass to Frank.

"I was keeping Mommy company." Angie smiled.

"I bet you were, honey." Frank winked at his daughter. "I want you to know how much I appreciate all you are doing to help your mother while she doesn't feel well."

"Is she going to be sick very long?"

Frank looked at both of his children. Erik was eating, but his head turned to see what his father's reaction would be. Angie was looking back at him with wide, innocent eyes.

"I don't know how long she's going to be down, honey," Frank finally answered. "I hope she'll be feeling better right away. But we need to be very quiet so she can rest."

"We will. Won't we, Erik."

"So how did you get back in your own bed, sweetie?" Frank asked as he poured some more batter.

"Erik carried me," Angie said impishly. "He thought I was sleeping, but I was fooling him."

"Why, you stinker," Erik retorted. "And you let me carry you all the way."

"It's good for you," Angie teased. "It will make your muscles get bigger."

Frank chuckled, happy to see Angie finally get the best of her older brother. "She's got you there, Son."

"Hey," Erik shot back, "is two against one fair?"

"You're twice as big as me." Angie stood up for herself. "So you're always two against one."

Erik finished his waffle. "And you're getting pretty smart for a squirt, aren't you." He smiled with good humor as he poured another tall glass of juice for himself.

"I'm going to be in second grade," Angie announced as if it were news.

"Is that so? Well, I think—" Erik looked at Frank, who was sending a warning look his way. "Uh, never mind," was all he ended up saying.

"Good idea," Frank said with another smile.

"I've got a good idea, too," Angie announced excitedly. "Let's take breakfast to Mommy in bed."

"Sounds good to me." Frank grinned.

"You can be the cook, Daddy," Angie stated, "and Erik, you can be the waiter. I'll be the nurse—"

Angie's excitement was interrupted by the ringing of the telephone.

"Are we going to get that answering machine hooked up today?" Erik asked his father.

"Oh, that's right." Frank grimaced. "I keep forgetting. Just a minute—

"Hello? . . . Oh, hello, Mark. . . . Yes, I tried to call you. . . . No, my wife is seriously ill, so I won't be in to meet with you today. I'm sorry, I hope the committee understands. . . . Yes, that'll be fine. I'm sure she'll be up and around by then. . . . Good, see you then. And thank you for calling back."

"You're not going to the university today?" Erik was preparing to down in one gulp a whole quarter of a waffle.

"Not today. Some things just take precedence over others."

"I can stick around and help until I go to work," Erik stated as he ate another quarter of waffle.

"You'd better watch out there," Frank scolded playfully. "You keep shoveling it in like that and we're going to have to be putting you on a diet."

"Just fuel, Dad. Just fuel. Gotta keep this lean, mean machine fueled. Erik grinned, patting his middle with both hands. Then, grabbing skin on his wrist, he added, "See, you can't pinch an inch."

"Enjoy it while you can." Frank winked. "There'll come a time—"

The telephone rang again. Erik shot a look at his father and picked it up.

"Hello. Greaves residence. No, Mom is sleeping right now. Can I take a message?" Erik grabbed for the post-it pad. "Oh, Sister Elder. No, I think she's going to be okay. She's just real tired. Okay, I'll tell her you called."

Frank was still cooking when the doorbell rang. "So,"

he said to Angie while Erik ran to answer the door, "are you ready for another one?"

"I can't, Daddy. My tummy is still full of last night's pizza."

Frank sighed. "Well, looks like I'm losing a customer."

Angie grinned her toothless grin. "I'll get dressed now. Okay, Daddy?"

"Okay, punkin. And be sure to brush your teeth. And then kind of watch to see when Mom wakes up. Okay, nurse? I'll get a tray ready for when she wakes up."

"Okay." Angie beamed. "Mommy will be real surprised, huh."

"What a softie," Erik teased his father as he passed Angie in the hall. He was carrying a delicate vase filled with leather leaf and baby's breath and one perfect red rose.

Frank smiled. "It didn't take the florist long to get that here."

"This is looking serious," Erik continued to tease as he set the rose on the counter.

"Yup. And you had better pay attention. These things make a difference to a woman, you know." Frank looked under the counter for a tray to put Jeanee's breakfast on. "Someday you're going to need to make an order from the florist yourself."

"What do you mean, 'someday?' " Erik teased. "How do you know I haven't ordered a few of these already?"

"You hadn't better have!"

Erik just smiled as he poured more syrup on the last of his cold waffle. Then, except for Frank's clanking around under the counter and the soft sizzle of the last waffle, there was a moment of quiet. The expression on Erik's face became serious as he looked pensively at the sticky syrup that remained on his plate.

"Dad," he finally asked, "what gives with the Blodgetts? Did Brother Blodgett really do . . . those things?"

Frank looked up at Erik, realizing for the first time that he was going to have to deal with his children's questions about all the publicity concerning his ex-counselor and friend.

Reaching up and pulling the plug on the waffle iron, he took a moment to collect his thoughts. "What have you heard?" he finally asked as he sat on another stool.

"A lot," Erik admitted. "That's all everyone was talking about last night at work."

Frank sighed heavily, realizing that the worst was yet ahead. "What is everyone saying?"

"Well, some people think Brother Blodgett is a real phony. Others think he's a great guy and it was terrible for his daughters to tell such lies about their own father."

"And you? What do you think, Erik?"

Erik shook his head. "I . . . I don't know what to think, Dad. It's just too much to even comprehend."

Frank nodded. "I know what you mean."

"Dad, did he do it?"

"If you mean, did he molest his daughters, the answer is yes."

"More than that?"

Frank shook his head. "The police don't think so."

"So, what's going to happen to them?" Erik asked. "What's going to happen to the family?"

Frank shook his head. "I don't know, Son. At this point, I honestly don't know. There's so much to consider, so many lives—"

"But how could he do such a thing, Dad?" Erik's eyes were moist. "He was always such a great guy—"

Frank wished he could take away Erik's pain, but he himself could make no more sense of what Mel had done than could his son. How could he explain to Erik what he couldn't even begin to comprehend? "Heavenly Father," he prayed silently, "please help all of us to understand.

"I think it's a matter of agency," Frank suddenly heard himself saying. "Choices. Simple choices, and honesty."

"But Dad, what he did—"

"I know, son, I know." Frank put his hand on Erik's shoulder. "We've just learned about it, but it didn't just start this week, or even this past year."

Erik looked at his father, his eyes cloudy with mixed emotions.

"It started a long time ago."

And as Frank explained to his son what his own heart ached to understand, he realized that he, himself, was being taught.

"A long time ago Brother Blodgett made a choice, a wrong choice. And that was bad. But then, everybody makes wrong choices, so that choice wasn't the culprit."

Erik didn't comprehend what his father was getting at.

"The culprit was that Mel decided to hide that wrong choice. He kept it a secret. He thought it was so terrible that he couldn't repent of it. He was awfully ashamed, and he didn't want anybody to know about it, especially his bishop. So he hid that secret in his heart.

"Erik, you know when I first taught you how to fish?"

"Yeah." Erik smiled.

"Well, remember how I taught you to let the fish have plenty of time to feel safe with the hook in its mouth before you reeled it in?"

"Yeah, you gotta play the line."

"Well, there's a reason for that."

"I know. If you reel him in too soon, he'll get away."

"And why is that?" Frank asked.

Erik was embarrassed by the simple questions his father was asking him. "That's pretty basic, Dad."

"But what is the answer?" Frank persisted.

"If the hook doesn't have a chance to work its way deep enough into the fish, he can fight himself loose."

"Exactly!"

"But what does this have to do with Brother Blodgett?"

"Erik, Brother Blodgett got hooked."

The youth furrowed his brow.

"Not by the kind of hook we use, of course. But hooked just the same. He could have fought his way free if he had only realized early on what was happening. But he didn't. Instead he ignored the fact that the hook was there. He pretended the choice he had made and the choices he kept right on making couldn't hurt him because they were so well hidden. No one could see them, so he figured he was safe. They were his secrets. Are you following me?"

"I think so."

Frank nodded. "Hidden in darkness, those secrets grew and found deeper and deeper places to hook themselves into Brother Blodgett's heart."

"How many years has he been doing this, Dad?"

"Far too many. And that's how it happens. It isn't all at once. You get hooked a little bit at a time."

"Like drugs," Erik announced.

Frank nodded. "That's right."

"But how . . . could he get hooked on . . . on something so . . . so gross?" Erik was not only hurt by the realization of what Mel had done, but he was also embarrassed by it.

"Pretty hard to comprehend, isn't it," Frank agreed. "Somewhere back in Brother Blodgett's past, he made a conscious choice to give in to lust and immorality. And the devil—who is the world's most patient fisherman, by the way—just smiled and sat back and waited for the day he could reel poor Brother Blodgett in."

"But think of what this is going to do to Tish and the other kids!" Erik squirmed. "How can they live with this? I feel so sorry for them! It's bad enough what their father did to them, but now what people are saying—"

"I know, son," Frank admitted.

"Dad, what can we do? How can we help them?"

Pleased with his son's desire to help, Frank smiled. "I

suppose we just need to continue being their friends, Erik, and to let them know that we love and care about them."

"And when people talk—"

"We let it be known that we don't want to hear the gossip."

"That's going to be a hard one," Erik stated uneasily.

"It won't be easy for any of us," Frank acknowledged. "Something like this doesn't just affect the people directly involved. It affects everyone around them—their family, friends, community—everyone! It's like a sickness that infects the whole society."

"I can't believe some of the gross things the guys were saying about Tish and Tess," Erik admitted. "I wanted to flatten them."

"It's hard, Erik. I don't know how it's all going to come out. But I do know they won't make it through this without a lot of help."

"Do you think Brother Blodgett can ever repent?" Erik was very serious.

"He can. The question is, will he?"

"You mean something this bad—"

"Erik, I don't want you to think that what he did is not very, very serious. It is. He will never be able to give back to his family what he has taken. But he can repent. That's why Christ suffered so heavily. For Mel, it will be just as rocky a road back."

Erik looked out the window, deep in thought. "I just wish there was more I could do for Tish and the others."

"I do too," Frank agreed. But our part is just to be their friends—and to say a lot of prayers for them."

"Robby Nichol came through the drive-through last night," Erik said, changing the subject. "He looked pretty rough."

Frank shook his head. "More choices. I need to call him."

"Daddy," Angie shouted as she came running down the stairs. "She's awake! Mommy's awake!"

"But I need to call him later," Frank said with a smile. Then, placing the rose on the tray with the covered waffle, he handed it to Erik. "Here," he said, smiling. "I believe you're the waiter today."

1:25 P.M.

"You asked to see me, Mel?"

Again Frank sat across from Mel Blodgett in the interrogation room of the county jail. This place, he thought ruefully, was beginning to seem all too familiar.

"I . . . uh . . . well, I just wanted to apologize for what I said yesterday."

"Apology accepted." Frank did not know what else to say, so he remained still, his heart yearning for this former companion and friend but waiting for Mel to make the next move.

"I . . . I feel like I want you to understand me, Frank. I don't want it to sound like I'm making excuses, but . . . well, you're probably my closest friend, and it hurts me to think that you might be feeling wrong things about me."

"Mel," Frank sighed, "I don't know what I feel anymore. All I know for sure is that you've done some horrible things that I can't understand, and that yesterday you hadn't faced up to them. As far as I can see, Satan has led you down the primrose path, and he still has you firmly by the old nose ring."

Mel dropped his gaze. "I know that's how you feel. It's why I asked Jerry to get you back in here. I misled you yesterday, and I want to set the record straight."

"All right, I'm listening."

Mel took a deep breath. "First, I acknowledge completely what I've done to my daughters. I know it was wrong, and I'm willing to accept full responsibility for it."

Frank looked deeply into Mel's eyes, searching for confirmation of his words. "Why did you deny it yesterday?" he finally asked.

"Because I was so embarrassed. You know, Frank, I still can't picture myself here in this place, among this filthy class of people. It was humiliating to have you see me here, and I was doing my best to drive you away so you wouldn't have to look at me."

"You weren't embarrassed about having repeatedly molested your daughters?" Frank asked incredulously.

"That, too. But yesterday I was still in shock about just being here."

Frank shook his head in wonderment. "It seems to me, Mel, that your priorities are awfully mixed up. You worry about how it looks to others when they see you in jail, and all the while your wife and daughters are out there going through hell? Doesn't that seem a little backward to you?"

"I'm trying to think of my family, Frank. I really am."

"Well, I hope so," Frank declared as he shook his head in frustration. "I just—How could you stoop so low? How could you justify such a thing?"

There was a long moment of silence. "I . . . told you yesterday that I thought I was giving them pleasure," Mel finally said quietly, "and that because they were my family—Frank, that really isn't so. I knew all along how wrong it was, but I wore blinders."

"What do you mean?"

"I didn't think I could change. I . . . I tried, but I kept failing. So I convinced myself that if I didn't hurt the girls physically, they could get over what I was doing to them.

"And, to compensate for what I did, I worked myself into the ground trying to give them the good things of life. To compensate for my lies to you and my other church leaders," Mel dropped his eyes to the floor, "I went overboard in all my church callings. I convinced myself that in some small way such things would make amends for what I was doing."

"But Mel," Frank pleaded, aching as he did for this man who had been such a powerful influence in his church and community, "blinders or not, you knew what you were doing was wrong. You knew you were injuring your girls!"

"I . . . know," Mel replied, anguish in his voice. "I know. I tried desperately to stop! One time I did — for three years. But then I let it start again, and it's like a drug addiction. I . . . I couldn't stop!"

Mel looked up at Frank, agony of soul burning in his eyes. And for a moment Frank felt that he was looking directly into hell itself.

"Were you involved in pornography?" he asked quietly.

Soberly Mel nodded. "I tried to stop that, too. But again, from the very beginning it was a losing battle! I couldn't keep my mind off it."

"Where did it all start, Mel?"

Mel looked away, beyond the concrete walls dividing him from the rest of the world. His mind was searching back, trying to put an answer together that would satisfy his friend.

"My sister," he finally conceded. "It started with my sister."

Frank felt restrained from speaking, and in a moment Mel continued.

"We played 'doctor,' you know. Lots of kids do it. I was curious. But then it grew into something more. Anyway, I knew it was wrong, but—"

"Mel," Frank interrupted, "was this an older sister, or younger?"

"Younger," Mel admitted. "I was bigger than she was, so I could force her—"

"Oh, Mel!" Frank agonized.

"I know," Mel whispered. "And it got worse. The older I got, the more I wanted to do. When I was sixteen, I got a girlfriend." Mel obviously wanted to open up, to share the burden he had been carrying. And Frank, horrified at the things he was hearing, nevertheless allowed the man to talk.

"What happened then, Mel?"

"That's the scary part! I still wanted little girls. I couldn't get them out of my mind. It's no different today. I still fantasize about children. Pornography just intensifies it."

Frank forced himself not to show his great discomfort at what he was hearing.

"One of the cops in here told me this morning," Mel continued, "that that characteristic makes me a pedophile—a guy who sexually preys on children. I . . . guess that's true. Maybe it means I'm crazy, I don't know. I guess a guy would have to be crazy to do to his daughters what I've been doing to mine."

"It's definitely not as God intended it."

"Will . . . will I be excommunicated from the Church, do you think?"

Frank looked hard at his former first counselor, trying to understand him. "I should think you'd want to be," he replied softly.

"Yeah, I guess you're right," Mel said as he placed his head in his hands. "I . . . I understand."

"Do you? Do you really understand?"

Lifting his eyes to Frank, Mel looked more miserable and lost than anyone else Frank had ever seen.

"I guess," Mel said, speaking mostly to himself, "I always thought I'd wake up someday and find it really wasn't happening, that it was a bad dream. And you don't get caught in dreams."

"Is that what you feel? Caught?"

Miserably Mel nodded. "I've felt caught from the beginning. Every time, even then, I convinced myself that it would be the last time. Finally I realized that I was just lying to myself. And then I thought if I could just hit bottom, I could change. But the hunger in me—it kept growing. Nothing would satisfy it. Everything I did just sent me deeper and deeper. And Frank," Mel stopped and looked at his friend, agony burning in his eyes, "*there is no bottom!*"

Searching his mind for something to say that would give this man hope, Frank finally spoke. "The truth," he said simply.

"That *is* truth," Mel declared miserably.

"I know," Frank acknowledged. "And it's where you have to begin now. What you've done is beyond anything I can even imagine, Mel. I can't tell you how many angry, helpless sermons I've carried around in my mind for you. Seeing what you've done to your family—letting me down. But right now, sitting across the table from you, I'm realizing that it isn't sermons you need. And it isn't blind, supportive friends, either. You need to know that, as terrible as your crime is, there is a way back.

"You're right, there is no bottom to sin. But there is a starting place for coming back. And that is in acknowledging your utter helplessness before the Lord. He's there for you, Mel. You've always been so strong, so self-willed. Maybe now you will see your need for the Lord's strength in your life."

Mel's expression was inscrutable. "Do you really think there's hope for me?" he finally asked. And the agony in his voice revealed the fact that Mel Blodgett had never in his life begun to comprehend the hope he had in Christ.

"How honest are you willing to be, Mel? For instance, was Trace one of your victims, as your family thinks? You can't deceive the Lord, you know. In spite of the old saw about a foolish or bumbling Gabriel guarding the gateway into heaven, the prophet Jacob teaches otherwise. He says, 'Behold, the way for a man is narrow, but it lieth in a straight course before him, and the keeper of the gate is the Holy One of Israel; and he employeth no servant there.'

"Mel, you must face and freely acknowledge every single particle of sin within yourself. That's the kind of truth that will set you free."

"Can I be free?" Mel asked.

"Can you be completely honest?"

"And if I can?"

"Then you also have to become completely repentant," Frank continued, feeling the power of the Spirit as he spoke.

"But I've *tried* repentance!" Mel objected. "It didn't work for me."

"You tried repentance in your own strength, Mel. It doesn't work that way." Frank grabbed his scriptures and quickly found Ether 12:27. "Here," he said. "Read this."

Mel took the scriptures and began reading. " 'And if men come unto me I will show unto them their weakness.' But this is more than mortal weakness, Frank. This is evil! Vile! Filthy!" Mel began rubbing his hands together as if he were trying to remove some spot that wouldn't come clean.

"Yes," Frank acknowledged forcefully, "it is! According to how I understand the gospel of Christ, Mel, only murder could be more evil than what you've done. And in a way you have murdered your girls, killing their childhoods, murdering their dignity, destroying their very sense of self. From what two or three women have been telling me lately, those dear little girls of yours may spend the rest of their lives trying to recover, sending out silent screams of agony that few but God can hear. But He can hear them, Mel, and those screams must surely stand as a witness against you."

Mel's face was in his hands. "I can't do it," he whispered. "I've tried, and I just can't do it!"

"There is a point in all of our lives when we must make

that very discovery," Frank encouraged. "As terrible as your sins are, and they *are* as scarlet, you've been promised that they can be white as snow. The Lord made that promise, Mel—for you, for me, for everyone, *without exception*. The rest of that scripture I asked you to read pertains to the sufficiency of Christ's grace in turning weakness into strength for the truly humble. Therefore, I believe that in time you can, according to your true desires and your level of humility, be able to come back.

"But it starts with that first step, Mel. The truth! You must honestly acknowledge your full responsibility in this, recognize how hopeless you are without the Savior, and then determine to let him carry the burden you have been unable to carry."

Mel looked up at his friend, hoping against hope that he was right. "How long?" he asked. "How long do you think it will take me to come back?"

Frank had no answer. He himself had asked that question too many times already. "I don't know, Mel," he finally said. "We can only live today. So I guess that's where you have to start, just being honest today. But whatever it takes, and however long it may be, there's something deep within me that says, 'It's worth the price.' "

15

WEDNESDAY, JULY 24

2:00 P.M.

Jeanee was awakened by a soft knock on her bedroom door.

"Mom, are you awake?" Erik spoke softly. "Sister Elder and Sister Martin are here to see you."

Turning over to look at the clock, Jeanee was surprised at how long she had been asleep. The shades were pulled, and a cool, welcome darkness surrounded her.

"I'm awake," she called sleepily to Erik. "Tell them to come in."

Sitting up and stretching, Jeanee did her best to pull her mind into coherency. "Let's see," she thought to herself, "it's Wednesday afternoon. Frank is—where's Frank? Oh, yes, he's gone to see Mel Blodgett. And yes, I guess it's okay to have company."

Just then Terri entered the room. "So you went and did it, huh?" she teased, pretending not to be worried. "What some people won't do for a little attention."

Jeanee smiled weakly. "I'm a case, aren't I?"

Abby Martin peeked around the corner. "Are you up to this?" she said with a smile, one hand held behind her back. "Nothing like barging in on you when you can't defend yourself."

"I'm just a lazy so-and-so," Jeanee nodded. "Maybe I just need you two to come over and kick me out of bed."

"You sure you don't mind?" Terri probed. "I was over

visiting Abby, and when I told her you weren't feeling well—"

"No, it's fine, Terri. Honest. I'm just catching up on a little sleep."

"These are for you," Abby said as she pulled a handful of roses from behind her back and handed them to Jeanee. "Out of my garden."

"Oh, Abby! They're beautiful. Such a gorgeous red."

"Thank you," Abby said. "I had them put in a few years back. I love red roses, and I could never get John convinced that—Oh, well, that's an old story."

"I'll get them in water for you," Terri offered, taking the flowers from Abby's hand. "You two visit for a minute, and I'll be right back."

"They aren't much," Abby said after Terri had left the room. "But when Terri told me you weren't feeling too well—"

"I love them!" Jeanee smiled broadly. "And besides, this stuff isn't even serious—just a royal pain in the neck!"

"I can't imagine how frustrating it must be."

Jeanee shrugged and smiled. "How's it going with you?" she asked, motioning Abby to sit at the foot of the bed.

"Rough," Abby acknowledged. "But—and this may sound very strange—I finally feel like my children and I have a safe place to live."

"It doesn't sound strange," Jeanee declared, reaching over and turning on the lamp. "After what you've been through with John, it isn't strange at all."

"But it doesn't do any good to dwell on it," Abby said as she sat down. "If I just keep focused on the things I have to be grateful for, I can make it through the day."

"Are you going to file for divorce?"

Abby looked at the pictures on the dresser and smiled. "Do you think there is anyone out there who could love me and my children the way Frank loves you and yours?"

Jeanee thought for a moment before answering. "I never knew there was a man alive who could love so completely as Frank loves, Abby. To tell you the truth, it is a gift the Lord has given him. But Abby, you deserve that kind of love."

Abby's careworn face relaxed as she sighed. "It's like I'm living in a whole new world. Every day it becomes more and more clear to me that John's leaving was a blessing."

"How are the children taking it?"

"They're surprising me."

"Do you want these in here or on the dining room table?" Terri interrupted as she brought the vase of roses into the bedroom.

"Oh, put them there on the desk," Jeanee directed. "They're too beautiful to hide where I won't be able to see them."

"Oh, and before I forget," Terri added as she set the flowers down, "will you please give this to Frank?" She pulled a piece of paper from her handbag. "I want him to consider using this message for the ward newsletter." Terri handed the paper to Jeanee.

"Do you mind if I read it?" Jeanee asked.

"You're not the one who needs it, but go ahead."

Jeanee held up the paper to the light. " 'Latter-day Gulls?' That's an interesting title."

"Read on." Terri smiled confidently.

> I used to enjoy watching sea gulls
> as they soared in high,
> sun-glinting circles.
> Their distant voices
> calling out stories
> of faraway horizons.
>
> I enjoyed them
> until the day

I watched the hay
being cut.

The farm machinery
mindlessly
swept up and spewed out
all that lay in its path:
trembling rabbits,
nesting, earth-bound birds.

Ever watchful, the gulls hovered,
then descended.
Like meticulously dressed
vultures
they tore at the weak and the wounded,
their hungry voices bruising the air.

I turned my eyes away,
sickened.

Today I watched as
gospel-clad members hovered,
then descended
to discuss the latest doings
in the lives of the weak and the wounded.
As each joined in
their hungry voices bruised my soul.

I turned my eyes away,
remembering the gulls

"And see that there is no iniquity in the church, neither hardness with each other, neither lying, backbiting, nor evil speaking." (D&C 20:54.)

There was silence as all three women considered the message of the poem. Finally Terri spoke. "I was at the store this morning, and Sister Byston came up to me and started in on how terrible it was for Tish and Tess to 'say those terrible things about their father.' As politely as I could, I let her know I wasn't comfortable talking about it. I thought that would end it, but a few minutes later I overheard her in the checkout line talking with Sister Bradshaw." Terri grimaced. "I wish her voice didn't carry like it does."

With a nod Jeanee agreed.

"She took up right where she left off with me about the total embarrassment for the whole Church having Mel in jail like he is. Then she started in on Claudia Nichol. I could hardly keep my silence."

"I don't think the woman realizes the damage she does."

"Probably not, Jeanee. And now we're sounding like gulls."

All three women started laughing.

"Anyway" — Terri sighed — "when I got home, this came to me. Maybe if it's printed it will reach someone — stop some of the gossip that is already started."

"That poor family," Abby said quietly. "It's bad enough without the talk."

Terri reached out and touched Abby on the shoulder, comforting her.

"I'll be sure Frank gets this," Jeanee assured her friend. "He's over visiting Mel right now. He's really been upset by all this."

"Frank's under a lot of pressure right now," Terri agreed. "I don't think I've ever seen him looking as rough as he did last night."

"It's been overwhelming for him," Jeanee admitted. "He can't comprehend how anyone could mistreat his own flesh and blood."

"How is he doing with *his* flesh and blood?" Terri asked softly.

"Meaning me?"

Terri nodded.

"Well, I got breakfast in bed this morning." Jeanee smiled.

"And how about the children? Is Angie handling this okay?"

Jeanee knew Terri was being concerned, and she didn't want to alarm her. But she couldn't stop a tear from escaping her eye as she thought of her conversation with Angie the night before. Blinking it quickly back, she forced another smile.

"My kids are the greatest," was all she would say. That and, "I don't know what I'd do without them."

7:32 P.M.

Frank's head was lowered, his chin on his chest, as he stared through the floor into nothingness. Across from him, President Richard Stone sat behind his desk, waiting for Frank to regain his composure.

"I'm sorry, President," Frank apologized, looking up. "I . . . I just don't know how to respond to this . . . this situation with Mel."

"Take as long as you need," President Stone replied. "There are few things I can think of that would be more difficult to deal with."

"It's so incredible," Frank acknowledged, taking a deep breath to steady himself. "I can't believe this kind of thing could even happen! In my own ward! My first counselor! I . . . I can't even begin to comprehend it!"

"I know how close you were."

Frank looked up. "President, he was my right-hand man! I depended on him! I loved him. Anything I needed, I could count on Mel to do it. And I would have done anything for him. He could see through any problem and make the solution seem so simple . . ." Frank's voice trailed off.

"It's pretty hard to imagine anything like this happening," President Stone agreed softly.

"And the publicity! That poor family! Already there is so much talk. And it's not pretty! Some of it's downright—" Frank paused, taking another deep breath. "President, how do I stop something like this from poisoning my whole ward?"

"What did you find out at the jail, Bishop?"

"The worst!" Frank answered in exasperation. "Everything's true, and maybe then some. He did it, and there may be more. He defiled his own daughters, I think all of them, and yesterday he defended his . . . his behavior as a beneficial thing to do!"

President Stone shook his head. "I'm sorry to hear that."

"President, it made me sick. Literally! I mean, how can a bright person like Mel do such a stupid, stupid thing?"

"We're going to need to move quickly," President Stone explained. "Just so you'll know, the high council is meeting with me tonight on this. Then Saturday we'll hold a council of discipline—"

Frank shook his head and looked at the floor. "I just don't understand it! An educated, capable man! How could he stoop so low? How could he have—And he was telling me yesterday he didn't belong in jail with the 'filth' that was there!"

"Are you going to be all right with this, Bishop?"

Again Frank shook his head. "I don't know. I've been trying to keep my perspective. I've tried to apply what I know to be true. And yet, I'm really struggling. I don't want to admit how really angry I am! When I went to the jail today—"

"You went again today?"

Frank nodded. "Mel asked me to come back so he could explain—"

There was a pause; neither man spoke.

"But . . . how can any man explain something like this?" Frank finally gave in to the emotion he had been holding back. "I keep asking myself, 'Why?' And there's no answer! And the darndest thing. Part of the reason I'm angry is that I feel . . . betrayed! I *trusted* him, President!" Frank's voice shook with frustration and anger. "I made him responsible for so much of the workings in the ward, believing that he had the Spirit! And he not only didn't have the Spirit, but he did *this!*

"I went to see Mel's wife, Carol, last night, and my heart nearly broke as I watched her. She's a good woman, strong, but this . . . It's like she's dying inside. And those poor little girls! How are they ever going to get past something like this? Carol told me they're all feeling guilty about breaking up the family and putting Mel in prison, but they shouldn't! That was the least he needed! If it had been left up to me, I think I'd have taken a knife and . . . and . . . "

Taking a deep breath to regain his composure, Frank reached into his pocket and withdrew a slip of paper. "Here are a couple of names—men I've prayed about. Either one would do a fine job as my counselor, though I would prefer the top name."

"You want your second counselor, Grant Harris, moved to first?"

"Yes, please. Will you be there to take care of this on Sunday?"

President Stone nodded. "Absolutely. Both of these names are good choices, Bishop. I'll present them to the high council tonight and let you know. If you don't mind, I think on Sunday I'd like to take a few minutes in meeting, maybe discussing such issues as gossip and judging unrighteously."

Frank smiled. "Take a look at this," he said as he handed a copy of Terri Elder's poem about seagulls to President Stone. "This is going into my bishop's message for the next ward newsletter."

President Stone scanned the verse. "A good decision. Sister Elder knows what she's saying. Despite what many would like to believe, the problem of gossip can't be ignored away, any more than abuse can be ignored away. It's going to take some real courage to deal with the challenge you've been given."

"It's going to take more than that, President," Frank replied huskily as the emotion of exhaustion and despair filled his voice. "Why is so much abuse suddenly appearing in my ward? Are the other bishops in the stake finding the same thing?"

"Some are," Richard Stone replied, being careful not to burden this good man unnecessarily. "Right now, however, the problems you are encountering are excessive."

"Satan is sure shaking things up, all right!" Frank shook his head in unbelief. "But why are the children having to pay the price? Why the children?"

"Did you see that article in the October 21, 1991, issue of *Time?*"

"I . . . don't remember . . . "

President Stone reached into his drawer and pulled out the magazine. "Actually, it's an interview with Randall Terry, the founder of a nationwide anti-abortion group. But listen to this comment on page 26:

> I believe that there is a devil, and here's Satan's agenda. First, he doesn't want anyone having kids. Secondly, if they do conceive, he wants them killed. If they're not killed through abortion, he wants them neglected or abused, physically, emotionally, sexually. Barring that, he wants to get them into some godless curriculum or setting, where their minds are filled with pollution. One way or another, the legions of hell want to destroy children because children become [our] future adults and leaders. If they can warp or wound a child, he or she becomes a warped or wounded adult who passes on this affliction to the next generation.

"Bishop, does that answer your question?"

Frank shook his head in agreement. "He's right on, isn't he?"

"All in the world you're encountering in your ward is this plot of Satan's."

Frank was still perplexed. "What's really distressing is that the people perpetrating this perversion are active members of the Church! Sure, their number is small. But even one is too many!"

President Stone nodded.

"And you can't spot them!" Frank continued in frustration. "They seem so normal! They help their neighbors, they pay tithing, they faithfully fulfil their callings. They attend the temple — and all the while they also molest their sons and daughters and mercilessly beat their wives, husbands, and children! It makes no sense!"

"Bishop, how much studying have you done on the issue of abuse?"

Soberly Frank considered. "I've read the priesthood handbook section on abuse three or four times, and I've studied the general conference talks that address it. I've also talked with a few people. But I still feel like I'm in the dark."

"You're in good company," President Stone reassured him. "A lot of Church leaders can relate to your challenge. And I'm sure that's why some incredibly powerful statements about abuse were made in the October 1991 General Conference."

"I remember," Frank replied quietly.

President Stone began going through his desk drawers. "I'm sure I have a copy of that *Ensign* in here somewhere. Let's see . . . Yes, here it is!

"Listen to this statement, one of the Brethren quoting a district judge: 'Sexual abuse of children is one of the most depraved, destructive, and demoralizing crimes in civilized society.' "

President Stone looked up from his reading, and then continued. "He goes on to say, 'The Church does not condone such heinous and vile conduct. Rather, we condemn in the harshest of terms such treatment of God's precious children. Let the child be rescued, nurtured, loved, and healed. Let the offender be brought to justice, to accountability for his actions, and receive professional treatment to curtail such wicked and devilish conduct.'

"And this is particularly pertinent to you and me, Bishop," the stake president continued. "It says here, 'When you and I know of such conduct and fail to take action to eradicate it, we become part of the problem. We share part of the guilt. We experience part of the punishment.' "

Frank said nothing for a moment, overcome with the responsibility he was feeling. President Stone also remained silent, pondering. Then, leafing through a few more pages, he continued reading.

" 'If only all children had loving parents, safe homes, and caring friends, what a wonderful world would be theirs. Unfortunately, not all children are so bounteously blessed. Some children witness their fathers savagely beating their mothers, while others are on the receiving end of such abuse. What cowardice, what depravity, what shame!' "

"I knew this kind of thing existed," Frank cut in, his voice barely above a whisper. "But in my ward?"

"Here's something that pertains to our sisters," President Stone continued. "A woman writes: 'Please remind the brethren that the physical and verbal abuse of women is *inexcusable, never acceptable, and a cowardly way of dealing with differences,* especially and particularly despicable if the abuser is a priesthood holder.' It's too bad that Brother Bob Nichol didn't hear or read that twenty years ago.

"And as for our brother John Martin," he continued, preparing to read again, "listen to this. 'Altogether too many men, leaving their wives at home in the morning and going to work, where they find attractively dressed and attractively made-up young women, regard themselves as young and handsome, and as an irresistible catch. They complain that their wives do not look the same as they did twenty years ago when they married them. To which I say, Who would, after living with you for twenty years?' "

Frank chuckled at the wry humor, but he was suddenly feeling a little nervous. "President," he said hesitantly, "are you sure it's John's problem and not Abby's?"

"Aren't you?" the president asked directly.

"No, not altogether. I mean, it just doesn't seem like John's type of problem."

"Can you explain what you mean?" President Stone seemed puzzled.

"Well, it's just a feeling, really. I've known John a long time, President. And he's bright, articulate, highly respected. He's been given all sorts of honors. I mean, take a look at him. He's a professor at the university!

"Then there's Mel Blodgett. You know where he is spiritually, and he was convinced that John was the problem. To tell you the truth, I'm not."

"Hmmm. Interesting point. What about the fact, Bishop, that he is already preparing to marry the young woman he left Sister Martin for."

"What?" Frank asked, shocked. "The last time I spoke with John, just a week or so ago, he told me he would be more than willing to discuss a reconciliation if Abby would only back down a little."

The stake president smiled sadly. "Well, we're getting some conflicting information here, Bishop. Would you mind following through on that and letting me know what you learn?"

"I'd be happy to," Frank said softly.

"Is there anything else?"

Frank shifted nervously in his chair. "This is really embarrassing, President. I hate to admit it even to myself, but I blew it pretty badly with a sister in my ward the other day." Frank readjusted his position in his chair and leaned forward, speaking directly to his priesthood leader. "It's a sad story—one I'm afraid I didn't help her with."

President Stone's expression showed concern as Frank continued.

"Her father molested her years ago when she was a child. And then—can you believe this?—when she was a young woman she was brutally raped. It's unbelievable that one woman would have to go through two such tragedies.

"I was concerned for her and wanted to help her get beyond the pain. Again, all this happened to her years and years ago. And to tell the truth, I was sure that if she would just forgive and forget—"

"Mmmmm," the President nodded, as if he had feelings concerning that line of counsel.

"Anyway, that's what I've always done, President, forgive and forget. And it's worked for me. You do what you can, and you let the rest of it go."

"This sister's name is—?"

"Marie Spencer. And she completely misunderstood what I was trying to say. Instead of feeling relieved, she felt censured. And as I've spoken with one or two other women who have survived childhood sexual abuse, I've learned that I made a serious blunder in telling her to forget her past and get on with her life."

"Brother Wixom from Church Social Services told me the same thing recently," President Stone acknowledged.

"But what am I supposed to tell her?" Frank asked helplessly. "Am I supposed to just let her go on wallowing in her pain, destroying any chance for happiness she might have?"

"First of all, Bishop, I hope you'll not be too hard on yourself. From your perspective, you did the right thing.

"But another thing to consider is timing. Maybe it wasn't so much what you said as when you said it. Brother Wixom told me that victims need to be given all the time they need, just remembering. When they're ready to move beyond that, they'll know, and they'll be open to receiving counsel in that regard. Like the writer of Ecclesiastes says, 'To every thing there is a season, and a time to every purpose under the heaven.'"

"It's—it's just so overwhelming to me, President. I know the path to healing is living the gospel of Jesus Christ. But when I offered the hope she had in the Savior, she became furious."

"As I am coming to understand it," President Stone explained, "her strong reaction at this point may be an important part of her healing. It simply indicates where she is on that road. Give her time, Bishop. Keep her in your prayers and keep in touch with her. And prayerfully search for answers for her and these other members of your ward. When the time is right, you'll know how to help this sister in her healing."

There was a long moment of silence while Frank fiddled uneasily with his watch.

"I wish I was confident of that." He shrugged. "Look how out of tune I was about Mel."

President Stone remained silent.

"Boy," Frank said softly, shaking his head, "we really do it to ourselves, don't we." For another moment he stared off into space. "You know," he finally continued, "I've been searching to know how I missed seeing what was happening with my first counselor. And the only thing I can come up with is that I was wearing blinders."

President Stone acknowledged his comment with a nod.

"A particular kind of blinders, President. And that's been troubling me as much as anything."

"What are you telling me, Bishop?" President Stone continued listening attentively.

"I'm telling you that I've been feeling uneasy about Mel for some time now. Certain things have made me nervous, like the way he's been conducting sacrament meeting, or the way Erik has been admiring him as a leader. And, well—I hate to admit this, but I'd come to the conclusion that my uneasy feelings were due to the fact that I was just plain jealous of the man."

"Ahhh." President Stone gave an understanding nod.

"I came across a scripture last night that had a particularly convicting effect on my heart."

President Stone leaned forward as Frank picked up his scriptures and turned to James 3:16 and began reading: " 'For where envying and strife is, there is confusion and every evil work. But the wisdom that is from above is first pure, then peaceable, gentle, and easy to be entreated, full of mercy and good fruits, without partiality, and without hypocrisy.'

"And," Frank continued, as he looked up, "I believe this scripture was the Lord's way of letting me know that my confusion in this matter came from comparing myself to the man and coming up short. I was so busy seeing in Mel all the things I couldn't see in myself that I haven't been seeing him as he really is. My envy blinded me."

"Someone once told me," President Stone said, "that Satan doesn't care if we think too much of ourselves or too little of ourselves, just as long as we always think of ourselves."

"Exactly," Frank agreed. "And with Sister Spencer, it was the same thing. I was uncomfortable when she was disclosing the details of her abuse. So I focused more on my discomfort than her need. If the message I gave her was premature, it was because I wanted her to hurry and get over her problem so I wouldn't have to deal with my own discomfort.

"In both situations, I was thinking more of myself than the people I was serving."

A wide smile spread across President Stone's face. "I think it's your honesty that I admire most about you, Bishop. Not many people would be willing to admit such weaknesses about themselves."

"But it's true." Frank disregarded the compliment. "In both of these situations, if I had been considering the needs of those I have been called to serve above my own, I would have been more in tune, more able to hear the Spirit.

"To think I might have stopped the damage Mel has done—"

"Now Bishop, don't be too harsh on yourself. The past twenty-four hours have been filled with some real introspection for me as well. Why didn't I hear the Spirit? Why didn't either of my counselors, or the high council? We approved him, you remember."

"And?" Frank asked softly.

"And, a thought keeps coming into my mind that might provide the answer. Do you remember how the Lord forbade Alma and Amulek from stopping the fiery destruction of the righteous women and children of Ammonihah?"

"I remember."

President Stone opened his copy of the Book of Mormon to the seventeenth chapter of Alma, which he quickly read. "Alma says here," he stated, looking up, "that they were forbidden to stop them so that the deeds of those committing the murders would be equal to their internal wickedness and stand as a witness against them. Frank, is it possible that the Lord withheld Mel Blodgett's wickedness from us—perhaps for the same reason?"

Frank thought for a moment. "I suppose it's possible," he finally stated. "But that certainly doesn't seem very fair to his wife and children."

"I agree. But then, it didn't seem very fair for those Nephite women and children to perish in the fire, either.

Yet the Lord allowed it to happen, afterward receiving them unto himself in glory, thus making the statement that fairness was an eternal principle, not a mortal one."

"Are you saying, President, that these victims of abuse will receive an eternal reward for their suffering?"

President Stone smiled. "Such a reward would certainly make sense. If God is a just God, and He is, then He cannot allow someone to take from the innocent their happiness and emotional well-being, literally their agency, without giving them just compensation in some other way and at some other time."

Reaching out, Frank took the open book of scriptures from the stake president, and for a moment he read down the column of verses.

"Well," he said finally, "I assume that those who suffer abuse today will also stand as eternal witnesses against their abusers. Justice will be done, in spite of what the abusers may be getting away with at the moment."

"Of course that's correct."

Frank looked up. "It terrifies me, President, to learn of people in the Church, people sometimes in leadership positions, who are leading double lives—Mel being one example. Tell me, how can an officer in the Church be involved in such immoral activities? How many of our brethren are there who are so unworthily serving?"

"Of course I can't answer that," President Stone replied slowly. "But like you, Bishop, I am deeply disturbed that a few of the men and women who hold leadership positions in the Church can be so incredibly unrighteous. My entire being cries out in protest, for I do not want to believe it!"

Silently Frank watched as emotion creased his stake president's face.

"But since I must face it and believe it," the president continued, "I will do so objectively. I will recognize that such wickedness is not common, and that no matter how common it might be, it in no way affects my personal testimony of Christ and the divinity of the work to which He has called me.

"This is His church and kingdom. As a whole, its people are righteous, though individually all have sinned and fallen short of the glory of God. Yet, through repentance, all can be cleansed and brought back into His presence, myself included.

"Bishop," President Stone concluded forcefully, "I know that Christ's suffering can remove the pains of sin from any and all who will wholeheartedly repent and turn to Him. On the other hand, all who will not repent, be they criminals or stake presidents or anybody else, will suffer the wrath of an offended God until full justice has been served."

16

THURSDAY, AUGUST 1

1:10 A.M.

It was late, long after Frank liked to be asleep. Yet tonight, as he lay in bed, sleep had not come. Part of it was the excitement of seeing Erik receive his Eagle award at the court of honor. Frank closed his eyes and remembered the tears of happiness Jeanee had shed as she shared her son's moment of success. That achievement and his recent acquisition of a driver's license had ushered Erik closer to the realm of adulthood, and Frank was understandably pleased.

In the early morning darkness, he considered his son. Erik's early years hadn't been easy. The loss of his natural father, accepting a new dad into his life — both had been very traumatic. And yet, even with those scars, he had seemed to be deeply grounded in a security that let him move, for the most part, successfully through life. Oh, he had his moments, of course. But he was easily a son his parents could be proud of.

Then, as Frank shifted to a more comfortable position, his thoughts moved to Robby Nichol. Robby had suffered different losses than Erik, probably even more traumatic. And Robby was paying a dear price for those losses. Once a sweet, tender young boy, Robby's countenance had begun to harden. At first Frank hadn't known what was causing the change. But now, thinking of what had happened in the Nichol family, he understood, and he was saddened.

"If parents only knew," he thought to himself, "the bitter seeds they plant when they fail to nurture their children."

Turning over, he again tried to get comfortable. But sleep wouldn't come. Next to him, in the darkness, he could feel Jeanee tossing and turning, tiny whimpering sounds escaping her lips.

Something was wrong with his wife. Frank knew that. Those were tiny sounds of pain, or of fear, or maybe they were the sounds of both. Yet Jeanee's cries were never loud or clear enough to understand, and in her waking moments, Frank could never get her to talk about what might be bothering her.

Finally, his mind in a turmoil, Frank rose and walked quietly down the stairs to his den, his music room. Always his favorite place in the house, he spent little time there anymore. Life had become too hectic. But now, for a little while at least, he would not be interrupted. Under those rare conditions, he thought ruefully, maybe he could come up with some sort of a solution to the destruction that was threatening his own family.

And it was destruction, he thought as he watched the LED indicators pulsing on his stereo. He had never felt so much distance from Jeanee. Nor could he understand why. When he tried to talk about anything beyond surface issues, she refused or made excuses. If he wanted to do something with her, she was too busy. Oh, she usually went with him wherever he asked her to go, but there was little enjoyment in it. Her mind was always preoccupied with one thing or another, and so there was an increasing distance between them. Thankfully, tonight, Jeanee had seemed to be her old self, at least at the court of honor.

Sighing, Frank pushed the buttons on his remote and bumped his FM receiver to another station, one that played the oldies twenty-four hours a day. The volume was very low, and he wasn't really listening to anything as much as he was giving his hands and eyes something to do while he pondered his problem.

In the days since his interview with President Stone, Frank had almost abandoned his work on his degree. Instead he had been focusing on the issue of abuse, trying to understand why it was happening. And as he read all he could find on the subject, he found himself trying to make whatever he was learning at the moment fit the difficult patterns of behavior that Jeanee was exhibiting.

Only not much really fit. As it was turning out, his wife appeared to be an enigma, a person who did not fit into the normal patterns of behavior he was slowly becoming acquainted with. Still, enough did fit that he was now convinced she had been abused in the past. Flicking off the stereo, Frank slid to his knees and poured out his soul to God, rehearsing before the Lord all he had learned from President Stone, Marie Spencer, Terri Elder, Mrs. O., and the others he had been dealing with. Of course, Frank also admitted in prayer that in fact he knew little of the real problems and damages associated with abuse. There were just too many of them, and he was simply not trained to see them all.

Still, he stated fervently, he would be eternally grateful if the Lord would just show him some way of communicating with his wife. Only through communication, Frank was certain, would he and Jeanee ever be able to get to the bottom of what was troubling her.

Much later, having received no impressions, Frank climbed to his feet and stretched. Before him on the wall was the certificate of excellence he had been given years before by a construction company he had briefly worked for. It had been a good summer job, he remembered as he looked at the certificate, a fun job. In fact, the only problem he had encountered was when the company had insisted on giving him trade credits instead of cash for his final two weeks of work. He had never used the credits, either, leaving them attached to the back of the certificate, where they most likely still were.

"I wonder if they're any good," Frank wondered absently as he picked up his remote and once again flicked on the stereo. "It's sure been a long time —"

As the speakers began their low throb, he was pleased to hear the mellow voice of Dan Seals, who was just beginning the song "Bop," one of Frank's favorite pieces.

Quickly transferring the sound to his earphones, he sat back down, turned up the volume, and leaned back in his chair, thoroughly immersed in the music. And it was then, with Dan Seals' words throbbing in his ears, that Heavenly Father gave Frank the inspiration he had been seeking.

PART THREE

PRETENDING

I close my eyes
Against the pain
And say
It isn't there
Hoping
Time, and
Love, and
Pretending
Will stop the
Sting

It
Doesn't

17

FRIDAY, OCTOBER 4

5:10 P.M.

A light October haze was in the air. Crimson and gold filled the trees lining the path of late afternoon traffic. Frank drove carefully, smiling to himself at Jeanee's reaction to his mysterious behavior. Thankfully she was taking this well. Frank had been concerned that, on this particular night, she might be having one of her "down-times," as they had come to call them. But luck was with him, and he smiled heavenward in appreciation.

Quiet for as long as she could force herself to be, Jeanee finally burst out, "So what is it? What's the big secret?"

"Secret? There's no secret about a weekly date."

"This is hardly the neighborhood for our weekly date, Frank Greaves. Now tell me where we're going."

"What, O great and wise one? You don't know?"

Giggling, Jeanee snuggled up to her husband. "Okay, I'll take a guess. We're going to the classiest restaurant in town."

"Close," Frank declared smugly. "Very close. But no brass ring."

"Next to the classiest?"

Frank grinned and said nothing.

"Way down from the classiest?"

Again, no response.

"The cheapest hamburger joint in the county?"

Frank shook his head.

"Come on! Am I getting warmer?"

Gently Frank took hold of his wife's hand. "Warmer?" he responded with mock seriousness. "I don't think so. At least your hand feels about the same as it did earlier."

Laughing, Jeanee hit him in the shoulder. "You bully! See if I ever agree to go out with you again. I won't—"

"You won't what?" Frank asked as he turned into a wide entrance lined with perfectly manicured evergreens and thousands of clear lights shimmering rhythmically in the late afternoon shadows.

Jeanee slid forward in her seat and looked upward. "Frank," she whispered as her gaze followed granite and glass upward for several stories, "why are we stopping here?"

"Why shouldn't we?"

"Because this is like the most exclusive and expensive hotel in the world!"

"Is it?" Frank asked innocently as he pulled into the spacious tile turnaround.

"Frank, what are you doing? We can't afford anything like this."

A man in uniform stepped to the car as Frank slowed to a stop. "Good evening, Mr. Greaves," he smiled as he opened the door. "May I park your car for you?"

"Frank," Jeanee whispered, "he knew your name! How did he know your name?"

"Thank you, Carlton," Frank answered as he stepped out into the crisp air, ignoring his wife's protestations.

Before he could get to Jeanee's side of the car, another uniformed man had opened her door, and she was obediently allowing herself to be helped out.

"May I take your hand, madam?"

Numbly Jeanee held out her hand.

"Will you be staying with us long, Mr. Greaves?" the doorman asked.

"Only as long as needed," Frank replied easily.

"Very good, sir. Ma'am. I hope each of you find your stay with us to your complete satisfaction."

"Thank you," Frank replied as he escorted his nearly speechless wife into the massive lobby.

5:33 P.M.

"This isn't real," Jeanee whispered to Frank as they moved slowly forward. "What are we doing here?"

"What do you think?"

"I'm not sure. I'm not sure it really — Does this place really exist?"

"Yup. It do."

"I don't believe it! Just look at that!" Jeanee pointed at the atrium, at least four stories high, filled with the most luxurious foliage imaginable. "Have you ever seen anything like it?"

Frank just smiled quietly as his wife took in the surroundings. Flowers and trees grew in profusion, shimmering fountains and waterfalls splashed musically, and two separate swimming pools lay unrippled beside them. A huge saltwater aquarium lined one wall, and soft music filled the air.

"Do you have the feeling we're in the garden of Eden?" Jeanee asked in amazement. But before Frank could respond, an important-appearing man came from behind a distant desk and hurried toward them.

"Good afternoon, Mister and Mrs. Greaves," he said with a wide and sincere smile. "In behalf of the owners, I welcome you. We are honored to have you as our guests. Mrs. Greaves," he nodded to Jeanee, "it is especially an honor to make your acquaintance. Mr. Greaves has spoken so highly of you, and I am very pleased to meet you at last."

"Why, uh . . . thank you," Jeanee said, feeling bewildered. "I . . . I'm happy to be here."

"Very good." He nodded again and then turned to Frank. "Mister Greaves, your suite is waiting, and Jimmy will escort you there on our private elevator. Please let me know if everything is not perfectly acceptable."

"I'll do that," Frank said with a gracious smile, and then he led his stunned wife by the arm as they followed what had to be the bellhop into the private elevator around the corner from the desk.

"Frank," she hissed as they sped upward, "what is going on? How much did you pay these people?"

Gently Frank squeezed his wife to him. "Relax, honey. They just like us here. Now take it easy and enjoy yourself."

"We're surely not staying?"

"Guess again."

"But . . . but I didn't pack a thing! Besides, Eric and Angie are expecting us back!"

"My, but you do worry," Frank replied easily.

"Here you are," the man named Jimmy said as the elevator stopped and the door opened. "Presidential penthouse suite. The door opens only to your handprint, Mr. Greaves. So if you will gently place your open palm against this glass plate —"

As Frank followed directions, there was a slight whir, and the door swung quietly open.

"We hope you enjoy your stay," Jimmy said with a wide smile. "Dinner will be served promptly at seven." With that the elevator doors closed, and Frank and Jeanee were left standing alone at the open door to the Presidential penthouse suite.

5:45 P.M.

"This is where I see if the old biceps are what they used to be," Frank said with a smile. And then he reached to pick up his wife.

"Frank, this is carrying it too—"

"The lady doth protest too much, methinks," Frank said, swooping Jeanee up in his arms. "Besides, you're eating this up, and you know it."

Crossing the threshold into a large sitting room, he kissed his wife tenderly, then added, "Now this is where the evening becomes interesting."

Jeanee shot an impish look at her husband, who was suddenly pretending to get weak in the knees.

"Put me down, Frank Greaves, before we both fall down."

"There, how's that?" Frank smiled as he set her neatly in the middle of one of the most incredible rooms she had ever seen.

"Now I know I'm dreaming!" Jeanee squealed. "This is unreal! Frank, look! You can see the whole city down there! And the river! Look on that side! It looks like gold from up here. Have you ever seen anything so beautiful?"

Jeanee twirled around, looking at all three sides of the room, where floor-to-ceiling windows seemed to spread the whole world out before them.

"I don't know which is more beautiful—the room, or what's outside. Look at this carpet! And the furniture! You could get lost in it. And don't you love this color? You knew I loved this color, didn't you . . . "

Frank stood grinning as his wife bubbled over with excitement. Finally he was seeing the side of her that had been missing for so long. *Yes*, he thought, *this was certainly the right thing to do.*

"And you even had a basket of fruit sent up? You didn't miss a thing."

Frank tilted his head and grinned some more.

"And—Oh, for the love of—Look at this!" Jeanee stepped to the jacuzzi whirlpool bath. "It's big enough to swim in!"

Next to the jacuzzi was a vase of a dozen red roses. Jeanee stood speechless, looking at them. Finally she opened the card, which read, "Forever—your Frank."

Tears filled her eyes, and she could say nothing.

Frank strolled over and nuzzled close to his wife. "Forever," he whispered as he kissed her tears. "That's what I feel when I'm with you." And then, pulling her close, he felt the warm excitement he had felt from the first time he had ever held her. It was a closeness, a perfect fit, that he had never known with another human being.

"How do you do that?" he whispered.

"Do what?"

"Here I have plans all made out, and you go getting me sidetracked."

"I'm sorry," Jeanee sniffed. "At these prices—"

"And I don't want to hear any more about prices," Frank scolded. Then, clearing his throat, he became a tour guide. "Over here," he motioned toward the kitchen, "you will find a fully stocked refrigerator. And to your left, if you will come with me, you will find the bathrooms—one for you, my lady, and the other for your"—he cleared his throat again—"for your hero."

"Oh, Frank, you are my hero. But how can we afford—"

Frank put one finger to Jeanee's mouth. "Shhh. I already told you. We will hear no more of that talk."

"But Frank, this bathroom is as big as our bedroom at home. And look at all that brass and glass. And a telephone?"

"If you will follow me," Frank continued his tour guiding tone of voice, "I will show my lady to her bedroom . . . "

7:10 P.M.

By the time dinner arrived, Jeanee was still overwhelmed by her surroundings.

"Do you believe this?" she continued in amazement. "It's like eating dinner at the top of the world! Look at the sunset! Honey, are you sure we can afford this?"

Frank lowered his fork and swallowed the bite of filet mignon he had been savoring. "I told you, Jeanee," he said in mock seriousness, "that you could talk about anything but money while we were eating. Now shape up!"

Jeanee giggled. "All right, Bishop. You'll hear nothing more about money."

"Then stop looking around and eat. You've got to try that lobster tail before it gets cold."

"You got it," she agreed as she tasted the lobster, then followed up with appropriate "ooohs" and "aaahs." Soft music wafted through the air, the scent of roses permeated the room, and candlelight and an ingenious system of indirect lighting bathed everything in the suite in a muted glow.

"I must have been treating you pretty rough," Jeanee responded quietly as she took another bite.

"What do you mean?"

"I mean, for you to go to this length to get my attention tells me how desperate you were."

Frank grinned. "Think you've finally got it all figured out, do you?"

Jeanee silently nodded.

"So, what do you think?"

"I think this is the most romantic setting you and I have ever been in."

"Uh huh."

"And that—Frank Lee Greaves, you're awfully transparent."

Frank smiled. "I am?"

"Yes, you are." Jeanee smiled alluringly. "But I don't mind."

Frank's smile grew even wider. "So I'm transparent, huh?"

"Totally. Is there another course to this meal?"

"Why? Are you still hungry?"

Giggling, Jeanee shook her head. "I just didn't want the waiter interrupting us in the jacuzzi."

"Ah," Frank said with soft understanding. "That's what you think you've figured out."

"You've got to admit it's crossed your mind."

Looking at his watch, Frank shook his head. "You'd better hold off. I expect we'll be having a visitor in about, oh, maybe another two minutes."

Now really puzzled, Jeanee tried to read her husband. But beyond the laughter dancing in his eyes, she could discern nothing that might even give her a clue as to what he was thinking.

"Someone's coming to clean up?" she said hopefully.

"We'll see," Frank replied, implying absolutely that her guess was wrong.

"Frank Lee Greaves!" she stormed.

"Jeanee Rae Greaves!" he teased back.

"Will you please tell me what's going on?"

"Well, we've just finished a delicious meal, and in about another sixty seconds we'll receive a visitor. Besides that, you seem to be quite put out, either because you can't jump into the bath or because you can't read my mind, I'm not sure which. But if I were to guess, I'd say the problem was with not being able to read my mind."

"Frank!"

Frank leaned back in the chair. "Hark," he said with

feigned alarm as he raised a finger into the air, "hear I footsteps beating in measured tread beyond yonder door?"

Jeanee started to laugh, and at that instant a chime sounded, alerting her to the accuracy of Frank's timing. *Merciful heavens,* she thought as she turned to watch. *What is going on?*

18

FRIDAY, OCTOBER 4

8:03 P.M.

"Let's see," Frank said as he held the two exquisitely wrapped gifts, "which one should you open first?" The delivery had just been made, and, with the door closing, Frank and Jeanee were once again alone.

Jeanee still sat at the table, smiling quizzically.

"Ahh," Frank said, enticing his wife, "this one feels most interesting. Why don't you open this one first, my darling."

Jeanee pushed herself away from the table, squinting her eyes and smiling at her husband. "This is too much, you know," she said as she took the gift and walked to the sofa.

It was obvious to her that it was clothing. Even through the wrapping paper she could see that the gift came from her favorite store.

"Frank," she said tenderly as she began to carefully untie the ribbons, "you really shouldn't have."

"Shouldn't have what?" Frank asked innocently.

"I have some really nice nighties at home. If I had just known—"

"Just open the box," Frank said with a grin.

"I am, I am. And in spite of the fact that I don't need this, the thought is so sweet—"

Suddenly she stopped. Lifting the top from the box, she stared in dumbfounded amazement. It was not the flimsy thing she had been expecting but her own well-worn powder-blue sweats and some fuzzy sox, the very things she wore when she wanted most to be warm and comfortable.

"What—" she asked, again trying to read the expression on her husband's face. "Frank, darling, what—"

"Go in the bedroom and put them on. Go on, get comfortable."

"But . . . but I thought—"

"I know." Frank laughed easily. "You thought I wanted to get you in the jacuzzi. Mighty transparent, am I? Now go on. You can't open this next gift until you're dressed."

Confused, and thoroughly enjoying it, Jeanee quickly changed.

"All right," she said, giggling as she walked back into the main room. "What do you think?" Twirling and bowing, she stopped in front of Frank, who remained seated on the sofa.

"Looks mighty comfortable." Frank smiled.

"Not exactly what I thought you had in mind," she conceded.

Frank looked shocked. "You mean maybe you don't know my every thought?"

"Actually, I do." Jeanee giggled. "I just don't want you to know that I know."

"So what's in this one then?" Frank winked as he handed her the second package.

Shaking the box, Jeanee sat on the sofa and faced her husband. "I don't know," she finally conceded.

"My goodness. Really?"

"Frank," Jeanee questioned, her smile one of true puzzlement, "what's going on? Why are you giving me these things?"

"Go ahead, funny face," he said gently. "Open it. Maybe then you'll know."

Quickly Jeanee ripped the package open and found a small cassette recorder.

"Huh?" She peered at Frank, totally puzzled.

"Play it."

"Now?"

"Now."

Jeanee shrugged her shoulders and smiled. "You're a man of mystery tonight, aren't you."

"Play the tape and I won't be such a mystery," Frank urged.

Eagerly Jeanee listened, and in seconds she recognized the rhythmic country beat and wailing saxophone of Dan Seal's hit tune "Bop."

This isn't new," she smiled, tapping her foot.

"I didn't say it was," Frank replied. "And you're not listening."

"I am too. It's about a man asking his wife to put on her old blue jeans and go bopping with him the way they used to back in the fifties when they were younger and she was happier and—"

The music stopped.

"It's going to play again," Frank stated. "And you'd better listen this time, because afterward there will be a brief quiz."

"Oh, brother!"

"Jeanee, I mean it."

Smiling at her husband's great seriousness, Jeanee sat back and closed her eyes in concentration. Just then "Bop" started all over again.

"What am I listening for?" she asked, making herself sound like one of Frank's students.

"The word *body*. Stop the recorder when you hear it."

Listening carefully, Jeanee pushed the button after just a few more seconds. "Okay, I heard it. Now give me the quiz."

"Question one," Frank said sternly. "Repeat the phrase in which the assigned word occurred."

"The phrase in which the assigned word—? Okay, I've

got it. 'I'm not after your body, baby, I just want to dance with you.' That's right, isn't it?"

"Bingo. One hundred percent."

"Okay, so—"

"Back the tape up a little and play it again."

Obediently Jeanee replayed the tape, this time singing along. Only, as she did, she suddenly realized that Frank's voice had been dubbed in over Dan Seals' voice, replacing the word *dance* with *talk*.

"Talk!" she laughed out loud, turning off the tape. "You just want to talk with me? That will be novel, huh?"

"No phones to answer, no kids, no interruptions at all. Just talk."

"And just you and me." Jeanee leaned back, smiling. "All right, what do you want to talk about?"

"About you—about us."

Frank reached over and took the tape deck. Then from his pocket he pulled out Jeanee's favorite pan flute cassette, walked over to the hotel's built-in stereo system, and dropped it in.

"And this time," he concluded as he started the music, "let's fill in the spaces."

"Spaces?" There was an uneasiness in Jeanee's voice.

"You know, the ones that have never been filled in. Like, where were you born? What kind of a family did you have? You know, minor things."

But Frank, I've told you where I was born."

"And about your family—" Frank sat carefully at a distance.

"There's nothing to tell," Jeanee protested.

"Come over here." Frank motioned for Jeanee to snuggle closer to him. "Honey," he continued as she curled up under his arm. "I know almost nothing about your family. You never talk about them."

"I never talk about them because there's not really

much to say." Jeanee struggled to hold her uneasiness under control. "My dad's dead. I told you that, didn't I?"

Frank nodded his head. "Yes, I guess you did."

"I thought I did. My mom and brother live up north in a little podunk town just this side of the Canadian border. There wasn't anything spectacular about us. I grew up in the Church, and we were just ordinary people." She cleared her throat. "And outside of that, no big deal. I moved away after I graduated, and I—just didn't want to go back."

"Or keep in touch with your own mother?"

"I know that may seem strange to you, Frank." Jeanee looked up at the ceiling. "There were—problems. I don't really want to talk about it."

"Jeanee," Frank urged, making his voice as soothing as possible. "You and I have been married for a lot of years—and I've never pried—"

"And I don't want to talk about it!" Jeanee interrupted. "Not tonight, honey. It's so beautiful here. I don't want to spoil it."

Frank reached back and rubbed his neck, trying to think of the right way of saying what he was about to say. "Jeanee," he finally ventured, "in the past few weeks I have been forced into contact with a problem so horrible that I can't even begin to comprehend it. In fact, for a time I denied that it could exist in our ward at all.

"Then the news about Amber, your friend Marie, Mel Blodgett—and there are other issues I can't tell you about—"

"Abuse." Jeanee sat forward, disconnecting with her husband. She loved him with all her heart. But she wasn't prepared to share the monstrous realities that her years of shame had hidden so well. Frank wanted her to reveal things she could not reveal! Now, just hearing the hint of it, her hands grew clammy with fear, and she fought the nausea swelling in the pit of her stomach.

"That's right. Abuse."

"I know. It's awful." Jeanee struggled for control.

"More awful than you can even believe," Frank whispered.

"You said you wanted to talk about me—about us?"

"Well, I am—I think." Frank reached forward and stroked the softness of his wife's hair. "I think abuse is what we're dealing with in our marriage right now."

Jeanee stood up, folded her arms, walked away from the sofa, and then walked back again. "Frank," she said, clearing her throat, "I'm sorry I've been so distant lately. I'm sorry I haven't been there for you. I'm sorry I haven't been as well aware of the kids. But abuse? I don't think—"

"No, honey." Frank stood and put his arms around his wife. "You're getting me wrong. I'm not saying that you've been abusing us."

"Then what *are* you saying?" Jeanee's arms remained folded, and with all her heart she hoped her ruse was being accepted.

"I'm saying I think maybe *you* were abused."

Jeanee stiffened in Frank's arms. "And who is saying that?"

"I think you're saying it. The way you keep having those catalepsy spells, or not being able to sleep at night, or the way you wake up gasping for air. Something happened to you, Jeanee. I don't know what or when or even if you remember it. But something happened!"

Jeanee could feel her heart beating harder with each sentence. A tightness increased its grip about her chest. "Just a minute." She excused herself and headed for the bathroom. "Would you please open a window, Frank? It's getting stuffy in here."

9:27 P.M.

Frank was standing on the balcony when Jeanee came out. The air was cool and refreshing, stars were scattered between soft purple-gray clouds, and, below, the city was alive with lights and motion.

"Look down over there." He motioned toward the seemingly endless ribbon of traffic. "Isn't it amazing how your perspective changes when you're looking down instead of up? It makes you feel so invincible."

"Or vulnerable," Jeanee added softly.

"Or cold?" Frank laughed as he felt his wife shivering beside him. "Come on, hon. Let's go in and snuggle."

"You're right," Jeanee said softly as she walked carefully in front of her husband.

"About what?" Frank asked, putting his arm about his wife and moving her inside.

"About the abuse. There was abuse."

"I thought maybe there might have—"

"But I deserved it."

There was a moment of silence as they both moved toward the sofa.

"I deserved it because I wasn't doing the things I was supposed to do. And when you make mistakes, you pay the price."

"Do you want to sit down and talk about it?" Frank encouraged.

Jeanee sat once again in the velvety plush pile of the overstuffed sofa. "No, I don't want to talk about it," she answered woodenly. "But unless I do, you'll continue to wonder. And—I guess I can't hide it any longer."

Frank sat next to his wife, waiting, praying that she would have the courage to tell him the things she needed to confront. "I know this is hard, honey," he finally said. "But you have been such a puzzle lately. When you started having problems after Amber was abused—"

"Raped!"

"Raped," Frank conceded reluctantly. "Anyway, after Tony called us, you just started going downhill."

"And you couldn't understand."

"I tried, honey. I honestly did. But it's so foreign to me."

"So now you have to know what happened to me." Jeanee stared straight ahead, fighting to hold her composure. At one point the previous spring she would have welcomed this chance to talk, to share her past with her husband. But the summer months had enforced a wall of silence that had separated her from her true feelings, and now she felt that sharing such secrets with him would be too dangerous.

Jeanee fidgeted nervously. This was not the surprise she would have chosen for herself.

"It's okay," Frank assured her. "It's just you and me here, and no one else will ever need to know."

"No one else will need to know?" she protested. "That's what my bishop told me when I went in to see him a thousand years ago. 'No one else will ever need to know.' Do you understand how overused that phrase is? And it isn't true! There is no end to it, Frank. I wanted to believe there was an end, but there isn't. I realized that when Amber—" Jeanee broke into sobs.

"Honey, I'm sorry." Frank was surprised at his wife's outburst.

"And this . . . is how you want to spend our night together?"

Frank waited as his wife braced herself.

"Well then, get ready for a ride, sweetheart," she declared as she wiped at her eyes, a course of action suddenly in her mind, "because you are going to have a shock."

Taking a deep breath, Jeanee began.

"You're right about my childhood. It wasn't great. But

the problems really began when I was old enough to start making some mistakes of my own."

A tear escaped, and Jeanee wiped it away immediately. "You think you married such a sweet, spiritual angel? Boy!" She laughed. "Far from it, I'm afraid. Oh, it was true for a while. I was the perfect Molly Mormon up until my senior year in high school. But then—" Jeanee sighed deeply and looked blankly at the wall. "I mean, I didn't date outside the Church. I didn't kiss the boys I dated. I didn't stay out late. I had a reputation for being so straight that I became a challenge for most of the boys in my graduating class."

"Jeanee—"

Ignoring her husband, Jeanee continued. "They teased me, and I ignored them. But then I met this one guy—I don't know why, but I just quit fighting. Years later I told myself it was the diet pills I was taking. They took them off the market a few months after I got pregnant, because they found out through further testing that they were a sexual stimulant."

"A what?" Frank wasn't sure of what he had heard.

"I know, it's a cop-out!" Jeanee was obviously flustered. "But they did take them off the market for that very reason. Still, I had my agency. I know that." She stared blankly at the floor. "I should have said no, and I didn't. So whatever the reason, it was too late for me."

Jeanee waited for a response. But there was none, and the quiet of the room was heavy around them. "Is this what you want to hear?" Jeanee flared angrily.

"If it's what you've been holding inside," Frank answered.

"Well, I got pregnant," Jeanee continued. "Shamed my family—had to get married. And then my husband started drinking heavily. And the baby came—Frank, this is so humiliating! I've gone through this before, and it doesn't get any easier."

"This was Tony?" Frank asked, trying to keep things straight.

"That's right."

"Tell me about the abuse, Jeanee," he prodded.

Jeanee sighed. "That started with the drinking. At first it wasn't anything but arguments, and, you know, just fighting over money, or really the lack of it. He didn't like to spend anything on frivolous things like food and clothes. It cut into his beer and party budget. And I felt like I didn't deserve to have anything nice. After all, look what I'd done! I figured, for me, that was okay. But," and then Jeanee's expression changed to helplessness as she added, "it wasn't okay for my baby!

"One night—it was winter and the snow was deep— and the baby was crying because there was no milk and he needed a bottle. But *his daddy* was watching TV, and he didn't want to go to the store until the movie was over. So I waited, and I tried to keep Tony quiet so he wouldn't make his daddy mad. Finally, after ten, the jerk started getting ready for bed.

" 'What about the milk?' I asked. He just said, 'I'm too tired. I'm not going.' Then he went to bed.

"It might seem like a little thing, but it was one of many. I couldn't drive. My dad hadn't let me get my driver's license, and neither would my husband. So I bundled Tony up and carried him out into the snow. And the only store that was open by then was the one clear across town. So I wrapped Tony's blanket close about him and walked all the way—just the two of us—in the dark and the snow.

"When I got back my husband accused me of getting a ride with someone. That's all he had to say. And we never talked about it again. But it scared me that he wouldn't even take care of his own baby. I mean, I deserved what he did to me. But the baby didn't."

"Jeanee," Frank cut in softly, "you didn't deserve to be abused, no matter what you did."

"Let me finish," Jeanee continued. "You wanted me to tell you, so I'm going to tell you."

Jeanee moved all the way to the other end of the sofa and wrapped her arms around herself as if she were chilling.

"Things weren't right with us—as a couple," she continued. "He wanted to do things that hurt me. He was into pornographic stuff, and just things that gave me the creeps. But he was my husband, and I had to make it work. So I tried.

"Then he stopped coming home at night when he was supposed to. Sometimes he'd be out all night. And then there would be no money in the checkbook. And when he came home sometimes, if I didn't have meals ready and waiting, even though there were no groceries in the house to make them with, he would get mean and start throwing things around."

"Did he ever hit you?" Frank asked tenderly.

"Oh, yeah." Jeanee trembled with emotion. "*He liked* to hit me. I thought he loved me! But it all got mixed up and ugly. And then—seeing the look in his eyes when he hit me—that scared me even more."

Jeanee curled her knees up against her chest and began rocking back and forth.

"One time when we were in the car, we were driving home from his mother's house. Tony was lying on the seat between us, and I was just wiping up some spit or something from the side of his little mouth. And all of a sudden— wham! A fist slammed right into the side of my face. I had a shiner by the time we got home. And my husband just turned his head and smiled as he drove down the road."

"Didn't you say anything?" Frank asked incredulously.

"Say anything? What *could* I say? Besides, if I said anything, what would he do to the baby? So I just pretended nothing had happened and then went home and put ice on it when he wasn't looking. And we never talked about it."

"This isn't Earl we're talking about, is it?" Frank questioned, finally understanding.

Jeanee fidgeted uncomfortably. "No, and now you know — I'm a bigger failure than you thought I was!"

"Jeanee!" Frank objected.

"Well, it's true! Earl came later — after my divorce. See, I failed! I started the marriage wrong! And I ended it wrong, and I'm not worthy — "

"Jeanee, babe, I'm so sorry. I had no idea!"

"I didn't want you to know," Jeanee replied softly, putting her chin against her knees. "I wanted you to think I was wonderful."

"But I do, honey! You are wonderful! None of this changes how I feel about you. Surely you know that!"

"But Frank, you're the bishop! I'm the bishop's wife. I'm supposed to be an example. Do you know how it feels to look at the sweet, pure young women that look up to me and to know that I've got a scarlet letter branded on my spirit?"

"But Jeanee, nothing's branded on your spirit! That's behind you."

"Oh, right! Is it? Then why are we talking about it? And why does little Amber have to pay?"

"Wait a minute! What does Amber have to do with this?"

"Scriptures say the sins of the parents will be visited onto their children unto the third and fourth generation, don't they?"

"Yes, but — "

"Well, look what I brought into Amber's life!"

"Jeanee, you can't possibly be blaming yourself for what's happened to Amber."

"Whether I do or not, it's the same!" Jeanee stood and began pacing the floor. "I thought I'd worked through all this. I really did! And now look! Old Satan just reaches back and it's all ugly again! It's like hell has no bottom! And here, this could have been a wonderful night. But no, we have to talk about the armpit of my life! And for what? Has it helped you to understand anything of what I've been going through? Has it done that?"

Frank stood up and walked slowly over to kneel in front of his trembling wife. "I'm sorry for how difficult this is for you, darling. If I could take this pain away, you know I would. But I had to know."

Jeanee looked helplessly at her husband. "Now that you know, now what?"

"Anything you want." Standing, Frank tenderly took Jeanee into his arms and held her close. "Anything you want . . ."

19

FRIDAY, OCTOBER 4

10:40 P.M.

"How does that feel?" Frank asked as he gently massaged Jeanee's back. "Any better?"

"Mmmmmm," she purred. "Feels wonderful. What did I ever do to deserve someone like you?"

"Jeanee?" Frank stopped his massage and sat beside his wife on the bed. "About that word *deserve.*"

"Yes?"

"I think you have something confused in your mind."

"That's entirely possible." Jeanee grimaced as she turned over, propping herself up on one elbow.

"The way your first husband treated you. Honey, I hope you know that you didn't deserve to be abused. That's not how the Lord works His plan."

Jeanee looked beyond her husband to the stars gleaming outside their room and sighed. But there was no expression on her face.

"When we make mistakes," Frank continued, "there are consequences. But abuse? That's not from the Lord, honey. That's from an entirely different source. Do you realize that?"

"Frank," Jeanee said, lifting herself into a sitting position on the bed, "once I started reading my scriptures, I discovered a place in Moroni that tells us how to judge whether or not something is from the Lord. As I understand it, only things that entice us to believe in Jesus Christ, and to do good, come from Him. Anything that entices us not to believe in Christ, and not to do good, is not from the Lord. So, yes. Mentally I know that abuse isn't the Lord's way of punishing us for wrongdoing. But Frank, honey, inside me where I feel—that's where I'm confused."

Frank twisted back and forth to relieve the strain on his shoulders, and then he looked over at her. "You know, hon, you're one of the most spiritual women I know. Your experiences have deepened you and made you more compassionate than those who haven't suffered as you have. And though the abuse wasn't the Lord's will in your life, He has turned it to your good. He has allowed you to develop depth in order to feel the suffering that others feel. That's why, when women come to you all ready to give up on life, you're able to give them the hope and courage to go on. You understand—really understand—and you give them sound gospel answers they can use.

"But when it comes to you? You're too hard on yourself. You always have been. And I don't understand that. As far as you're concerned, you're never good enough. Maybe that comes from what your first husband did to you. I don't know. But I do know there's a way to get beyond this suffering. Maybe it's counseling—maybe it's even a principle we haven't been applying in our lives—"

"Frank, there's more," Jeanee interrupted. "I haven't told you the whole story. I haven't told you about my . . . leaving the church."

"Wait a minute." Frank made the time-out signal with his hands. "You dropped out of the Church?"

Jeanee looked up at the ceiling and nodded affirmatively. "After I got married the first time."

"Guess that's something we share," Frank said. "But tell me, what was it that got you active again?"

Jeanee's expression became almost careless. She pulled her legs in so she was sitting cross-legged on the bed. "It's amazing that I did, actually. I was so far gone after the divorce. I was angry and rebellious, and I was sure I could never fit in with all the good Mormons I had grown up with. So, for a couple of years, I didn't want anything to do with the Church. Not anything! Tony and I moved to another town, and I got a job. I don't even want to talk about how rough that was! But I wouldn't go on welfare. I had been taught that taking welfare was shameful, and I had enough shame in my life already."

"Was that when you met Earl?"

"Uh-huh. It was that first summer."

"And Earl was good to you?"

Once again, Jeanee stared off into the expanse of stars scattered beyond their room. "He was good to us."

"A member? Right?"

"Yeah, a member. Not real active, but he encouraged me, and that's when I finally started going back to church."

Again Jeanee became quiet and distant.

"It's funny," Frank mused. "I always thought Earl was Tony's father."

"I know." Jeanee's eyes began misting over. "Earl was a wonderful man. I'll never get over how he kept that insurance policy a secret from me. And in the hospital, when he said he'd be better to me dead than—"

"It's okay, honey." Frank comforted, putting his arm around his trembling wife. "I won't ask any more questions. Let's take a break, okay?"

Jeanee sniffed back her tears.

"One last thing—this idea that you deserved all that happened to you? Jeanee, you've neither said or shown me anything that would make me believe that."

"I just know it in my heart," Jeanee whispered.

"Well, maybe that's something you need to talk with someone about—someone who understands these things better than I do. This abuse issue is so complicated, Jeanee. And the more I learn about it, the more I realize that the best tool Satan has to use in this game of his is confusion.

If he can get you feeling guilty about something that isn't your fault and make someone who is abusing you think they have the right to abuse, or, worse yet, think that their abuse is making their victim's life better—if he can do that—and it looks like he is doing very well—then he can get everyone wrapped up in his web of deceit, and he can control them."

Jeanee had never heard her husband talk this way. But in a way she couldn't understand, it made her uncomfortable. Almost unconsciously she moved closer, breaking his train of thought.

"Frank, darling," she whispered, running her fingers gently up the side of his cheek and around his ear. "We've put in a full night's work, don't you think?"

"It's been quite a night," Frank agreed, smiling.

"What do you say," she continued, kissing his temples, "if for the next little while we just pretend there's no one but the two of us—and the rest of the world and their problems don't exist?"

"Does that mean it's time for the sparkling cider?" Frank smiled, totally accepting his wife's deliberate turn-around.

Jeanee moved slowly off the bed. "That's a good place to start," she whispered. Then, winking, she headed toward the other room and the jacuzzi.

20

SATURDAY, OCTOBER 5

12:55 A.M.

An hour had passed since the jacuzzi had finally stopped draining, and Frank and Jeanee were lying together on the massive bed, watching reflections from the city lights below play across their ceiling.

"I have a confession to make myself," Frank whispered.

"Mmmm." Jeanee purred as she ran her fingers through Frank's thinning hair.

"I have you here under false pretenses."

"This I want to hear. But it's a bit late for a warning."

"I'm not suddenly rich and impetuous," Frank smiled, holding his wife close to him, "just desperate and resourceful."

"Sounds intriguing."

"And — the hotel bill — " Frank began.

"Sorry. I don't have enough in my allowance to go dutch!"

"That's not necessary." Frank grinned. "And that's what I want to tell you, just so you won't be worried."

"I know we haven't been saving that much on our phone bill," Jeanee teased. "So you must have got the money somewhere else."

"Actually, it's been in a time capsule, gathering dust."

"Huh?"

Frank smiled at the dimple that appeared on Jeanee's

chin every time she was perplexed. "Yeah. It's been exactly ten years, so that makes it a time capsule."

Jeanne turned and lifted herself on her pillow. "Okay, any time now you can start making sense."

Frank chuckled. "Actually, I've had a credit here since before we got married. Do you remember me telling you about the summer after my wife died, when I worked construction?"

"Mmm hmm."

"Well, this was the project."

"You're kidding!"

"No." Frank grinned. "I helped build this hotel. I did quite a bit of the finish carpentry here, including the molding in this very room."

"Amazing."

"And when it came time to pick up my last check, they handed me some trade credits for lodging instead of money. Until a few weeks ago I had forgotten all about them. Then one night I remembered, and that's when I got the idea of bringing you here."

"You mean we don't have to live on our food storage until Christmas?"

"Put your mind at ease. Though I may get a little desperate from time to time, I never get crazy."

Frank began to tickle his wife playfully. But instead of responding, Jeanee snuggled sullenly back down in bed.

"If you want to put my mind at ease"—her voice was too serious—"maybe you can explain why I've started having these catalepsy spells."

She was suddenly sorry for her comment.

"I might be able to help you there, too." Frank was effusive as Jeanee made a concentrated mental effort to lighten her mood.

"It's the message for my next monthly ward newsletter."

"Have you already written it?"

"Mostly. It's the one I tried to finish for August—you know, the one about praying for our enemies."

"Oh, you mean the one that got replaced by Terri's poem, the warning to Sister By—"

"A warning for all of us," Frank scolded.

"Mmm." Jeanee snuggled closer. "Praying for our enemies. Sounds familiar."

Raising up on one arm, Frank continued. "I didn't know, Jeanee, when I was first prompted to do the message, just why it was so important. I thought it was for the Nichols. Now I realize it applies to every situation of abuse I've been dealing with."

"I wouldn't be surprised."

"And"—Frank hesitated—"I think it's really important for you right now, too."

"Oh?"

"I'm discovering that something happens to our hearts when we pray for our enemies."

Jeanee looked up.

"The Lord takes away the bitterness we feel."

"That's true."

"Well, don't you see?"

"See what?"

"It's bitterness, pent-up angry feelings, that are making you sick. If you would just start praying for—What was your first husband's name?"

"It doesn't matter."

"Well, whatever his name is, if you'll just start praying for him, all this bitterness you feel toward him will be taken away, and you'll be able to get on with your life."

Jeanee did not protest. She had led Frank to believe her pain was coming from the abuse in her first marriage, so it was logical that he would counsel her concerning it.

"And what's more, this young boy who hurt Amber, this Benny—"

"Benjamin!" Jeanee bristled. "His name is Benjamin. Benny sounds too benign."

"Benjamin," Frank conceded. "Anyway, he needs our prayers too. He's a lost, sick boy, and we need to soften our hearts toward him."

"Frank, I know you're right about praying for Benjamin. I need to do that. And if you think it will help, I'll even pray for my first husband."

Smiling, Frank snuggled down and held his wife close. "If you will," he whispered, "then I'm positive you will begin getting better. And Jeanee, honey, thanks for being so open with me tonight. I can only imagine how hard it was for you. I want you to know how much I admire your honesty and courage. To me, you're one of the greatest women in the world."

"You're—sweet," Jeanee whispered as she stared past Frank and out through the huge picture window into the darkness. "Thank you for tonight."

"I love you," Frank whispered huskily, "more than I knew I could ever love anyone. And it is—forever."

Frank wrapped his arm around his wife and settled back, ready to drop off to sleep, totally unaware of the distance that still remained between them.

"Oh, Frank," Jeanee thought to herself a little later as she listened to the soft rhythm of his breathing, "if you only knew."

For years Jeanee had been praying for her enemies. How could she tell him that, despite her prayers, there were still secrets, secrets deeper than anything she dared to share with him? And even with all her prayers, those secrets kept coming back to haunt her. Of course she felt guilty for not fully opening up to her husband. Maybe his love was strong enough to handle it. But then, maybe it wasn't. And if she told him, and it wasn't strong enough, what then?

Sighing, Jeanee knew it might be hours before she

could drop off to sleep, hours of fighting an unseen enemy while the city pulsed beneath her in the night, hours of watching Frank in his private world of slumber.

Turning over on her side, she did her best not to disturb him. Well, she thought with another sigh, at least she hadn't lied. No need for guilt over that. And she had protected the life she now had, far from the secrets she kept hidden. No matter what happened to her personal health, her marriage and family would at least be preserved. And to Jeanee Greaves, who was hiding more secrets than even she could know, nothing on earth was more important than that!

Nothing.

BOOK TWO

THE HEALING

PART FOUR

A SAFE PLACE

Hear me
Open your
Heart
To me
Unlock the
Riddle
Of my
Tears

Show me the
Safety
Of your
Love

21

MONDAY, MARCH 30

4:07 P.M.

"Today's shopper's special is at the deli bar," a voice blared over the supermarket speaker system. "Barbecue beef sandwiches at half price, and roast chicken—"

Frank did his best to ignore the faceless voice so that he could better concentrate on the list in his hand.

Shopping for his family had once been something he enjoyed. It had even been considered a "date night" for him and Jeanee in months and years past. But now, except for the occasional trips when Angie would accompany him, it was a solitary chore—a chore that today was keeping him from Erik's baseball game.

Despite Jeanee's acknowledgment of her past in the hotel the previous fall, her health had taken a turn for the worse during the winter months. When her doctor had diagnosed a nervous breakdown, something in her had given up. Frank remembered with a shudder the night Angie came running in from the garage, screaming that something was wrong with her mother. He had hurried out to find his wife slumped over the steering wheel muttering something about not letting the bad people hurt the little children anymore. She had been unable to walk inside a grocery store from that day on.

Standing in front of the produce section, Frank shook his head, not knowing if his wife would want the two-and-a-half- or five-pound bag of carrots, or if instead she wanted the fresh untopped carrots stacked before him. In frustration he reached for the five-pound bag. After all, it was the best buy—

"Bishop Greaves?"

Looking up, Frank gazed at the woman who had spoken. "Yes?"

"Bishop, don't you know me?"

"I . . . uh . . . " Frank stammered as he tried to place her. She certainly looked familiar, but for some reason he couldn't tie a name to her. "I'm . . . sorry . . . "

The woman laughed with delight. "Bishop, I'm Claudia. Claudia Nichol."

"Claudia!" Frank exclaimed with amazement. "My goodness. It's only been six months since you moved out of the ward, but look at you . . . Claudia, this is a whole new you."

"Well," Claudia said modestly, "I think I've lost a little weight . . . "

"It's more than that," Frank said positively. And he was right. Besides losing weight and looking quite attractive in her peachy-pink jogging suit, Claudia Nichol had a new hairstyle. She was even standing taller than he had ever seen her stand. But what Frank noticed most was the sparkle in her eyes, in her countenance. The woman before him was a happy person, or at least a person who felt comfortable about herself.

"One of the aims of our women's support group," Claudia explained, "is to help us discover the 'beautiful woman' hiding inside each of us. I never realized how much I had put my own needs in the closet until I started meeting with the women from the shelter."

Frank nodded. "Have you been seeing Brother Wixom from Social Services?" he asked as they pushed their carts down the aisle together.

"Every time he's in the area. Between his help and the

weekly meetings with my support group, and the daily talks with my sponsor—"

"Sponsor?" Frank didn't want to pry, but seeing the amazing transformation in Claudia piqued his curiosity.

"That's what we call the person who takes us under her wing. We've patterned our group after the twelve-step program that Alcoholics Anonymous uses. Each of us helps each other to get through our addiction to abuse, just as the recovering alcoholic helps the new AA member gain abstinence and learn the principles that will help him stay away from alcohol."

"Addiction to abuse?" Frank was puzzled.

"Sounds sadistic, doesn't it," Claudia stated. "But that's exactly what it is. Victims get so used to being abused that they actually start setting themselves up for it. Bishop, I used to think I deserved it!"

Claudia parked her cart by the cold cereals section. "With the counseling I've been going through with Brother Wixom," she continued, "and the things I'm learning through my support group, I'm finally realizing that I was set up to be a victim very early in my life."

"You were abused before you met Bob?"

"I don't know that it was actual abuse, but it was certainly a prelude to it. Looking back, I can see that my agency was taken from me, and that is always the start. I was taught that I couldn't trust my own decisions or feelings, and that set me up for anyone with an abusive nature to come in and take right over."

Frank listened, still not understanding. "Who set you up, Claudia?"

Claudia became silent for a moment, apparently embarrassed to admit her own discovery. Then, with a deep breath, she plunged ahead. "My parents," she declared, looking Frank squarely in the eye. "My parents set me up to be abused. It's hard to say it, even now. I love them so much, and I know they didn't mean to hurt me. But—"

"Claudia, your parents are wonderful people." Frank's response was automatic but sincere.

"I know, Bishop. And they always have been."

"Then I don't understand."

"I haven't understood for a long time either. The only way I can explain it is to ask you to think of a little baby just learning to walk. Bear with me a moment, will you?"

Frank nodded, and Claudia continued.

"When a baby falls, we want to pick him up and carry him and keep him from ever falling again. Right?"

"Maybe. But the baby would never learn to walk if his parents didn't let him fall."

"Exactly! The baby would need to be carried for the rest of his life. But we know that, so we let him fall and get up again as many times as it takes for him to learn." Claudia looked deeply at Frank to make sure he was comprehending what she was saying.

"And yet," she continued, "far too many parents can't make themselves allow their children to learn accountability, simply because they are afraid their children might make mistakes. So they overprotect them, overcontrol them. And without meaning to, they take agency away from the children they love. Thus the children, and I'm one of them, grow up letting others make their decisions for them. They've never learned to trust their own inner guidance system. They're outwardly controlled rather than inwardly motivated.

"When they are teenagers, their friends control them," Claudia went on. "If they're lucky enough to have good friends, they seem okay. But if they don't get good friends," she paused, fighting emotion, "like Robby hasn't . . . ."

Both she and Frank thought of what was happening in Robby's life. Since he had moved into foster care, he had almost completely withdrawn from his mother and from the Church, following the pattern of the children in the family he was staying with. There was no doubt who was controlling his decisions.

"Then," Claudia continued, swallowing hard, "when these children are married, they seek out a husband or wife who will control them — make their decisions for them. If they marry well, they still seem to be okay. But if they marry someone with an abusive or evil nature, as I did, they're in deep trouble! And so are the children who will come into their homes. Because when something like abuse occurs, these well-trained victims will step back and do nothing, even when they should be defending their little ones. Does that make sense to you, Bishop?"

Frank seemed far away, his thoughts spinning as he considered the implications of what Claudia was saying.

"Bishop, are you with me?"

"Do I understand you to be saying," Frank asked, "that overprotecting our children and not allowing them to learn by their own mistakes is wrong?"

"Considering that the plan for control of others was voted down in heaven, it couldn't be any other way." Claudia stood firm. "Everyone on earth fought for the right to choose. Lucifer opposed that and was expelled."

Frank had to agree. Moses 4:3 and D&C 121:39 supported that concept. And, as he listened, he was impressed with Claudia's understanding. But, more than even by what she was saying, Frank was impressed with Claudia's ability to say it. In their interviews, when she had lived in his ward, he had needed to pry almost every response out of her. She had always hidden behind her husband's smooth way of controlling the conversation. Yes, this was indeed a new Claudia Nichol that Frank was seeing.

"Tell me," he said, changing the subject, "how you are getting along. We miss seeing you in the ward."

Claudia was quiet for a moment, almost blushing. "I'm — hoping that won't be for too much longer," she offered.

Frank was surprised. "You're moving back home?"

Claudia smiled. "I haven't spoken with Bob, but that's certainly what I'm hoping for."

"Excuse me," a woman interrupted, "but might I get to the Fruity Pebbles over there?"

As Frank pushed his cart out of the way, Claudia looked at her watch. "And I really must be going. Bishop, thanks for all you've done for Robby and me. I don't know what it's going to take to make us a family again, or even to get Robby past his anger and back in church. But I know, God willing, that we'll do it. And this time it will be right."

Watching Claudia walk away, Frank felt continued amazement at the transformation that had taken place in such a short time. The physical changes were impressive, but Frank was more astounded with Claudia's newfound ability to speak for herself. It was something he had never before seen in her. Funny how he had never connected that character flaw with abuse. He had always thought of it as meekness or timidity. But thinking back on their conversation, he realized that it was her abusive relationship with Bob, combined with her victim's mentality, that had kept her silent. Instead of meekness or timidity, it was her fear of being wrong, of upsetting the perverted balance of her life and so incurring Bob's wrath, that had kept her silent.

As Frank loaded his car with groceries he thought of Bob Nichol. He hadn't been in church in months. And with both Claudia and Robby in other ward boundaries, as well as all that continued to happen within his own ward, Frank had simply lost touch with the family. But at least his prayers for Claudia were being answered. "Now," he said to himself, "if only Jeanee could make that same kind of progress."

But sadly, she wasn't! Despite the fact that she was seeing a counselor, Frank could see no sign of improvement.

"Maybe," he said to himself as he closed the trunk, "it's time I paid a visit to Jeanee's therapist."

22

TUESDAY, MARCH 31

12:25 P.M.

"It's like my mind is a closet." Jeanee's voice was barely above a whisper. "And in my closet, I have these little drawers, all separate and neat, with nothing out of place, at least when you first look in."

"And what happens when you open the drawers?" A gentle but direct woman sat across the room from Jeanee, probing carefully.

"I don't open the drawers," Jeanee answered, staring out the window at the fury of the March wind. "Unless I'm forced to, like when Amber—"

Jeanee's voice quivered and she pulled her gaze from the window. "Is there any point to this, Peggy?" she asked. "I mean, after six months, why is it still so impossible for me to resolve?"

"It's been a difficult six months," came the calm reply.

"It's been hell!" Jeanee flung her anger. "I have a few good days, and just when I think I'm going to finally get some perspective, wham! I'm back in the muck all over again."

"Tell me once more about Megan's phone call."

Jeanee looked over at her gentle interrogator, a small woman with short, dark hair and deeply perceptive eyes. Peggy was finally, after several months of therapy, beginning to gain her trust.

"I know—that's when my depression hit. But it isn't

what's really bothering me," Jeanee declared, pulling her defenses up.

"Do you want to talk about it?"

"About what?"

"The phone call."

"We can talk about it, but what good will it do?"

There was silence, and Jeanee looked away from Peggy to the trees swaying in the gusty weather outside.

"Jeanee," Peggy asked, breaking the silence, "what are you feeling right now?"

"If I knew what I was feeling . . . " Jeanee didn't finish her sentence. Instead, she dropped her head in her hands and shook it back and forth.

"Are you angry? Are you feeling anger?"

"Yes, I guess I'm feeling anger."

"Do you want to tell me about it?"

"No! I want to forget it. I want to forget *all* of it! Is that too much to ask? To just forget everything that hurts, and not have to remember it again?"

"Just stuff it all in neat little drawers—"

"And never look at it again!" Jeanee finished the sentence.

"I'm afraid that's not the way it works," Peggy declared as a wry little smile lifted the corners of her mouth.

"But why not?" Jeanee flared.

"I suppose because that isn't the way the mind works."

"And how *does* the mind work? Tell me! I don't understand it. Isn't it enough that you feel pain when you're hurt? Do you have to keep going back and feeling the same pain over and over again?"

"Is that what it feels like you're doing?"

"Yes, it does! You know I keep writing these crazy little poems in my journal. They don't make any more sense than I do. In fact, I think I have one here in my weekly planner." Jeanee reached down in her purse, pulled out a small notebook, and began to leaf through it. "Here it is! Listen to this. *I've lived through hell again and again. And it keeps coming back. Seems it will never end.'* What do you think of that? Pretty grim, huh?"

"Sounds pretty good to me. Very accurate." Peggy smiled. "You're a poet, huh?"

"I don't know. I just get these thoughts tumbling into my head. Then they won't leave me until I write them down."

"This poem in particular—is this how you really feel?"

"Yes." Jeanee nodded her head as she tucked the day planner away in her purse. "And that doesn't make sense either. It goes against everything I believe. I know God doesn't give us more than we can handle. And I know he wants us to have joy. So why is it so hard now? I'm doing all the things I'm supposed to be doing. Why am I so mixed up inside?"

"Tell me about your journals."

Jeanee laughed. "I've got volumes tucked away in Tony's old room, gathering dust."

"What kinds of things do you keep in your journals?"

"What's happening—my feelings—stuff like that. Only lately I'm so up and down, I'm embarrassed to go back and read what I've written."

"But you keep writing?"

"Yes, but I don't know why. I just feel better once I've written my feelings down."

"And your feelings. Are you able to be honest about the way you feel?"

"Oooh, yes," Jeanee said sarcastically. "Honesty, that's the hard one. But yes, I think I'm honest."

Peggy regarded her, knowing that Jeanee had no idea how dishonest she was being, even then. She ignored her feelings, or was unaware of them, until they became so demanding and confused that her body simply shut itself off and went into paralytic hiding. But she could not tell

Jeanee that. Instead, for it to do any good, Jeanee needed to discover it on her own.

"Would you like to share more of the things you write—in our sessions together?" Peggy probed gently.

Again Jeanee looked out the window. "What do you think is causing these catalepsy spells to come back?" she asked, changing the subject. "Is it just stress?"

Peggy had worked with Jeanee long enough to recognize that she was feeling threatened. Each time they came close to a sensitive issue, Jeanee would back up and introduce a different subject.

"Jeanee," Peggy followed her lead, "your catalepsy spells returned after you learned of Amber's abuse. Right?"

Jeanee nodded in agreement.

"That suggests there might be a connection between the two problems."

"Frank thinks I keep having trouble because I have too much anger toward Benjamin. He thinks if I would forgive him, I would be okay."

"Jeanee," Peggy spoke directly, "Frank came in to see me yesterday afternoon."

Jeanee's whole body became erect in her chair.

"He's concerned—"

"But he didn't tell me he was coming!"

"He asked me to tell you of his visit. He was very open, and—"

Jeanee folded her arms defensively against her chest. "He's waited six months, and now he wants me to get off my pity pot and get on with life as the bishop's wife!"

Both Jeanee and Peggy were surprised at the outburst.

"I'm sorry," Jeanee offered meekly. "I didn't mean . . ."

"Jeanee," Peggy said, leaning forward in her chair and speaking calmly and directly, "let me tell you something. And I hope you really hear what I'm going to say."

Peggy paused to be sure that Jeanee was listening.

"Jeanee, I do not share anything you tell me with anyone, including your husband. In fact, especially your husband! Not unless you ask me to."

Another pause, while Peggy visually monitored Jeanee's reaction.

"You are completely safe here," she continued. "Nothing ever goes beyond this room. But there's nothing wrong with feeling this anger, either. It's an honest emotion, and honesty is the only way we're going to get you through to the other side of this pain you're experiencing."

"But I don't want to feel this way!" Jeanee's voice literally shook with emotion.

"Let me tell you about my conversation with your husband," Peggy continued carefully. "He asked me to share any of what he and I talked about that I felt would be helpful to you."

"I'm sorry." Jeanee looked at the floor. "I know Frank loves me and only wants the best for me. But he just keeps simplifying everything that's happened until I'm sure if I ever told him what really happened to me, he'd just—" Jeanee stopped.

"Just what?" Peggy encouraged.

"Just—just—" Jeanee became more agitated. "He could never comprehend what this is really all about!"

Peggy gave no response.

"And Megan is so blind!"

"Did you and Megan argue when she called?" Peggy probed carefully.

"No!" Jeanee was emphatic. "It does no good to argue. She has her mind set. She just refuses to see her own daughter crying out for help! She thinks that if you just don't dwell on the problem, it will go away!"

"Are we talking about Amber?" Peggy asked gently.

"Yes!" Jeanee's voice shook with emotion. "She won't take Amber in for counseling! She's too busy being a new mommy to see anything—except which baby powder to

buy and which disposable diapers don't leak into the crib!
I know what it's like to have a new baby. But you can't just
turn your back on the children you already have because
there's a new baby in the house!"

"And Tony?" Peggy asked calmly. "How is Tony feeling
about all this?"

"Who knows how Tony feels?" Jeanee stormed. "He
just goes along with what Megan says is best for Amber.
And she doesn't have a clue!"

"Does Tony know about your concerns?"

Jeanee shook her head and looked out the window
again. "I don't dare tell him," she almost whispered, tears
moistening her eyes. "He has such a tender heart. He'd
be torn if he knew how I felt."

"So Megan's the only one who really knows you think
Amber needs counseling?"

"For all the good it does." Jeanee sighed. "And Frank's
no help. He can't see either! He just thinks that in
time—"

"You're upset with Frank," Peggy observed.

"I don't want to be." Jeanee sighed. "I want to be able
to talk to him. But if I did—if I really opened up to
him . . . "

Jeanee's voice trailed off. Peggy waited a few moments
before she moved ahead.

"What is it that causes you to trust me and feel safe
with me that doesn't exist in your relationship with Frank?"

Jeanee searched her mind for the right answer. She bit
her lip and searched deep within her thoughts. Finally she
spoke, and as she did, she realized for the first time what
the missing element in her marriage actually was.

"Honesty," she answered simply.

Peggy smiled. "And were you able to be honest with
me in the very beginning?"

"No. I was afraid."

"Of what?"

"Aughh!" Jeanee let out a deep, throaty groan and shook her head in memory of the experience. "I was *so* scared!" she continued. "I . . . I just knew I was at the edge of the universe, and—I was going to have to jump off. And no one was there to catch me!"

"It took an awful lot of courage to come in."

"It took more than I had by myself," Jeanee acknowledged. "I prayed so hard to know if this was what I was supposed to do. I was afraid that because your religious background was different than mine, you might try to interfere with my most basic beliefs."

"And how did you get over that hurdle?" Peggy continued.

"I let you know what I believed. I told you that my relationship with God was the most important relationship in my life, and I didn't want you trying to undermine that."

"And have you felt supported in your values?"

"Very much! I remember you telling me that you wouldn't take those basic values away. We would just clean out the pockets of abscess. That's what you used as a term to describe my memories. Do you remember that?"

"Uh huh."

"You said that once I had them cleaned out, I would be stronger in my values."

Peggy nodded. "What if I couldn't have supported you, Jeanee? What if I had said that I didn't accept what you believe?"

"I would have walked right out of your office!"

Peggy leaned back in her chair. "Jeanee, is that what you are doing with Frank?"

"Walking out on him?"

"Not literally, obviously. But emotionally, isn't that what you are doing?"

Jeanee took a deep breath. "I guess that's what it seems like, doesn't it."

Peggy tipped her head slightly and raised one hand. "Is that what it feels like to you?"

"But he doesn't understand!" Jeanee was emphatic.

"Jeanee," Peggy proceeded in her gentle but firm way, "I spoke with Frank about flashbacks."

Jeanee remained silent.

"I explained to him — he's a 50's–60's music buff, isn't he?"

"Yes."

"Well, we talked about how certain songs can trigger memories from years before."

"That's something he can relate to."

"Yes," Peggy smiled, nodding, "he did. We talked about how when some songs come on the radio, you almost feel transported back in time to when you had your first date or when you first fell in love."

"He's a real nostalgia freak," Jeanee said with a smile.

"And that's good, because it made it easy to explain to him some of what you are experiencing."

"He thinks when I get upset that I'm upset with him."

"He told me that."

"And what did you say?"

"I explained trigger experiences. We talked about how some of the servicemen came home from Viet Nam with post traumatic stress disorder — how they experience feelings that are totally unconnected with their present circumstances. And yet those feelings are very real, and at times terribly uncomfortable."

"Do you think he understood?"

"As I said, he was very open."

"But did he understand?"

"As much as he can — with the information he's been given."

Jeanee looked out the window again, sighing.

"Until you feel safe enough to tell him what you are really dealing with, Jeanee, he will struggle to understand."

"But do you think he can? Understand, I mean?"

"Are you so sure he can't?"

Jeanee fought emotion. "It's just scary."

"Understandably."

"I thought if I just remembered the things my father did—and forgave him—that all this would be behind me."

"We have a lot of work to do on that one, too."

Jeanee looked puzzled.

"One of these days," Peggy explained, "we will need to talk about how really sick your father was."

"But . . . I've dealt with that already."

Peggy put her head to one side. "Maybe."

Instantly Jeanee became uncomfortable.

"Remember," Peggy continued, "healing happens in layers. It's like peeling an onion. You may have more peeling to do."

"But I have all the memories out!" Jeanee was adamant. "I know I do!"

"I want to get back to something you said earlier." Peggy had begun tying the session together. "You said you felt like hell keeps coming back—like it will never end."

"That's right."

"Let me explain something about how the mind works. Okay?"

For Jeanee this was her favorite part of her sessions with Peggy. Invariably toward the end of their hour together, her therapist would bring some little piece of their conversation out and give her something pertaining to it—something she could mentally work on until the next session.

"The mind," Peggy continued, "has an amazing capacity to protect us. When a little child is abused as severely as you were abused, the mind of the little child just tucks the pain of the abuse away in forgetfulness. In fact, often during the abuse itself, the child's mind will block out the pain of the abuse entirely and not even experience it. This keeps the child safe, even though that forgetfulness is the only safety the child may know.

"As time passes, the child grows into adulthood, and the memory is still tucked safely away in the forgetfulness of the mind. But then, as the adult develops skills to help cope with the reality of the abuse, the mind begins letting go of the memories. That's when trigger experiences begin happening. Like the music I talked with your husband about, something happens to open a channel deep within the recesses of your mind. And then you begin experiencing things that may not make any sense to you at all.

"At first you just feel the emotions, or remember a sound, or feel a texture. Or there may be a certain time of the day when you are extremely anxious."

"Like the trouble I have going to bed at night!" Jeanee interrupted. "Because I'm so nervous."

Peggy nodded in agreement. "All these things are just ways your mind has of telling you that it has something for you to take a closer look at."

"But what if I don't *want* to take a closer look?"

"Well, at this point you only have two choices, Jeanee. The first is to force the memory back inside, in which case your mind will find some other way of reminding you that it's there."

"Like my catalepsy spells?"

"And the way you wake up in the night gasping for air. Though you may not understand them, all these things are perfectly logical."

"What's logical about a nervous breakdown? Tell me! Do you know how it felt to see that on my chart?" Jeanee began twisting the padding on the arm of the chair she was sitting in.

Peggy was silent for a moment. Then she quietly continued. "Jeanee, 'nervous breakdown' isn't the term I would use to describe what you have experienced."

"But that's what Dr. —"

"It means nothing. I know the medical profession uses the term. But for our purposes it doesn't apply. What is happening with you is perfectly logical, and as we unravel what's happened—"

"I don't want to know what's happened! I was working so hard! Why wasn't God there for me this time? Why didn't He stop all this from happening?"

"Perhaps because He knows that, to be fully whole, you need to finish the process. Goodness knows you have support now, which you never had before. Perhaps God is now helping you to finish healing, and you just aren't recognizing Him."

"You said I had two choices," Jeanee pressed. "What's the second one?"

"To do what I believe your inner soul wants you to do—embrace the memory and then experience the feelings you were never allowed to have when you endured the abuse."

"But I've felt those feelings!" Jeanee objected again. "That's why I don't understand why this keeps happening. It makes no sense. I've remembered. I've forgiven! What else do I have to do?!"

"That's something we'll keep working on until you have your answers. And something that would help? You said you keep a journal. Why don't you begin to record when you experience your spells of depression, and what you think might have triggered them. And keep in mind, Jeanee, that when you begin remembering, such memories are your body's reassurance that you are strong enough, and healthy enough, to handle it.

"And one final thing," Peggy added as Jeanee stood to leave. "I've been noticing that you're losing weight."

Jeanee smiled a little self-consciously. "Yes, well, I put on a few pounds after I learned about Amber."

"And now you're on a diet?"

"Actually, I'm just not eating a couple of meals a day."

"You might watch that," Peggy warned. "Eating patterns affect your moods, too. What we eat, as well as what's eating on us, can create real problems."

"Okay," Jeanee agreed, not wanting to admit that there were frequent days when she drank nothing but water and ate nothing at all. Yet she was trying to drop the weight she had put on the previous fall. Her life the past few months had been a roller coaster. Compulsive, out-of-control behaviors were becoming a real problem for her.

"Maybe," she thought to herself as she bundled up for the walk to the car, "I need to stop trying to carry this by myself. Maybe I really do need to tell Frank."

1:17 P.M.

The house was quiet when Jeanee returned from her counseling appointment — too quiet. Except for the ticking of the grandfather clock in the living room, she felt that she might have been in a tomb.

Slowly Jeanee's mind surveyed her home. It seemed unkempt, and there was a heaviness in the air that she didn't understand. Dust seemed to collect faster than it used to, and her plants looked withered and limp, crying for attention. But Jeanee couldn't force herself to sprinkle life-giving moisture on them. It was as if she had a silent wish that everything around her would cease to be, and that the vacuum she was feeling in her mind would suck everything into its insidious wake, leaving blessed nothingness.

She thought of what she would fix for dinner, and immediately pushed the thought out of her mind. She couldn't stay another minute in the suffocating confines of her home. Grabbing Frank's winter parka from the hall closet, and pulling on her oldest Reeboks, she hurried out the door for some air.

Wind howled through bare branches on the cottonwood trees lining the park across from her home. Dead leaves and debris scurried ahead of her in the gravel lining the road. She breathed in the brisk air and pushed faster, faster, ignoring the cold, feeling little more than the need to move ahead.

One foot in front of the other, she moved as if she was propelled by a force beyond herself. Inside the warmth of Frank's parka, she seemed separate from the starkness of the March afternoon.

"How can I tell Frank?" she thought, agonizing over the question. "Even if Peggy is right, how can I tell him?" The past six months had created a gap in their relationship that had never been there before. And communication in their marriage was surface only.

"It's my fault," Jeanee told herself. "I don't know how to pull myself out of this."

More and more Jeanee had been pulling away from others too, retreating behind a gray wall of fear. Nights were fitful. Days were a blur. She pushed herself to exhaustion, then fell into the paralysis of her catalepsy. Frank had urged her to get the doctor to prescribe some medication that might help. She had refused. Instead, she was determined to search for the answers within herself.

And she had found some.

Almost miraculously, from time to time, she would have a reprieve where all the wonderful promises she read in her scriptures would seem to apply. And each time, she believed that finally her faith had been proven, that she had been found worthy of being healed. But each reprieve would be short-lived. Something would happen to trigger her fear again, and once more she would plunge deep into depression.

Peggy had been her link with sanity. Of course, she had an Advocate far more powerful than her therapist. But when the depression took hold, she was sure she was so unworthy that even He couldn't look beyond the stain on her soul.

"Dear God," she prayed, "what is happening to me? Why can't I tell Frank? Why am I destroying what we have together?"

Wind whistled through the bright yellow of a forsythia bush at the corner of the park, whipping it against the fence. As Jeanee walked into the entrance, she could see daffodils and tulips dropping their petals at the abuse of the weather, while colorful crocus and grape hyacinths merely bent before the wind's onslaught. No one else seemed to have braved the elements, and so she was alone with the fury of the wind and her thoughts, her determined stride carrying her directly into each howling gust.

"My fault," she thought each time her feet hit the pavement. "My fault, my fault, my fault." Over and over it played in her mind. Her head was down to protect her face, but her hair, once neatly pulled back, was blowing against it. She could feel her heart pounding as she inhaled and exhaled. Her heaving, burning breath seemed another symbolic assault on her body.

"Oh Father," she silently pleaded. "What's wrong with me?"

Tears began escaping down her cheeks, stinging almost instantly with the cold. "What is it that I have to do? Why do I keep experiencing this terrible grief?"

Whether by coincidence or divine plan, a shaft of sunlight shot through the clouds overhead, sending a golden ray onto the path before her. And at that very moment Jeanee heard a quiet, peaceful thought enter her mind. It said simply, "Be thankful. I am healing you."

"Be thankful," Jeanee said to herself. "Is that it? Is that what I need to be doing? Being thankful for how impossible my life has become?" And then, as if the wind had abated, she felt a warmth suddenly filling her soul.

Her mind raced back to years earlier when she had

first learned the principle of gratitude, before she knew
there was a healing Power. Second Corinthians chapter
four jumped immediately into her mind.

*"For all things are for your sakes, that the abundant grace
might through the thanksgiving of many redound to the glory of
God. . . . For our light affliction, which is but for a moment,
worketh for us a far more exceeding and eternal weight of glory."*

" 'For all things are for your sakes,' " she repeated to
herself. " 'All things.' Even this?" Then again that warm
glow filled her being. "Even this." She accepted the confirmation.

A veil seemed to fall from her mind, and the dark,
foreboding spirit she had carried for so long began lifting,
opening a place for a Spirit of Healing and Light. "Even
this!" she repeated out loud, smiling as she continued to
push ahead. "Even this! Somehow God is going to work
even this for my good."

If it were possible for angels to sing at that moment,
Jeanee almost thought she could have heard them. It was
as if her entire being was changed, in an instant. She could
feel deep, passionate laughter welling up inside. And in
the wind, by herself, she gave in and set her emotions
free—not in tears this time, not in frozen anger, but in
free-flowing, bubbling laughter.

Turning around, she headed back away from the wind,
letting it push her forward, realizing that literally and fig-
uratively, forward was the only way she could move com-
fortably.

"It is time," she told herself. "I need to tell Frank what
this is all about."

6:15 P.M.

"Is there any more cornbread, Mommy?"

"Mmmm," Jeanee responded absently as she passed

the plate of Mexican chili and corn to her confused daughter.

"Mommy, I asked for the cornbread, not the chili."

"Sorry, Angie," Jeanee murmured. "I . . . I'm just not thinking clearly tonight."

"Something happen today that upset you?" Frank asked gently.

"No, no. I . . . I just . . . " Jeanee stopped speaking, not knowing what she could possibly say. All afternoon she had been filled with the most wonderful peace.

"Jeanee, what is it?"

"Yeah, Mom. You look all spaced out tonight."

Jeanee smiled awkwardly. "Maybe I'm just tired," she replied. "There was so much laundry—"

"I noticed you got all that done," Frank said. "I was going to do it tonight. In fact, the kids and I—"

"Yeah, Mommy, I was going to iron all Daddy's shirts."

Jeanee laughed. "I should have left them, darling. Maybe next time."

"Please leave them," Frank said, taking his wife's hand. "I don't want you overdoing when it's something we can do."

"But you're so busy—"

Jeanee was interrupted by the ringing of the telephone. Erik rose to answer it.

"Hi, Tony. Uh-huh. Yeah, he's here. Just a sec."

Taking the phone, Frank leaned back in his chair. "Hi, kid. What's going on?"

Jeanee watched as Frank's face grew serious. "Well, let me ask your mother. Hold on a minute."

Frank put his hand over the mouthpiece as he turned to his wife. "Jeanee, Tony has to go to a convention, and today his boss told him he could take Megan if he wanted. He thinks it would do her good to have a vacation right about now. But—"

"But it would mean we would need to take Amber and Nicole."

Frank nodded. "That's right. But Jeanee, you need rest every bit as much as Megan, if not more. If we take the girls, the bulk of the work will be on your shoulders. I really don't think we should do it."

"How long will they be gone?"

"A week. Next week. But—"

"Frank," Jeanee said with a smile, "a week is nothing. I'd love to have them here. Besides, it will give me the excuse to fix up Tony's old room, to make it pretty and frilly like I always wanted it to be. You tell him yes, we'd be delighted to take care of them."

"Are you sure?" Frank was dubious.

"Absolutely. Those little girls will be good for me. Angie can help, and we'll have a great time."

Angie smiled brightly. "I'll help with Amber and Nicole, Daddy. And I'll keep the family room picked up, too! I promise I will."

10:45 P.M.

"You awake, honey?" Jeanee whispered into the darkness of the bedroom.

"Mmm mmm," Frank answered.

"You okay?"

"I'm okay," he assured her. "You?"

"Well, yes. And no. Something has been bothering me. And I finally decided—"

Frank reached over and turned on the lamp on the nightstand.

"It's going to be too much for you, isn't it?"

"What?"

"Having the girls here. Is it going to be too much?"

Jeanee snuggled next to her husband and smiled. "No

Frank. It's not going to be too much. Actually, it couldn't have come at a better time."

"Are you sure?" Frank looked puzzled.

"I'm sure. In fact, I think probably a lot of things are going to be timely from now on."

Frank smiled a lopsided smile. "Now you've got me curious. What's this big secret?"

Jeanee scooted backward on the bed so she could prop her head up on her pillow and look directly at her husband.

"Frank," she began, "this isn't going to be easy."

There was silence.

"I don't know where to begin or how to say it—"

"Just say it," Frank urged.

Jeanee looked deeply into her husband's eyes and realized it had been literally months since she had been able to do that.

"Frank," she began again. "I haven't been honest with you."

Again silence.

"You're not going to make this easy, are you?" Jeanee whined.

"I'm listening."

"Okay. Here goes."

Frank could feel a tremble in his soul, and he realized this disclosure, whatever it was, would shake him deeply. And yet he knew at the same time that it was the very thing he had been praying would happen.

"Peggy told me," Jeanee continued, "that you stopped by to see her."

"I've been awfully worried," Frank admitted.

"And you had a right to be." Jeanee continued to hedge. "But—oh, honey—I don't know any other way to tell you than just to come out and say it. But—"

"Whatever it is, we'll work through it together."

"Well, it's terrible. More terrible than I—"

"Jeanee," Frank interrupted, "what can be more ter-

rible than this awful distance that has grown between us?
Sweetheart, I love you. I may not be the greatest catch in
all the world, but I'm devoted to you. And nothing you
could tell me would ever change that—not even one—"

"Oh, Frank!" Jeanee's lip began to tremble and her
eyes filled instantly with tears. "Frank, I'm so ashamed! I
haven't lied to you. But I haven't been honest either. I
thought it was the best thing to do. I was afraid. I didn't
want you to know. I thought you would—"

Frank reached over and stroked his wife's hair. "Just
tell me," he said encouragingly. "I'm not going anywhere."

Jeanee swallowed hard and sniffed back a tear. "I—I
didn't tell you everything. Last fall, when—when you took
me to that wonderful hotel. I didn't tell you—

"Oh, Frank, my daddy . . . he . . . he . . . Oh, Frank,
he . . . "

Immediately Frank knew what his wife was trying to
say—what he'd suspected but never dared ask. And finally
Jeanee was opening up to him, trusting him. He pulled
her tightly to his chest and began rocking her. "He hurt
you, didn't he, Jeanee."

"Yes. He made me—he made me do bad things. I didn't
want to do them. But he made me. And I was so afraid to
tell. And—Oh, Frank, can you love me? Can you still love
me?"

Jeanee was sobbing deep sobs of grief. And Frank,
gently cradling her in his arms, began to weep himself,
tears of gratitude that the barrier of silence was finally
broken. Finally he knew. Finally he understood.

"Jeanee," he whispered, "Oh, Jeanee, if you only knew
how *much* I love you . . . "

23

WEDNESDAY, APRIL 1

7:30 P.M.

"Mom, if this is your idea of an April Fool's joke, it isn't funny!"

Pulling a stray wisp of hair back from her face, Jeanee sat back on her heels and sighed. "April Fool's. My goodness, Erik, I'd forgotten what day it is."

"Yeah," Erik grumbled, "I'll bet."

"I had! Oh, look! You got a whole strip off that time!"

Erik shook his head as he held the piece of paper in the air. "Big deal. Three inches wide and fifteen inches long. Mom, are we really going to do both walls?"

"It isn't hard, Erik," Angie declared brightly. "See, I just got a big piece, too."

Erik snarled at his sister, stood to stretch, and then picked up the compressed-air garden-spray canister. Pumping it quickly, he turned the nozzle on the area of the wall where he had been working, giving the wallpaper a thorough soaking with the mixture of water and fabric softener. "Sheesh but this smells awful!"

"It smells clean," Angie stated.

"Do you always have to be so cheerful?" Erik glared fiercely at his sister.

"Only when I am," Angie retorted brightly. "Can you spray here by me, Erik?"

"Mom," Erik muttered as he stepped over behind Angie, "this isn't doing a bit of good. This is our second gallon of fabric softener, and we haven't even got a fourth of this stupid paper off."

"It just takes patience," Jeanee declared as she scraped at a moist area with one of her kitchen spatulas. "Another couple of hours and we'll have both walls clean and ready for paint."

"Sure! And day after tomorrow night the Millennium will be here."

"Erik!"

Quickly Erik looked up. "I'm sorry, Mom, but this just isn't how I planned on spending my one night off. I've got homework, and the guys and I were going to toilet paper Cara Bradshaw's Rabbit."

"You're going to mess up that poor girl's car?" Jeanee scowled.

"Fair's fair. You should see what she and Shannon Michelson did to—"

"Hey!" Frank said as he walked into the room, "who's doing all the laundry in here?"

Angie giggled. "It isn't laundry, Daddy. It's the spray water."

"Well," Frank smiled, "that's a relief. Now will somebody tell me what we're really doing?"

"And me," Erik groused sullenly.

Again Jeanee sat back on her heels. She was still not at full strength, but for some reason she was filled with energy as she contemplated the project of redecorating Tony's old room.

"We're redecorating for Nicole and Amber," she said simply.

"Redecorating? Why? What was wrong with the way it was?"

"Frank," Jeanee said, pouting, "surely you can't expect two little girls to be happy in a room decorated with baseball and basketball players."

For an instant Frank looked at his wife, wondering.

And then he smiled. "Is there by chance an extra spatula around here?"

"Come work by me, Daddy."

"Okay, punkin," Frank agreed as he took the spatula from his relieved wife. "You show me where, and I'll scrape. Bet ya in ten minutes I can scrape twice as much off this wall as Erik can on his."

Looking over, Erik frowned. "Dad, you can't make me work harder with that old trick."

"Who's trying to make you work harder? Just watch and see what I can do."

Folding his arms Erik watched smugly and then was chagrined as Frank's first efforts worked loose a large strip of paper.

"Lucky, that's all."

"Skill," Frank countered. "And the right attitude. Watch, and I'll do it again."

Sullenly Erik watched as, to everyone's amazement, another large strip tore loose under Frank's careful scraping.

"See," Frank said as he held the paper up triumphantly before his startled son. "I'm already up with you. Ten more minutes and you'll never catch me."

"We'll see," Erik snarled good-naturedly, and with a vengeance he tore back into his work.

The project didn't prove to be as easy as it had first appeared to Jeanee. The old paper had been nonstrippable, and even the liquid mixture they were spraying on it did little more than soften the edges around where they had scraped before. Yet slowly the wall was bared, and though Jeanee and Frank were alone when the project was coming to an end, finally there was nothing left to do but wash everything down again and clean up the mess on the floor.

"So what are your plans?" Frank asked as he gathered little strips of paper into a plastic garbage bag.

"To make it beautiful," Jeanee responded as she sat in

a heap in the corner. "Could you build a ceiling shelf along that wall?"

Frank squinted his eyes in mock concentration. "Oh, I suppose I could do that—for you."

Jeanee smiled tiredly. "I knew I could count on you. By the way, honey, thanks for your help tonight."

"Hey, I like stripping walls."

"What I meant was, thank you for helping me with Erik. He did not have a great attitude!"

"I thought he worked pretty hard." Frank smiled.

"After you came."

Reaching into the bag, Frank pushed the paper down to make room for more. "Jeanee, you have to understand boys. Most won't get too excited about projects like this. In fact, about the only way to motivate them is to let them have the idea in the first place, or to turn it into some sort of contest where they can show off their developing prowess."

"Is that what you do with the Aaronic Priesthood boys?" Jeanee smiled.

"All the time. I wonder what Erik's up to with those friends of his."

"You don't want to know." Jeanee sighed tiredly. "You can bet, though, that the girls will love the attention."

"How are you doing, honey?" Frank questioned. "Are you okay?"

"Yeah," Jeanee smiled. "Just tired."

"Is there anything you want to talk about?"

Jeanee looked pleadingly at Frank. "Later, hon. Is that okay? I know you probably have questions—"

"When you're ready."

"Just one thing," Jeanee continued. "I want you to know. I forgave him."

Frank looked lovingly at his wife.

"I forgave everything he ever did to me. I prayed for him—for years. And then he died. But before he did—"

Frank walked over and took Jeanee in his arms.

"We've got plenty of time, honey. You can tell me when you're ready. I'm not going anywhere."

9:50 P.M.

"Mommy, this is Abby Martin." Angie was up late because of the project in the bedroom, and she was at the kitchen counter, finishing a glass of milk, when the telephone rang.

Wiping her forehead with her sleeve as she walked in the door, Jeanee took the phone and smiled. "Hi, Abby. What's up?"

"I . . . I'm sorry it's so late, Jeanee. Are you in bed?"

Jeanee laughed. "Not hardly. We've been stripping wallpaper all evening."

"Oh, then I shouldn't disturb you."

"Abby, this is a perfect time," Jeanee said, stretching the truth. "Now, how can I help you?"

Abby took a deep breath. "May I please speak with your husband?"

"Of course, Abby. Just a minute."

"Hello?" Frank said a moment later as he picked up the phone in his music room.

"Bishop," Abby abruptly declared, "I know you're not going to want to hear this. But I'm seeking an injunction against John. I don't want him entering my home or associating in any way with the children."

"Just a minute, Abby," Frank responded uneasily. "I thought you were getting some of those differences worked out."

Abby sighed. "You know I've tried, Bishop. I've done all the things you've suggested these past few months. And I know you've done your best. But I've had it."

"Do you want to get together and talk about it, Abby?" Frank asked.

"I'm through talking!" Abby's voice was suddenly filled with anger. "And I'm through allowing that man access to our home! All winter long I've done that. I haven't complained when he's been late on his support payments. I've encouraged the children to show him respect. And when things broke up between him and his girlfriend, I even thought maybe—"

"You've been more than a stalwart, Abby," Frank agreed. "And I know it hasn't been an easy few months. But John has been making progress, hasn't he? I know in my interviews with him, he seems to have been more willing to accept responsibility for your family."

"Accept responsibility? I guess that just depends on your definition. If you call terrifying his own children accepting responsibility, then yes, I guess he has been accepting responsibility! And as far as progress is concerned? If you call verbally abusing me every chance he gets as progress, then yes, he's been making great strides in that department, too."

"Is he really doing those things, Abby?" Frank asked, not wanting to believe what he was hearing. "You see no hope of any sort of reconciliation?"

Abby laughed harshly. "Are you kidding, Bishop? I know he's got you convinced that he's doing wonderfully, but let me tell you something. I have two volumes of my journal right here beside me, and if you would like, you may read the day-by-day, blow-by-blow accounts just exactly as I wrote them when they occurred."

"If you'd like me to read them," Frank said slowly, thoughtfully, "I will."

"Yes," Abby quickly replied, "I think I would. And let me tell you something else about John. I know you think a great deal of him. But Bishop, he's not the man you think he is, or the man he's led you to believe he is. Oh, he's impressive. And I know he makes a great appearance. But

let me tell you, Bishop, that's all there is to him. None of
it's real. His whole life has been a phony front!

"If you knew, really knew how he has treated his
family—" Abby was crying now, unable to stop the tide of
emotions tearing at her heart. And Frank, suddenly aware
of her great pain, waited as she fought to regain control.

"Really, Bishop," she finally concluded, "how can you
ask if there can be a reconciliation? Though I have nothing,
at least I have freedom. Though my children have nothing,
they can finally discover what it means not to be hysterical
with fear or seething with anger. They might even learn
what it's like to laugh in their own home!

"Knowing what we've had to put up with, Bishop, how
can you even think to question my decision about getting
a restraining order?"

Abby Martin grew silent. Frank wanted to respond, to
say something profound or helpful, for he knew, abruptly,
that what she had told him was true. The Spirit had borne
witness even as she had spoken. But all that would come
into his mind was an apology—an apology that she and
her children had been so wronged by a fellow brother.
And maybe, the Spirit whispered, for the time being, that
was all he really needed to say.

11:44 P.M.

Standing in the freshly stripped room that had once
been Tony's, Jeanee stared into the open closet. Frank had
just gone to bed, but she had made an excuse for herself
and had left him alone. Now she stood in Tony's room,
the door closed, trying to overcome the uneasiness tugging
at her mind.

On the shelf above her, stretching from wall to wall,
were volumes of journals. Twice that evening they had
been brought to her mind, and so now she stared at them
fearfully, feeling driven to examine them and yet knowing

that they contained secrets she didn't want back in her memory.

Her entire body trembling with emotion, Jeanee finally reached forward and randomly pulled a volume free of the shelf. Then, dropping to her knees, she slowly opened the cover and forced herself to look at the first page.

With a sigh of relief she realized that the entry pertained to some antics Tony had pulled on the day she had written. Quickly she read on, visualizing in her mind the two-year-old boy and the delightful time they had shared together. Smiling, Jeanee continued, knowing that the entries had been after her first marriage had ended. How interesting that she could still feel the heady sense of freedom that had been hers, knowing that no one would be coming home to beat or berate her. She could even smell the odors of the tiny apartment where she had lived, poverty-stricken but free, knowing that somehow all was going to be fine.

Reaching back into the closet, Jeanee pulled out more volumes, earlier volumes, and back on the floor she opened the first one of them.

And laughed aloud.

Tony Walton. It had been years since she had thought of him. But now here he was in her journal, and she was fourteen again and madly in love with the dark, curly-haired sophomore neighbor who had not yet even noticed that she existed.

Sighing with all the emotions of first love, Jeanee read on and found herself both smiling and weeping as she read of the school dance when Tony had first asked her to dance.

Certain she was in heaven, Jeanee had danced two whole dances with him and had known that she was forever in love. That had been confirmed moments later when Tony had defended her in the face of two other boys who were calling her spindle-legs — a name bestowed on her by her brother.

Reading on, Jeanee realized only gradually that she had never spoken with Tony again. She had written of him often enough, but on a dark day in the middle of the winter his family had moved away, and the broken heart so eloquently manifest in her writings still ached in her chest.

Drying her tears, Jeanee pressed forward, reading over and over of the dreams of this young girl who had been so alone that her only confidant was a boy who had really existed only in her dreams.

Finally putting the small book down, Jeanee thought of that, knowing that her own Tony had been named after this dream and wondering why it was that a dream had given her such solace, such amazing motivation.

The next volume she picked up, a little girl's diary with a lock on it, had been written when she was nine. For a moment Jeanee wondered how she could possibly unlock it, but then she also knew, abruptly, that years ago she had hidden the key to it up between the layers of fabric on the spine.

Quickly retrieving the key and opening the book, Jeanee smiled at the childish handwriting. But again she was transported back somehow so that the emotions recorded on the pages were still hers. She read of a family picnic out on the river, at Ash Park. It had been a happy affair — the warm summer afternoon, aunts and uncles and cousins playing games on the grass or sleeping in the shade of the willow trees. And then suddenly the words on the pages weren't all that Jeanee was remembering. There was more. And it was ugly.

She could see her father, laughing and joking with everyone around him, nobody suspecting what he was really doing. But Jeanee knew, and the horror of it suddenly sickened her. Clearly she could see herself standing next to him. He was holding her so she could not move. But worse, while others stood innocently by, he was violating her, touching her—

Jeanee slammed the book shut, shivering. And immediately a single page caught her eye. It had been stuffed in the back of one of her more recent journals and was dated just a few days after her father's funeral.

Pulling it free, she read:

To My Dad

What did you see
When you looked at me?
Wide blue eyes and
Wisps of white-blond hair
And dimples when
I smiled
And saw you coming?
I was your shadow
You were my hero.
Next to God
There was none greater.

Until
At night
You began stealing into
My room
Stealing more than sleep.
How could you call me
"Daddy's little angel"
When you knew
My silent struggle
To make you stop?
You saw my eyes
Grow sad and
Deep
As years of
Innocence
You ripped
From me.

I'm still a
Little girl
Inside.
And wide blue eyes
Now fill with
Tears
I couldn't cry.
And in the night
I fight an
Unseen enemy
For you are
Gone.

What do you see
When you look at
Me
From your new home
Beyond this earth?
Do you see my eyes?
Do you hear my pain?
I wonder.
Are you sorry?

Eyes brimming with tears, Jeanee gathered the journals together and jammed them back among the others on the closet shelf. Then, breathing heavily as if from great physical effort, she forced closed the closet doors and hurried to leave.

Yet even as she ran toward the bedroom and her sleeping husband, part of Jeanee knew that she was not through with those journals . . .

24

THURSDAY, APRIL 2

6:25 A.M.

"Hi, sleepyhead."

Squinting her eyes against the glare from the closet light, Jeanee yawned and sat up. "Frank, honey, why are you dressed so early?"

"Big day," Frank responded as he sat down to pull on his socks. "I've got a bunch of papers to grade for tomorrow. And since my monthly interview with President Stone is scheduled for this afternoon, and my calendar is full with interviews tonight, this is the only time to do them."

Jeanee smiled. "You're such a good guy."

"Yeah," Frank responded with a lopsided grin. "Real good. Jeanee, I've been thinking—I'm going to ask President Stone for a release."

Jeanee's eyes opened wide. "What?"

"I think I need to be released," Frank continued as he tied his tie. "I mean, I just feel maybe I need to spend more time with the people I love—you especially. So I think today's the day."

Her mind whirling, Jeanee tried to respond. "Are . . . you certain, Frank?"

"Yeah, pretty certain. The idea sure does make sense, don't you think?"

"No," Jeanee said, shaking her head, "I don't."

"You don't?" Frank asked, surprised. "I thought for sure you'd cheer."

Slowly Jeanee shook her head.

"Hmmm. Well, I still think it's the right thing to do."

"Have you prayed about it?" Jeanee asked carefully.

"Well, I've certainly prayed."

"Have you felt a confirmation from the Spirit that you should resign?"

Frank smiled patiently. "Not exactly. But it took a while for me to get a confirmation that the Lord wanted me to be the bishop, too."

"But you got one." It was a statement, not a question, and Frank acknowledged it.

"Well, honey," Jeanee said with a slight smile of her own, "if the Lord wanted you to have the calling, don't you think you ought to clear it with Him before you quit?"

Suddenly uncomfortable, Frank rose to his feet. "I've thought of that, Jeanee. But I've also thought of how much my family needs me. I can't bear leaving you alone all the time, especially the way you've been feeling. I've fought this a long time now, and I think Heavenly Father would understand."

"Of course He'd understand," Jeanee said as she slid from the bed. "But God's understanding something doesn't make it right."

Frank tilted his head to one side and squinted his eyes.

Jeanee continued, "For instance, I'm quite sure He understands why we sin. But that's no reason to advocate committing it."

Shaking his head, Frank picked up his suit coat. "You should be a lawyer, you know. You're very good."

"Good enough to convince you?" Jeanee asked as she slipped her arms around her husband.

Frank hugged her in return. "Almost. I gotta go."

"Honey?"

"Huh?"

"Promise me. If you won't pray any more about this, will you at least do what President Stone feels is right?"

"He'll do whatever I ask, Jeanee."

"Then don't approach it that way. Tell him your feelings and ask him what he thinks you should do."

"Why is this so important to you?" Frank looked down into his wife's eyes and was surprised when almost instantly they filled with tears.

"Because," she said hesitantly, "I . . . couldn't stand to be even part of the reason that you . . . would . . . let the Lord down." Jeanee's eyes became deeply troubled as she sniffed back tears. "Besides, I know He's going to heal me. He . . . He promised me that. And He said nothing about your resigning, or being released."

Startled by the depth of feeling in Jeanee's voice, Frank pulled back. "What are you talking about?" he quizzed half-jokingly. "You make it sound like you've had some sort of conference with God."

Jeanee smiled up through her tears. "Do I?" she asked, becoming distant and serious. "Well—Frank, just please do as President Stone suggests. Please."

9:10 A.M.

"Claudia, it's me, Bob."

Bob Nichol's voice was shaking, he was so nervous, and he knew there was little he could do about it.

"Hi, Bob."

"Hi Claudia. It . . . it's been a long time . . . I mean, before you called me . . . yesterday, it was a long time." Bob shook his head in dismay. He couldn't believe how much he was sounding like a blundering fool. Yet just the sound of his wife's voice electrified him.

"I enjoyed visiting with you," Claudia said, sounding so casual that Bob grew even more nervous.

"So did I. I mean, well, Claudia, I . . . I've really missed you." To Bob, Claudia still sounded distant, cautious.

"I . . . uh . . . I was wondering if we might get together for lunch? Today, I mean?"

"Today? Gee, Bob, I have some other plans."

"It can be a late lunch, Claudia. You just tell me the time and place, and I'll be there. I . . . I really need to talk . . . about us, I mean—"

"Well, I . . . '" Claudia hesitated.

Bob Nichol took a deep breath to steady his nerves, to push back the empty feeling that she might refuse him.

"I promise," he said, trying desperately to be light, "I'll be on my best behavior."

Claudia laughed at that, and Bob couldn't believe how the sound of her laughter affected him. He was literally aching to see her again, to talk with her in person. It was a real pain, such a feeling as he had never before experienced.

"All right," she finally responded, and Bob could tell by the sound of her voice that she was smiling. "Three o'clock, at the Sizzler on Fourth Street."

"It's a date," Bob said with relief.

"And Bob," Claudia added suddenly, firmly, "you do know the conditions—"

10:20 A.M.

"Bishop Greaves?"

Looking up from the papers he was reading, Frank was surprised to see June McCrasky standing in his doorway.

"Well, if it isn't one of my favorite McCrasky girls," he declared with a wide smile. "What can I do for you, young lady?"

June was obviously embarrassed, but slowly she made her way into the recess-emptied room.

"Could I . . . use your room . . . for a few minutes, I mean?"

"Absolutely," Frank declared as he leaned back with

his hands behind his head. "What do you want to do? Move out the chairs and go roller-skating?"

June giggled and shook her head. "No. I just need to write . . . some things in my book."

"Great. Pick a chair and have at it. Uh . . . why not use Mrs. O.'s room?"

June pulled a face. "She has some parents in there."

"Ahh," Frank declared knowingly. "Tell me, is she treating you all right?"

"Mrs. O.?"

Frank nodded.

"Oh," June said enthusiastically, "she's wonderful! I just love her!"

"Me, too," Frank admitted. "But don't worry. She's my cousin, so I can love her all I want."

"Really?"

"You bet. My favorite cousin, in fact. Tell me, June. Why do you love Mrs. O.?"

Slowly June sat down, her mind churning. "Because she loves me," she finally answered.

Frank was impressed. "Good answer. How do you know she loves you?"

June smiled brightly, "I can just tell. She talks to me. And she listens to me when I talk. Her mommy died, too, and she told me it's okay to be angry about that, and to feel sad. She told me that's the only way to grow past it. So now I have a mad book Mrs. O. gave me. I write all my mad feelings in it."

"A mad book?" Frank questioned.

"Yeah," June answered simply. "I also have a happy book. Every time I write in my mad book, Mrs. O. told me I also have to write something in my happy book. That way I'll be a balanced person. When somebody says mean things and hurts my feelings, I just go in Mrs. O.'s room at recess or lunch and write it all out in my mad book. Mrs. O. says that's a lot more healthy than locking my angry feelings down inside myself and screaming at other people later on."

"And the happy book?" Frank asked, growing more and more impressed.

June smiled as she held up a yellow notebook. "This has all my good feelings in it. Some days I can't think of much to say, but Mrs. O. says if I just think about it real hard, something good will come into my mind."

"And it works?"

Again June nodded. "Last week I had a really bad day, and I thought and thought before I remembered that you had waved and smiled at me that morning when I walked past your class."

"And that's in there?" Frank was dumbfounded.

"Yes. In fact," and now June grew embarrassed again, "there are lots of days when the only thing I can think to write in my happy book is something nice that you or Sister Greaves or Erik or even Angie said to me or my brothers. You have a real nice family, Bishop. I . . . I think we're real lucky to be your neighbors."

Stunned, Frank was at a loss for words. He admired such honesty, but not often did he encounter it in adults.

"I told my Mom about my mad book," June continued, apparently not noticing Frank's silence. "I thought it might help her, too."

"Did it?"

Slowly June shook her head. "Uh-uh. She just got mad at me for saying she was always mad. Bishop, if Mom would just start one of these mad books so she could get all her anger out on paper, I know it would help her be more happy."

3:10 P.M.

Bob Nichol could not get his eyes off his wife. She had changed so thoroughly and so wonderfully that he had almost not recognized her when she had come through the door. And now, as she sat talking, he realized that her voice and even her vocabulary had changed. In spite of the fact that her name was Claudia Nichol, this was a completely different woman sitting across the table from him — different from the woman he had married, different from what he was able, even yet, to grasp.

"Wh-what's happened to you?" he finally stammered. "I mean, you look so great!"

"It's amazing what a little exercise can do." Claudia smiled sweetly.

"No," Bob shook his head firmly. "It's more than that, Claudia. You're just . . . well . . . you're just a whole different person!"

For a long moment Claudia gazed at her husband, wondering how far she should go. "You're right," she finally said, deciding that complete honesty was the only way. "Now, I'm me."

"What?"

"You heard me," she said gently. "For the first time in my life, Bob, I've discovered who I am. Oh, I'm still getting used to my discovery, still changing old habits. But it's incredible how high people can fly if they aren't being constantly hammered into the ground by someone they love."

"I . . . had that coming," Bob acknowledged quietly.

"Yes, you did. But I also owe you an apology, Bob, a sincere apology, which I freely give. I am truly sorry that, in all the years we were together, I never had the courage to stand up to you. Had I done that, all of this pain and agony might have been avoided."

Bob didn't know what to say. He knew Claudia meant every word of her apology, but all it did was make him feel lower than he already did. Yet again, the implied rebuke was more than deserved, and he knew that, too.

At length he grinned lopsidedly. "Apology accepted. I . . . I wish it was as easy to . . . offer an apology to you."

"Isn't it?"

Bob shook his head. "Are you kidding? How can a stupid apology wipe out nearly twenty years of me treating you and Robby the way I did?"

"Maybe it can't wipe it out, Bob," Claudia said softly, tears suddenly in her eyes. "But it could certainly ease the pain I feel in my heart."

Slowly, hesitantly, Bob reached his hand out until the tips of his fingers were touching the back of Claudia's wrist. "Then . . . I'm sorry," he said as his own eyes flooded. "I'm really, truly sorry . . . "

3:30 P.M.

"Bishop, how are you?"

The stake president's question was sincere, and Frank sat silently for a moment, trying to think of the appropriate response to give this man he had grown to love and respect.

"I'm all right, President," he finally stated. "But I'm really not doing very well."

"You've been dealing with a lot," President Stone said empathetically. "I understand your wife still isn't feeling well?"

"Actually, she's having a few good days right now. But that may not last."

"Anything I can do?"

"Not really."

"Have you been using the priesthood in her behalf?" President Stone asked.

"As often as she asks, she gets a blessing."

"That's good." President Stone's voice showed concern. "You let me know if there is any way I can be of assistance."

"I have some thoughts on that subject. But I'd like to cover them a bit later, if that's okay."

President Stone nodded agreement.

"I ran into Claudia Nichol the other day in the grocery store," Frank declared, beginning an update on members of his ward, "and she seems to be doing very well. But both Bob and Robby have stopped coming to Church, and I haven't been able to meet with either of them in several months. Of course, Robby is in a foster home somewhere across town."

"What's Bob's legal status now? Were charges ever filed against him?"

"Not really," Frank responded. "An investigation was conducted, but with Robby's placement in foster care, and with Bob's separation from Claudia, the officers concluded tht no criminal charges were necessary. At least that's my understanding."

"I hope they made the right decision. How about the Martins? Any developments there?"

"Actually, yes. Abby had me read her journals, and she has a tight case for both physical and emotional abuse against her husband. The divorce is close to being finalized, and the judge has issued a restraining order keeping John from the children without her close supervision."

"You've been counseling with them both these past few months?"

Frank shrugged. "Obviously not effectively."

"Is she receiving assistance from the fast offering fund?"

Frank nodded. "Right now we're helping her with food and utilities, and she is keeping the house payments up with her part-time work."

The stake president smiled sadly. "Wasn't it Paul who said to Timothy that if a man provides not for his own, and especially for those of his own house, he has denied the faith and is worse than an infidel? Brother Martin seems to fall into that category."

Soberly Frank nodded. "He does, and I don't know

what to do about it. In fact, President, so much is going on right now that I don't comprehend! I need to work with Bob Nichol and his family, I need to work with Carol Blodgett and her girls, I need to work with Abby Martin and her children, I need to work with Elaine McCrasky and her children — President, the list doesn't seem to end. But I . . . I can't seem to get a handle on it."

"Your ward is experiencing some unusually demanding problems," President Stone stated sympathetically.

Frank's eyes were bleak. "Every time I think of these people, I get this empty, sick feeling in the pit of my stomach that tells me I'm in so far over my head that there's no way I can address their needs.

"Even worse, I can't even help my wife! President, Jeanee has undergone some serious problems in her life. She's just begun to talk about it. And I want to help her. But I don't know how.

"So I ask myself, if I can't even help my own wife, then what on earth am I doing trying to help all these other people? To tell you the truth, I think it's time you found a replacement for me."

President Stone looked across the desk at Frank, knowing his tender heart was close to breaking, and remained silent.

"There's more," Frank continued softly. "President, I . . . I don't know how to say this, but I can't stop seeing myself in the men and women in my ward who have been perpetrators of abuse. I mean, there have been times lately when it would be so easy to totally lose control of my own temper. That's something I really used to struggle with, and now, with some of the things Jeanee does when she is having a difficult time — well, remaining in control is almost more than I can do.

"Then there's something else I can't come to grips with." Frank paused and breathed deeply. "As a young man, I had a tough time overcoming lustful thoughts. I've made some of the same mistakes I'm seeing in my ward members. I'm really no better than they are, so how can I possibly judge them righteously, especially when I'm so far from being righteous myself?"

President Stone leaned back in his chair and took a deep breath. "You're right, of course," he declared gently. "Uncontrolled anger and unrighteous thoughts are something to be concerned about. And they seem to be weaknesses that nearly all of us must overcome."

Frank sighed. "I keep thinking of that scripture in Matthew where Jesus tells us to judge not that we be not judged. As I go around my ward, I feel like I have a beam in my eye while I'm looking for motes in the eyes of others."

Thoughtfully President Stone regarded Frank. Finally he picked up his scriptures again, turned the pages for a moment or so, read, then nodded with satisfaction and looked back up.

"Bishop, there are some major differences between you and those we are discussing. To point them out, may I ask you a few more questions?"

"Sure."

"When you lose your temper, do you allow it to become a pattern of daily activity, or do you attempt to curb it and keep it under control?"

"Well, so far I'm keeping it under control."

"When those unrighteous thoughts assault you, do you harbor them and find joy in them, or do you try to get rid of them?"

"I try to get rid of them, of course."

"In fact, you probably have a tried and proven method of doing so."

Frank grinned. "Yeah, I do. In my mind I just go climb a certain mountain where Erik and I had a great afternoon a few years ago. With that and prayer, it works every time."

The president nodded. "That's the first difference, Bishop. When those thoughts assail you, you eliminate them as quickly as possible, and the Holy Ghost remains your companion. Unrighteous men and women don't do that. They not only harbor angry and lustful thoughts, but they also cherish them, they invite them, and they mentally embellish them. Thus Lucifer gains power over them."

"You said there were two differences?"

"Remind me again of your calling in the Church."

"Uh . . . " Frank was puzzled, "I'm a bishop. I guess that's what you want."

"That makes you a servant of God and a common judge in Israel. Right?"

"Yes."

"Have you ever read Joseph Smith's inspired revision of the scripture you used a few minutes ago?"

"I . . . don't think so."

"Then listen, and see if you can detect a different meaning. 'And Jesus said unto his disciples, Beholdest thou the Scribes, and the Pharisees, and the Priests, and the Levites? They teach in their synagogues, but do not observe the law, nor the commandments; and all have gone out of the way, and are under sin. Go thou and say unto them, Why teach ye men the law and the commandments, when ye yourselves are the children of corruption? Say unto them, Ye hypocrites, first cast out the beam out of thine own eye; and then shalt thou see clearly to cast out the mote out of thy brother's eye.'

"Frank, tell me the difference between the two versions."

Reaching out, Frank took the president's Bible and read the Joseph Smith Translation. Then he turned to Matthew and read the first five verses of chapter 7. "Interesting," he said when he was finished. "Very interesting."

"What were Christ's disciples counseled to do?" the president asked.

"They were to judge the unrighteous and call them to repentance."

"Exactly. So what is your responsibility as a servant of God and judge in Israel?"

Frank sighed. "To judge these people and call them to repentance."

"Bishop Greaves," the president said softly, "as I have said, you have some unusually serious problems to deal with in your ward right now. But I bear testimony to you that the Lord inspired me to recommend you as the bishop. Further, and this surprises me, but in spite of the needs in your own home, He has not inspired me to release you. To me the message is clear—you are the one man in that ward whom the Lord considers best prepared to deal as a righteous judge with the problems you are encountering.

"Would you now take a look at the Doctrine and Covenants, section 1 verse 3?"

Frank thumbed through the scriptures until he found the passage. " 'And the rebellious shall be pierced with much sorrow,' " he read, " 'for their iniquities shall be spoken upon the housetops, and their secret acts shall be revealed.'

"Boy, that sure describes what happened to Mel," Frank concluded.

"And Bob Nichol, and John Martin, and so on. Bishop, I'm convinced that the time has arrived that the Lord is cleansing His Church. No longer will He allow secrets to remain secrets! Satan's code of silence is being broken, both in and out of the Church, and you have been called of God to be a part of that process. Do you have the faith to allow God to continue using you in accomplishing His purposes?"

President Stone smiled, knowing full well the innate goodness of this dedicated bishop. "I look at you," the president continued resolutely, "and I see other good priesthood leaders, all struggling just as you are, to serve in righteousness despite their own personal inadequacies. Yet how thankful I am to know that the Church is being guided by such leaders as you."

"Thank you, President," Frank said humbly. "Jeanee said I shouldn't resign. She also asked me to do what you recommended."

"You have an uncommonly wise wife."

"I know. President, I'll continue to serve, but I really think I could use a priesthood blessing myself . . . "

4:15 P.M.

"Do you ever see Robby?"

Bob and Claudia stood in the chill air in front of the restaurant, waiting for Claudia's bus. She had turned down a ride from Bob, her way of telling him she did not yet consider him safe enough to reveal the location of her apartment.

"Yes," Claudia replied as she looked up the street expectantly. "I see him at least every week, and usually more than that."

"How does he feel? About me, I mean?"

"He's angry."

"Do . . . do you think he'll ever be able to forgive me?"

Claudia sighed. "You've hurt him pretty deeply."

"But I've changed, Claudia. I mean it."

"Have you?" She peered into his eyes.

Startled, Bob did not know how to reply.

"I mean," Claudia explained, sensing his confusion, "that I want with all my heart to believe you. But I wonder how truly committed to change you really are."

"What . . . do you mean?"

Again Claudia looked up the street. "Bob," she said when she saw no bus, "the kind of change you need to make is not superficial. I've experienced some radical changes, and as you have been forced to admit, they're noticeable. The only change I see in you is loneliness."

"Isn't that enough?" Bob asked, trying to be funny.

"Not hardly."

"But—"

"Radical change, Bob, begins with your basic beliefs. Unfortunately, your basic belief is that a woman is an object to be used for your own selfish pleasure, and that children are little more than slaves. Were we to spend any more time together, as soon as your loneliness wore off you would treat both Robby and me as you did before."

"How do you know that?" Bob demanded almost angrily.

"Because I saw the way you looked at our waitress today," Claudia replied with total candor. "Every time your physical needs were great, I'd see you looking at me in that exact, same way."

"My gosh, Claudia! It's been almost a year—"

Claudia smiled patiently. "You see, Bob? You're still justifying yourself, accepting no responsibility for your own behavior. It's been almost a year for me, too, you know."

Bleakly Bob Nichol stared into the street. Was Claudia right? Was he practicing self-justification? He really thought he'd changed. But in his mind he could still see that waitress quite clearly—

"Are you going to Church anymore, Bob?"

"Not too much," he admitted.

"Reading the scriptures?"

Bob shook his head.

"I didn't think so," Claudia said quietly.

"But that's easy enough to change," Bob insisted, raising his voice to be heard above the approaching bus.

"Oh, Bob." Claudia looked sadly back as she waved for the bus to stop, "It isn't easy. I just wish I knew you wanted it badly enough to do what needs to be done."

With that Claudia was gone, and Bob Nichol was so busy trying to understand the terrible ache in his heart that he didn't even notice the tears of disappointment and loneliness that Claudia herself was no longer able to hold inside.

25

TUESDAY, APRIL 7

6:45 A.M.

"Mighty pretty," Frank declared as he gazed around the newly redecorated room.

"You like it?" Jeanee was in her robe, having just awakened from a restless night's sleep.

"I'll say!" Frank gave his wife a hug. And he did like it. The roses and pale blues on the walls were soft and feminine. The white area rug accented the white moldings and shelf he had somehow found the time to build, as well as the white curtains and white bedspreads Jeanee had found at a garage sale just the day before. And all Jeanee's little stuffed animals that lined the shelf, bedraggled as they had looked in her storage boxes after years of being tucked away, somehow looked resurrected. It was a little girl's room, all right. Of course Frank still didn't understand why such a radical change was necessary when the girls would only be with them a week. But, on the other hand, Jeanee had done particularly well during the time she had been working on the room. So who was he to complain?

"You did a great job, honey," he reiterated, squeezing his wife to him. "I didn't think you'd finish in time, but here it is Tuesday morning, and the girls won't be here for several hours yet. I'm impressed."

Jeanee sighed. "Well, I hope it's worth a week of my life, because I haven't done one other thing since we started."

"That's almost true for me, too," Frank acknowledged.

"I'm sorry, honey." Jeanee winced. "I guess I really went a little overboard. But that shelf you did turned out beautifully."

Frank grinned. "No problem — I just wish there was more I could do to help. About the girls — are you going to be able to go to the airport without me? I mean, I can't get out of my meeting, but if it will help, I can put off my temple trip until tomorrow."

Jeanee shook her head. "Actually, it's better that you go today, before they get here. Besides, Erik will be with me for the drive to the airport, and we'll be just fine."

Frank smiled. "You're wonderful. You know that?"

"But you'll be home as soon as you can?" Jeanee said, ignoring her husband's remark. "Right?"

Frank smiled and nodded. "It's a promise. After all, nobody can spoil granddaughters like a happy grandpa."

12:10 P.M.

"Bishop, it's good of you to come in."

Frank smiled as he took a seat in the classroom of his ward meetinghouse. "Well, it's very good of you to see me, Brother Wixom."

"Please, call me Hark."

"Hark?"

"That's right. Like, 'Hark, the herald angels sing.' "

"That's an unusual name."

Hark Wixom grinned. "Well, my mother was big on family names. Her maiden name was Harkness, and my grandmother's maiden name was Jewell. So I came out Harkness Jewell Wixom." His grin grew wider. "You can understand why I use Hark."

Frank chuckled. "I can. And would you please call me Frank?"

Hark nodded agreeably. "All right. Now, Frank, what can I do for you?"

Frank settled back in his chair. "This is a long story, Hark, which I don't want to take much time with. But, to put it briefly, my ward seems plagued with problems of abuse. I mean, all kinds — verbal, emotional, physical, sexual. Are there more than that?"

Hark shrugged noncommittally.

"My former first counselor is even in prison for molesting his daughters."

"Ahh," Hark said knowingly, "now I know who you are."

"Yeah, pretty sad situation, especially for the Blodgett family."

Frank cleared his throat and then moved forward. "My problem, Hark, is that I don't understand abuse. I've been researching it these past few months, but the more I learn the more I'm convinced I don't understand the least little thing about it. I guess I just want someone to explain it to me."

Hark Wixom took a deep breath. "That's a tall order, Frank. Have you read the handbook?"

"Yes," Frank acknowledged. "Twice. But that's pretty basic stuff."

"It's a good place to start."

Frank nodded. "But I need to do more than get started. I have several people very close to me that need me to understand."

Hark Wixom smiled approval.

"In fact," Frank confessed, "it's precisely because I didn't understand that I seriously offended a woman a few months ago. She came to me with a tragic history, and I told her all was well, to put it behind her and get on with her life."

"Ouch!"

"No kidding! Now I'm so gun-shy, I'm hesitant to talk

to anyone who's been abused. Literally I don't know what to say."

Hark Wixom looked at his watch. "And in the next fifteen minutes we're going to train you as a therapist?" There was a note of friendly sarcasm in his question.

"I don't think so," Frank answered candidly. "I'm a schoolteacher, and I intend to stay one. But I'm also a bishop, and for right now I have a role to play in these people's lives. I . . . think if I understood abuse better, I could better help my people. Does that make sense to you?"

"It does." Hark nodded. "It takes experience to have the kind of compassion to help these poor victims out of their destructive past. And, sadly, few have the courage to really open up and gain that experience."

"Well," Frank squirmed uneasily, "I have another motivation. My wife has been a victim of abuse. She told me last fall that she was abused by her first husband. But the other night she finally admitted that her own father abused her, though she won't tell me just how bad it was."

"That's not surprising."

"It isn't?" Frank was startled.

Feeling the constraints of time, Brother Wixom moved quickly forward. "Not if you understand shame."

Frank sent a puzzled look as the man continued. "Abuse is shame-producing, Frank. Though it isn't logical, probably 99.9 percent of abuse victims blame themselves for their trauma."

"Wait a minute." Frank stopped him. "Can you explain that for me?"

Wixom smiled. "Got your attention, huh?"

"I've just never heard that one. But I'm listening."

"Let me give you an example. Children who are forced into an incestuous relationship with a respected family member, such as a father, cannot conceive that the person they love would intentionally hurt them. So they blame themselves, and shame grows."

"So innocent children who are molested or abused by a parent believe it is their own fault?"

"Sad, huh?"

"It makes no sense!" Frank was emphatic. "Obviously the adult is the one at fault. Why would a child believe otherwise?"

"You have to understand the way a child thinks to comprehend it. But it's true. Shame is one of the greatest barriers to healing. And a major portion of our society, which sadly includes some of our Church members, encourages and magnifies that shame by insisting that it is unacceptable to reveal such problems. So the poor victims, still caught in the emotional blackmail they experienced as children, are further abused.

"Take your wife, for instance, if we may?" Brother Wixom proceeded carefully. "If she is deeply troubled and has never recovered from her abuse, it makes perfect sense that she would hide that abuse from you. Don't you hide things from her that you're ashamed of?"

"Yeah," Frank responded quietly, "now and then, I guess I do."

"Then you're normal." Brother Wixom chuckled. "And there's something else you may consider. Am I going too fast for you?"

"No, this is fine." Frank glanced at the notes he was taking. "I'm keeping up—somewhat."

"There's something else that's even harder to explain. And if it isn't dealt with properly, it is a powerful barrier to healing."

Frank took a deep breath, realizing as he did that the next statement was somehow going to apply to his Jeanee. He could feel the tingling that preceded a moment of inspiration or revelation, and he was open.

"Frank, sometimes victims of abuse, especially very severe abuse, dissociate. Do you know what that term means?"

Frank thought for a moment. "They stop associating with other people? That would certainly make sense in light of Jeanee's recent behavior."

"Even more damaging than that," Hark explained. *"They stop associating with their own feelings.* Let me explain. Because the pain and horror of the abuse is so great, they separate themselves mentally from the experience. They go into a form of denial where they can't admit, even to themselves, that their experience is real. In fact, in their minds it is not real. It becomes something that happens to another person whom they really don't know. Thus they may see the abuse happening but from a distance, and to someone else, even while they are in the middle of the actual experience."

"Let me understand what you're telling me," Frank asked in amazement. "Are you saying that they — leave their body?"

"Well, the research is insufficient to answer that question. Suffice it to say they are somehow able to separate themselves from the act of abuse, as well as the feelings resulting from the act, even as it is happening. The more terrifying and confusing the abuse, the stronger the barrier they build in their mind."

"Until they can actually seem like more than one person?" Frank was amazed.

"That's right!" Brother Wixom confirmed. "Continued dissociation results in memory blocking, which can be so effective that the victim absolutely can't remember that the abuse ever occurred. Or if it can be remembered, the memories will be vague and sketchy. Such memory blocking, whether partial or complete, may go on for years, though the body itself will likely be screaming out the truth in whatever way it can."

"Distress signals," Frank said softly.

"That's an interesting term."

Frank nodded. "It came from my Relief Society president. She told me a long time ago that my wife's poor health is a distress signal from her body."

"It may be."

"I believe that."

"The next item," Hark Wixom declared, "is that boys who have been abused tend to act out their anger, hurting others. They become next-generation abusers. On the other hand, girls who have been abused generally act inwardly, hurting themselves. Their lives are filled with trauma, and it is nearly impossible for them to live healthy, happy, complete lives – until healing occurs."

Feeling a chill of recognition, Frank thought of Robby Nichol and June McCraskey.

"Third," the man from Church Social Services stated, "there is no such thing as 'worse' abuse. We cannot say that one person was abused 'worse' than another. The reason for that, Frank, is that no two people are alike. Everyone reacts differently to circumstances, and they have a right to do so. So, one person may be totally traumatized by a single experience with fondling, while another may recover quite rapidly from an extremely violent rape. To say to a recovering victim, 'But your abuse was not all that bad,' puts the victim in the position of trying to defend his or her own experiences, which is completely counter-productive to healing.

"A therapist whose work I'm acquainted with, Jan Hindman, puts it this way: 'We need to find out how each kiddo is hurt. It's not generic. And treatment shouldn't be generic either.' She says that not to assess how each victim has been traumatized is the same as telling the person, 'You have cancer, but I'm not going to find out where. We'll just treat it generally.' "

"Scary thought," Frank observed.

"I'll say. The other problem with assigning a value level to a particular abuse is that it tends to invalidate the individual's experience. Most victims are already terrified that others won't believe them, or will belittle what they've gone through. If we say, 'Well, your abuse wasn't as bad as Susie's,' we are telling the victim, in effect, that we don't believe his or her experience. In actuality, that is heaping new abuse on top of old, and a victim does not need new pain."

Frank looked thoughtfully at his instructor. "Does everyone who experiences abuse have such deep scars as the ones I'm encountering? I mean, is it possible for someone who has been abused to simply go about living the gospel and letting the past quietly work itself out?"

Hark smiled. "Absolutely! In fact, a good many abuse experiences can be resolved in that way. The gospel is intended to heal. And it does. Complications come into play and counseling is mandatory when the abuse was so pervasive and destructive that the victim was essentially programed to reject the simple healing message the gospel offers.

"However, a good many well-meaning friends and family members may unintentionally damage a severely traumatized victim by insisting that all abuse can be resolved in this way. It can't. But then, that's where education comes in.

"You see, not all victims are affected the same way. Some may be content to let matters rest. Others feel driven to discover the root of their discomfort and confusion. I find it's important to encourage whomever I'm counseling to let their own feelings be their guide.

"Now, any other questions?"

Frank smiled. "I wish I had more time to spend with you."

Hark Wixom nodded. "So do I. But truthfully, I'm expecting someone shortly. I do have a few more points to make, however.

"Remember, deeply troubled victims won't discuss their abuse, or even begin to remember it, unless they feel safe. That's because while they were being victimized, they could find no safety anywhere. As an example, home to most of us is a place of safety, a castle of security. But to a child being abused by a father or mother, home becomes a prison, a dungeon of pain and fear.

"I don't know how you should do this, Frank, but if your wife has such an abusive past, and if you ever expect her to open up to you, you must convince her that she is completely safe."

"I've tried to do that." Frank's voice was filled with frustration. "So far, even though she's admitted the abuse, she's still holding back."

"That could be because a part of her still doesn't know she can trust you, or maybe even trust herself. Bishop, this is hard for a lot of people to comprehend. But somewhere inside of each of these victims is an emotional self who was never able to grow up—to mature. That child-like emotional self is very powerful, and if he or she feels in the least bit threatened, that part will control what the adult self actually does."

Frank stared ahead, remembering Mrs. O.'s thoughts about the inner child. "You know," he said, "sometimes when I'm talking to Jeanee, she does sound like a little girl."

Hark Wixom shrugged. "That's what I'm talking about."

"So, how do I deal with her when that happens?"

"Just as you'd deal with any little child," Hark answered good- naturedly. "You teach school. Elementary or high school?"

"Sixth grade."

Hark smiled. "Perfect. When you hear that change in her voice, act as though she's become one of your students—one who needs endless understanding and compassion. Don't expect her to think or act like an adult. If her childlike emotional self has taken over, she won't be able to."

"But won't she even know what's happening?"

"Most likely she will. No matter which part of her is in control, the adult you know as Jeanee will be there. She'll see and hear everything that's going on. But she may feel like a bystander, and it will be almost impossible for her to connect back as an adult until it's time."

"Which is when?" Frank looked perplexed.

"When she's finished having her memory, or whatever portion of it she's ready to deal with."

"I've heard talk of some people who experience memories that are more imagination and fantasy than reality."

"That happens occasionally," Hark agreed.

"Is there a way to tell them apart?"

"Sure." Hark smiled. "One is true, the other isn't."

Frank chuckled.

"I'm being facetious," Hark admitted, "but then again, I'm not. To discover the truthfulness of memories, we must constantly seek truth.

"When I counsel with people who have been abused, I encourage them throughout their healing to seek Christ and become new creatures through His atonement. I encourage them to seek the guidance of the Holy Ghost as a constant companion. Additionally, and this is pretty important, I encourage them never to seek to blame someone else or some incident for the problems they are having.

"Though abuse victims are never responsible for someone else's mistreatment of them, they are always responsible for their own healing."

"Wait a minute." Frank stopped him. "That's a pretty strong statement. You say abuse victims are responsible for their own healing?"

"Bear with me a moment, Bishop," Brother Wixom urged. "This is a point a lot of people get hung up on. But let me share this thought with you.

"Probably the most devastating wound left by abuse is the loss of personal freedom. Victims are forced to give up their agency to their abusers. Accustomed to this, they remain a victim until they discover that their freedom has to be reclaimed. That, by the way, only happens when they are strong enough to accept personal responsibility for their own choices, not the abuse that was forced upon them.

"My task, and the task of every righteous counselor, is to help victims sort through their blind spots and discover they have the right to reclaim their own personal freedom."

"Then, it's a message of hope," Frank agreed, "and not condemnation."

"Exactly! The next step," Brother Wixom continued, "is the same for everyone—to take their own personal weaknesses, whatever they may be, before the Lord and honestly acknowledge culpability. This, by the way, is called repentance in the Sunday School manual.

"Then, as the Lord heals us, he will bring us closer and closer to all truth. 'Howbeit,' it says in John 16:13, 'when he, the Spirit of truth, is come, he will guide you into all truth.' And Jeremiah 33:6 says, 'I will cure them, and will reveal unto them the abundance of peace and truth.'

"Interesting how peace and truth are spoken of together. And it's no coincidence. As a true memory is revealed, peace is also revealed.

"Bishop, 'all truth' includes painful truths about the past—when and if they are there. But the Lord will only reveal them as it is in His wisdom for us to know them. 'Behold,' He says in D&C 50:40, 'ye are little children and ye cannot bear all things now: ye must grow in grace and in the knowledge of the truth.' I believe He prepares us to receive His grace before He reveals truths that are hard for us to bear. And when He does reveal them, they will come naturally, without coercion, and they will be true memories. As we accept them and trust the Lord enough to lay them on the altar of His love, we will be healed."

Frank was writing the scriptural references in his notepad when a knock came at the door. Brother Wixom excused himself and asked his next interview to wait in the foyer.

"Again, any more questions?" he asked as he turned back.

"Just one." Frank nodded. "You said 'totally false memory.' Is there any such thing as a partially false memory?"

"Frank," Hark explained, "these are my personal conclusions, so bear that in mind. But I've discovered that totally false or partially false memories come from the mind's determination to make sense of what the person has experienced. Very few people, I mean *very* few, would consciously create a lie. In fact, a good many false memories are simply the result of a victim's not remembering the details clearly.

"For instance, one young woman I have been counseling with remembered that her uncle had incested her. In reality, through therapy, we discovered that it was her older brother. However, it was safer for her mind to remember her uncle as the perpetrator because he had died by the time she began remembering, and her brother lived in the same house with her."

"There's so much to learn," Frank declared, rising to his feet. "I always thought remembering was what everyone did. It was part of living. My dad taught me years ago that memories were what God gave us to help us avoid making the same mistakes time after time."

"I agree with that. It's just that abuse victims bury them. But when they start coming back, then Katie bar the door, get out of the road! They'll be the most real memories you've ever heard of—more real even than reality itself. And unless those real memories are exposed to the light of day, discussed fully with trusted others, and then dealt with honestly — and let me underline that word *honestly* — unless that happens, the poor victims who have buried these painful memories in the first place will never, ever be fully healed."

5:15 P.M.

Frank sat silently, enjoying the plush comfort of the chair he had located. As always the temple was serene and beautiful, and he was feeling a remarkable closeness to the Spirit of the Lord. A few feet away a young couple, preparing to join hands in eternal wedlock within a few short minutes, whispered excitedly with their parents.

Bowing his head in prayer, Frank struggled for a few moments with his concentration. But finally the small sounds of the room faded in his ears, and he was able to forge ahead.

"Heavenly Father," he prayed, "years ago Thou taught me how to feel Thy Spirit. Today I have a great need to feel that power, that I may know Thy divine will concerning the people I love. President Stone has asked that I not be released, and I am willing to be obedient. But Father, wilt Thou manifest unto me that my staying on as bishop is also Thy will?"

For a moment Frank paused, and suddenly he realized that he was being affected by the sweet power of the Spirit, just as he had been many times in the past.

"I thank Thee, Father, for hearing my pleas. Is it Thy will, I pray, that I remain in my calling as —"

Instantaneously, even before he had finished the question, the Spirit gave a powerful response, and Frank was left with no doubt as to the Lord's will. He was to remain as bishop!

For some time Frank prayed about the people in his ward, and in each instance an impression came as to what he should do to help them. Some impressions were more clear than others, and in a couple of instances he could feel nothing at all. Yet overall he was more than elated, and he was finally ready to broach the subject of his wife.

"Dear God," he prayed, "Thou knowest Jeanee and her needs. I would ask if the memories she is experiencing are a good thing?"

Again the response was instantaneous, and again it was overwhelming. From that moment Frank knew that whatever Jeanee was going through, it was all according to a divine plan that he might or might not need to understand.

"Father," he asked, "may I understand what Jeanee is experiencing?"

Waiting then, Frank felt hard-pressed to tell what he was feeling. He was certain the Lord was saying he could indeed understand it. But beyond that, his mind was receiving no information whatsoever. "Does this mean, Father," he finally asked, "that I will have to wait—"

For an instant Frank was overcome by the powerful influence of the Holy Spirit. As he wiped away his tears, he knew that all the answers would come, but that he would need to be patient until they did. Interestingly, he also felt that he needed to continue to learn, seeking out such people as Hark Wixom and Peggy, as well as any others who could teach him.

"Father in Heaven, I thank Thee that Thou hast heard my pleas this day. I have one question left concerning my wife. If I am not to resign as bishop, then surely there must be some other way for me to help her through this experience. Father, I have no idea what this might be. If there is something I can do, wilt Thou please put it into my mind . . ."

6:45 P.M.

"Grandpa! Grandpa!"

Frank stood in the doorway, smiling from ear to ear, as Amber and Nicole rushed across the family room toward him with outstretched arms. And Jeanee, already exhausted by the girls' exuberance, sank thankfully onto the couch. Nicole, five years old, and Amber, three, were a handful in anybody's home. But in hers—

"How was your day?" Frank asked as he reached down to hug both children.

Jeanee smiled weakly. "Good, actually. Though I am tired."

"I'll bet. Have you girls been wearing Grandma out already?"

Nicole shook her head, but Amber looked confused.

"What's the matter, punkin?" Frank asked, tickling the tiny girl gently in the ribs with his finger. "You look bothered."

"Don't frow Gramma away," Amber replied simply, not reacting to being tickled.

"What?" Frank questioned, surprised. "Who said anything about throwing Grandma away?"

Amber's brow puckered. "You said she gots wored out, Grampa. Mommy frows wored out fings away."

Frank laughed while Jeanee frowned thoughtfully at the child's innocent statement. "Well, Grandpa isn't going to throw Grandma away," Frank assured. "You can bet on that. Say, do you girls want to come boogeying with Grandpa and Angie?"

"What's boogeying?" Nicole asked seriously.

"Dancing, silly," Angie shouted as she jumped up from the floor. "In Daddy's music room. We do it all the time. Come on! We'll show you how."

"Thank you." Jeanee mouthed the words as Frank smiled back at her.

"Okay, girls," he instructed to the three excited children, "you go in and wait for Grandpa. I have to talk to Grandma for a minute, and then I'll be in."

With a squeal they were gone, and then he turned back to his wife. "You know, hon, you really don't look so good."

Jeanee smiled weakly. "That's a strange sort of compliment."

Frank smiled. "I know you're doing better, sweetheart. But there's something I want you to know." Frank walked over and, taking Jeanee's hand in his, knelt in front of the sofa. "In the temple today I felt strongly to do something. And I don't want you to say anything until you've heard me out. Okay?"

Jeanee nooded her head in agreement. "I won't say a word."

"Good," Frank said, "because it won't do any good even if you oppose me on this."

"I'm listening," Jeanee agreed, curious to know what her husband was leading up to.

"Okay." Frank cleared his throat. "This next summer, instead of spending my days at the university working on my degree, I'm going to spend all three months with you. Period! That's the way it's going to be. No work on my degree. Just the bishoping stuff I have to do—and you."

Jeanee's eyes were suddenly brimming with tears. "And you thought I'd oppose that?"

"Well, I didn't know. But it wouldn't do any good if you did. My mind's made up." Frank was adamant.

"Thank you," she whispered as she drew her husband close. "I know what that degree means to you."

"Let's get something clear. Nothing means more to me than you do." Frank kissed the top of his wife's head. And then smiling and standing in a '60s twister stance, he added, "Now, stay clear of the music room or plug your ears, because we gonna get way way down and boogey."

11:10 P.M.

"Oh, Frank," Jeanee gasped as she threw herself back on the bed, "why am I so tired?"

"Little kids do that to grandmas," Frank replied lightly as he began unbuttoning his shirt.

"Well, then, tomorrow will you buy me a cane and a rocking chair?"

Frank grinned. "They really got to you, huh?"

"Oh, I love them with all my heart. But their energy is so inexhaustible. I feel like I've been through a war."

"Well, your nightmares can't be helping you very much."

"Nightmares?" Jeanee asked cautiously.

"That's right. Nightmares." Frank was incredulous. "You don't remember them?"

"I . . . remember."

Frank sat down in the chair. "I've been wanting to talk to you about them, honey. They're getting to be a regular thing lately, aren't they?"

"I've been thinking, maybe there's some kind of a problem with my breathing." Jeanee was matter-of-fact. "Maybe it's an allergy problem or something that's triggering the dreams."

"Whatever, they're getting worse."

Jeanee looked at Frank with total dismay.

"You start out moaning, then gasping for air. Then you end up kneeling face down on the bed. Last night it happened twice."

"I . . . I don't want to talk about this anymore."

Frank, who had fully intended to tell his wife about his visit with Hark Wixom, suddenly decided that now was not the time. "So the little girls are both asleep?" he asked, changing the subject.

Jeanee sighed. "Yes, but for a little while I didn't think it was going to happen."

"I could tell you had quite a discussion in there. Did they like the bedroom?"

Jeanee sighed. "They didn't notice it. But Nicole said some of the most interesting things tonight. You know, she's a very perceptive little girl."

Carefully Frank hung his shirt over the back of the chair. "Oh, yeah?"

"She looked at that picture of Jesus, the one we have hanging above the bed?"

"Mmm hmm."

"And she got a really sad look in her eyes and asked me why Jesus had to die. Well, I explained how He was the only perfect Son of God and He had to show us the way. I told her, 'He walked through the door of death and came back to be resurrected so we could follow Him and live again with Heavenly Father.' And I thought that would be the end of it."

"And it wasn't?"

"No. She said, 'But Gramma, why did He have to bleed?' "

"What did you tell her?" Frank had an amused, impressed look on his face.

"I told her that He had to bleed because His blood washes our sins away. And she said, 'Oh, you mean, when we do a sin and say sorry to Jesus, He takes it and Heavenly Father throws it in the garbage?' "

"She said that?" Frank asked, smiling from ear to ear.

"She did!" Jeanee confirmed, sitting on the bed and taking off her shoes. "Do you believe it?"

Chuckling, Frank mused. "Well, it sure lets you know why the Lord told us a little child would lead us. Take a look at Amber. After all she's been through, she's amazing. And her little lisp is so cute. While they were in the music room, she saw a spider on the wall. She wanted me to stop the music, and then she asked me, 'Grampa, does that 'pider have teeth?' I told her it didn't and asked if she was afraid of the spider. But she said, 'No, he's a nice 'pider. He can 'tay here. Jesus wants 'piders to be alive.'

"I tell you, Jeanee, it's wonderful to see her doing so well. Tony and Megan are doing a fine job with both those little girls. It's because of that kind of faith that she is being healed of what that Brattles boy did to her."

"I'm not so sure," Jeanee said hesitantly as she rose to her feet and turned toward the bathroom. "Her comment about not throwing me away, and the look in her eyes— I'm not convinced she's healing. Something is really bothering her."

MONDAY, APRIL 13

8:05 A.M.

"Morning, Frank."

Looking up, Frank saw his principal leaning in his class-room door. "Hi, Kent," he said with a smile. "How are you today?"

Kent Bailey shook his head and grinned. "Just about like yesterday. Except for some good news — we got your telephone approved."

"Well, will wonders never cease!"

Kent Bailey's smile grew wider. "Yeah. Too bad it isn't installed. You're wanted on the phone — Bishop. A woman named Claudia Nichol."

With a sinking feeling, Frank rose to his feet. What, he wondered as he hurried down the hall, could be going wrong now.

11:05 A.M.

Shadows of late morning shrouded Jeanee's bedroom. The girls were down for early naps, and Jeanee was alone, sobbing into her pillow. The memory of a terrifying presence was still with her, a presence that had ripped her from her own sleep.

It had been huge, massive, crushing her down into the bed, smothering her so that she had been certain she would

361

die. But the monster had also been dark, so dark that Jeanee could remember nothing but its size.

"Dear God," she pleaded as she continued sobbing, "what *was* that? *Who* was it? What have I *done!* If . . . if I've done something wrong that is making this happen, please tell me. In Jesus' name I ask, whatever I've done wrong, please let me know.

"I thought I'd repented of everything, but if I haven't remembered something, and the Holy Ghost is trying to recall it to my mind, please bring it back. I don't care how badly it hurts! I . . . I need to know what I've done wrong, so I can repent. I can't live this way. I can't go on in this world of shadows and terror. I can't stand it! Please, Father! Please!"

11:55 A.M.

"Good to see you again, Claudia. Sit down, and tell me what I can do for you."

Claudia Nichol sat purposefully in one of the student desks. "Actually, Bishop," she said softly, "I don't think you can do anything."

"Oh?"

"I ate lunch with Bob last week. In spite of my desires and my hopes and my prayers, he hasn't changed a bit. I've decided I need to file for divorce and get on with my life."

His heart suddenly pounding, Frank sent a frantic plea heavenward. He had felt this was coming, but for the life of him he hadn't been able to shake the feeling that Bob and Claudia needed to remain together.

"And . . . you're sure he hasn't changed?" he asked, pressing for time.

Claudia shook her head. "He hasn't. Trust me. So, when I leave here, I'm going to go see a lawyer."

"I . . . I think you've made a good decision." Frank was

dumbfounded to hear the words come out of his mouth, but no more dumbfounded than Claudia Nichol.

"You do?"

"I do," Frank declared, suddenly feeling a sense of confidence. "What are the conditions?"

"Conditions?"

Frank nodded. "Yes, conditions for him to meet before you'll call off the divorce and take him back."

Now Claudia was even more surprised. "I . . . I hadn't thought of doing that."

"You hadn't? But you still love him, don't you?"

Claudia dropped her eyes. "Yes," she breathed, "I do."

"And yet you're considering just cutting him off forever? You're willing to say, 'Sorry, Bob, but you've already proven you're a bad guy. I don't care if you do change, or even if you've started to change. I won't believe it, and I won't accept it.' Is that the message you want to give this man you love?"

It was obvious that Claudia did not know what to say.

"Sister Nichol," Frank pressed on, his mind suddenly thinking of Mrs. O. and June McCrasky, "if you had two empty notebooks in front of you and had the assignment of writing in one the things you know about Bob that make you mad, and in the other the happy things, what would you write?"

Claudia was at first puzzled by Frank's comments. And then, seeing a way to validate her decision, she began. "In the mad book I'd write that he is dishonest and cruel. He makes a good impression, but he hides a dark side that comes up when you least expect it, destroying every hope. I wanted to believe things could work out for us, Bishop. I really did. But after this last attempt, well, there's no hope for us, not as a couple.

"And what he's done to Robby? It was bad when I was there, but I'm finding he was even worse when I wasn't around."

Frank nodded his head. "And in the happy book?"

Claudia paused and then reluctantly began. "In the happy book I'd write that he does everything well, always knows the right thing to say, even if he doesn't mean it—"

Claudia caught herself, "Sorry Bishop. I guess I'm just a little bitter."

Frank smiled and waited for Claudia to continue.

"It's just that I had such hopes," she apologized.

"What else would you write in the happy book?" Frank put her back on track.

"I'd have to say that he reached a lot of lonely boys when he was Scoutmaster. And when he taught Sunday School, he had a way of making it fun to learn. You remember?"

Frank smiled. "So he has both good and bad qualities?"

Claudia nodded. "Unfortunately, the bad qualities outweigh the good."

"I agree," Frank said carefully. "But what if you could tip the scales? Would you be interested?"

"I don't think I can."

"If you could, Claudia, would you be willing to give it a try?"

For a long moment the woman was silent, thinking. "What," she finally asked, "are you suggesting?"

Frank leaned back in his chair. "A simple thing, really. When he is served with the divorce papers, give him a list of changes you feel he should make immediately if he wants your marriage to work. Can you think of any, right off-hand?"

Claudia thought for a moment. "That would be easy!" she began. "No more criticisms of Robby or me, no more temper tantrums and profanity, no more treating me like an un-person, daily prayer and scripture study, weekly visits to a therapist. You get the picture?"

Frank nodded. "I do. And those all sound reasonable.

If he solemnly agreed to every one of them, plus any others you think of, would you be willing to get back together with him and give your marriage another try?"

"Bishop," Claudia asked, looking askance at Frank, "why are you doing this? You know what he's done to me. You know what he's done to Robby. Why do you want me to subject our family to more of it?"

Soberly Frank gazed back at Claudia. "I don't. What I want is for you to give Bob a chance to change for you."

"But why?"

Frank took a deep breath. "I am convinced that the Lord does not want you and Bob to divorce."

"But . . . I've prayed about it, Bishop."

"And what have you felt?"

"I . . . don't know. I've prayed that Bob would repent and change his ways, and nothing's happened."

"But you haven't been given a clear direction concerning divorce?"

Slowly Claudia shook her head.

"Then, for one more try, will you accept mine?"

"You mean file, see if he accepts my conditions, and then, if he does, get back together for three months?"

"That's right."

"But . . . what if he agrees . . . and then goes back on it?"

Frank could see the fear in Claudia Nichol's eyes, and he didn't blame her for it. Nor did he have any idea if what he was about to suggest would even work. On the other hand —

"Any time you decide, Claudia, you leave again. But before that, there is one other thing I want you to do."

Claudia sighed. "What's that?"

"A young lady here at the school has been really struggling since her mother's death a few years ago."

Claudia regarded him quizzically.

"This year another teacher in my school is having a

dramatic impact on her. As we talked about what she is doing a little while ago, it brought to mind a story I want to tell you. Can you spare another few minutes?"

Claudia nodded.

"Good. I think you may find it very encouraging. It's about a woman, LDS, very active, who raised her children to be righteous and to marry in the temple. But through it all, her husband remained a vile, wicked man. He drank, had an evil temper, smoked, profaned, and was an all-around unpleasant person.

"Everyone expected that when the children were grown and gone, the woman would divorce her husband and not have to put up with him any longer. That didn't happen. She continued to love him, and he continued to be vile and wicked.

"One evening when he was out of town, the home teacher gathered the man's wife and children together and proposed a simple plan. He challenged them not to let a day go by that they didn't tell their husband or father at least one good thing about himself. He also had them promise that they would never point out his weaknesses again — just his good points.

"Well, the home teacher was inspired, because a miracle happened in that family. The father and husband, who had a very low self-image, was just fulfilling the role he believed was his. Once he started hearing only good mirrored to him, his behavior began changing. Within a year he had quit smoking, drinking, and swearing. He had joined the Church and was preparing to take his family to be sealed eternally in the temple."

"Is that what that other teacher is doing?"

Frank nodded. "Some days, Claudia, she can't think of a good thing to say to this girl. So she finds me or some other teacher and asks us to think of something good we can say about her. We do, and she goes back to the child and says, 'I heard the nicest thing about you today.' Well, you can't believe the impact that little bit of thoughtfulness is having on the girl. She is making remarkable changes."

"So you want me to do that with Bob? Say only nice things and disregard the others?"

"That's right—with only one exception. There will be times when you will need to confront your husband with concerns. At those times, remember the value of speaking the truth, in love. Don't accuse or blame. That will only destroy your good efforts. But speak honestly, with the attitude of love. Can you do that?"

"That's a tall order, Bishop."

"I know," Frank agreed. "And you're the only one in a position to fill it, Claudia. But only for the ninety days it will take the divorce decree to become final. At that time—or even before if you feel you simply can't stand it any longer—if you see no changes, then you'll never hear another argument from me about giving Bob another chance. In fact, I'll help you leave."

Claudia smiled weakly. "You really believe in this, don't you."

"I do. Some amazing results are right down the hall. Claudia, you pray about this. I'm sure you'll receive a witness that I am asking you to do the right thing. Okay?"

Claudia sighed. "All right, Bishop. I'll trust you. I'll add that list to the divorce papers right now, and then we'll see what happens next."

"Thanks, Claudia," Frank said as he rose to his feet. "I pray Bob will soon come to realize what a remarkable woman he married."

11:10 P.M.

"Frank, what's *that*?" Jeanee's voice was urgent. "You have to wake up! I'm scared!"

Quickly Frank shook himself awake.

"Am I dreaming? Am I here?" Jeanee was trembling and disoriented. "What's that sound. Is it me?"

It took Frank a moment to focus his mind.

"It's one of the girls," he exclaimed as he threw back the covers and leaped to his feet. "She sounds terrified!"

Not realizing how frightened Jeanee was herself, Frank hurried down the darkened hall and burst into the room where Amber and Nicole had fallen asleep a couple of hours before.

"What is it?" he demanded as he turned on the lamp. "What's going on?"

Nicole sat up and began rubbing her eyes. But Amber lay cowering against the wall, sobbing and whining even as she tried to pull the covers over her.

With great relief, Frank sat on the bed next to Amber. "It's only a nightmare," he comforted, reaching out gently to stroke his little granddaughter's hair. "You just wake up, punkin, and you'll be okay."

He hadn't noticed Jeanee standing in the doorway, hugging the frame. But looking up, he saw horror in her face.

"*Listen* to her!" Jeanee demanded, trembling. "Listen to what she's *saying!*"

Paying more attention, Frank was suddenly aware that Amber, in the midst of her sobs, was pleading for someone not to 'frow' her away.

"Why is she afraid of that?" Frank asked, puzzled.

"It's what she always says," Nicole volunteered as she perched on the side of her bed.

"Always? You mean this happens a lot?"

"Uh-huh." Nicole nodded. "Daddy and Mommy don't understand her. But I do."

"Do . . . you know why she says it?" Jeanee asked, her voice little more than a whisper of fear.

Again Nicole nodded. "Uh-huh. It's 'cause of what that mean Benny boy said to her."

Jeanee shot a look at Frank. "What did he say to her?" Frank asked, acutely aware of his wife's nonverbal accusation. "Do you know, Nicole?"

"Uh-huh. He said if she ever told the secret, he'd put her in a garbage bag and Mommy would throw her away."

With a stifled moan of agony and grief Jeanee rushed to the side of her still sobbing little granddaughter. Picking her up and sitting on the side of the bed, she began rocking her trembling little body.

"Do you . . . know the secret?" Frank continued to press Nicole.

Slowly the six-year-old nodded her head. "Amber can't tell, or she'll get thrown away."

"No, she won't!" Frank declared forcefully. "Nicole, do you know anything about her secret?"

"Easy, Frank," Jeanee urged through her pain. "Be soft with her."

Taking a deep breath, Frank nodded. "I . . . I'm sorry, punkin. I'm just upset about Amber's bad dreams. Now, do you know anything about her secret?"

Again the girl nodded affirmatively. "Uh-huh. That mean Benny boy wants to hurt her potty place again."

A gasp escaped Jeanee's mouth.

"Grandma, are you okay?"

Unable to speak, Jeanee only nodded.

"Grandma is just terribly sad that Amber was hurt," Frank explained as he took Nicole onto his lap. "So am I. It isn't fair, is it."

"I wish that mean Benny boy would die!" Nicole declared vehemently.

"Has he ever done mean things to you?" Frank asked.

"Uh-uh," Nicole answered, shaking her head. "I won't let him. But Amber isn't big like me. She's just little and she's afraid."

"You mean he's still being mean?" Frank was shocked.

Nicole nodded again. "Sometimes he says bad things

to us through the fence. I take Amber into the house. But she's still scared. And her bad dreams keep scaring her, too."

"I . . . I think," Jeanee said, her voice still filled with pain, "that we all need to . . . to say a prayer for Benjamin."

"But why, Grandma?"

"Because," Jeanee explained as she continued to rock the finally quiet Amber, "Heavenly Father is the only one who can help Benjamin stop being mean. If we pray for him and ask Heavenly Father to take away his meanness, then little Amber won't ever have to be scared anymore. Do you understand that, Nicole?"

"Then will Heavenly Father throw his sins in the garbage?"

"I . . . hope so. But Benjamin has to want Heavenly Father to throw his sins in the garbage before that will happen."

"Then he'll be nice to us?"

Jeanee looked to Frank for help. But he was formulating some thoughts of his own.

"You're a very brave little girl," Frank whispered, turning to Amber, "and it's good for you to tell the secret. Nobody's going to throw you away. Not ever. Heavenly Father will make sure of that, because He loves you very much." Then turning to Nicole, he added, "The secret is Benjamin's, and he's the one who is being bad. So we need to ask Heavenly Father to take that secret from Amber and share it with the right people, so Benjamin can get help. Heavenly Father loves him, too, but he doesn't want him to keep being mean to little girls. Do you understand that, Nicole?"

"Uh-huh."

"Good. Do you understand, Amber? You are safe here with Grandma and Grandpa. Benny is not going to hurt you again. You can tell us what he did and we'll make sure you are always safe. Do you understand what Grandpa is saying?"

Sniffing back her tears and clinging to her grandmother, the tiny girl nodded. "Will . . . Benny . . . make Mommy frow me away?" she asked tremulously.

"No!" Jeanee said forcefully. "Grandpa Frank and I will make certain of that!"

"And Heavenly Father won't throw Benny away, either." Nicole spoke excitedly. "He'll just throw his bad sins away. Right, Grandpa?"

"Right, Angel." Frank's eyes sparkled at her comprehension. "And Father in Heaven will help us, too. Would you like Grandpa Frank to say a prayer for Benjamin so he will stop being mean to you?"

With a slight smile Amber nodded.

"Okay," Frank said as he slid Nicole off his lap, "let's all kneel down by Amber's bed, shall we? Then we can all say a prayer for this mean enemy . . . "

27

THURSDAY, APRIL 16

10:20 A.M.

"President Stone? This is Frank Greaves."

"Hello, Bishop," the stake president responded warmly through the telephone. "What's up?"

"I need to talk with you for a minute, but if this isn't a good time . . . "

President Stone laughed. "You caught me, didn't you? That means it's a great time."

Frank smiled for a moment, and then the look on his face became serious. "President," he said hesitantly as he looked out at his empty class room, "I probably should have mentioned this before. But we . . . uh . . . recently learned that our little granddaughter—" He paused a moment, realizing that, in this setting, verbalizing what had happened to little Amber might take more control than he could manage.

Sensing Frank's grief, President Stone waited patiently. "Do you want to come in to see me about this, Bishop?" he encouraged.

There was a long pause as Frank regained his composure. And then quietly he stated what had happened to little Amber.

"I'm so sorry, Frank," President Stone responded quietly.

"Me, too." Frank took a deep breath and continued. "The police didn't do anything to him because Amber was too young to testify. Besides, the boy denied it, and even though the hospital examination verified what Amber said, they didn't consider it proof that this particular boy was the one who did it."

"Incredible."

"I guess I haven't been letting myself realize how terribly she was damaged," Frank admitted. "But our granddaughters have been staying with us the past week, and the other night the little one it happened to had a terrible nightmare. Since then she's been drawing pictures of what happened to her.

"President, the pictures are, well, they're horrible. It's amazing that a little girl could come up with such graphic horror. There's no way she could have just made this up. And she draws several different settings. I'm afraid that little Amber was severely abused frequently over a long period of time, maybe even a year."

"I'm very sorry to hear this, Bishop."

"It's especially hard on Jeanee," Frank continued. "But I have a twofold question. First, both Amber and her older sister say the boy is still abusing her, though more by terror now than anything else." Frank cleared his throat in an effort to distance himself from the pain this conversation was stirring in his heart. "I have to do *something!* As helpless as I feel as a grandfather, I have to do something! And as a bishop, I need to know what my responsibility is. President, what are the guidelines for these sorts of things?"

"Well," the president said after thinking for a moment, "if you have evidence that abuse is occurring, evidence that you obtained from someone other than the perpetrator, you are required by law to report it to the proper authorities."

"How do I do that when I don't even know who the authorities are? I mean, they're way out of this area."

President Stone paused. "What I would do," he finally responded, "is write a letter detailing who you are and what you have observed and send it to the chief of police in the city where your family lives. Also tell the chief that he will be contacted with further information by the child's parents—I presume Tony and his wife?"

"That's right. Should I send the police chief copies of the pictures Amber has drawn?"

"I think I'd let Tony and his wife take them in."

Frank nodded. "That makes sense."

"Now, your next question was concerning your ecclesiastical responsibility?"

"That's right," Frank affirmed.

"And the boy who abused your granddaughter is LDS?"

"He is."

There was a moment of silence on the other end of the phone. "Do you know the ward where he lives?" the president finally asked.

"I do."

"Okay, good. You need to write to his bishop. But I'd make this a more complete letter, and I would definitely include copies of the things your granddaughter has drawn. Put your letter on your ward letterhead so he'll understand you are making an official report about a problem within his ward."

"All right, President. I'll take care of it today."

"Good. And Frank, this is only a suggestion, but if I were you I'd call Brother Wixom from Social Services. It seems likely to me that your little granddaughter should receive counseling."

Frank was surprised. "Already? But she's so young!"

"Not too young to be traumatized, apparently."

"Good point," Frank said thoughtfully.

"But you ask Brother Wixom about her age, Frank. He'll know better than I do if she's too young or not. How's Jeanee taking this?"

"Well, President," Frank replied carefully, "it's real hard on her."

"I can imagine. Did I ask you if she's in therapy?"

"I . . . don't remember, President. But she is."

"I'm glad to hear that. How are you doing?"

Frank grinned lopsidedly. "Up and down. But I do have more hope, President. In fact, since we talked I've had a couple of great experiences, and I think maybe things are going to work out."

"That's wonderful. I'm happy to hear it."

Then President Stone's voice filled with empathy. "I'm terribly sorry to hear about your little granddaughter, Frank. I can only imagine what you and Jeanee must be going through."

1:15 P.M.

"Augh! I just want to scream!" Jeanee was seated in her therapist's office, Amber's drawings spread out on the floor in front of her. "Can you *see* what that boy *did* to our baby?"

"I see." Peggy's voice was low and calm.

"It makes me sick! Why would he do that to a little child? Why would anybody? I'm telling you, Peggy, I feel like I'm going to explode! And my mind is screaming, 'Somebody stop this! Please! Somebody has to stop it!' "

"Try to slow down, Jeanee." Peggy's voice was very calm. She was well aware of how such incredibly graphic drawings might affect Jeanee.

"Why?" Jeanee asked.

"The faster you talk, the more it will make you feel wound up—like a closed loop."

"Oh," Jeanee replied, surprised. "I didn't know that. Okay, I'll talk more slowly."

"Good. Now, you were telling me about your granddaughter."

"She has nightmares, and the other night after one of them, Frank and I had prayer with her and Nicole, and then she started talking. Only she didn't know the words, so she started drawing me these pictures."

"It was Amber's idea?"

"Yes. But the drawings make me so sick—"

"Why is that?"

"Well, look at them. They're sickening!"

Jeanee spread the large pieces of butcher paper in front of them. "See this!" she was emphatic. "And this! See, that's Benjamin, and Amber drew herself here. Do you see what's happening."

It was very clear to Peggy, as she scrutinized the pictures, what Amber was depicting. Though children's drawings might normally leave a lot open to interpretation, Amber's stick drawings left no doubt.

"Well?" Jeanee demanded. "Aren't they sickening?"

"Jeanee," Peggy sat back and asked, "how did you respond when Amber drew these pictures for you?"

"I can't believe how calm I was! It was like I could hear your voice asking her about what she was doing."

"And how did she respond?"

"She just kept drawing and telling me more about how he—I can't say it!"

"Do you realize what you've done?"

Jeanee looked blankly at her gentle interrogator.

"You've opened a door for Amber. A door to her own healing."

"Are . . . you sure?"

"Yes! But I must caution you, Jeanee. Amber needs professional help. This boy has filled her mind with a lot of lies, very sick lies that she can't help but believe, and in my opinion, only a trained therapist can help her get rid of them."

"I know that!" Jeanee was adamant. "That's why I've been so upset that no one will get her into therapy!"

"Still," Peggy continued, "this is wonderful. Look at that picture, for instance. What is she doing there?"

"She said she was tying Benjamin up and running out the door and closing it behind her."

"You see? This is a very good sign. When did she draw this?"

"After I told her to draw a picture making her big and Benjamin little. I told her what Benjamin did made his spirit small. And her courage made her big. So I had her draw herself bigger than Benjamin."

"And then she drew this one — of tying him up?"

"Uh-huh."

A smile crept over Peggy's face. "Amber's a lucky little girl to have a grandmother like you. Already her healing has started."

Jeanee was suddenly overcome with tears.

"Now tell me why the pictures are sickening to you, Jeanee."

Jeanee took a deep breath. "Because . . . because . . . Oh, I can't say it!"

"Is it because they might have been your drawings, if somebody had helped you draw them when you were smaller?"

Jeanee couldn't answer. The question stung so sharply and unexpectedly that it took her breath away. And she couldn't even begin to consider an answer.

They had been talking about Amber, not her. For a moment Jeanee wept silently. But then, with a deep breath, she regained some control. "Frank didn't think she was still suffering, but then he saw her having the nightmare and watched her do the drawings and explain them. Now he believes."

"What were you feeling just then, Jeanee?"

"Huh?" Jeanee seemed unaware of suddenly changing the subject.

"We were just talking about the drawings maybe being

the same as if you had drawn them." Peggy paused, waiting for Jeanee to realize what she had just done.

Jeanee hugged her arms close to her body and began rocking in her chair. Her bottom lip began to quiver as she blinked a tear back.

"Would you like to talk about that?"

There was a long pause. Peggy waited calmly as Jeanee's expression changed to that of a lost child.

"I . . . had a dream," she almost whispered.

"Go on."

"I don't want to think about it."

"Take as much time as you need," Peggy said reassuringly.

"There . . . was . . . there was . . ." Jeanee pulled her knees up against her chest and hugged them tight. "It's so hard," she whimpered.

"I know," Peggy assured her calmly.

Again, there was a long pause.

"This huge monster was on top of me, and the pain was so bad I thought I was dying. Even after I woke up I could feel the pain—" Again Jeanee broke into tears.

"Can you tell me any more about the dream?" Peggy asked gently.

Silently Jeanee nodded. "It . . . was my . . . daddy." She began to tremble. "He hurt me. He hurt me bad. And I tried to stop him. I really did!" Tears were streaming down Jeanee's face.

"And you were just a tiny girl," Peggy concluded.

"I tried so hard. And he wouldn't stop!" Jeanee wept again.

"And you couldn't have stopped him."

"And I didn't know what he was *doing!*" Jeanee cried. "He just kept hurting me—and I couldn't tell anyone. He said if I did—" Jeanee began weeping uncontrollably.

"If you did?" Peggy pressed. "What would happen if you did?"

Jeanee continued to weep as Peggy waited. Finally, as she began to calm down, Peggy spoke again. "What would happen if you told, Jeanee?"

Jeanee looked straight ahead. Her face took on a frozen expression, and her eyes glazed over as if she were in a trance.

Again Peggy pressed. "Jeanee, can you tell me?"

"My mother," Jeanee whispered. "My mother — he said she would die."

There was a long moment of silence, and then with an abrupt change of emotions, as if she had changed them by flipping a switch, Jeanee looked Peggy directly in the eye. "I told Frank," she said with controlled calmness. "I told him the other night. And he still loves me."

"Did you think he wouldn't?" Peggy asked.

"I didn't tell him everything," Jeanee continued. "He doesn't know how bad it was. But he knows it was bad."

"And that's a beginning," Peggy acknowledged.

"I couldn't tell him everything. I don't want to remember it. I just want to let it stay in the closet."

"Have you gone through your journals?"

Jeanee again stared straight ahead. "The girls are going home tonight."

"How are you feeling about that?" Peggy questioned.

"I'm not sure," Jeanee answered quietly. "I'm just not sure."

The session continued disjointedly from there on. Peggy took mental notes while Jeanee jumped from one topic to another. It became obvious that she was in too much pain to stay on one subject or deal with the great emotional load she was carrying.

The children's visit had opened drawers in the closet of Jeanee's mind, drawers that hadn't been opened in many long years. And until some time had passed, Peggy knew, it would do no good to press ahead.

4:10 P.M.

"Carol, how are you doing?"

Frank sat in Carol Blodgett's living room, keenly aware of the quiet in the home—and of the difference. In the two weeks since he had been there, the furniture had been changed or rearranged. But there was something else, something more than a mere change in furniture.

"I'm fine, Bishop. What do you hear from Mel?"

"Not much," Frank replied. "In fact, he hasn't responded to my last three letters. I've been thinking of taking a Saturday and driving over to see him."

"He'd like that," Carol said softly. "He thinks the world of you, you know."

Frank shifted uneasily. "Anything new on his status?"

"Well, he's still in treatment. As for getting out, who knows? Apparently no decision can be made until his evaluations are completed. And they won't even be started until he has reached a certain point in his treatment—which he has not yet reached."

"Troubles?"

Silently Carol nodded.

"Do you want to talk, Carol?"

Bleakly the woman looked at him. "Mel's going backward, Bishop. He really is. He's denying things again, blaming me for his being in prison, becoming very bitter."

"Poor Mel."

"That's what I've always said. But no more. I'm through feeling sorry for the man. If he doesn't want to accept responsibility, then I'm not going to waste my life waiting around for him. I've contacted my lawyer, Bishop. I want a divorce."

Frank sighed. "I'm sorry to hear that, Carol. But under the circumstances, I understand."

Carol smiled sadly. "I just wish all of us did. Even now my little Trace will come up to me and ask, 'Where's

Daddy?' She still can't understand what it means that her daddy is in prison. And we haven't just abandoned him, either. All this time we've been fighting for him. We've been to see him many times. I didn't want the kids to be bitter toward him because I knew it wouldn't do any of us any good. But I guess there comes a time when you see the rewards are not worth the effort."

"Are you angry with him, Carol?"

Slowly the woman nodded affirmatively. "I wasn't at first, but I am now!"

"Are you in counseling?"

Carol nodded. "And that's been an interesting experience. For some reason I thought all counselors would be the same, but they aren't. I visited with two before I found one I was comfortable with. He's a spiritual person, and he understands my spiritual concerns. He's helping me deal with my anger."

Frank nodded. "Well, I'm happy to hear that, Carol. All of you will do better with appropriate counseling."

"Oh, we're going to make it, Bishop." Carol smiled. "I've had to get a couple of blessings from my father, because every once in a while I feel complete fear. I mean, I have three struggling kids at home, and financially there's no way."

"Do you need help?"

The woman shook her head. "Not yet, at least. If I do, I'll call you."

"Please do that, Carol. In the Lord's church there is no reason for people to go hungry."

For a moment Frank looked deeply into Carol Blodgett's eyes, seeing there the pain and desperation brought about by his friend, but also seeing the resolute determination that was growing within her.

"Heavenly Father," he pleaded silently as he squeezed her hand, "please bless this dear woman, and please protect her wounded little children."

9:05 P.M.

"Hi. Is your daddy home?"

Angie, dressed in her pajamas, looked up at the man on the doorstep. "I'll get him. Will you come in, please?"

Smiling slightly at the child's politeness, Bob Nichol stepped into the entryway and closed the door behind him. He was nervously fighting his emotions, and he had no clear idea of what he wanted to say.

"Bob, it's good to see you!"

Turning, Bob Nichol looked up at the smiling countenance of Frank Greaves, automatically reaching out and shaking his hand.

"H . . . hi, Bishop," he finally stammered. "You got a minute or two?"

Frank immediately grew serious. "You bet. Would you like to come in the living room, or do you need more privacy than that?"

Bob shook his head. "No, this will be fine. I just . . . well, I wanted to ask you a question or two. I won't be very long, I promise."

"Hey," Frank said as he clapped his hand on Bob's shoulder to lead him into the living room, "don't worry about that. We just got back from the airport a little while ago — sending our granddaughters home to their parents. So it's bound to be a quiet night in the Greaves home. Here, sit down and tell me what's on your mind."

For a moment Bob sat silently, his emotions threatening to spin out of control. "I . . . I haven't been to . . . church lately," he finally ventured.

"We've missed you," Frank responded gently.

Bob looked up, his face creased with worry. "Well, I — Bishop, did you know? My wife and I are back together."

"I'm pleased to hear that, Bob."

"She also filed for divorce and gave me a list of ultimatums that I had to agree to."

Frank wondered if Bob would say anything about Claudia's efforts to praise him.

"She says she loves me, and she sure talks like she does. But Bishop, she's given me ninety days to prove I can change, and I don't have the faintest idea what to do about it. I mean, I think I've changed—but she says I haven't, and she's the one who makes the final decision."

Frank shifted position on the couch, mentally praying for help. "Bob," he questioned, voicing the first thing that came into his mind, "do you think Claudia has changed?"

"Oh, yeah!" The man was emphatic.

"For the better?"

Bob nodded. "Absolutely."

"Would she have made those changes had she remained with you these past several months?" The question was asked quietly, yet Frank could see that it had a great impact on Bob Nichol's mind. For long moments he made no answer. Instead he sat unmoving, his eyes never leaving the far upper corner of the wall.

"Bob?" Frank pressed.

"Uh . . . obviously not," Bob slowly answered, his voice hardly above a whisper. And it was only then that Frank could see the tears brimming in the man's upturned eyes.

"Why not?" Frank pressed.

Now the tears splashed down Bob's cheeks, and with a swipe of frustration he wiped them away with the back of his hand.

"Because," he responded, his voice filled with anguish. "Because . . . well . . . because I turned her into what she was before she left me! Me! And I didn't even know it! But now that she's been away from me, she's . . . she's so wonderful . . . " Bob cursed softly. "Bishop Greaves, what did I do to her?"

Watching the man's anguish, Frank wisely ignored the profanity.

"Bishop," Bob finally spoke again, "Claudia isn't the

only one I hurt. You know what I've done to Robby!" Bob buried his face in his hands. "What am I ever going to do? I am a lost soul, damned for what I have done to them, and I deserve it! I truly do . . . "

As Bob wept openly, Frank silently continued his prayer, asking that he be directed in how he might help this man who was finally beginning to acknowledge his errors.

"Bob," he questioned a moment or so later, "when did you first see Claudia after your separation?"

"Two weeks ago. We got together for lunch. I was scared, Bishop. I mean, real scared, just seeing her. It was lots worse than when we were kids. Back then I didn't know much of anything. I mean, I was a returned missionary, but I was so dumb! Why would I have treated her like I did, Bishop? Why?"

"I don't know, Bob. How did your meeting with her go?"

"Lousy, I guess. I couldn't think of anything much to say. I mean, I was so blown away by how she had changed! Then I happened to look at a waitress, I guess, and that was it! The way she left me, I figured it was all over. I was even sort of expecting to be served with divorce papers. But the ultimatum and the offer for a ninety-day trial reconciliation about blew me away."

Soberly Frank looked at the man before him, the man who had for so long terrorized both Claudia and Robby. "How have you felt about the past few days?"

"Besides feeling like I'm hanging on the edge of heaven but losing my fingernails as I slip off, you mean?"

Frank smiled. "In other words, you'd really like to change enough to stay with her?"

"I'll say I would." Bob's words were emphatic.

"Enough to meet Claudia's ultimatums, as you call them?"

"I . . . don't know," Bob responded slowly, doubt again in his voice. "Some of them are pretty tough."

"Such as?" Frank asked.

"Such as praying regularly. I . . . I don't know if I can do that, Bishop. I feel too evil."

"Are you reading the scriptures?"

Again the man shook his head. "But that's another one of her items."

"All right, Bob. It's bottom-line, brass-tacks time. You do what Claudia asks and you keep her and maybe even get Robby back. You don't do as she asks, and your family is history. How high a price are you willing to pay for happiness?"

For a moment the look of anguish remained. But then gradually it was replaced by one of hope. "Do you think I can do it, Bishop?"

"I know you can, with the Lord's help."

"You mean He'd help me, after what I've done?"

"Yes. And I'll help you, too," Frank said. "Whatever you've done in the past, you can change and become a completely new man, if you'll let the Lord help you."

"You really believe that, Bishop?" Bob asked.

Soberly Frank nodded.

"Even after what I've done?"

Again Frank nodded, a smile filling his whole face. "He's just waiting for you to openly acknowledge and confess all your sins."

"Then I'm going to do it!" Bob declared. "I mean that, Bishop. If there's even the smallest chance that I can have my family back, I'll do whatever I have to do.

28

MONDAY, APRIL 20

12:27 P.M.

"Frank, sit me down and throw a rope on me!"

Looking up, Frank grinned at Mrs. O. "What's up, cousin?" It was only then that he realized how upset the woman was.

"I am so angry!" Mrs. O. fumed as she sat in a student desk in front of Frank. "You'd better stop me, or I'll do something we'll all be sorry for!"

"Hey," Frank said as he tried to calm her, "what's wrong?"

"That *woman* is what's wrong! She's out of control, Frank, and I can't stand to watch it anymore!"

"What woman? Who are you talking about?"

Mrs. O. took a deep breath. "Mrs. McCrasky, Frank. June McCrasky's mother."

"Ahhh."

"Yeah, I'd say ahhh! Do you know what she's done now? I happened to glance in June's mad book a few minutes ago. She left it out, and as I was putting it away I noticed today's entry."

Mrs. O. was trembling, and Frank walked to her and put his hand on her shoulder. "Settle down, cuz. Just take it easy, and we'll see what we can do."

"I . . . I'm okay," Mrs. O. said finally. "I just—Oh, what's the use?"

"We'll see. Now, about Elaine McCrasky?"

386

"Is that her name? Interesting. That sounds like such a calm, gentle name. Ha!" Mrs. O.'s expression changed from anger to concern.

"Frank, remember how we've worried that June doesn't eat with her friends? Well, there's a reason why she doesn't."

"Which is?"

"Because for some reason or other June's step-mother — Elaine — has a phobia about weight. She's forever on June's case about getting fat — that to a little girl who, soaking wet, couldn't weigh eighty pounds."

"That's why June eats alone?"

Mrs. O. nodded. "You'd eat alone, too, if you were given the skimpy lunches June brings to school. Many days she isn't even *allowed* to eat lunch. In fact, two weeks ago the poor thing got so hungry she stole a lunch from one of the other children and ate it in the bathroom. Then she felt so guilty she came and told me about it. And all because Elaine McCrasky thinks she's going to grow up to be fat.

"Anyway, Saturday morning the woman baked an angel food cake. Someone came along and picked off the little points on the cake's whirls, and June got the blame. Never mind that she denied it. She was slapped along into the mother's bedroom, forced into one of the mother's tight girdles — over her clothes, I might add — forced to eat that entire cake, and made to sit on a low stool all day, still in the girdle. And all the while she was being called names, such as stupid, fat, ugly, obese, and so on, and receiving a continual lecture about dishonesty, stealing, and mostly about how ugly and fat she was going to grow up to be."

"Are you sure about this, Mrs. O.?"

Mrs. O. looked incredulous. "Am I sure? Can I read? Can I see all the signs of a little girl so traumatized that she's being destroyed? Yes, Frank, I'm sure! Would you like to read what she wrote?"

Slowly Frank shook his head. "I . . . don't think so. I think maybe it's better if I don't read June's book."

Mrs. O. sighed. "There's more. About noon June's two little brothers confessed to the crime of pinching off the cake tips."

"Well, that's good, isn't it?"

"You'd think so. And Mrs. McCrasky acknowledged the two boys' confessions, all right. But then she declared nonetheless that June had gotten away with enough in the past to justify the punishment continuing until the end of the day. And it did — names, diatribe, the girdle, the low stool — every bit of it!

"I'm telling you, Frank, something's got to be done! That little girl is being beaten up in ways she can't even begin to deal with. Not only is she being abused and labeled for now, which is bad enough, but she is being told exactly what she'll be like in the future — stupid, fat, and ugly. And of course what will happen is that these horrendous pronouncements will become a self-fulfilling prophecy, because people tend to become their labels. I'm telling you, June will end up just the way Elaine McCrasky is telling her she will."

"Does that have to happen?" Frank asked.

"Of course not, if somebody can break the cycle of abuse. But I'm not having much luck from my classroom. In one afternoon that woman has undone everything I've tried to do this whole past year!

"Frank, you're her bishop. You know it's you who needs to step in with this. Don't you?"

Slowly Frank nodded, his heart heavy with trepidation. "Yes," he sighed heavily, "I know."

1:45 P.M.

Jeanee sat in the rocking chair in Tony's newly decorated bedroom. The house was empty and quiet. Outside the window little white clouds passed overhead. And the azure blue of the sky was a reminder that spring was about to begin.

Jeanee was numb, her mind confused. She had moped around the house over the weekend, trying to get interested in something, unable to focus on anything but the emptiness she felt inside.

On the wall beside her hung the picture of the Savior with the children. It was the only picture in the room. Jeanee thought of Nicole's innocent comprehension of His atonement. She remembered Amber's nightmares and her drawings and wondered if Tony and Megan would finally do something about getting their little daughter in for counseling. With those drawings as tangible evidence, maybe they wouldn't put it off any longer.

Rocking back and forth, Jeanee almost felt a kind of comfort in her innermost self, as if another part of her was being cradled and comforted as she rocked. She looked around the safety of her beautiful little room and almost felt another presence, separate from her. But who?

"Why am I so empty?" she agonized in silence. "What is wrong with me?"

For a moment she looked up at the little stuffed animals she used to go to for comfort, and without realizing what she was doing, she reached up and grabbed her favorite and most worn teddy bear and snuggled it close.

"Oh, bear," she whispered. "Sad little no-name bear. Are you empty too? Do you live in a vacuum like I do?"

Walking out the door, still hugging the teddy bear close, Jeanee moved down the stairs to Frank's music room. His life was so full. He knew who he was, and this room reflected it. On the walls, pictures and posters of his teenage years were hung everywhere. Little mementoes he had gathered from his youth were also scattered about. This room was him. All his things spoke of who he was.

A tear escaped Jeanee's eyes as she thought of how

patient he had been with her lately. Did that come from the security he knew from his childhood?

Just above his desk was a picture of Frank and his parents when they had first taken him home from the hospital. They looked so proud. His face was scrunched, but even then he was beautiful. Above that was a collage of pictures from his childhood and early teens that his mother had sent one year for Christmas. What a neat gift that had been! And scattered around the pictures were his Scout achievements, all framed and impressive.

Frank had experienced life. Jeanee had hidden hers in the journals of her closet. There were no mementoes on the wall from her childhood, no pictures—

Suddenly Jeanee was seized with an idea. The room—the room she had decorated for Amber and Nicole. It had really been for her! It was her room—a safe place for her to go when she needed to get in touch with her feelings—the safe room she had never had when she was a little girl.

Only, it was missing something. It needed pictures of *her* childhood. Did she dare call her mother and ask for them? Jeanee struggled against the idea. But it was no use. A deep yearning had entered her soul.

She *had* to reach back into her past. She had to have those photographs. She didn't know why, but she was sure that once she had them, she would be able to start once again to live her life.

9:00 P.M.

"Bishop, do you have a minute?"

Frank, listening carefully into the telephone, was not certain he recognized the voice. "Sure I do," he replied. "This is . . . ?"

"Bob Nichol," the man responded. "Bishop, something's going on, something I don't understand. I feel awful, and no matter how I pray or what I do, things just get more bleak. I've never felt such despair—"

Bob was speaking so rapidly that Frank had a hard time following him. His voice was different, higher maybe, or more strained.

"Bob," Frank said, interrupting, "slow down. Better yet, start at the beginning. What's happened since we visited here in my living room?"

"Wow," Bob replied, taking a deep breath, "that's a question, all right. Okay, the beginning. After we talked I thought about things all that night. I decided I wanted to start this right, so yesterday morning I began a fast—"

"A complete fast?"

"Yeah, from all food and drink. I fasted all day yesterday, and then this morning I took off work and drove to the mountains. I spent all day there, just hiking and thinking. At one point, knowing I was absolutely alone, I covenanted with the Lord that if He would show me how to get my family back, I would give up all my sins."

"I'm glad to hear that," Frank declared sincerely.

"Well, I had just been reading in the Book of Mormon about Lamoni's father and how he had done that, and—Bishop, you can't know how great that felt! It was the most wonderful feeling. I know He heard my prayer, and I really felt close to Him. In fact, and I hope you don't think I'm weird, Bishop, but I think maybe angels were rejoicing over my decision."

"I can easily believe that," Frank said softly.

"Well, anyway, I came home higher than a kite. I felt so excited, so ready for what I was sure was coming. I couldn't wait to tell Claudia. Only, only now—"

"What is it, Bob?"

"I . . . I don't know. I am in such incredible despair that I can't even describe it. Everything seems hopeless, impossible. I pray and nothing happens, I read the scriptures and feel nothing—"

"Bob?"

"Yes?"

"What about your sins? Do you find yourself thinking more and more about them?"

There was a long silence, and Frank had the feeling that Bob was struggling with his emotions. "Y-yes," the man finally whispered. "I'm experiencing some really convicting memories of my sins."

"Did you ask the Lord to help you repent?"

"I . . . did."

"Then it's started," Frank said quietly. "Bob, this is what you prayed for, and now you must bear up while you come to grips with how Heavenly Father perceives your actions."

"I didn't know He would do this."

"Well, He's done it for others. Do you have your Doctrine and Covenants handy?"

"Uh-huh."

"Good. Read me verse 3 of section 66."

There was a moment's pause, and then Bob began reading.

"Verily I say unto you, my servant William, that you are clean, but not all; repent, therefore, of those things which are not pleasing in my sight, saith the Lord, for the Lord will show them unto you."

"He's showing my sins to me?" Bob asked incredulously.

"I'd say so."

"But . . . but what can I do about them?"

"What do you feel directed to do?"

Again there was a pause. "I . . . I have to . . . tell Claudia. I have to . . . apologize to her . . . "

"Then do it, as soon as you can. And Bob, once you have this taken care of?"

"Yes?"

"Get ready for memories of more sins for which you

have never repented. They won't come any faster than you can handle them. But neither will they stop until, with the Lord's grace, you have taken care of every obstacle that is keeping you from full fellowship with His Spirit."

"Serious?"

"I'm very serious."

"O-okay," Bob said, and Frank could almost see his shoulders slumping with despair. "And Bishop, pray for me, please pray—"

29

TUESDAY, APRIL 21

6:40 P.M.

"Are you sure you're okay?" Frank asked into the telephone. Jeanee hadn't looked good at dinner. And when he had come home from school that afternoon, she had been sitting in Tony's redecorated bedroom, rocking and humming to herself. He was worried.

"I'm fine," Jeanee assured him. "I just need some time to work through . . . some feelings. Thanks for taking Angie to Trace's."

Out of habit Frank looked at his planner. But he knew he couldn't cancel his interview with Elaine McCraskey. Still, if it were an emergency—

"Really, Jeanee," he coaxed. "If you need me to come home, you know I will. I worry about you when you're there all alone and feeling the way you do."

"Frank, really. I'm . . . just a little down. But I'm not alone—not really. You do your interviews and forget about me. Besides, when summer comes, you're going to have more of me than you know what to do with."

"Now, that I can handle!" Frank said. "I won't be late tonight, honey. Not much after eight. Then I'll stop by Blodgett's and pick up Angie, and we'll be home."

Just then there was a knock on the door of the bishop's office.

"Gotta go, Babe," Frank apologized. "Looks like I have a customer."

6:45 P.M.

"Why didn't I stop him? What have I *done* to my family?"

Tish Blodgett sat across the desk from Frank, her dark eyes filled with tears of desperation.

"My family is breaking apart, Bishop. The one thing I feared the most. And it's all my fault!"

"You feel responsible for your parent's divorce?" Frank asked, handing a couple of tissues to the sobbing young woman.

"Well, who else? I'm the one who insisted we tell!"

"But Tish," Frank insisted, "you did the right thing."

"Really, bishop? Try telling that to my insides!"

Tish dapped at tears that returned each time she wiped them away. "You know, if I really pleaded, Dad wouldn't do it to me. So now I think, 'Why didn't I plead more often?' Sometimes I used to warn Tess to stay away from him, too. But I didn't warn her all the time. Why didn't I? I knew what was going on."

"You feel responsible for all of this?" Frank asked, carefully trying to comprehend the guilt this young girl was feeling.

"Who else, Bishop? I could tell when Dad got with one of my sisters. I knew. It was always the same. After it happened, he'd always get so sweet with Mom, real sugary, and I would know. Then I'd go into my room and bawl, because I hadn't stopped it again.

"One time, Bishop, I knew Dad had Tess in the bathroom. I knew it! So what did I do? Instead of barging in on them and making Dad stop it, I timidly knocked on the door and told Tess I needed her in the kitchen. Boy, if only I had that one to do over again!"

"But Tish," Frank explained gently, "you were only a little girl, and your father is a big man. I think you're being too hard on yourself."

"Do you know how little?"

Frank was at a loss. "No Tish, I don't."

"I was four, Bishop. Four years old." Tish's eyes dropped to the floor. "That's when it started. All those years and I never told! I wanted to so many times. But I didn't!"

"You were probably afraid." Frank stated.

"Oh, I was," Tish agreed. "I was so afraid! I mean, I didn't want to hurt Mom. And I didn't want to see Dad get in trouble. But my real fear—my real fear, Bishop, was that he and Mom would get a divorce. And now look at what's happening!"

Tears brimmed in the young girl's eyes, and Frank remained silent, waiting.

"You know," she finally continued, "he did it with Trace, too. We all know he did. But now he's denying it and blaming Mom, denying that it was really his problem. How can he do that?"

Frank shook his head, thinking to himself about his own conversation with Mel about being totally honest.

"That's why Mom has had it with him," Tish continued. "I . . . I just wish she'd waited until he got out of jail. Did you hear Tess ran away again?"

"Again?" Frank asked, surprised.

"Yeah, Sunday. With some kid from the other school. She was gone all afternoon and night. I know why she's running away, Bishop. She told me."

Frank sat forward. "Why?"

"Because she thinks she's a slut. She's called herself that for a long time. Then when all this about Dad and us hit the papers, some of the kids, including some of them here in the ward, started calling both of us that—and other things that are even worse. So Tess gave up and said, 'Okay, I'll be a slut.' And that's what she's doing."

"But . . . but she isn't that way, Tish." Frank was frustrated, and it showed in his voice. "She's a sweet little girl who has been terribly victimized by her father."

Tish was scornful. "Other people aren't quite that kind, Bishop. You should have heard some of the things Sister Byston said to Mom a couple of weeks ago. Tess and I happened to be in the hall, so we could hear everything she said. I even tried to drag Tess away, but she wouldn't go. It was that night that she first ran away."

Sadly Frank shook his head. "Oh, Tish, if only your dad could have seen the damage he was doing."

"I just wish he could see it now."

Frank nodded his agreement. "Is Tess in therapy?"

"Mom's trying to get her in, but she says it makes her feel yucky talking about it, and besides, she doesn't believe it will do any good."

"Well, from what I'm learning, it does take time."

Tish shook her head. "She isn't going to have much of that if she doesn't shape up. That kid she goes with scares me. But she won't listen, so I don't know what to do anymore. Besides," and tears again filled her eyes, "what good can I do for somebody else when I can't even keep my own boat from tipping over?"

There was a knock at the door, and Tish blew her nose and wiped at her eyes with the back of her hand. "That's for me," she explained, standing up. "I'm conducting the Young Women's meeting tonight, and I asked Michelle to knock for me when it was time. Thanks, Bishop. I appreciate you talking to me."

"Are you going to be okay?" Frank asked, standing behind his desk.

Tish took a deep breath to steady herself and forced a smile. "Oh yeah, Bishop" she answered, "I'm getting pretty good at faking it."

Concern in his voice, Bishop Greaves walked closer. "Let's do this again, Tish. Next week, same time?"

"You sure?" Tish asked, looking puzzled.

"Absolutely. Somebody once told me there's nothing better for getting rid of painful memories than talking them away. Whatever else I am, I'm a good listener."

Tish grinned. "Angie says you're a good boogeyer, too."

"Hey," Frank teased, "don't go spreading that around the ward. I wouldn't want to spoil my reputation."

Then, a note of seriousness in his voice, he added, "Tish, I hope you know what a choice young woman you are. I mean that. I want you to know how much I love and admire you."

Smiling through tears, Tish barely whispered. "I . . . love you, too, Bishop Greaves. And thanks."

7:00 P.M.

Elaine McCrasky sighed as she sat down. "Was that Tish Blodgett I saw leaving here with Michelle?"

Silently Frank nodded.

"The poor child! I . . . feel so sorry for that family."

"How are you getting along?" Frank asked, considering the task that lay ahead.

"I . . . I'm fine. I just—" Elaine's voice faltered and stopped. Then, with a deep breath that was more like a sob, she looked with pleading eyes toward Frank. "No, no I'm not fine, and I'm tired of pretending I am! There's something wrong with me, something terribly wrong!"

Frank regarded his neighbor without speaking. He had been praying for some way to get Sister McCrasky to open up. But he hadn't expected such a direct answer.

"I . . . I'm out of control," Elaine continued. "And I don't know why. I scream at my kids, I'm always losing my temper over the most foolish little things, I . . . But you probably know all this already. The way I sound, I'm sure the whole neighborhood thinks I'm a real witch!

"Do you know what I found myself doing a little while ago? I mean this very night? June is terribly hard for me to deal with, Bishop. I . . . I don't know why. It feels like she's always trying to put something over on me — to get away with something. I know she's only a little girl, but the way she looks at me, never saying a word —

"Anyway, tonight she was outside with the boys and I could hear all this screaming going on. When I looked, there she was, screaming at one of the boys and slapping his face.

"Well, I just lost it. I grabbed her, dragged her into the kitchen, and lit into her. I mean, I started slapping her face, hard, and screaming at her. And do you know what I was saying? 'We don't hit people in this family!' All the time I was slapping her face I was yelling that, over and over again. Can you imagine that, Bishop? Here I am, hitting my child and yelling at the same time that we don't do that in our family!"

Elaine took a tissue from her purse and wiped nervously at her eyes.

"Bishop, what's wrong with me? Have I gone . . . crazy?"

Slowly Frank shook his head to the contrary. "No, I don't think so. But I know what you do with the kids isn't good," he stated softly.

Elaine McCrasky shuddered and lowered her eyes. "I know that, too. And I hate myself for it! But I always start out trying to help them. I really do. When I married Ralph I promised myself that I'd be as good a mother to those kids as their real mother had been. But something went wrong, Bishop. I . . . I don't know what, but I can't make them love me.

"Ralph isn't any help, either!" she continued angrily after a deep breath. "He's never home, and when he is, he refuses to get involved in any discipline. They're his kids! But he leaves everything to me!"

In the silence that followed, Frank found his mind racing. For a long time he had been wanting to give this woman a piece of his mind. As her bishop, he had felt inclined to call her to repentance. But now, listening to the poor woman's struggles, he had no such inclinations.

"Elaine," Frank said gently, his words guided from something beyond himself, "tell me about your parents and the home where you grew up."

The woman's face softened. "My parents. They were wonderful. My mother was sick a lot, but I really loved her."

"And your father?"

"Daddy," Elaine smiled. "It wasn't easy for him to make a living. He had to go where the work was, which meant he was sometimes gone for days and weeks at a time. But oh, I loved him, too."

"If he was gone, Elaine, and your mother was sick so much, how did she ever run the house?"

"Oh, she didn't run it," Elaine replied quickly, her expression turning from tenderness to anger. "My oldest sister did that. She was the boss, and all of us knew it, too. She got very upset if we didn't obey her instantly—me especially."

"Did your oldest sister do a lot of yelling?" Frank asked carefully.

"Yelling? I . . . don't remember, but I don't think so. Why are you asking these questions, Bishop?"

For a moment Frank paused. "Before I answer that, let me ask one more question. Was your mother heavy?"

Elaine laughed. "Mother heavy? Not hardly. In fact, she was very tiny. No, the only one in my family who was heavy, at least back then, was my sister."

"The one who was the boss?"

"No." Elaine smiled a puzzled smile. "The other one. The talented one. She was gone all the time, doing this, that, and the other, so she got out of everything. Now, what is all this about?"

Frank leaned forward. "Elaine, I'm not a therapist. But may I point out some things that I find interesting?"

The woman nodded.

"First, you admit that you have become a harsh disciplinarian. Right?"

"Unfortunately, yes." Elaine looked down at her hands.

"Second, you have special problems with June, who is the eldest daughter."

"Correct."

"Third, you have some very bitter feelings about Ralph not being there to help you with the children. And fourth, you have a real problem about the possibility of June's becoming overweight."

"How do you know that?" Elaine's face instantly showed her dismay.

"Because," Frank said as quietly as he could, "I'm June's bishop, too."

Blinking, Elaine digested that news, which she had obviously never before considered. "Then . . . you probably know all about the girdle incident," she said quietly.

"I do."

"Did she tell you she was innocent?" Elaine demanded, her voice suddenly filled with anger.

Frank shook his head. "Actually, Elaine, she never told me a thing. She wrote about it in her mad book, not knowing that anyone else would ever see it."

"But you did?"

Again Frank shook his head to the contrary. "Elaine, I don't want you to get hung up on this. That the incident occurred is sufficient for our discussion."

"But . . . but you're accusing me—"

Raising his hand, Frank interrupted the woman. "I'm not accusing you of anything. Now, take a deep breath and then tell me whether or not you are deeply concerned about June's possible weight gain."

Elaine did as she was told and slowly nodded.

"Very well, now let's look at four more items. One, you were essentially raised by a harsh disciplinarian — your sister. Two, that same sister was the eldest girl in your family. Three, frequently neither your father nor your mother were there to save you from her stern anger. And four, your sister who seemed to get away with everything was overweight."

Elaine took a deep breath. "I . . . haven't ever thought of this. Bishop, might this be why . . . Oh, I would give anything to know why I do the things I do!"

"Elaine," Frank declared, "as I said, I don't pretend to know why or even if these things are related. But I am slowly learning that everything we do is influenced by our experiences and attitudes from the past.

"Now, you said you would give anything to know?"

Elaine nodded vigorously. "Yes, yes, I would."

"Very well. Do you know Brother Hark Wixom?"

"I . . . don't think so."

"He's over LDS Social Services for this area. I want you to go see him, Elaine. With your permission I'd like to tell him what you and I have discussed — "

"A therapist?"

"Brother Wixom is a very knowledgeable counselor."

"But can he help? I mean, really help?"

"I'm very confidant that he can," Frank assured her.

"This is a scary step you're suggesting, Bishop." Elaine fidgeted in her chair.

"Change takes courage, Sister McCrasky. Would you rather leave things as they are?"

Elaine shuddered. "No. Absolutely not. Things can't stay that way, not if June and I are to survive."

"Then — "

"Call Brother Wixom, Bishop. If you believe it will help, I'm willing."

Standing, Elaine McCrasky reached her hand forward

to shake Frank's hand. "Thank you, Bishop," she smiled hopefully. "Thank you for taking the time to hear me out."

9:00 P.M.

Jeanee was sitting on the floor of the room she was coming to accept as her "safe room" when Frank and Angie walked in the front door. Her journals were scattered around her in piles. And she was reading them through tears of joy.

"Anyone alive in here?" Frank asked, coming up the stairs and peaking his head through the door. "All the lights were out. I thought maybe you had gone to bed."

Jeanee looked up and smiled. "I'm more alive than I've maybe ever been."

With a curious look, Frank stepped in. "Angie," he called back out into the hall, "go and get your jammies on, punkin, and then Daddy will be in to kiss you goodnight."

"Without family prayer?" Angie peaked her head in the door.

"We'll both be in," Jeanee smiled.

"Okay." And Angie was off.

"So tell me," Frank said, seating himself on the bed. "What miracles have been happening in the Greaves home tonight?"

"Miracles?"

"I detect a major change in your countenance, my love," Frank stated tenderly.

"Oh, Frank," Jeanee breathed, "I can't tell you. There are no words! But let me show you something here in my journal. It was something I wrote before my father died, about—well, you read it."

Frank took the journal Jeanee handed him and began reading.

I have been praying for my father for years now, asking
Heavenly Father to help me to forgive him. Years—and nothing

*happened, except turmoil and occasional times of happiness.
But one morning last week, as I was praying, I felt prompted
to get up and go to the shelf to get a particular book. It was
an old book, the cover was torn. But I felt an overwhelming
power drawing me to pick it up. I did, and it fell open to a
chapter entitled "The Healing of The Memories."*

*Strange, but as I began reading the first sentence, my whole
body began sobbing. From the very center of my being this
heaving sorrow came pouring out. I read about the Savior's
ability to go through the wreckage of our past with us, and how
when we were children, we didn't understand some of the things
that happened to us. But if, as adults, we would invite Him to
go back and journey through those years with us, He would be
able to heal us and make us whole. The book suggested we
imagine Him there with us during the time we were being
abused, holding and comforting us and telling us He would
protect us and take the pain Himself so we wouldn't have to
suffer it.*

*I was so impressed with this message. It was a marvelous,
powerful message that entered my very soul. And I knew this
was what I was supposed to do. So I picked up my pen and
began writing the memories as they came to my mind, imagining
as I did that the Savior was there with the little child I used to
be.*

*As I did, I experienced a lot of pain. I remembered some
terrible things. And they ripped at my soul. I realized my father
wasn't my only abuser, there had been others. These memories
came to my mind so vividly. It was as if they were all super-
imposed over what I was experiencing at that very moment. It
was as if I were reliving everything I was writing. And as I
wrote, I felt the same relief on a spiritual level I had felt as a
child when a large boil had been lanced. And I had perfect
faith that this was what I was to be doing, even though it was
painful.*

*My husband was aware of what I was experiencing. I kept
writing for days, weeping, going through agony of soul. Even
though he wasn't active in the Church at the time, he went to
my bishop and told him he was worried I was going off the deep
end. And the bishop tried to convince me I should leave the past*

*alone and not allow myself to remember such terrible things,
that it would very likely bring me unhappiness and not effect
any improvement in my life at all. I listened to what he had to
say. And I wanted to be obedient. But there was this deeper
message in my soul from the Spirit. It told me, "Keep writing.
Keep writing."*

Frank put the journal down and looked at his wife, who
was still sitting on the floor, smiling.

"Did this happen while you were still married to Earl?"
he asked.

"Mmm hmm."

"You've never told me about it."

"I couldn't, without telling you things I was afraid for
you to know." Jeanee stood up and turned the page.
"Here," she said, "please read — this."

Frank looked down and continued reading.

*After a few days, my whole world was shrouded in pain,
physical and spiritual pain beyond anything I had ever experienced. It felt like there was a band around my mind, squeezing
tighter and tighter until I just couldn't bear it. And I wondered
if I shouldn't have remembered all the terrible things my father
had done to me. I pleaded with Heavenly Father to stop the
pain. And it only got worse, till I thought it might destroy me
completely.*

*Then I went to my bedroom and knelt again in prayer. Not
that I wasn't praying already — I had continued praying for
days as the pain became increasingly worse.*

*Finally exhausted, I lay on my bed. Everything in my world
was pain. Everything was shrouded with a pervading fog of
anguish. There was no peace. I was alone. My body began
drifting off to sleep. And as I had been doing in the previous
days, even as I was falling to sleep, I was pleading with Heavenly Father. And all through my prayer the pain was excruciating. In fact, I was sure I would die. Finally, in anguish,
thinking I might be destroyed, I prayed for the first time in the
name of Jesus.*

I can remember saying "Heavenly Father, if you would do it for Alma, wouldn't you do it for me? If I pray in the name of Jesus Christ, wouldn't you take this terrible pain from me?"

I can't adequately describe what happened next. It was like my soul was being drawn to a very center place. It happened so fast. All the pain I was feeling was drawn, like a current of water, through a small opening, then expanded with such a brightness that every grief was washed and burned away. And I was aware only of a beautiful, piercing, peaceful voice. Every cell of my body heard it, like a mighty rushing of water, shaking and cleansing. Yet it was still, perfect and more beautiful than any voice I've ever heard.

"Jeanee," Frank looked down at his wife with tears in his eyes. "You heard the Savior's voice."

Jeanee could only nod her head and smile through the tears falling down her cheeks.

"But this was several years ago."

"And I've asked myself," Jeanee whispered, "why, if I forgave him, if I *really* forgave him, why have I started having problems again?

"Frank, it was an incredible experience! From the moment I heard His voice, there was no pain! I opened my eyes to a room that moments before had held so much heaviness and sorrow. But suddenly, it was beautiful! The only thing I can compare it to is, as a child, seeing something for the first time, seeing a butterfly or silver dew on the web of a spider, or feeling rain in your mouth, or smelling a flower—for the first time. When I opened my eyes in that room, everything was new!

"I was new." Jeanee added quietly.

Frank shook his head and looked lovingly at his wife. "I had no idea you had been going through this for such a long time."

"I had felt such bitterness toward my father." Jeanee spoke through tears. "But, after this experience, it was completely gone! The Savior took every angry unforgiving thought I had ever had—and made me clean.

"Frank, I've made some serious mistakes in my life."

"We all have, Jeanee."

"And He forgave me. And the years since then have been wonderful. In spite of Earl's death, the Lord has blessed me so much, meeting you the way I did, starting our family together. But then, what happened to Amber—

"Frank, I don't fully understand what has been going on with me these past few months. And I'm sorry for the worry I've put you through. But I've been so confused! There have been times when I've even doubted that the Lord knew I was here.

"And then, tonight, alone here reading my journals, I felt His love so profoundly." Jeanee's voice was shaking with emotion, and she was almost overcome with the feeling that she was being lifted off the floor. "Oh, Frank," she breathed, "I don't know what He has in store for me. But, I'm willing to go through it, whatever it is, because I know, somehow, He is going to turn it for good."

PART FIVE

REMEMBERING

I see
Yesterday
That great hole
That left me
Empty and
Wounded

And
In remembering
I am open
To be
Healed

30

FRIDAY, JUNE 12

7:15 A.M.

"Hi, Claudia." Frank stood holding the telephone and trying to do up the last of his shirt buttons.

"I hope I haven't called you too early?" the woman asked.

"No," Frank smiled, "it isn't too early. In fact, another few minutes and you'd have missed me. Two-day youth outing, you know. Angie, Erik, and I are all going."

"That's right," Claudia responded, remembering. "I wish Robby was going too."

"So do I," Frank agreed. "I asked him, you know. Last week. But he said he was too busy."

Claudia sighed. "That's just an excuse, Bishop. Nothing more."

"I guessed as much. How can I help you, Claudia?"

The woman took a deep breath. "It . . . it's Bob. Bishop, I'm scared for him. I really am. I don't know exactly what's happening, but I don't think it's good."

"What do you mean?"

"I've never seen him like this. I say something nice to him and he cries. He looks out the window and cries. He reads his scriptures and cries. And something else. When he's home I'll bet he goes in that bedroom to pray twenty times a day! Who knows what goes on at work? I don't know what's going on, but I'm scared for him. I think you need to talk to him and see if you can get some stability back into his life."

Frank took a deep breath. "Have you prayed about this, Claudia?"

"No, I haven't. But I think I see signs of a nervous breakdown."

Frank's expression was sober. "How long has it been, Claudia, since you read Alma the Younger's experience with the mighty change?"

"I . . . don't know."

"I'd like you to read it again."

"Are you saying that Bob is experiencing the mighty change?"

"I believe so."

"Then this is what I've been praying for?"

"Again, I think so. The scriptures call it Godly sorrow, Claudia, meaning that it is a righteous sorrow that leads to God. Read 2 Corinthians chapter 7 verse 10, and you'll see that it's not something you'll want to stop."

Frank reached for his other sock. "Christ taught that every individual needs to be born again, and, after his mighty spiritual rebirth, Alma reiterated the same thing. Every individual needs to experience the mighty change. But as for suffering the degree of sorrow that Bob is enduring, I suspect that depends on the individual. Bob has done some pretty wicked things, so I believe this awful remembering he is going through is the consequence of the choices he has made."

Frank stood and stepped into his old shoes.

"Then I shouldn't try to talk him out of it," Claudia declared thoughtfully.

"Certainly not. Claudia, read Alma's experience again and see if you don't agree that what happened to him and what is now happening to your husband have some remarkable similarities. Oh, and one other thing. Let's keep this discussion to ourselves for now. Bob deserves the right to make a few more discoveries on his own."

10:30 A.M.

Jeanee was in the kitchen cleaning cherries to take to Abby Martin when the doorbell rang.

"Just a minute, please!" she called to the insistent chimes. "I'm coming." And tucking her towel over the oven door handle, she hurried toward the front of the house.

"Marie!" her whole countenance beamed. "Marie! What a pleasant surprise."

"Am I still welcome here?" Marie smiled apologetically.

Jeanee just laughed. "Well, if you're not, no one is! My gosh but it's good to see you! What's happening in your life? What have you been doing with yourself?"

Following Jeanee into the kitchen, Marie laughed agreeably. "In the order of questions asked: My life is changing drastically. And I'm doing a lot of reading."

For a moment the two women simply looked at each other. Then they sat at the counter.

"Are you mad at me?" Marie asked cautiously, breaking the silence.

"You mean about never returning my calls?" Jeanee shook her head in mock disgust. "No. I take that kind of rejection real well."

"I've been terrible," Marie conceded.

"Actually, yes. But then I've had a few rough months myself, so who am I to—"

"What's been wrong?" Marie was suddenly concerned.

"The doctors tell me I had your nervous breakdown."

"No!"

"That's what I keep saying. But it looks like that's what happened."

"And I probably helped cause it." Marie was suddenly serious.

Jeanee shook her head. "No, hon. I managed that all by myself. But I'm working on it, too. I'm in therapy and—"

"Jeanee, you hide it well."

"From what I'm hearing, that's part of my problem. But let's talk about you, Marie. I can't wait to hear what's been happening in your life."

Marie reached inside her oversized purse and pulled out Jeanee's well-worn copy of *The Miracle of Forgiveness*. "I'm eating a lot of humble pie," she answered.

Without saying a word, Jeanee arose and filled two glasses with ice.

"I've got some apologizing to do to your husband," Jeanee's old friend admitted. "And he's not the only one."

"So the book is helping?" Jeanee asked, filing the glasses with cool water from the fridge.

"Helping? Ha! That darn book!" Marie shook her head. "You knew how it would affect me, didn't you?"

"I know how it affected me." Jeanee sat down beside her friend and handed her a glass.

"Well, at first I hated it!" Marie flared. "I got so depressed when I first started reading it, I couldn't go on."

Jeanee nodded knowingly. The book had affected her the same way—at first.

"So I went therapist shopping." Marie laughed irreverently. "The first one suggested I was too straitlaced. Can you imagine? Me, straitlaced? He suggested I should be open to extramarital affairs to regain the feeling of sexual control that my abuse took from me."

"You're kidding!" Jeanee almost choked on her water.

"True story." Marie shook her head. "The second therapist I didn't care for. He insisted that I go back into all the painful details. The third one simply didn't know anything. I mean, that woman needed her own therapist! But then I ran into someone down in the professional building, a Doctor Witt."

"You mean Peggy?" Jeanee was beaming.

"You know her?"

"And love her!" Jeanee smiled.

"Well," Marie nodded her head, "she knows what she's doing. I've made more progress since I've been seeing her than I've made in the past ten—twenty years!

"She helped me find the courage to read your book. I've even started praying again. And—I'm ready to see your husband to confess *my* sins, instead of someone else's."

10:55 A.M.

Jeanee was laughing through tears of joy. "Oh, Marie, that's how I felt when I finished that book. I had been convinced that there was no hope for me, that I was a lost cause. But once I endured that book—"

"It was a monster!" Marie teased. "And now I'm returning it to its rightful owner. And I'm boldly collecting on a promise."

"Promise?" Jeanee was puzzled.

"You promised to answer some of my questions."

Jeanee became uneasy.

"When I first came to see you, you told me it was no coincidence that I was here—"

"I can vaguely remember that," Jeanee admitted.

"Don't say anything," Marie continued forthrightly. "Because I'm not really going to collect on that promise. I just want you to know I've come to realize something. While I was reading the book, as I read the places you marked, I knew why you understood what I was going through."

Jeanee remained quiet.

"You're no stranger to the path I walk."

It was a statement, not a question. And no answer was required. Relieved and gratified, Jeanee realized that without revealing anything about her past, she had been able to share her testimony of hope with her friend.

"We're totally different people," Marie continued. "And I guess it's only natural we'd find our own different ways to travel that path and find our answers."

"What do you mean?" Jeanee asked.

"Well, I'm prolifically abrasive at times, in case your husband hasn't told you." Marie laughed easily. "You, you're the subtle, reticent type."

"Not always." Jeanee laughed. "Just ask Frank!"

"You mean you've put him through it too?" Marie shook her head.

"Still am, I'm afraid." Jeanee grimaced.

"Well, good." Marie smiled approvingly. "It's good to know you're developing an assertive edge."

"Assertive edge, huh?" Jeanee smiled. "Is that what you call it?"

Her friend nodded, and Jeanee reached over to squeeze her hand. "I've missed you, Marie," she whispered. "Let's not make it so long between visits next time."

"I promise," Marie reassured her as she stood to leave. "I don't understand this mixed-up path I'm walking right now. But I do know my next step is to get in to see your husband. Let him know I'd like to talk to him. Soon."

"I'll have him call you," Jeanee promised. "As soon as he gets back in town. And Marie, whatever our differences, we have more in common than probably either of us realizes."

11:20 A.M.

The quiet of the summer morning was all around Jeanee. The mailman had just gone, and now she was alone in her safe room with the package he had brought her.

She recognized the handwriting on the address label. It was her mother's, a bit more delicate than Jeanee had remembered, as if age had taken the boldness from the pen. But it was unmistakably hers.

Jeanee sat for a moment, looking at the unopened package, following each loop of her mother's writing with her finger. And as tears moistened her eyes, she remembered her mother signing school papers, Christmas cards, letters. She remembered having taken those precious, carefully signed items to school or to the mailbox, always admiring the graceful curves and artistic loops her mother had penned.

"Oh, Mom!" She sighed. "Where did those years go? Why have I let such a terrible distance grow between us?"

And the distance was there. Jeanee was the one who had insisted on it. Her mother had just quietly agreed.

Remembering back to her recent phone call, she thought of how fragile her mother's voice had sounded, almost frail. As difficult as the call had been for her to make, she realized, it had probably been the first step toward opening a door to healing within her family. Maybe that, as much as anything, had been the reason she had felt so strongly that she had to make it.

Carefully opening the package, Jeanee found a note:

> Dear Jeanee,
> I am sorry for the condition of the photographs I am sending you. Maybe you don't remember, but you used to destroy your pictures and throw them away. There are only half a dozen here, but I hope they will help you discover what it is you are searching for.
> I am also sending a recent picture of me with your brother's family. It was taken last Easter. I thought you might want to see what we look like today. Take care, and God bless you.
> I love you.
> Mom.

Trembling through tears, Jeanee held the letter to her

heart. She didn't understand herself why she had put such a distance between the two of them. She loved her mother. And yet—

Jeanee picked up two large brown envelopes from where they had been nestled in tissue paper. From the first envelope, she slipped the picture taken at Easter and smiled sadly as she realized how small and aged her mother looked. Her brother and his wife had changed so much they almost looked like distant relatives. And Jeanee didn't recognize any of the children.

Where had the years gone?

Turning the second envelope upside down, Jeanee shook it vigorously. Her heart was beating faster, and a strange excitement filled her mind. Somehow she felt certain that this would be a major piece to the massive puzzle she was fitting together in her mind—something more to help her resolve the questions she had about her childhood.

The photographs caught on each other as they fell onto the bed. Ragged and bent, they were not an impressive collection. But they were of her, and eagerly Jeanee picked up the one on top.

It was of her riding her tricycle when she was about three. The wind had been blowing the wisps of her white-blond hair, and she was bundled in a coat she could remember her mother had sewn. Jeanee giggled at the fat little cheeks and the scowl on her face. She looked so determined, so ready to conquer the world.

The next picture was of her swinging in the park. She would have been about six. Her head was down, and her hair covered most of her face. And there was a deep sadness in her posture and expression that Jeanee could now understand.

Holding back her emotions, Jeanee next examined what had to be a school picture. It was black and white like the rest, a portrait. She would have been seven or eight when it had been taken — second grade. There was a smile on her face, but the eyes! Jeanee looked at the eyes and was overcome with the empty darkness hidden there. It was as if a shade had been drawn and there was no one inside.

"Oh no!" Jeanee whispered. "I can see it! I never saw it before, but I can see it now. Oh, you poor little child. You were so alone."

Jeanee didn't realize she was talking to someone who no longer existed, someone who had become herself. She just saw the deep sadness in the tiny face, and she couldn't help but feel great empathy for the little child looking out at her through those eyes.

There were two more photographs of her, both playing with other children. One of them was her brother, with his red wagon. But there were none of her in her early teens. Jeanee searched through again and wondered where they had gone. Had she really thrown them out? And if she had, why?

Holding the envelope open with her fingers, she began shaking it again, harder, and finally one last picture fell out, face down. Reaching for it, Jeanee realized that part of it had been torn off. Turning it over, Jeanee was seized with sudden horror. The mouth! There was no mouth on this teenage portrait of herself! Who had torn her mouth off, she wondered. Who would have done such a thing?

31

SATURDAY, JUNE 13

3:30 A.M.

The darkness was overwhelming. Jeanee was trapped on her bed, unable to move, paralyzed. And above her a dark, evil, menacing cloud was gaining strength and threatening to reach down and devour her.

"Where am I?" her mind screamed. "Where is everyone?"

She was alone. She knew that much. But where?

"Don't look up!" her mind continued in horror. "Don't look at it, and maybe it will go away!" So she closed her eyes and tried to forget the rising terror in her heart. It was alive! The cloud was alive! And it was moving, churning, belching its evil intentions.

Smother! Consume! Destroy!

And Jeanee was its target.

"I can't move!" her mind screamed again. "I can't move! Someone get me out of here!"

But there was no one.

"Scream!" Her mind convulsed. "Scream for help!" And with every ounce of strength she could muster, Jeanee forced herself to form the word "Help!"

But nothing came out.

She was mute.

Without opening her eyes, Jeanee could feel the cold movement of the cloud, its dark, convulsive plumes diving

420

toward her helpless body. "Don't look!" her mind ordered once again. "Move! Scream! But don't you dare look!"

But Jeanee could do nothing.

"Oh, please!" She struggled in silent paralysis. "Please, someone, somewhere, come get me out of here! I can't move! I can't scream! And I'm going to die!"

Jeanee was certain that death was just moments away. And she was helpless to stay its hand, just as she was helpless to comprehend her assailant — or assailants — for the cloud seemed alive with thousands of dark faces, leering at her, reaching down to claim her soul.

"I *have* to look!" She fought against her own fears. "I can't just lie here and be overcome. I have to do *something!*"

And opening her eyes, she saw the devilish mass of heaving darkness plunging and reveling in its power, filled with the fluid wisps of laughing, leering legions, sure of their victim.

"What do I do?" she silently agonized. "It's too strong! I can't get away!"

And as she conceded her helplessness, the horrid cloud seemed to gain an even greater energy. The vapors of darkness gathered in density, adding evil to greater evil.

And still Jeanee could do nothing.

"Scream! You've got to scream!" her mind pleaded, reeling. But no sound, no movement, nothing came forth from her vocal cords.

"I'm lost," she thought in despair. "I can't run, I can't crawl. And I have no voice! I'm doomed."

Then, just as she was ready to give in to the eternal abyss, Jeanee felt a quickening within her, an entity — a child? It had to be a child. For it was the voice of a child trying to speak. And yet — it was her own voice.

As if she were floating somewhere above her body, Jeanee watched and listened as the child's voice strained to speak. And suddenly, as if a door had opened into her soul, the child's voice was released.

"I know you're stronger than me," Jeanee could hear her saying. "But I know someone who's stronger than you. And I'm going to ask Him to help."

There was no fear in the tiny voice, no railing accusation, no pride or taunting. It was just a simple stating of fact. The child knew. The child spoke. And as she did, brilliant light filled the room, instantly dispelling the awful darkness—

Jeanee awakened with a start, gasping for air, feeling incredibly thankful that it had been only a dream. But the threat the dream had posed was well etched in her mind, as was the message.

She *did* know Someone stronger than evil. And she needed to call on Him!

Silently Jeanee slid down beside her bed and prayed that, no matter what it was, she would come to understand what He was trying to reveal to her.

4:47 P.M.

Jeanee was poring through stacks of her journals on the kitchen counter when Frank walked in the door, smiling from behind a two-day beard.

"Don't tell me," he teased as he dropped his backpack on the floor, "you're going to go through and condense them all into one volume so we won't have to cut a hole in a mountain somewhere to store them."

Jeanee looked up blankly. "Uh, well—no," she stammered, closing the volume she had open in front of her. "I was just—looking for some answers."

"I have claim on the bathroom!" Erik announced as he stuck his head in the kitchen. "Angie can have it when she gets home." Then he disappeared.

Jeanee sent a questioning look to her husband.

"She wanted to ride down the mountain with Tish," he explained, reaching down to kiss his wife on the temple.

"She'll be here in a few minutes. What do you say you and I hit the swimming pool for a few minutes?"

Jeanee looked pensively at the stack of journals before her, then at her husband. "I'm sorry, honey." she responded quietly. "I'm glad you're home. But I'm in the middle of something here, and I just have to get some answers."

Frank's expression became serious. "Are you okay?"

Jeanee smiled weakly, nodding her head. "Just going through more of the same. And suddenly I can't ignore this feeling that my answer might be hidden in these journals somewhere. I'm so confused! Why, Frank? Why do these things keep happening?"

Silently Frank pulled a bar stool around so he could sit next to his wife. Then tenderly he reached over and took her hand.

"If the Lord has really forgiven me," Jeanee continued, "and if I've really forgiven my father, why do these awful dreams keep coming back? Why do I keep struggling?

"Look at this." Jeanee handed her husband an article from the *Sunday Magazine* that had been delivered earlier that day. "It's about a woman who never came to terms with her past until she had prosecuted her father."

Frank picked it up and began reading, and Jeanee reached for her Doctrine and Covenants.

"Jeanee," Frank offered tenderly after a few minutes of reading, "this brings up something I've wanted to ask you about, but I haven't known just how to approach the subject."

Jeanee was silent, waiting.

"This woman had to see her father prosecuted and justice done before she could let go of the past."

Frank read from the article. " 'And justice really does matter, after all that time. . . . He had to stand there and face the music. Now, at last, everyone knows I was not the one with the problem.'

"This is terrible." he continued. "The man got off for years without having to pay for what he did, and he abused others besides his daughter.

"Jeanee, honey, I know your father's dead, but is it possible you still need to see some kind of justice done before you can let go?"

Jeanee was prepared. "Read this," she said, handing Frank her scriptures, which she had opened to D&C 132:26, "the part I have marked."

Frank read: "They shall be destroyed in the flesh, and shall be delivered unto the buffetings of Satan unto the day of redemption, saith the Lord God."

"My father was destroyed in the flesh," Jeanee explained firmly. "He died a horrible, lingering death. Then he was delivered over to the buffetings of Satan. Eternal justice was done.

"When I read that article, I wondered myself if that was what was bothering me. But it isn't. It's something deeper. And I've been searching all day to discover why, when I started searching to know Christ—"

Tears welled up in Jeanee's eyes. "Isn't it supposed to get better once you've committed your life to Him?"

Frank sent a tender look of compassion to his wife, and then, smiling, he quickly thumbed to D&C 93:24. "Take a look at this," he responded. "And there's another one in John 16:13. I've been doing some searching of my own."

Jeanee read: "And truth is knowledge of things as they are, and as they were, and as they are to come."

"And this." Frank handed her the Bible.

"Howbeit when he, the Spirit of truth, is come," she read, "he will guide you into all truth."

"And this one in D&C 93:37: 'Light and truth forsake that evil one.'

"Jeanee." Frank turned and looked tenderly into his wife's searching blue eyes. "I've done a lot of thinking on those mountain trails. And my thoughts and prayers keep coming back to what you have shared with me. You know, hon, you have endured what I can never even imagine. And you've been blessed wonderfully at the hands of the Savior. I know with all my heart that you have experienced the mighty change. That's what that journal entry was about that you had me read up in your room."

Tears were falling from Jeanee's wide eyes.

"But this mighty change principle is an interesting one," Frank went on. "It is an absolutely necessary step we all must take if we intend to come to Christ. Jesus said that all of us must be born again, and this is what He was talking about.

"But it is a beginning step, hon, not an ending step as so many believe. Through the mighty change we become children of Christ — His sons and daughters, as King Benjamin described it, or His seed, as Abinadi put it to King Noah. As Christ's sons and daughters, our quest should then become a single-minded effort to know Him, to seek His face, and to become personally acquainted with Him."

"It's not enough to be born again," Jeanee whispered. "You have to keep seeking the face of Christ."

"That's right. Nephi said that after the mighty change, we must press forward with a steadfastness in Christ, having a perfect brightness of hope, and a love of God and of all men. As we do that, the Spirit of truth opens as much truth to us as we are capable of accepting and enduring at that time."

"The Lord won't force us immediately into His presence," Jeanee agreed.

"No. It's a progressive experience. Once we are made clean through the blood of Christ and our sins are forgiven, then we really begin our quest in earnest. But it's not easy to maintain our new purity. Soon after the mighty change, each person, despite the abhorrence of sin, finds that new sins are being committed. Of course they're usually not being committed intentionally because one who has been born again really does find sin reprehensible. Still, because old habits do die hard, daily repentance must go into effect. Thus, forgiveness is quickly granted, and growth occurs.

"In time, each of us realizes that our tendencies to commit new sins seem to fall into general areas or patterns."

"Like self-doubt?" Jeanee asked.

"Or discouragement," Frank added. "Personally, I fight tremendous discouragement. But we all seem to have our own areas of mortal weakness. As we discover them and go before the Lord concerning them, He begins to provide a way for us to deal with them, one at a time."

"You're talking about repentance?" Jeanee asked.

"At this point we have a repentant spirit, so repentance does continue to be a daily process. But more than the initial repentance that leads us to receive the Savior's image and become spiritually born of God, the person is now seeking to discover the underlying weakness he or she inherited with mortality, and this weakness will be at the root of the particular sins the person struggles with most. In other words, the person begins to seek all truth.

"And mortal weakness, 'the natural man,' the scriptures call it, which God has given us to aid in our humility, must be made a strength through the grace of Christ before we can ever become pure enough to obtain all earthly blessings, know all truth, and, as D&C 93:1 says, behold the face of Christ."

Jeanee was stunned. "You mean," she almost gasped, "the weaknesses I have because of what happened in my childhood are part of the truth I must accept? Without acknowledging the damage from my childhood, I can't fully come to Christ?"

Silently Frank nodded.

"Then that," Jeanee stated in amazement, "could be what this turmoil I keep going through is all about. The dreams. The—Oh, my word! I didn't understand. I've always thought it was because I wasn't doing something I was supposed to be doing. Or vice versa."

"When in reality," Frank stated, "you're being allowed to remember the problems in your past because you are doing precisely what He is asking of you. You are striving to seek Him and His truth with your whole heart.

"Take a look at what happened to Nephi, Jeanee, if you think that having problems means you're doing something wrong. He had his calling and election made sure. He was taken above the earth and shown marvelous things. And yet he struggled. Just take a look at 2 Nephi 4:17–19: 'Nevertheless, notwithstanding the great goodness of the Lord, in showing me his great and marvelous works, my heart exclaimeth: O wretched man that I am! Yea, my heart sorroweth because of my flesh; my soul grieveth because of mine iniquities. I am encompassed about because of the temptations and the sins which do so easily beset me. And when I desire to rejoice, my heart groaneth because of my sins; nevertheless, I know in whom I have trusted.'

"Nephi wasn't spared his struggles because he had committed his life to Christ and had been blessed of Him. And take a look at Joseph Smith. Despite all that God had granted him, he walked in some pretty deep water himself, struggling to overcome his mortal weaknesses.

"No, Jeanee, if you're thinking of your struggles as proof that you're doing something wrong, then you haven't comprehended how the Lord uses our our pain to refine us. Quite honestly, the only way I know to escape such mortal agony is to be translated or to die, and neither will happen until they happen. For you and me, they haven't."

Smiling at Frank's humor, Jeanee was nevertheless overcome with what she was learning. Tears shown brightly in her eyes as she thought of the years she had doubted herself. She thought of how she had distanced herself from her family because she was so unsure of her own conclusions. She had thought, for too many years, that pain was punishment, pure and simple. And since she was going through pain, she must have deserved to be punished. Somehow she had never realized that pain was a purifying power in her life.

"And, my precious wife," continued Frank, "as you progress in your healing, the Lord will continue to reveal truth, until He has helped you completely overcome all impurity. Then your weakness will have become a strength, and the promise made in Ether 12:27 will be fulfilled.

"You've had a marvelous experience with the Savior, hon, but my impression is that after you have completed what the Lord is now allowing you to experience, He will bring you even closer. Jeanee, don't be discouraged. You are being healed. And one day, either here or hereafter, you will be pure enough to see His face and to be brought fully into His presence."

32

TUESDAY, JUNE 16

8:30 A.M.

"Morning, all you wonderful people," Frank said cheerfully as he came in the door, toweling himself off after his morning swim. "You too, Erik."

Knowing he was being teased, Erik grinned. "Ha ha, Dad. Get too much chlorine again?"

"Not more than I can handle."

"Yeah, Erik," Angie declared. "Daddy can handle anything."

"Except long hikes," Erik snickered, referring to the previous weekend's activity.

Frank grinned. "You're right. I don't go up mountains like I used to. Especially when I'm dragging an Angie-pie behind me."

"You didn't drag me very much, Daddy. I even carried my pack sometimes."

"That's right," Erik agreed. "And when she wasn't carrying it, I was. So you've no excuse there, Dad."

Sighing, Frank sat down at the table next to his wife. "They're right, you know. I really am starting to feel my age."

"And show it," Erik said with a laugh.

Frank nodded agreeably. "And show it. I'm only now starting to walk normally. Jeanee, how're you feeling today?"

Jeanee looked up from her journal. "Tired." she answered. "That's why I didn't come swimming."

"You look tired," Frank said sympathetically.

"And it's not all physical, either," Jeanee admitted. "It's this stuff I'm wrestling with. I just need some clear answers. And they're not coming.

"Frank, do you have time to go to the temple today?"

"That's a good idea." Frank agreed. "I have some calls that have to be made this morning. But, yeah. You bet! Erik, do you work today?"

The teenager shook his head. "Not until tonight."

"Good. Will you—"

"Yes," Erik interrupted as he polished off a quart of milk, "I'll let Angie keep an eye on me."

"How come I can't keep my eye on Eri—" Angie, suddenly realizing what her brother had actually said, broke into a giggle, and soon the entire family was laughing with her—

12:05 P.M.

Frank was opening the front door for his wife when the phone rang.

"I'll be just a minute, honey." he promised.

"Sure." Jeanee smiled knowingly. "I'll be waiting in the car."

"Perilous times." Frank smiled and winked. Then hurrying to pick up the wall phone in the kitchen, he was surprised at the sound of weakness in the man's voice at the other end.

"I . . . think maybe I'm going crazy over . . . here," the voice admitted.

"Is that you, Brother Nichol?"

"Yeah, it's me, Bishop." Bob's voice was filled with despair.

"What's happening?"

"I . . . don't know. Yesterday I got a good day's work done. Then this morning after prayer, I walked into the living room and picked up my Bible. It came open to Luke chapter 17. I just started to read, and in verses 1 and 2 it says . . . wo unto those who . . . offend His little ones . . .

"Bishop," Bob cried brokenly, "it says it would be better for me if . . . a millstone were hanged around my neck and . . . and I was drowned in the depths of the sea."

Bob's emotions overcame him, and Frank remained still, praying to know what to say.

"What have I done?" Bob continued. "I hear myself yelling at Robby, I see myself losing my temper every time I talk to him, I feel . . . I feel the skin of his face on my hand when I sl . . . slap him . . .

"I . . . I don't know, Bishop Greaves. Maybe this is hell. It all looks so hopeless to me. I've destroyed my wife, I've destroyed my son, and . . . and . . . How can I ever face my God? What can I say to Him, knowing the incredible evil I have done to these two people He entrusted to my care? Bishop, what am I ever going to do?"

"What do you think you should do?" Frank asked softly.

"I . . . I don't know. I wish I could take all those years back again—just start over! But I can't! The damage is done, and I . . . I can't stand the horror of knowing what I am—what I did to them when they were only trying to love me. Am I naturally evil?

"You know, I always pictured myself as a good man with a few problems that I would one day take care of. There have been times when I even thought of myself as religious. But this, this that I am seeing in myself, is evil!"

"You're right, Bob," Frank stated quietly. "Abuse is evil, satanic. In fact, it's hard for me to imagine a sin more reprehensible before God. As for you being naturally evil, can you remember what King Benjamin said about it?" Frank grabbed Jeanee's scriptures and flipped them open. "Here. Let me read it to you. 'For the natural man is an

enemy to God, and has been from the fall of Adam, and
will be, forever and ever, unless he yields to the enticings
of the Holy Spirit, and putteth off the natural man and
becometh a saint through the atonement of Christ the
Lord, and becometh as a child, submissive, meek, humble,
patient, full of love, willing to submit to all things which
the Lord seeth fit to inflict upon him, even as a child doth
submit to his father.' "

"Where . . . is that?"

"Mosiah 3:19. We are all natural men, Bob, and we
remain so until we yield to the enticings of the Holy Ghost
and repent of all our sins. Then we become childlike in
our natures, and God is able to prepare us to return to
His presence."

"You know the part about a child submitting to
his . . . father?"

"Yes," Frank said.

"I . . . I . . . Oh, Bishop, this just convicts me further!"

Again Frank waited while the man wept bitterly.

"So . . . so what do I do now?" Bob finally asked, his
emotions once again under control.

"What do you think you should do?"

For a moment there was silence on the line. "I want,"
Bob finally stated, "to let Robby know how sorry I am. But
I'm so embarrassed, so ashamed! Bishop, what if he won't
even listen to me?"

"Do you think he might not?"

"I . . . don't know. I'm not sure I would listen, knowing
what I did to him. But I've got to apologize! I have to let
him know how wrong I've been, how . . . evil!"

"Then do it," Frank urged. "I can tell you this, Bob.
No forgiveness from God will ever come until you've done
your part to make peace with your son. I don't know how
he will respond, but I do know you can't proceed without
a sincere and genuine apology."

"But . . . how can that really help? I mean, it will only

be words! Words! What can words do to turn back the pain I've caused him for so many years?"

"You can't turn it back, Bob. It's done, and there's nothing you can do to change that. But you can change what happens from today forward. Since the Lord hasn't taken your life yet, and I imagine you've even prayed for that—"

"I . . . have—" Bob's voice was almost a whisper.

"Then there must be something ahead for you that only He knows about. More time to live your life means more time to alter the course you've been living. I suppose the degree of your remorse will equal the degree to which you are willing to change."

"Then . . . it will be . . . a hundred and eighty degrees," Bob declared fiercely.

"Good. Start that change with the apologies, and leave what comes after that to God. Have you apologized to Claudia?"

"Only a thousand times."

"Does she accept it?"

"I . . . I can't tell. You know the ninety days are . . . nearly over?"

"I've thought of that," Frank responded.

"Me too. Constantly. And . . . I don't know what Claudia's going to do—" Breaking down again, Bob's tears sounded bitter.

"Bob," Frank said gently, "you can't worry about that. You worry about your repentance and let the Lord take care of Claudia's decision. If you do all you can, it'll be right. I promise you that—"

4:20 P.M.

The sound of the car and the steady rhythm of the road was almost mesmerizing. Frank blinked and shook his head to stay awake.

"Sleepy, honey?" Jeanee asked tenderly.

"Mmm." Frank agreed, smiling. "The old man isn't what he used to be. Just ask Erik."

Jeanee reached over and began massaging the back of her husband's neck. "Does that help?"

"Over here." Frank pointed to a tight muscle in his shoulder.

"That better?" Jeanee continued working.

"Much! Any chance you're available on a regular basis?"

Jeanee smiled. "I think that can be arranged." She was quiet for a moment. "Speaking of arrangements, did you ever get hold of Marie?"

"Marie Spencer?"

"That's right. She really did want to see you."

"She and her husband have been out of town this last little while. But I left a message with their baby-sitter. Why do you ask?"

"I was just talking with Terri this morning and—Oh, Frank, something wonderful has happened to her."

"Terri, or Marie?"

Jeanee laughed. "Terri, silly. Can't you follow me?"

"Of course I can," Frank fibbed, still not understanding what Terri had to do with him calling Marie. "Tell me about Terri."

"She told me I could share this with you," Jeanee explained. "I wish I could say it the way she did on the telephone. And I wish I could explain how it makes me feel."

Frank was puzzled.

"I was telling her how I was struggling these past few days," Jeanee explained. "And how it's hard not to blame myself for what I'm feeling. And she told me she doesn't do that anymore."

Frank turned his head from the road for a moment. Remembering his interview with Terri, he was very interested.

"I was telling her about what I've been going through, and out of the blue she very calmly said that she doesn't hear her voices anymore."

"What happened?" Frank asked, amazed.

"They just simply went away." Jeanee grinned. "She kept reading her scriptures and praying and following what the Spirit directed her to do. And one day she woke up and realized the voices were no longer there. They haven't been for months. She's been healed, sweetheart! Terri's been healed!

"And listen to this." Jeanee reached inside her purse and pulled out a slip of paper. "She shared this with me, something she calls 'Benediction':

> *Willingly I sit*
> *beneath*
> *The Polisher's hand*
>
> *Reflecting God's love*
> *with my*
> *pain-buffed heart*

"Isn't that beautiful!?"

"Yeah," Frank agreed, "that's really something."

"It says so much in those few short words! And when I heard it, it was as if I could feel a radiant warmth coming through the telephone into my heart, telling me there will come a time when I will feel the same way.

"Oh, Frank, I'm going to have my own benediction. One day this is all going to be a thing of the past, and I will be healed!"

"I know, sweetheart." Frank smiled. "I've been promised that, too."

"And Marie is going to get beyond her pain as well," Jeanee continued. "She's really been doing some changing these past few months. Honey, she was so badly hurt!"

"I know," Frank acknowledged as he checked the rear-view mirror to make a lane change. "It's pretty terrible what some people have to endure in this life. But you know — I was reading in the New Testament last night, and I came upon something I'd marked in 1 Peter 3:17 and 4:1 and 2 a long time ago.

"Peter says: 'For it is better, if the will of God be so, that ye suffer for well doing, than for evil doing. . . .Forasmuch then as Christ hath suffered for us in the flesh, arm yourselves likewise with the same mind: for he that hath suffered in the flesh hath ceased from sin; that he no longer should live the rest of his time in the flesh to the lusts of men, but to the will of God.'

"What I think that tells us, hon, is that those who suffer, as you and Terri and Marie have suffered, having not committed the sins that have caused your suffering, are doing as Christ did. He, too, suffered for well doing. As you suffer patiently, as He did, you are enjoined with Christ."

Jeanee snuggled down in her seat, "I've been praying so hard for clear answers, trying to understand what has been happening to me. And today —" Tears misted over in her eyes. "Today I had a wonderful experience in the temple."

Jeanee was quiet for a moment, then she continued. "I felt the Spirit so close to me. And all through the session I had this overwhelming peace. I just know the Lord is aware of what I have been going through. And He is going to be right here to carry me through the rest of it."

Frank reached over and touched his wife's cheek tenderly.

"Jeanee," he whispered huskily, "I know He is too. And something else — no matter what it takes, no matter how long, I'm going to be here too —"

10:10 P.M.

"Sit down, Bob. From the look on your face, things didn't go so well with Robby."

In agony of spirit, Bob shook his head. "They didn't," he responded slowly. "Oh, I talked to him. I apologized. But it felt so . . . so superficial to me! But what else could I expect? How can you wipe out a lifetime of hell with a few selected words?"

"You can't," Frank agreed. "On the other hand, a few selected words are the only way you can ever start to wipe it out. How did Claudia feel about your visit with Robby?"

"She's a class act, Bishop. She really supported me. But then, she always treats me with respect. I . . . I don't deserve that, God knows I don't!

"Good grief! Why am I always bawling? I . . . could hardly say what I wanted to say to Robby. Not that I didn't want to. I just . . . just . . . Oh, Bishop, the enormity of what I've done to Claudia and Robby is more than I can bear! Every time I think of it I go to pieces! And I can't ever stop thinking of it! I want to die and I can't. I want them to know how sorry I am, and the words sound so hollow and empty, I feel so empty and . . . unworthy—"

"How did Robby respond?"

Bob looked up, his eyes bleak. "He didn't say a word. He just stared at the ground until I had stopped talking. Then he . . . he turned and walked away."

"Is that what you expected?"

"I don't know what I expected. I know it hurt to watch him turn his back on me, more than I can say. Have I . . . lost him? Have I?"

"I don't know," Frank replied honestly. "He's a fine boy, but he's been badly wounded. Wounds like his must surely take a long time to heal."

"It doesn't matter. If it takes the rest of my life, I'm going to find a way to let him know how sorry I am!

Whether God forgives me or not, I won't rest until Robby knows I'm sorry, and that I won't ever hurt him again!"

Frank reached for his open Book of Mormon and handed it to Bob.

"Here," he urged, " I hope you don't mind if I share a few of my favorite scriptures with you." Frank pointed to a marked passage. "This is Alma the Younger's account of what he experienced after he had been brought to a realization of his own wickedness. Right there, chapter 36, verse 12."

Reaching out, Bob took the book and, after wiping his eyes, began to read.

> But I was racked with eternal torment, for my soul was harrowed up to the greatest degree and racked with all my sins.

"This sounds awfully familiar, Bishop!"
"I thought it might. Read on. It'll get even more so."

> Yea, I did remember all my sins and iniquities, for which I was tormented with the pains of hell; yea, I saw that I had rebelled against my God, and that I had not kept his holy commandments.
> Yea, and I had murdered many of his children, or rather led them away unto destruction; yea, and in fine so great had been my iniquities, that the very thought of coming into the presence of my God did rack my soul with inexpressible horror.
> Oh, thought I, that I could be banished and become extinct both soul and body, that I might not be brought to stand in the presence of my God, to be judged of my deeds.
> And now, for three days and for three nights was I racked, even with the pains of a damned soul.

Looking up, Bob wiped at the new tears that were streaming down his face. "Bishop, he knew! He knew just as I know! I've read this maybe a dozen times. But until now I've never seen it. Now it is all so clear, so damnably clear. I have led Claudia and Robby to destruction, which Alma says is the same as murdering their eternal souls. Oh, dear God, what have I done? What have I done?"

Reaching out, Frank put his hand on the man's shoulder. "As bleak as it looks, you know there is hope."

"But . . . how can that be? When you see what I have done, how can you possibly say there's hope?"

"Read on."

Wiping again at his eyes, Bob once more began to read.

> And it came to pass that as I was thus racked with torment, while I was harrowed up by the memory of my many sins, behold, I remembered also to have heard my father prophesy unto the people concerning the coming of one Jesus Christ, a Son of God, to atone for the sins of the world.
>
> Now, as my mind caught hold upon this thought, I cried within my heart: O Jesus, thou Son of God, have mercy on me, who am in the gall of bitterness, and am encircled about by the everlasting chains of death.
>
> And now, behold, when I thought this, I could remember my pains no more; yea, I was harrowed up by the memory of my sins no more.
>
> And oh, what joy, and what marvelous light I did behold; yea, my soul was filled with joy as exceeding as was my pain!
>
> Yea, I say unto you . . . that there could be nothing so exquisite and so bitter as were my pains. Yea, and again I say unto you . . . that on the other hand, there can be nothing so exquisite and sweet as was my joy.

Again Bob looked up at Frank, his eyes filled with questions even as he pleaded for understanding. "Bishop, I . . . I've done this, and nothing's happened! For days on end I've been praying for forgiveness —"

"That isn't what Alma did," Frank explained. "Read it

again, Bob. You see, Alma cried out to Christ, declaring his sins to Him and pleading for mercy from the very One who would, and has, taken upon Him all the sins of the entire human race."

"But . . . can I do that?"

"Why can't you? Why can't you, during your prayer to the Father, apologize directly to Christ and plead for His forgiveness? Besides, you've apologized to Claudia and Robby. Don't you think an apology is due to the Great God our Savior, whom you have also wounded?"

His face betraying his shock, Bob simply stared. Such a thought had never entered his mind, and now that Frank had placed it there, the power of it was overwhelming to him.

"Do you now see what your next step must be?" Frank questioned.

Numbly Bob rose to his feet and turned toward the door. Taking a deep breath, he turned and looked Frank squarely in the eye. "I . . . just hope I have the nerve to face Him—"

33

SATURDAY, JUNE 20

1:15 P.M.

"Bishop Greaves?"

Looking up from his chrysanthemums, Frank was surprised to see a man standing in his driveway, a man he had never seen before.

"Yes?"

"Are you . . . Bishop Greaves?"

"I am," Frank said as he rose to his feet. "What can I do for you?"

"Don't stop on account of me." The visitor spoke apologetically as he walked closer. He was elderly, mostly bald with a fringe of white hair. His face was deeply tanned and wrinkled, probably from a life outdoors, and his hands were gnarled and knotted with rheumatism.

"I don't think I caught your name." Frank smiled, wiping his own hands on his coveralls.

The man smiled. "I'm Henry Winston. I believe you know my daughter. Marie Spencer?"

"Oh," Frank said, his mind spinning. "Of course. Why don't we walk around to the patio, Brother Winston, and then we can talk privately."

"A beautiful yard," the man acknowledged as they passed a bed of roses.

"It likes to be pampered." Frank smiled. "Usually I don't have the time to putter around like I want to. But this summer I planned it so I could have more time to be

441

at home with my family." Frank motioned for Brother
Winston to sit in the shaded area of the patio. Both men
sat down facing each other, and for a moment there was
silence.

"I hardly know where to begin," Henry Winston finally
said. "But Bishop—May I call you Bishop?"

Frank nodded.

"Thank you. Bishop Greaves, I have a real dilemma,
and I don't know who else to turn to. Are . . . you sure this
is a good time—"

"This is an ideal time," Frank assured his visitor.

Henry Winston looked around, trying to get comfortable with what he would be revealing about himself.
"Bishop," he finally began, "I've made some serious mistakes in my life."

Frank remained silent.

"When I decided to join the Church, the wonderful
man who was bishop guided me through my repentance
and healing. And now—" Anguish was written in every
crease of his brow.

Frank spoke softly. "Does this have to do with your
daughter?"

"Yes," Brother Winston admitted. "This has to do with
Marie." Then he looked Frank squarely in the eye. "I have
been so harrowed up in my mind. With all my heart I have
wanted to tell her how terribly sorry I am that I hurt
her—"

"Then why haven't you done it?" Frank asked bluntly.

Brother Winston was silent for a moment. And then,
taking a deep breath, he explained. "Fear, I suppose. Not
fear for myself, Bishop. I've dealt with that, and I deserve
whatever suffering I have to bear. But Marie's innocent,
and I've been so worried that if I said anything to her, I
would hurt her further—"

"I'm sorry," Frank interrupted, "but I don't understand."

Henry Winston sighed. "I'm not doing this very well, am I? Let me put it this way. I came to see you today because I don't know how much Marie remembers. I have been so concerned that if I were to start talking about things, painful things concerning situations that she might not remember, well, I don't know what that would do to her."

Frank nodded. "Now I understand. To tell you the truth, Marie has suffered terribly because she *does* remember some things, and she struggles with those memories."

The man was staring at the brick floor of the patio, holding back tears. Frank also remained silent, sorting through his own thoughts. For months, Marie had kept a measured distance. And until recently, she had even refused Jeanee's attempts at closeness. But now—

"Brother Winston," Frank finally ventured. "I've not known how to help Marie. My wife and I have both been quite concerned about her."

"I understand." Henry Winston nodded quietly.

"You do?" Frank questioned.

"Yes—I do."

There was a long pause, and then the old man sitting across from Frank began unfolding the sad story of his own childhood abuse at the hands of a maiden aunt, and of how it had affected his own search for happiness.

"Bishop Greaves," he agonized, "I had no idea what I was doing to my little girl. I thought I was simply sharing a special kind of love, like my aunt did to me. I'm thankful I finally recognize my lust for what it was."

Is it possible, Frank wondered silently, *that this could be Mel Blodgett several years from now?*

"Bishop," Brother Winston continued, "do you think it would be helpful for me to talk to her, to apologize?"

"Is the Spirit prompting you to apologize?" Frank countered.

Henry Winston nodded. "I think so. My problem is

that I know it can be dangerous for a victim to be forced to remember before he or she is ready to deal with the devastating emotions associated with the memory. That's why I didn't come earlier. I didn't know if Marie remembered. I've been praying she would so that we could get this out of the darkness and into the light. I think the Spirit is telling me that Marie is finally ready."

Frank smiled, his eyes moistening with emotion. "Brother Winston, you're a courageous man."

Henry Winston remained silent.

"And you are right. I believe your daughter is ready—"

2:25 P.M.

"Hello, Bishop."

"Well, if it isn't the McCrasky girls!" Frank beamed as he glanced at June and her mother.

"Do you have a minute?"

"Absolutely." Easily he led the way around the house. "This patio's been busy today. Sit down and tell me what I can do for you."

"My," Elaine said as she gazed around. "This is even more beautiful than it appears from across the fence."

Grinning, Frank nodded toward the fence. "Well, a lot of the credit for that goes to Jimmy and Willy. They're both real helpers over here."

"They really love you, Bishop."

Frank's smile grew wider. "I love them, too. And this young lady," he winked at June, "is one of my favorites in all the world. I don't know what our school is going to do without her."

"I . . . I'm nervous about junior high," June said softly.

"You should be! Once you get going, that school will never be the same." Frank chuckled.

"Mom's got a mad book." June beamed.

"She does?"

"And a happy book," Elaine added with a smile. "More important, I'm using them."

"That's wonderful," Frank said enthusiastically.

"I just wanted to give you an update," Elaine continued. "I called Brother Wixom, and he got me with a therapist who is absolutely wonderful! I go once a week, and he has really helped me."

"That's great."

"And you were right on track, Bishop. There is a definite link between my childhood traumas and my behavior now that I am an adult. My two older sisters, my parents, my husband, my feelings of being picked on and overworked, even my hatred of too much weight—all of it is related to my behavior."

"But you can change?"

"Mom's mad book is really working," June declared. "Now, instead of yelling at us, she goes in and writes in her book."

"Well," Elaine admitted, "almost always. But I am getting better at controlling myself. I do have a lot of anger pent up inside, which I am slowly acknowledging and taking care of. Sometimes it still comes out, even when I don't want it to. My counselor calls that 'spontaneous recovery,' which means that my mind recovers my inappropriate anger spontaneously when some particular thing triggers it. He says it's to be expected but that as I work through my memories, my incidents of spontaneous recovery will grow less and less violent and less and less frequent. Ultimately they'll stop altogether."

"That'll be wonderful," Frank stated.

"Yes, it will. Interestingly, Ralph has noticed the change and is spending less time away from home. Funny, I didn't even know he had a choice—"

"Guess what, Bishop?"

"What, June?"

"I'm seeing the counselor, too."

"That's a good idea!"

Elaine looked proudly at her daughter. "You know, Bishop, the more I thought of it, the more I didn't want to see June going through this same sort of nonsense after she was married. My counselor said therapy would help her, so she's been going to see him for three weeks now."

June nodded. "He told me I could go ahead and be sad about my Mommy being dead and not feel guilty about hurting Mom here." She smiled up at Elaine. "Mommy will always be my mommy, but I can love other moms, too. That's what everybody does when they get married."

Frank smiled. "That's right."

"And I don't have to take Mommy's place with the boys, either," June continued. "I thought Daddy wanted me to. I thought I had to be a grown-up. Then when Mom came to live with us, I got real confused because I didn't know who to be anymore. But the counselor says I'm really not old enough to be a mommy. So now I guess I'm just back to being a young woman."

"And a very wise one," Elaine said softly.

"Well, Bishop," she said as she rose to her feet, "we just wanted to give you an update. If you hear me screaming across the fence again, wave a flag or something. I just need to be reminded that it's that spontaneous recovery stuff, and that I need to back down and go write in my book —"

3:30 P.M.

Bob Nichol stood at his front door, staring out at Frank. His face looked gaunt, his eyes swollen and sunken, and overall he gave the impression of a man consumed with the greatest grief imaginable.

"Bishop?"

"Claudia called, Bob. Are you okay?"

Slowly Bob nodded. "Come . . . in, Bishop. I need . . . to talk to you . . . "

Silently Frank followed the man into his home and seated himself on the sofa.

Bob gazed at the floor, not raising his eyes. "I'm still trying to comprehend what happened, to understand what I was shown —"

"Shown? What do you mean?"

Bob looked up, his expression bleak. "I . . . I don't know. I was praying, and my eyes were closed. But all of a sudden I saw this, I guess in my mind. Only, it was more real than anything I have ever seen in my life, including you sitting in front of me. Is that a vision, Bishop?"

"Was what you saw edifying?"

"It was certainly instructive."

Frank nodded. "It sounds like some sort of manifestation from the Holy Ghost, all right."

"I've always said I believed in visions," Bob declared, shaking his head. "But I never expected to have one. I thought they were for prophets and apostles, but today —"

"Bob, what exactly did you see?"

Again Bob began to weep uncontrollably. "I . . . I did what you said," Bob muttered a moment or so later. "Only, you can't imagine how terrified I was to begin. I was so embarrassed, so humiliated. I've been in the Church all my life, and now, here I was kneeling before the Lord, trying to find some way of apologizing for my sins when all along I had intentionally committed them.

"I . . . I thought I knew Christ, I really did. But there I was, and I . . . didn't even know how to address Him —

"Anyway, I finally muttered some sort of lame apology and then cried out for Jesus to have mercy on me, just as Alma did. I was kneeling right here at this chair, in the midst of begging for mercy and forgiveness, when I became aware that I was someplace else. I don't know how to

explain it. I was just there, standing in some rocks on a
hill watching a group of men a few yards in front of me.
At first I couldn't tell what they were doing, but as I looked
more closely, I saw that they were holding a man down
on his back, doing something to his hands.

"Somehow I moved closer, and that was when I finally
realized that I was watching Christ being secured to the
cross.

Again Bob buried his face in his hands. "Oh, Bishop,
I was horrified! I wanted to stop it, to stop them from what
they were doing. I even yelled at the men, calling them
fools and worse, trying to get their attention so they would
stop. But they paid me no mind.

"Then one of them took a spike, not like anything I
have ever seen, and held it in place in the curled palm of
Jesus' hand. I watched that hand, Bishop—I couldn't take
my eyes from it—and I even saw the muscles in it tense in
anticipation of the blow from the mallet. While I was watching that, my head felt like it was going to explode, my heart
was pounding until I thought it would burst from my chest,
and I heard myself begging and pleading for the men to
stop! Yet nothing seemed able to stop them, to affect them.

"Then, for some reason my gaze left Jesus' hand and
lifted to the face of the man who was wielding the mallet,
the huge wooden hammer that would drive the spike
through that hand I had been watching. And . . . and—"

Emotions contorted Bob Nichol's face. But then, with
another swipe at his eyes, he continued. "Bishop, the man
holding that mallet, the man who would be driving that
horrid spike through the Savior's flesh—was me! I, myself,
because of my pride and cruelty and unrighteousness, was
driving those spikes into the flesh of my Redeemer!"

For a moment Bob grew still, his breath coming in
ragged gasps as he saw again in memory his experience
of that morning. At length, however, he spoke again.
"I . . . I can't describe the grief I felt as I saw that awful

scene. But when I pleaded for it to be taken away so that I could see myself no longer, it was not. Instead I was left for some time to watch the consequences of my behavior upon my Lord Jesus Christ. I wept uncontrollably, Bishop, and in that brief time my sins became so reprehensible to me that I lost all desire to commit more of them, even the tiny little things you mentioned that I have always tended to overlook, or to secretly enjoy. It was then, finally, that I made the personal covenant before Heavenly Father that if I should somehow survive what I was experiencing, I would never again sin intentionally."

"Do you have peace now?" Frank asked softly.

Bleakly Bob Nichol looked back at him. "How could I possibly have peace, knowing that I added to the pain of my Lord, that I helped to . . . to crucify him—"

11:58 P.M.

It was late, almost midnight, and it seemed like hours since Jeanee had said goodnight to Frank. She might have been completely asleep, or only very close to it. She wasn't sure. But a moment or so before, right on the edge of sleep, she had become aware that a very strange thing was happening to her.

It had to do with her hands. She was aware of them, very aware, and yet she could feel no other part of her body. It was as if the only parts of her that existed were her hands. Carefully she kept touching them, feeling the sensations of skin on skin, and yet being aware that the hands she was feeling—her own—were strangely unfamiliar. They felt too big, and the skin was somehow thicker, as if they belonged to someone else.

Frightened, Jeanee tried to determine if she was having a dream or if she was awake. Except for small fidgeting movements, she could hardly move. And to her distress, they continued, threatening to arouse Frank from his deep sleep.

"Jeanee," he finally mumbled as he rolled over, "what's wrong? What is it?"

Jeanee could not answer. She could only writhe on the bed and feel her hands. And the more she felt them, the more aware she was that they were all she dared to feel. If she felt more than her hands, something very frightening would happen.

"Jeanee!" Frank was now speaking loudly. "Jeanee, wake up! Come on, snap out of this! Can you feel me shaking you? I'm right here, Jeanee! Can you hear me?"

Jeanee could hear. But she could not respond. It was better to stay asleep, safe asleep where the only things she could feel were her hands—

"Jeanee!"

"No!" her mind cried. "You can't wake up. Please—"

Only there was nothing she could do to stop it. Her body was waking, and suddenly feeling shot into her arms and legs, excruciatingly painful feeling that almost threw her into convulsions.

Desperately Jeanee fought not to feel. She couldn't let herself! It was too awful, too painful! Yet she was feeling anyway, and great heaving sobs were shaking her body, sobs that she could not stop.

"I tried," she wept in anguish. "I tried, I tried, I tried! But he wouldn't stop—"

Jeanee could hear herself crying out, sobbing, but it was as if she were listening to someone else. She had no control over what she was saying or feeling. It was all rushing out like air from a ruptured balloon, gushing from a dark painful hole in the center of her. And she couldn't stop it. No matter what she tried, it wouldn't stop!

"Jeanee," Frank was calling from somewhere nearby, "wake up! Snap out of it!"

"I tried—" A little girl's voice began whimpering

through Jeanee's mouth as she fought to contain the agony and prevent the horrible sounds from escaping.

With a mighty effort she attempted to come fully awake so she wouldn't upset Frank. Regardless of her own pain, she didn't want to upset him. But the harder she tried, the more she felt an overwhelming grief ripping her open.

Still caught in her half-sleep state, Jeanee turned over on the bed, clawing at the sheets. Her fingers were rigid, pressing harder and harder against the weave of the fabric. "I couldn't cry," she sobbed, "I couldn't cry! It hurt so bad. And I could never cry!"

At the very edge of wakefulness, terror consumed her. She knew that no matter how badly it hurt, if she cried someone would die. And it would be her fault. But she could hold it in no longer. It was exploding inside of her, breaking through the fabric of yesterday into today — ripping, tearing. And then again, unbearable agony consuming her, she burst into heaving, convulsive sobs.

"Aaaoooh, nooo! Please no! Don't do it!" She could hear her own agony. She could feel the consuming terror. She knew she was in her own bed. And yet, it was another bed, stolen from yesterday.

And she was helpless to stop the horror.

"Jeanee, honey," Frank said soothingly as he did his best to hold and comfort his wife, "why are you so frightened? You don't need to be afraid. I'm here, honey, I'm holding you. I won't let go, I promise! Now please, don't be afraid — "

"I tried, but I couldn't stop him — !" Her whole body was shaking uncontrollably. "I couldn't stop him! I tried — but I — couldn't!"

"Of course you couldn't," Frank said. "He was a man, Jeanee. He was too big for you to stop. You couldn't have stopped him."

"Who are you?" the thought seized her mind.

And just as quickly her mind answered. "That's Frank, your husband."

But at the same moment, she wasn't even sure who she was. So how could she be certain of anyone else?

Jeanee's whole soul was in turmoil, not knowing how to respond to the confusion of thoughts and emotions flooding her mind, or how to stop the incessant moans and agony coming from her mouth.

"How does Frank know to be so gentle?" The question shot through her consciousness? With a feeling of awe, the adult Jeanee wondered at his tenderness. He was listening, trying his best to tenderly understand.

"It's okay, Jeanee. I'm here."

Suddenly Jeanee felt safe, incredibly, completely safe. And in that moment the horror abated, and the terrified child who had hidden within her for so many years opened her eyes to a world she didn't fully recognize.

"What do you want me to do?" Frank asked tenderly.

"You know what to do," she heard herself sobbing.

Instantly Frank was holding her close, rocking gently as he repeated, "I love you, Jeanee. I'll take care of you."

And that was what she needed to hear—

34

SATURDAY, JUNE 27

9:55 A.M.

"What's happening to me?" Jeanee's voice was barely a whisper.

"It sounds like you may have a memory coming through." Peggy's voice was calming, even through the telephone.

"But it doesn't make any sense," Jeanee gasped. She was crouched in the fetal position in Frank's den, hugging her knees to her chest, shivering. "None of this—"

"We've talked about those drawers in your closet?" Peggy spoke deliberately. "It sounds like one of them just might be opening up."

"But I'm afraid. The other night I had an experience—" Jeanee stopped in midsentence.

"Jeanee, are you alone?"

"Frank . . . went somewhere. He had a phone call—but Angie is here. Only, she's so little, and I don't want to scare her."

"It would be best if you had someone there to help you, right now. Do you have a friend or neighbor who could come over?"

"My friend—Terri, I could see if she could come by." Jeanee was trembling even as she was speaking.

"Do that." Peggy sounded relieved. "And see if a neighbor could help with Angie for a few hours. You're probably going to be in for a trying day. And Jeanee, just let whatever is going to happen, happen. Don't fight it. And don't force it, either. If that drawer is supposed to open, it will. And if it isn't, then don't push it."

"But why do I keep waking up in that position? I did that five times in the night last night, and the last time—" Jeanee felt a groan coming from the very center of her soul. "Peggy, are you sure . . . this is what I'm supposed to be doing?"

"Don't try to make sense of this right now, Jeanee. If you do, it might be too much for you to handle."

"Am I going crazy?"

"I know this is difficult." Peggy's voice was firm. "But please accept that, just for the moment, you might not make sense. And it's okay. We'll fit the pieces together once you're through this. But for now, just accept it."

"I feel like my soul is scattered all over through time, like I have no center, just pieces and no me."

"I hate to leave you," Peggy apologized. "But I have another appointment coming in right now. Hang on. I'll be checking back within the hour."

"I'll be okay." Jeanee forced optimism. "I'll call Terri. And Peggy, thank you for being there—"

10:15 A.M.

"I . . . I don't know how to talk about this," Bob Nichol said softly as he sat across from Frank in the Nichols' living room. "It's so . . . so incomprehensible!"

"Take your time," Frank said. "If you're supposed to tell me, it will come."

"Oh, I'm supposed to tell you, all right. You're the one who told me it could happen. Alma was right, too! I see that now, more clearly than I ever imagined."

"The scriptures have a way of always telling it like it really is." Frank smiled.

"Something happened early yesterday afternoon," Bob

continued, "while I was writing in my journal, trying to record all that has happened to me the past little while."

"I'm glad you've been recording all this, Bob."

"I guess I thought if somehow I had to die to atone for the evil I've done, at least there would be something that Robby and Claudia could read so they could see how I've been trying to change."

"You thought you might die?"

Soberly Bob nodded. "I . . . I offered my life," he replied quietly. "I told God I had nothing but that to give Him to show my sorrow for my past. I didn't know if . . . if He wanted it, but I had nothing else left, Bishop. I felt like I needed to sacrifice something —

"Anyway, since then I've sort of been waiting, thinking I'd be standing on a corner or something, when along would come a truck — the truck — and I would be gone. I haven't been *seeking* it, you know. I know that would be wrong. But I sort of thought God might orchestrate it somehow."

"Your feelings certainly show your sincerity," Frank said. "My impression, though, is that God wants a spiritual sacrifice from us — the sacrifce of a broken heart and a contrite spirit. The physical sacrifice was already offered up by Christ."

"That's right! But . . . well — you just have to understand the way I've been thinking.

"Anyway — yesterday, while I was writing, in the back of my mind was the thought that at any moment I could be gone, and those few words would be all that would be left of me to help Claudia and Robby understand that the abuse was my fault, not theirs, and that I've been trying to change.

"Then, at 4:10 in the afternoon, it happened. In the middle of writing I was suddenly and abruptly overcome by the Holy Spirit in such a marvelous manner that it felt as if I were being consumed in the flesh. Ever since then

I have tried to find words sufficient to describe this experience, and I can only do so by saying that it felt like someone stood above me with a 5,000-gallon drum of burning warmth, which was poured over me in slow, continual waves of ecstasy."

Again tears were falling from Bob's eyes, but Frank could see that there was no more agony associated with them. They were at last tears of joy, and Frank felt his own spirit swelling with happiness as he listened to the words of this humbled man.

"As I experienced this indescribable joy, Bishop, my natural strength left me, and for an hour or more I lay trembling on the floor, weeping uncontrollably and filled with the absolute certainty that my guilt had been swept away through the marvelous redemptive powers of the blood of Christ. Like Alma, I had been redeemed of the Spirit, born again, led through repentance to experience the mighty change. As of that hour I was clean before the Lord, every whit, and I knew it!

"The crazy thing was, at that moment, I really did want to die! Not because of all the horrible things I know I've done. I still thought of them. In fact, I have a perfect recollection and understanding of them. But the pain, the guilt I had been going through, had been removed from me by this incredible feeling of warmth and light that was filling me with such ecstasy. I wanted to go to the source of it, my Savior, and remain with Him forever. I couldn't bear the thought that the glory of that warmth and light might leave me.

"I knew Alma had felt the same way, which was comforting to me. Of course I didn't see God like Alma did, but I knew He was there, and I knew what I was feeling was coming directly from Him."

"And do you understand the drum full of burning warmth?" Frank asked.

Bob was silent.

"Here, let me show you a couple of verses from the scriptures. This first one is from 2 Nephi 31, verse 17. Why don't you read it."

Bob took the book and read:

> Wherefore, do the things which I have told you I have seen that your Lord and your Redeemer should do; for, for this cause have they been shown unto me, that ye might know the gate by which ye should enter. For the gate by which ye should enter is repentance and baptism by water; *and then cometh a remission of your sins by fire and by the Holy Ghost.*

"After repentance," Frank declared, "comes a remission of sins by fire and by the Holy Ghost, who witnesses to you that your sins have been burned away. It is perfectly logical that you would feel those burning waves of ecstasy and know that your sins have been removed. The Doctrine and Covenants says the same thing in section 19, verse 31. As I understand it, Bob, that particular kind of fire is a manifestation of the Holy Ghost. It comes only after a person completely forsakes his sins and exercises faith in the Lord Jesus Christ. As King Benjamin taught, you have now become a son of Christ."

Lowering Frank's copy of the scriptures, Bob Nichol smiled. "I hadn't realized this until now," he said slowly, "but you've experienced this same joy, haven't you."

It was a statement, not a question, and Frank nodded his response. "Bob," he said, "let me read something to you here, from Mosiah 27.

" 'Marvel not that all mankind, yea, *men and women*, all nations, kindreds, tongues and people, *must be born again*; yea, born of God, changed from their carnal and fallen state, to a state of righteousness, being redeemed of God, becoming his sons and daughters; and thus they become new creatures; and *unless they do this, they can in nowise inherit the kingdom of God.'*

"No one is exempt here, Bob." Frank looked up from his reading. "Regardless of our experience or degree of commitment, we all must come to Christ through complete repentance and spiritual rebirth.

"My own experience was several years ago, after my wife died. She was not a member of the Church, and after she had gone, I felt the greatest sense of helplessness and sorrow. I had never been very religious, but a good friend put his arm around me and told me I could only find peace if I came to Christ. Then he . . . showed me how—"

"And since then, you've been helping others do the same thing."

"Trying. But I've found, Bob, that the only people I can help are those who are honestly seeking to put their lives right with the Lord. You've faced some difficult truths about yourself, and it hasn't been an easy path."

Bob nodded in agreement. "No, it hasn't been."

"But you've held on," Frank continued. "Regardless of the price you were being asked to pay."

Bob's face seemed almost illuminated with joy.

"Have you told Claudia?" Frank asked.

"She's been pretty worried about Robby. In fact, she spent yesterday and today with him. So no, I haven't. But I will, Bishop. As soon as I can, I'm going to tell her."

Frank stood and looked briefly at his watch. "For some reason, Bob, I'm feeling like I need to be with my wife right now. What do you say we talk again tomorrow, after church?"

"I'll be looking forward to it."

As Frank walked down the path to his car, he was almost trembling with spiritual energy. "Thank you, Father," he breathed heavenward. "Thank you for bringing this dear brother back home. And bless Jeanee—"

10:40 A.M.

"Jeanee, hon, what is it?" Terri came in the front door without knocking. Jeanee was huddled on the sofa, her face buried in a large pillow.

"I don't know Terri," she said, looking up. "Peggy says it might be a memory." Then, trembling with emotion, she continued. "Only, how can a memory hurt so much?"

"I'm so glad I was home." Terri spoke deliberately as she walked over to sit beside her friend. "I had a feeling I wasn't supposed to be going to the mall with Doug." And then very tenderly she urged, "Tell me, Jeanee, what's happening?"

Jeanee sniffed back her tears and sat up straight. "I wish I knew! This past week has been unbelievable!"

Jeanee looked at Terri and then began to whimper, "Oh, Terri, I . . . I'm sorry to be such a mess."

Terri reached over and drew Jeanee close. "You're doing just what you're supposed to be doing—"

"But all this awful stuff is trying to come out!" Jeanee protested.

"Better out than in," Terri stated calmly.

And then both women, suddenly struck with the humor of her statement, began to laugh.

"Oh, Terri," Jeanee finally said with a sigh, "I'm sooo glad you're here!"

"Me, too. Now tell me what's going on with my best friend?"

Jeanee looked up at the ceiling and tucked her left foot under her. "This has been crazy!" She shook her head. "For several nights now I've been waking up—"

"More than usual?"

"Five times last night!"

Terri raised one eyebrow. "Something good is happening."

"Are you sure?"

Terri nodded. "When it gets that intense, you know you're close to a breakthrough."

Jeanee again protested. "But I'm so scared of what I've been thinking. I keep praying that whatever is trying to come out isn't just some crazy creation of my own mind. Terri, you won't believe what I've been thinking! I'm so afraid this might just be my imagination."

Terri reached down and squeezed Jeanee's hand. "Don't be afraid." She spoke tenderly. "The Lord didn't give us the spirit of fear."

"But—" Jeanee protested.

"What are you afraid of, Jeanee?" Terri asked.

"The truth! Oh, Terri, it's so terrible. Why does the Lord ask so much?"

"He doesn't ask so much," Terri said soothingly. "He asks everything."

"Right." Jeanee sobbed and laughed in the same breath. "Everything!"

"It's true. Be grateful that this is happening."

Jeanee's eyes searched for an explanation.

"The very fact that this memory is finally coming through is confirmation that the Lord knows you are strong enough to accept it. He's been guiding all this. He protected you from your memories before because He knew you couldn't deal with them. But now you can. Do you understand that? Now you can! And He's allowing them to come out into the open, where you can face them squarely. So don't be afraid. It's okay for this to be happening right now."

Jeanee took a deep breath. "But the other night— Terri, something very strange happened."

"Tell me," Terri encouraged.

"I woke up, or rather part of me woke up. But it was as if that part had been asleep for . . . years!" Jeanee looked at Terri for courage to go on. Terri squeezed her hand and smiled.

"I wasn't me."

There was a pause. Then Jeanee continued. "I was me. But I was little. Terri, does this sound too crazy?"

"It doesn't sound crazy at all."

"I woke up feeling my hands — nothing else — just my hands."

Terri nodded.

"And then I did feel. And — Oh, Terri!" Jeanee began sobbing again.

"Jeanee." Frank's voice suddenly boomed from the front door, startling both women. "Where are you? Honey, are you okay — "

10:58 P.M.

"No! Don't!" Jeanee sat up in bed, her words driven with fear. "I'll scream! I'll scream!"

Frank had been only half asleep, wondering at his wife's incredible anxiety that afternoon. Now he was fully awake.

"What is it, Jeanee? What's happening?"

"No! Don't!" she kept repeating, unaware of where she was.

"It's okay, honey," Frank said, putting his arm around his wife.

"No! Don't touch me!" Jeanee's eyes were bright with terror, her trembling hands pushing him away. "Go away! Don't touch me!"

"You don't want me to touch you?" Frank asked, puzzled. But Jeanee was unaware of her husband. The terror ripping her awake was so intense that it blocked out all perceptions of time and place. Cowering in her bed, she was totally lost in yesterday.

"He's coming into my room," Jeanee gasped, her face contorted, her voice sounding like that of a terrified little girl. "I'm asleep, but I can hear him coming —

"Daddy, don't . . . don't, please. It isn't nice. I don't

want you to do—" Suddenly Jeanee's voice was muffled.
And there was silence, broken only by Jeanee's movement
in the bed and her gasping for air.

"I can't breathe! I can't breathe! No, Daddy, don't!"

And suddenly, as in her most recent nightmares, Jeanee
raised up on her knees and began gasping furiously for
air.

"No! No! Oh, nooo!" she groaned in horrified gasps.
"Please don't! Please!

"Daddy, I can't breathe! I can't breathe! No, Daddy!
Mommy told me to scream! Nooommmmmph—"

Writhing in agony, Jeanee began moaning almost silently, seemingly unable to speak further.

"Jeanee," Frank questioned urgently, "what's happening? Tell me what's happening."

Gasping for air, Jeanee tried to sit up. "He . . . he's
smothering—" Another gasp. "His hand—I can't
breathe—it's over my mouth—my nose!

"Oh, nooo!" Jeanee screamed in agony. "I'm being
ripped inside out! My insides—they're exploding! Oh, help
me! Help me! No, Daddy! I can't stand—It hurts—"

Jeanee was clawing at the sheets, her hands digging
deeper and deeper, fighting to get away from the pain,
fighting the unseen enemy.

"I want to get out of my body! I can't stay in my body!
It hurts too bad—"

For a moment Jeanee was silent, her body trembling,
and Frank stared at her. "What do I do?" he pleaded
heavenward. "Dear Father, what am I supposed to do?"

And then the silence was broken.

"My hands! My hands!" Jeanee was moaning. "It was
my hands. My hands saved me. I felt with my hands. They
took all the pain away, and I was saved.

"I can feel the sheets. They're cold and rough. I can
feel my hands. But I can't feel—

"Oh, no! I can't believe what I . . . I'm remembering," Jeanee moaned. "Oh, dear God, please help me—"

Doubling over again, Jeanee began screaming, long agonizing screams that tore at Frank's very soul.

"Oh, no, I *know* what he did to me!" she gasped. "I know what he did! Only . . . I can't say it! It hurts so bad! He . . . he—"

And giving in to the writhing agony of her memory, Jeanee's mind only then became aware of the secret hidden within her body, a secret so heinous she had never been able to remember it—

"He . . . did . . . that . . . to me." Jeanee's voice was tortured. "Oh, nooo! He did *that* to me!" She screamed in horror. And then doubling over, great sobs of pain racked her body.

Frank sat close, not touching his wife, continuing to plead in mighty prayer for his poor Jeanee, as her very soul seemed to be ripping asunder.

"Dear God," he wept silently, "bless this child. Bless her—Oh Lord, I don't know what to do! But please, dear Father, help her make it through this night—"

35

MONDAY, JUNE 29

10:00 A.M.

"It's been a difficult weekend," Peggy stated calmly as she sat across the room from Frank and Jeanee.

Jeanee turned to Frank, hesitant to speak.

"It's been — unusual," he admitted.

"And *difficult*," Peggy emphasized. "For both of you."

"Were you able to get a neighbor to help with your little daughter?"

"She spent the day with a friend," Frank answered. "Our son Erik is at baseball camp, or he could have helped out."

"Erik is a baseball player?" Peggy asked.

"He was just named second team all-state." Frank smiled. "And he just keeps getting better. His coach expects he'll be first team next year, and he's already getting feelers from various universities. So yes, I guess you could say he's a baseball player."

Jeanee remained silent.

"That's wonderful!" Peggy then sent a probing look across the room. "Jeanee, do you want to tell me how you're feeling?"

Jeanee sat without moving, saying nothing. Then her eyes dropped to the floor, and, in a quiet, almost childlike voice, she answered, "I feel like I've been raped."

"That's because you have been." Peggy validated Jeanee's statement.

464

"But I feel like it's real, like it just happened."

"It is, and it did," Peggy reconfirmed.

Both Frank and Jeanee looked surprised.

"Let me explain," Peggy went on, searching Jeanee's countenance to be sure she could handle an explanation. "What happened to you is a phenomenon of which we are becoming more and more aware.

"Jeanee, are you all right?"

Jeanee nodded silently, and Peggy continued.

"It's common when the abuse is severe and perpetrated at such an early age. But it is difficult for most people to accept and understand. Still it's very real, and it's important that you accept it as such."

Frank sent a look of comfort to his dazed wife.

"Jeanee," Peggy continued, "remember how we've talked about those little drawers?"

Jeanee nodded.

"Well, that's a very good way of looking at this—as if the memory of what happened has been in a drawer all these years. It was too painful for you to have dealt with when you were so small. Your mind couldn't process the magnitude of the experience. So it simply tucked it away. Does that make sense?"

Jeanee showed no expression, but she was hearing everything that was being said.

"Frank," Peggy asked, "are you with me?"

Frank nodded and, reaching over, he covered his wife's hand with his own.

"Okay, Jeanee," Peggy continued, "there's a reason why the memory felt so real. It has to do with the way a child's mind processes something as painful as this."

Peggy knew how fragile Jeanee's emotions were. She knew, just as well, that honesty was vital at this point.

"When your father sodomized you," she proceeded carefully, "your mind was too young to accept it. So it stored the memory away in a compartment—in your little drawers. You had no conscious awareness of it. It was hidden in darkness, just waiting for the right trigger to bring it out."

"Is this the darkness I have felt for so long?" Jeanee asked. "Is this why I have had all those terrible dreams?"

"That would make sense," Peggy responded. "The recent stresses in your life—Amber's rape—your friend Marie's problems—they triggered this compartment, or drawer, and opened the memory to the light of day."

"And I fought to keep it in darkness—because it was so ugly." Jeanee shuddered.

"Understandably. It's normal to avoid those things that cause great pain."

"But I couldn't stop it from coming out."

"No more than you can stop a baby from being born, once labor has begun." Peggy smiled tenderly.

Jeanee made no response, so Peggy continued. "But unlike other memories that lose their vividness as time passes, this memory was kept clear and undiluted because it was held separate in that drawer. And so, when it was tapped into and ready to come out, the memory was as vivid and graphic as if it were actually happening.

"Jeanee, for all intents and purposes, you *were* just raped. What you are feeling is very valid and very understandable. It makes a lot of sense."

"But how is it possible for something like that to happen?" Jeanee's expression was bleak.

"Something like what?" Peggy questioned.

"You know—I was so small. How could he—"

"Jeanee, we've talked before about your father being more disturbed than you've been able to admit."

Tears sprang immediately to Jeanee's eyes.

"Believe me, it is possible. There are ways. And obviously, he found those ways, severely damaging your physical body while he was damging your soul."

"Do you mind my asking," Frank said solemnly, "why

it is that Jeanee has to keep dealing with these memories? She dealt with difficult memories from the past once. Isn't that enough?"

Peggy smiled. "It's difficult to see someone you love so deeply go through this kind of agony."

Frank nodded.

"So many loving family members and friends of abuse victims, those who have suffered as Jeanee has, feel this very thing. That's why they keep trying to convince these victim/survivors to 'put it behind them.'

"Sadly, it's this concern, or discomfort, that prompts them to undermine the kind of excruciating honesty that Jeanee, and others going through this amazing process, have to have if they are to heal."

"You're saying that they sabotage the healing process?" Frank asked.

"All too often," Peggy concurred. "Some husbands even refuse to allow their wives to continue therapy when the healing memories start coming out, because they don't understand that to clean a closet, you have to raise a little dust—in some cases a lot of dust."

"It was amazing to me," Frank shook his head, "being there with her as it was happening. It was as if Jeanee were experiencing it that very moment. I still don't understand how she could have held that kind of pain inside her for so long."

"It is amazing," Peggy responded, "how the mind of the child is protected. Frank, let me try to explain something. Okay?"

Frank nodded agreement.

"What Jeanee is experiencing is sometimes difficult to comprehend. But as close as I can see, it's as if the memory had been trapped in layers of forgetfulness. These layers peel off one at a time. Imagine peeling an onion."

Again, Frank nodded.

"When you get one layer peeled off, there's another

waiting, and another. Remembering can be compared to that.

"For example, a first indication might be feeling nervous or depressed around a certain person or situation. Then might come nightmares, then unexplained anger, memories of fondling, and finally memories of serious violation, such as this sodomy she has just remembered."

"Are there more to come?" Jeanee asked.

Peggy looked at Jeanee with great compassion in her face and spoke deliberately. "Whatever is there that needs to come out, will come out—in it's own time. You don't want to force it. And you don't want to fight it, either."

Jeanee was deep in thought as Peggy continued explaining. "Once your mind has accepted what your body has been trying to tell it all these years, you won't be troubled by these kinds of things anymore. And Jeanee, it won't happen until you are ready. Remember that."

Jeanee was deep in thought. "My body," she said, almost to herself. "My body has been trying to tell me."

"That's right."

"I've been poring through my journals, trying to discover what dark secrets might be hidden there. And all the time it was recorded in my body."

"Mmm hmm." Peggy smiled in agreement. "Amazing isn't it?"

"My body has been my journal! Frank, my body held the secrets." Jeanee looked at her husband, who was still trying to process what she was discovering.

"And the catalepsy?" Jeanee asked, hope radiating from her face. "Is that over? And the waking up in the night, gasping for air. Will it be gone now that I have remembered?"

"Time will tell," Peggy responded. "But keep this in mind—just because you have gone through hell doesn't mean you're consigned to live there for the rest of your life." A smile brightened her face. "It may take more time,

Jeanee. But you're making significant progress. And with the support of your husband—"

"Jeanee?" Frank asked. "How do you feel about your father, knowing what he did to you?"

Peggy showed concern for Frank's pushing another issue. But Jeanee didn't seem troubled by his question.

"I used to try to tell myself that he loved me. But now, remembering what he did—"

Jeanee was suddenly silent, a look of distant comprehension on her face.

"I understand now." Jeanee spoke as if from another dimension. "I understand what He meant."

"Your father?" Peggy asked.

"No." A serene smile lifted the corners of Jeanee's mouth. "When I forgave my father, I understand what Jesus meant."

Jeanee's thoughts were transporting her back to years earlier, when she had heard the Savior's voice. His message had been simple but profound in its application to Jeanee.

" 'Accept what is . . . ' " she whispered. "That's what He told me. " 'Accept what is. And trust me.' " Tears were welling up in her wet blue eyes. "Oh Frank! This is what He was talking about! He knew I couldn't be healed until I could do that. He knew I couldn't go through these past few months if I hadn't forgiven my dad. And He gave me all these years to get ready for—for *this* step.

"Oh, Frank, He does know I'm here!" Jeanee's eyes burned with the witness of the Spirit. "He knows I'm here. And He *is* working everything for good!"

As they walked to the car, Jeanee was still physically weak from her ordeal. But holding Frank's hand tightly, she knew strength was on its way. And with each step she was increasingly amazed at how new the world around her seemed. Birds seemed to sing more clearly. Even the air seemed to be fresher and sweeter. As excruciating as her recent experience had been, she had the unmistakable feeling that she was climbing out of a very dark hole — into the light —

1:20 P.M.

"Mister Greaves?"

Looking up from the rosebush he was trimming, Frank smiled. "Hi, Robby."

"You got a minute?"

Walking to the curb, Frank leaned in the open window of the car. "Nice wheels."

"Yeah, I bought it. Or I'm buying it, I mean."

Frank grinned. "That's usually how it works."

"Bishop," Robby said abruptly, changing the subject, "do you believe my dad's changed?"

"Yes," Frank said thoughtfully, "I do."

"You're buying all this religious crap he's trying to pull? Hey! Not me!" Robby swore viciously. "And it makes me sick!"

"You feel pretty strongly about that." Frank was taken aback.

"No offense, Bishop," Robby protested, "but if he's back in church, that's the last place I want to be!

"For all my life he beats the crap out of me and Mom," the boy continued, "and just like that he expects us to get over it! Do you know he even wants me to move back in with them?"

"But you don't want to?"

Robby laughed harshly. "No way! He may have suckered Mom, but he isn't going to sucker me!"

"What does your mom say?"

"She wants me to give him another chance. Can you believe that?"

"She must really believe he's changed."

"Well, he probably has," Robby said scornfully. "For this week! Or this month! He's done this before, Bishop.

I've seen it, and I'm scared for Mom. One day he'll go BOOM, and that'll be it. I know. A leopard doesn't change its spots. You know that old fable."

Frank nodded. "I know it. I'm glad somebody didn't teach it to Jesus."

"Huh?"

"Well, Jesus taught that anybody can change. He called it repentance. Doesn't do much for the leopard story, though."

"The leopard didn't need a shrink like he does!" Robby gripped the steering wheel and revved the engine. "If he thinks I'm going to come back and let him—"

"Do you think counseling would help your dad, Robby?" Frank asked above the roar of the engine.

"What do you mean?"

"Counseling—do you think that would help your father?"

"Humpff! It's not helping me. But then, I'm not the one with the problem!"

"Robby," Frank spoke sincerely, "you have a lot of reasons to be angry." Wisely, after months of dearly earned experience, Frank knew to accept Robby where he was.

"You bet I do! After what he's done!"

"Your father has treated you pretty badly."

"Then you don't think I should move back with him either?"

"Robby, I think you should do exactly what you feel you should do. But let me share an observation with you, if I might."

Robby turned the engine off and leaned back in his seat, listening.

"I've discovered," Frank stated, "that when I have unresolved anger, however justified it may be, it tends to get in my way of seeing things clearly."

"But I can see this clearly. He hasn't changed, Bishop! I know that!"

"I'll tell you what," Frank said gently, "why don't you reserve judgement for a little while longer. Do what you want about moving back, but keep an open mind about your dad. If he hasn't changed, it shouldn't take too long to discover it."

"You really think he's changed?" Robby asked again.

Frank leaned closer into the car window and smiled easily. "I'm confidant, Robby, that not only has he changed, but that he's continuing to improve every day."

There was a look of distant sadness in Robby's eyes as he reached down and turned the key in his ignition.

"I think a lot of you, Bishop. And you almost have me believing it could be true. But no—I don't believe it.

"I gotta go," he said with a shrug as he put his car in gear. "This is just too much for me."

And as Frank backed hurriedly away from the curb, Robby accelerated sharply and took off down the street and around the corner—

5:11 P.M.

"Phone's for you, honey." Frank brought the remote out onto the patio where Jeanee was resting. "Terri."

Jeanee took the phone and thanked Frank as he disappeared into the house to prepare dinner.

"Hello, friend," she said, managing a smile.

Terri laughed. "Do you feel as bad as you sound?"

"Is this a trick question?" Jeanee countered weakly.

"No. But if it will help, I'm bringing dinner over."

"Frank and Angie are just starting the meatloaf." The fatigue was obvious in Jeanee's voice.

"Tell them they can do that tomorrow. Doug and I are bringing lasagna. And we won't stay. We'll just be in and out. Okay?"

"Fine." Jeanee smiled.

"And another thing. As soon as you're able, I think you

and Frank should take a few days and use our place up at the lake. It's beautiful this time of year."

"A real vacation? What a wonderful offer."

"I think you ought to consider it."

"Frank has something he has to take care of here, as soon as I'm more ambulatory," Jeanee explained. "It has to do with Marie. Her father came to see her, you know."

"So I heard."

"Amazing timing." Jeanee smiled. "Frank won't tell me exactly what happened, but he seems pretty pleased about it."

"I think that's wonderful."

"And so's this," Jeanee said. "Frank has also decided that he needs to hold a special adult fireside."

"Oh?" Terri responded. "What's the topic?"

"Abuse."

"Good for him!"

Jeanee was quiet.

"Still pretty shaky?" Terri asked.

"It's strange how fragile I feel. I go through periods of time when every breath is an effort."

"It was pretty painful, wasn't it." Terri spoke tenderly.

"It was the most difficult thing I've ever gone through in my life." Jeanee almost whispered. "But Terri," she paused and her voice filled with sudden elation, "I feel so clean! Like all the rotten stuff has been cut away."

"By the Lord's spiritual scalpel." Terri's smile could be felt through the telephone. "And there will come a time, Jeanee, when all this that you're dealing with will no longer be the focus or primary motivation in your life. It will simply be a memory—a distant memory."

Tears filled Jeanee's eyes. "You mean it won't keep breaking my heart?"

"That's right. The grief will be gone, and it will just be an almost forgotten memory."

Jeanee's spirit leapt within her, confirming the truth of that revelation.

"But Jeanee," Terri added wisely, "while it's here, let yourself feel the grief. Don't fight it. Release it. It's honest and healing to be with it for as long as it's yours. That's what has hurt you all these years, fighting not to feel the grief, trying so hard to deny it and stuff it back inside.

"Let it out, hon, let it all out. Take as long as it takes, but let it all come out—"

9:45 P.M.

"Mommy." Angie came into the bedroom with a note in her hand. This is from Sister Elder. Daddy found it taped to the pan the lasagna came in. It's for you."

Jeanee sat up in bed. "What are you doing up so late, punkin?"

"Daddy said it was okay." The little girl giggled. "Now that you're not feeling good, I'm being the 'woman of the house.' "

Just then the telephone rang. Jeanee could hear Frank picking it up in the kitchen.

"Yes," he said loudly. "It's great to hear from you. How are things?" Jeanee listened, trying to make out who was calling. "Well, that's good, Tony. I'm glad to hear it. I'm sure your mother will be happy about that. Yes, I'll tell her."

Then there was a pause, Frank's voice became low and serious, and Jeanee couldn't make out the words. She strained, still couldn't, and finally heard Frank telling Tony good-bye.

Jeanee's heart started beating faster as Frank took the stairs two by two. Expectantly she waited for what she hoped would be good news.

Looking serious, he came into the bedroom.

"Tony called," he announced. "Amber and the whole family are working with Church Social Services."

"The whole family?" Jeanee smiled her relief.

"Their therapist said there were issues they all needed to deal with in order to put things back together. Tony said he's happy with the progress they're all making."

"Oh, Frank! That's wonderful!"

"And there's more news—"

Jeanee waited, realizing it was something serious.

Frank turned to Angie and then to his wife. You know how we have been praying for Benjamin Brattles?" he asked his little daughter.

She nodded her head, her eyes wide.

"Well, I guess he chose not to turn his heart back to the Lord. He had an accident the other night. He and a bunch of his friends were out drinking, and the car—" Frank could hardly get the words out.

"He's dead?" Jeanee gasped.

"No." Frank struggled with his emotions. "His neck is broken. From what they can tell, he'll be completely paralyzed for the rest of his life."

"Daddy." Angie walked over and looked up at her tearful father. "Why are you crying? He was a bad boy."

Frank knelt down to his bewildered little girl. "I know what he did was bad, sweetheart. It was very bad. But he's Heavenly Father's child, just like you and me. Now maybe he'll change so the Lord can heal his spirit."

"Can Jesus make bad boys be good?" Angie asked innocently.

"Yes, He can, sweetheart. If they'll let Him."

"Then maybe," Jeanee said softly, "this will be what it takes."

"What was in the note?" Frank asked, wiping his eyes and turning to Jeanee.

"I haven't even opened it yet," Jeanee admitted. "Let me see."

Ripping the top from the envelope, Jeanee opened it and read.

Dear Jeanee,

When you come to the end of everything you know
And the next step is into the darkness
   of the great unknown
You must believe one of two things:
Either you will step out onto firm ground
Or you will be taught to fly.

I wish I knew who the author was so I could give credit. But I don't.

Our prayers continue in your behalf. "The effectual fervent prayer of a righteous [person] availeth much."

I love you and accept you wherever you are at any given point.

Your forever friend and sister,
Terri

P.S. Once I decided to love the Lord more than I feared the pain, He healed me—

PART SIX

TRUTH

I am
Learning
Truth is
My only safety

And
Emerging
From my
Pain-stretched
Soul
I am free!

36

SUNDAY, AUGUST 9

6:20 P.M.

"I thought we were going to the church." Jeanee shifted uncomfortably.

"We are. I just have to make a little detour—"

"You're not going to tell me, are you."

Frank smiled. "Tell you what?"

"Frank, honey," Jeanee teased, "you are so devious! I can't believe the Lord lets you stay in as bishop."

"Well, I did think of resigning. But then a certain woman, beautiful of countenance and uncommonly curious—Ouch!"

"You tell me where we're going, Frank Greaves, or you'll get more than that."

"Just around the corner up here, and then down the road a little farther."

In frustration Jeanee shook her head. "Are you nervous?" she finally asked.

"You mean about my talk? Piece of cake, as Erik would say."

"I mean it, Frank. Are you sure this is the right thing to do?"

Frank put his arm around his wife and squeezed her gently toward him. "Hey, it's the truth, isn't it? Since when was it not right for the truth to be preached in the Lord's church?"

479

"But . . . there are people who don't want to hear it, Frank."

"I'm sure you're right," Frank agreed with a smile. "But maybe they're the very ones who need to hear it the most. All I know, hon, is that I have felt the Holy Spirit incredibly strongly while I have been writing it. As far as it is possible for me to do, I have written a talk that is the mind and the will of the Lord for these people in my ward. All I can do now is give it."

"I know," Jeanee said as she pressed her cheek against Frank's arm. "You're in my prayers, sweetheart."

"Speaking of prayers," Frank changed the tone of his voice, "what did you think of Erik's prayer tonight? Is he growing up, or what?"

"Are you talking about that comment he made about healing the hearts of the wounded and inviting the unrepentant to partake of the truth?" Jeanee asked.

"You got it. He sounded like a poet."

"He understands a lot more than I've given him credit for."

Frank smiled. "That's because you've been so open and honest with him about your difficulties. While we've been learning, so has he."

"I'm glad we didn't try to shield him from our pain."

"So am I, hon. While we've been learning, so has he. By the way, President Stone will be there tonight. Great, huh? Oh, here we are."

Curiously Jeanee watched as Frank pulled to a stop in front of a large brick home. He got out of the car and strode to the front door, and she searched for some clue as to why they were there.

The neighborhood was new to her, and the homes were quite nice. She was looking appraisingly at the well-manicured yard when the front door opened and a man stepped out and shook hands with Frank. For a moment the two men visited, and then Frank turned and walked back to the car.

"Who was that?" Jeanee asked as Frank got back in the car.

"A fellow by the name of Dave," Frank responded non-chalantly.

"And?"

"And what?" Frank smiled sweetly.

"What is going on?" Jeanee was getting frustrated again.

"And now we wait."

"But Frank, we need to get there a little early—"

Abruptly the front door opened again, and two people stepped out and walked toward the car—the man Frank had called Dave, and his wife, who, to Jeanee's great amazement, was her prodigal friend, Marie Winston Spencer—

7:15 P.M.

"Brothers and sisters," Frank began from the pulpit, "as you note on the program, I am the only speaker tonight. President Stone is here because he has read and approved my talk and wanted to show his support. I want him to know how much I appreciate him. I bear witness that he is a man of God who has the best interest of each of us in the stake at heart."

Frank looked down at his congregation. The love he felt for them had grown immeasurably in the past year and a half. *Father,* he pleaded silently, *help me to get through this without breaking down.*

"After the meeting tonight," he continued, "we will be handing out copies of my talk to every family in the ward. Please study it thoroughly. Please study it prayerfully and honestly. And if you see the need, or if the Lord's Spirit whispers that the need is there even if you don't see it, please take the appropriate steps to see that your family obtains relief."

Taking a deep breath, Frank pushed ahead. "I will also be speaking on this subject to the young men and women, and, in a slightly different vein, to the Primary children. I would suggest that you prepare yourself for the possibility of questions from them."

There was a stir of interest, and Frank smiled. "In the Book of Mormon we read of a day when the Lord commanded the prophet Jacob, who was Nephi's younger brother, to address his people on a particularly reprehensible subject. In chapter 2 of the book of Jacob he says: 'Now, my beloved brethren, I, Jacob, according to the responsibility which I am under to God, to magnify mine office with soberness, and that I might rid my garments of your sins, I come . . . this day that I might declare unto you the word of God.

" 'And ye yourselves know that I have hitherto been diligent in the office of my calling; but I this day am weighed down with much more desire and anxiety for the welfare of your souls than I have hitherto been. . . .

" 'But behold, hearken ye unto me, and know that by the help of the all-powerful Creator of heaven and earth I can tell you concerning your thoughts, how that ye are beginning to labor in sin, which sin appeareth very abominable unto me, yea, and abominable unto God.

" 'Yea, it grieveth my soul and causeth me to shrink with shame before the presence of my Maker, that I must testify unto you concerning the wickedness of your hearts.

" 'And also it grieveth me that I must use so much boldness of speech concerning you, before your wives and your children, many of whose feelings are exceedingly tender and chaste and delicate before God, which thing is pleasing unto God;

" 'And it supposeth me that they have come up hither

to hear the pleasing word of God, yea, the word which healeth the wounded soul.

" 'Wherefore, it burdeneth my soul that I should be constrained, because of the strict commandment which I have received from God, to admonish you according to your crimes, to enlarge the wounds of those who are already wounded, instead of consoling and healing their wounds; and those who have not been wounded, instead of feasting upon the pleasing word of God have daggers placed to pierce their souls and wound their delicate minds.

" 'But, notwithstanding the greatness of the task, I must do according to the strict commands of God, and tell you concerning your wickedness and abominations, in the presence of the pure in heart, and the broken heart, and under the glance of the piercing eye of the Almighty God.

" 'Wherefore, I must tell you the truth according to the plainness of the word of God.'

"Brothers and sisters, in that spirit I feel constrained to speak to you tonight about the abomination of abuse. As most of you know, in the past two years some in our ward have suffered excruciatingly from this horrid sin. I suppose there are many reasons why abuse is so rampant, but as I have met again and again with both victims and perpetrators of abuse within this ward, one reason always rises to the top.

"That reason is selfishness. And though this is not always the case, in most instances the selfish perpetrators of abuse, at least in our ward, have been the brethren.

"If I might again quote from Jacob's address: 'For behold, I, the Lord, have seen the sorrow, and heard the mourning of the daughters of my people . . . in all the lands of my people, because of the wickedness and abominations of their husbands.

" 'And I will not suffer, saith the Lord of Hosts, that the cries of the fair daughters of this people . . . shall come up unto me against the men of my people, saith the Lord of Hosts.

" 'For they shall not lead away captive the daughters of my people because of their tenderness, save I shall visit them with a sore curse, even unto destruction; for they shall not commit whoredoms, like unto them of old, saith the Lord of Hosts.'

"Unfortunately, not much has changed since Jacob's day. Nor has the Lord changed his position. If this evil is not brought to a stop, if the selfish abusing of others to satisfy our own lusts is not ended, then the Lord's promise of a sore curse, even unto destruction, will be fulfilled!"

In the very center of the front row were the Mc-Craskeys, Ralph sitting next to his wife, and both paying close attention. Back a little farther sat Abby Martin, with an attractive man sitting next to her. Her arm was in his, and Frank smiled, thinking of how drastically her life was beginning to change since her divorce had become final. *If John had only given himself a chance—* he thought to himself.

"But let's look at a few more things." His talk proceeded. "The Lord warned in Doctrine and Covenants section 38 verse 39 that we are to beware of pride lest we become as the Nephites of old. Can there be any greater manifestation of pride, Brothers and Sisters, than to exhibit the total selfishness, or gratification of self, that is at the heart of every act of abuse?

"Anciently the prophet Mormon wrote his son, Moroni, concerning this very issue, which seems to have been as rampant in his doomed society as it is in ours today. He says in Moroni chapter 9: 'And notwithstanding this great abomination of the Lamanites [enforced cannibalism], it doth not exceed that of our people in Moriantum. For behold, many of the daughters of the Lamanites have they taken prisoners; *and after depriving them of that which was most dear and precious above all things, which is chastity and virtue —*

'And after they had done this thing, they did murder them in a most cruel manner, *torturing their bodies* even unto death; . . .

" 'And again, my son, there are many widows and their daughters who . . . [have been] left . . . [by their awful brutality] *to wander whithersoever they can for food;* and many old women do faint by the way and die. . . .

" '*O the depravity* of my people! They are *without order and without mercy.* . . .

'And [this people] have become strong in their perversion; and they are alike *brutal,* sparing none, neither old nor young; and *they delight in everything save that which is good; and the suffering of our women and our children upon all the face of this land doth exceed everything; yea, tongue cannot tell, neither can it be written.'*

"Brothers and Sisters, as your bishop, your judge in Israel, I have felt impressed to mark for you certain portions of these verses so that you might not miss them. Nowhere in the scriptures have I read a more graphic account of the abominations of abuse — child, spouse, physical, sexual, and otherwise. Please let me explain.

"In verse 9 Mormon deals with rape and sexual abuse, calling them the abominations that they are. In verse 10 he describes physical abuse as cruel torture. In verses 16 and 17 he refers to the awful brutality of abandonment. In verse 18 he says that the whole scenario of abuse is a depravity wrought by a people who are without order and without mercy. Finally, in verse 19, he declares that the suffering of the Nephite women and children is the result of strong perversion, brutality, and the delighting of the abusers in everything except that which is good.

"Can sins that have been so graphically described, aptly named, and roundly condemned in that ancient society be any less serious today? Knowing the incredible pain that

these sins have brought upon so many members of our
ward, I feel compelled, as Mormon does in verses 13
through 15 and 21, to exclaim: 'O my [dear ward mem-
bers], how can a people like this, whose delight is in so
much abomination—

" 'When we commit such sins,] How can we expect that
God will stay his hand in judgment against us?

" 'Behold, my heart cries: Wo unto this people. Come
out in judgment, O God, and hide their sins, and wickedness, and abominations from before thy face! . . .

" 'Behold . . . I cannot recommend them unto God lest
he should smite me.'

"Then Mormon says something very significant. In order that he and his son might profit from the experiences
and mistakes of the people around them, Mormon likens
his people to another, more ancient, civilization. He says,
'And if [our people] perish it will be like unto the Jaredites,
because of the wilfulness of their hearts.'

"As I pointed out earlier, in D&C 38:39 the Lord commands us to do the same thing that Mormon did with the
Jaredites—liken ourselves to the Nephites so we might see
ourselves more clearly and adjust our course of action to
suit our desired end—exaltation in the celestial kingdom.
It is one of the primary reasons why the Lord gave us the
Book of Mormon. Thus we must also say: 'And if we perish
it will be like unto the Nephites, because of the wilfulness
of our hearts.' "Wilfulness in what? At least partially the
answer must be, as it was for Jacob's and Mormon's
Nephites, wilfulness in gratifying our basest natures at the
expense of others—the wilfulness, or selfish arrogance, or
pride of abuse.

"Fortunately, brothers and sisters, at least so far, the
Lord has not stretched forth his hand to destroy us as a
people or a nation. Instead, He has given us incredible
blessings, blessings that should have been inherited by the
Nephites. As Mormon says: " 'And behold, the Lord hath

reserved [my peoples'] blessings, which they might have received in the land, for the Gentiles who shall possess the land.'

"Those gentiles, my fellow Saints, are you and I. But in the same breath, Mormon issues a dire warning to those of us who have been given the blessings originally intended for the Nephites. He declares: " 'But behold, it shall come to pass that [my people] shall be driven and scattered by the Gentiles; and after they have been driven and scattered by the Gentiles, behold, then will the Lord remember the covenant which he made unto Abraham and unto all the house of Israel.

" 'And also the Lord will remember the prayers of the righteous, which have been put up unto him for them.

" 'And then, O ye Gentiles, *how can ye stand before the power of God, except ye shall repent and turn from your evil ways?'* (Mormon 5:19–22.)

"In my opinion, this prophetic warning needs no interpretation. We as a people called the Gentiles, both collectively and individually, will be swept from before the face of the Lord if we do not repent and forsake our evil ways.

"Therefore, Brothers and Sisters, if such depraved and brutal wickedness as abuse has place in your heart or in your home; if your pride and selfishness leads you to inflict such pain upon others, if your selfishness aligns you with Lucifer to the point where you are depriving another of his or her God-given agency; and if you will not, by seeking appropriate help and taking the appropriate steps, wholly repent and turn altogether therefrom, then as your common judge I declare that you, individually, will incur the wrath and judgement of God unto your ultimate destruction. Like both the Nephites and the Jaredites, you, personally must lose the blessings that have been reserved for you, and perish. There is no other course for you. As Mormon said, 'I speak it boldly; God hath commanded me. Listen unto [these words] and give heed, or they stand

against you at the judgement-seat of Christ.' (Moroni
8:21.)"

For a moment Frank paused, breathing deeply. Those
were strong words he had just uttered, stronger than he
had ever spoken from the pulpit. But even yet the Holy
Ghost was resting upon him with great power, and he knew
that he had spoken truly.

Yet just as powerful as that confirmation had been,
Frank found his entire being flooded with a feeling of
compassion, a feeling so strong that he found his heart
and mind yearning to reach out with love to all who had
been involved with abuse.

"Now, my dear fellow Saints," he quickly continued,
"please understand that this is not a message of despair,
nor is it a message of condemnation. Instead, I give it
entirely as a message of hope. For those of you who have
been suffering because of abuse, having been called as your
bishop, I declare to you with words of soberness: *There is
hope! There is a way out!* You do not need to continue as an
abuser! You do not need to remain a victim!

"Escaping this abomination cannot occur, however, until you acknowledge that the problem exists. For you who
are adults, if you are an abuser or a victim or both, you
must recognize the problem and accept personal responsibility for what it is doing to you. Once this acknowledgment and acceptance is made, then your next step is to
talk about it with an appropriate person.

"For you who have sinned as perpetrators of abuse, my
calling as bishop is to serve as your common judge, which
at least for today is a spiritual judgeship. In that capacity,
and with the Lord's help, I must assist in your repentance.
When you desire this, I will do all that I can to be of service
to you.

"I will also, if necessary . . . " Suddenly Frank stopped
speaking, once again amazed at the manifestation of the
Holy Spirit within him, and even more amazed at the un-

derstanding that the words he was speaking were the words of Christ.

"I will also, if necessary, steer you toward appropriate professional help. Besides counseling, that may include legal help, for you should understand that I am required by law to report certain facets of abuse. To do what a few in this ward may be doing is absolutely against the laws of this land. But even in that, my dear friends, painful though it may be, you will only be moving back toward Christ. And isn't eternal union with Him what we are all seeking, no matter the price we must pay?"

In the congregation, Bob Nichol beamed up at Frank, his eyes clear and bright. Claudia held his arm lovingly. Frank smiled down at them.

"If you are or have been a victim of abuse and have not also been a perpetrator, then despite the harrowing up in your mind, you are *not* guilty of wrongdoing. You have been violated, you have been wronged, and you suffer not because of a stricken conscience but because of a massive wounding to your soul. If you are suffering from such a wound and cannot find peace, then I would recommend that you also talk with someone appropriate, such as an understanding priesthood or Relief Society leader. Begin to unburden yourself by obtaining the clearer perspective of an inspired viewpoint, the comfort of one who has been called of God to be a guide and a comfort to you. Such a person, if necessary, can also lead you to additional, professional help.

"And to you priesthood and Relief Society leaders, may I say that never in earth's history has greater patience and compassion been required than will be expected of you as you hear the tragic tales of these wounded souls. Know that they did not sin, nor have they been less a person than you. Despite their pain and the ugliness that exists in their memories, each of these individuals is every whit as precious before God as any of the rest of us, and every whit as pure.

"Through sad experience we are learning that before these wounded souls can heal, they must verbally walk through their memories with trusted others." Frank trembled with emotion and the strength of the Spirit. "To be deprived of that privilege is to heap upon them further abuse. Therefore, if you are appropriately called upon, be a trusted other. Be patient as they remember again and again, for we are also learning that most victims must relate their memories as often as it takes for them to gain understanding. While they are doing so, be tender, be kind, be gentle, be long-suffering. As the Lord declared scripturally to those of us who serve as leaders, 'No power or influence can or ought to be maintained by virtue of the priesthood, only by persuasion, by long-suffering, by gentleness and meekness, and by love unfeigned; by kindness, and pure knowledge, which shall greatly enlarge the soul without hypocrisy, and without guile . . . Let thy bowels also be full of charity towards all men, and to the household of faith, and let virtue garnish thy thoughts unceasingly.' (D&C 121:41–42, 45.)

"Finally, do not hesitate to encourage or support these people should they require professional counseling. Part of the healing for victims, my dear friends, is for them to gain an understanding of their past. This does not need to include every tiny detail, but victims of childhood abuse must regain a general picture of their past before they can honestly deal with it. Many do not have that. Many do not even have any memories, for their abuse was so horrendous that their memories have been blocked out. To unblock them properly often requires the help of properly trained, righteous counselors—men and women who have prepared themselves through extensive training to assist these people in their healing. It is our responsibility to encourage our brothers and sisters in this therapy, and to both spiritually and emotionally support them while they are struggling to be made whole."

Again Frank paused, overwhelmed with the powerful words that were on the paper before him, words that President Stone, having read, had declared came directly through inspiration.

"But please remember, fellow ward members," he finally continued, "that the ultimate solution to all abuse, as it is to everything else in this life, is in the precious blood of our Lord and Savior, Jesus Christ. Christ's gospel is one of pure love, and love is the only weapon that can destroy the old serpent's plan.

"If you are an abuser, then I plead with you to come in and see me, for I love you and have been appointed to render judgment upon your spiritual health during this facet of your mortality. By doing so, and unburdening your soul, you will begin the process of turning to Christ through repentance. Remember, if you will turn to Christ, who loves you with a perfect love, then through His atonement He has already paid the full price for your enormous sin, and you need not carry your horrible burden of guilt any longer.

"He says: 'I, God, have suffered these things for all, that they might not suffer if they would repent.' (D&C 19:16).

"My dear ward members who are guilty of these things, may I remind you of who you are — Latter-day Saint priesthood holders and spouses who have been 'called and prepared from the foundation of the world according to the foreknowledge of God, on account of [your] exceeding faith and good works; in the first place being left to choose good or evil; therefore [you] having chosen good, and exercising exceedingly great faith, are called with a holy calling.' (Alma 13:3.)

"Brothers and Sisters, that was Alma's description of you! Have you ever heard anything that filled you with greater hope? Imagine, you and I, chosen by God in the premortal existence because of our exceeding faith and good works. As I read that, I know that if I was capable of choosing righteousness then, I am just as capable of doing so today. Further, I know that each of you are in that same category. On account of your exceeding great faith, you can choose righteousness!

"But like the ancient Zeezrom, Satan has determined in his wicked subtlety to destroy you and your mortal mission by exercising his power in you, laying a snare through the weakness of your own more base natures that he might catch you and bring you into eternal subjection to him. (See Alma 12:4–6.) His phony gospel is to use fear, guilt, anger, secrets, and shame to control and conquer, and he is exercising that gospel to destroy you.

"Through the foreknowledge of God, however, being aware not only of your weaknesses but also of Lucifer's intentions to destroy you through them, our Father in Heaven has provided for you a Savior, to redeem you not in, but from, your sins. (See Alma 11:36–37.):

" 'And he shall come into the world to redeem his people; and he shall take upon him the transgressions of those who believe on his name; and these are they that shall have eternal life, and salvation cometh to none else' (Alma 11:40).

"Thus, redemption can come only through believing on Christ's name, which is the beginning of true repentance. God says: 'Whosoever repenteth, and hardeneth not his heart, he shall have claim on mercy through mine Only Begotten Son, unto a remission of his sins; and these shall enter into my rest.' (Alma 12:34.)

"Did you notice how the Lord speaks of hardening the heart? He also says that if we allow our hearts to be hardened, then we 'will do iniquity' (Alma 12:35), which iniquity will provoke the Lord to send down his wrath upon us to the everlasting destruction of our souls (v. 36). In that

condition, having hardened our hearts against the word
of God, our state would be awful (v. 13), and we would be
condemned by our words, our works, and even our very
thoughts, causing us to shrink from the presence of God
and His representatives (v. 14).

"From what I can learn, if our hearts are hardened we
are not teachable, nor are we even approachable. Though
we know right from wrong, we refuse to hear or accept
the promptings of the Holy Spirit. We resist the entreaties
of all who reach out to help us, and, above all, we are not
interested in repentance. It matters not whether this is
because we are enjoying our sins and seeking happiness
through them, or because we believe that we have gone
so far that we cannot repent. Either way our hearts are
hardened, and thus we refuse to partake of the cleansing
blood of Christ.

"But as Zeezrom was lied to by the devil, so is Lucifer
lying to us today who have become hardened of heart and
will not begin to repent. And what is the truth about the
devil's lies? First, that no one can ever find happiness in
doing evil (Alma 41:10), and second, that no one is beyond
the power of the atonement of Christ through repentance
(2 Nephi 2:21). Thus, the very reasons for hardness of
heart are lies, and they fly in the face of all that the Lord
declares through His holy prophets.

"Thus, with Alma I say to you who have been guilty of
abusing others, 'And now, my brethren, I wish from the
inmost part of my heart, yea, with great anxiety even unto
pain, that ye would hearken unto my words, and cast off
your sins, and not procrastinate the day of your repentance; but that ye would humble yourselves before the
Lord, and call on his holy name, and watch and pray continually, that ye may not be tempted above that which ye
can bear, and thus be led by the Holy Spirit, becoming
humble, meek, submissive, patient, full of love and all long-
suffering; having faith on the Lord; having a hope that ye

shall receive eternal life; having the love of God always in your hearts, that ye may be lifted up at the last day and enter into his rest. And may the Lord grant unto you repentance, that ye may not bring down his wrath upon you, that ye may not be bound down by the chains of hell, that ye may not suffer the second death.' (Alma 13:27–30.)

"Now, Brothers and Sisters—"

Suddenly Carol Blodgett caught Frank's eye. Fighting tears, she sat unmoving as Frank spoke. She had been grievously wounded, Frank knew. But hopefully, through Christ, healing was beginning to occur in her family.

"For those of us who have been victimized by another and have not yet found peace," Frank continued, "the true end of your pain is also in Christ. Please, please, remember that He suffered for our sorrows and troubles as well as for our sins. As the great prophet Isaiah declared, "Surely he hath borne our griefs, and carried our sorrows.' (Isaiah 53:4.)

"Interestingly, though you were abused by forces over which you had no control, the peace you are seeking, though it originates with Christ, can come only through your own efforts. Let me explain.

"Where abuse has been suffered and wounds have been opened, almost always the unjustly inflicted pain sinks from righteous anger into bitterness, a satanically inspired emotion that is even more destructive eternally than the abuse has been. In other words, the devil is not satisfied that he has tempted the abuser into great iniquity. Since his goal is to see that all people become miserable like unto himself (2 Nephi 2:27), he will treat as weaknesses the wounds our souls have received, and, like throwing dirt into an open wound on our bodies, he will do all he can to cause bitterness to infect and fester in the wounding to our souls.

"But for such wounds, too, God has provided a Savior, a perfect being who has borne, through incomprehensible unjust suffering of His own, our griefs and our sorrows.

To transfer our pain and suffering to Him, even if it has festered into these and other unhealthy emotions or feelings, we must take three significant steps.

"We shed our wounds and their frequent consequences by, first, *softening our hearts enough, through prayerful pleading, to learn from the Spirit if our wounds have festered into unrighteous emotions such as bitterness.* If they have, and if we are brought by the Spirit to recognize that this is so, then we must remember that such emotions cannot prosper unless we want them to. By clinging to our pain, continually rehearsing the injustices inflicted upon us, and regularly condemning our abusers, we blind ourselves to the fact that we are choosing to make these emotions our own. Thus our pain grows, and our condition worsens. As Alma taught, this is the meaning of the word restoration — bringing back again evil for that which is evil, or bitterness for that which is bitterness. (Alma 41:13.)

"But no matter what has harmed us or how severely we have been abused, we can also have the opposite experience — of bringing back good for that which is good, mercy for that which is merciful, and peace for that which is peace. As Alma says, we do this, and it is the second step in shifting our burdens to Christ, *by being merciful, dealing justly, judging righteously, and doing good continually.* Then " 'shall ye receive your reward; yea, ye shall have mercy restored unto you again; ye shall have justice restored unto you again; ye shall have a righteous judgment restored unto you again; and ye shall have good rewarded unto you again.' (Alma 41:14.)

"Finally, we shift our burdens to Christ *by humbling ourselves enough to accept the comforting influence of the Spirit, rather than refusing to be comforted; by humbly praying for meekness and lowliness of heart instead of setting ourselves up as judge and jury for our abuser; by humbly praying for understanding as we study the scriptures for guidance; and by humbly asking the*

Lord, in fervent prayer, to lift our burdens from us in order that we might have peace.

"By taking these three Christ-like actions—softening our hearts, taking positive action, and humbling ourselves, we shall have peace restored to us again. As Christ declared, 'Come unto me, all ye that labour and are heavy laden, and I will give you rest. Take my yoke upon you, and learn of me; for I am meek and lowly in heart; and ye shall find rest unto your souls.' (Matthew 11:28–29.)

"I bear humble and solemn witness that by turning to Christ with all our hearts, we can be freed from the bondage and pain of this most abominable form of wickedness, or from anything else that has become a wounding to our souls."

Frank smiled tenderly at his wife, who was smiling through her tears. Next to her Marie was nodding her head, her arm in her husband's. They both looked as though they had always belonged in the congregation.

Frank was amazed at the calm, sweet spirit that had subdued his emotions as he spoke. And yet his heart was overflowing with love for all those before him. What choice people they all were! How he cherished the opportunity God had given him of coming to love them as he had.

"In conclusion," he finally stated, "may I once again echo the thoughts of Mormon as he ended his revelatory letter: 'My [beloved brothers and sisters], be faithful in Christ; and may not the things which I have written grieve thee, to weigh thee down unto death; but may Christ lift thee up, and may his sufferings and death, and the showing his body unto our fathers, and his mercy and long-suffering, and the hope of his glory and of eternal life, rest in your mind forever. And may the grace of God the Father, whose throne is high in the heavens, and our Lord Jesus Christ, who sitteth on the right hand of his power, until all things shall become subject unto him, be, and abide with you forever. Amen.' "

9:35 P.M.

"That was quite a sermon."

In his rear-view mirror Frank could see Marie, and he could tell that she had been affected.

"I'll say," Dave Spencer agreed. "In my church they'd pay a guy a lot to give a sermon like that."

"Did you agree with it, Dave?" Jeanee surprised herself with her boldness.

The man shrugged. "Who can argue? Of course, I'd never heard of nine-tenths of the scriptures being quoted, so I can't comment about that. But from personal experience as Marie and I have tried to come to grips with her background, I'd say your husband was right on."

"All I can say, Bishop," Marie added quietly, "is that you've come a thousand miles in the past year and a half. Thank you."

Frank acknowledged the compliment with a nod, and for a moment there was silence, the only sounds coming from outside the car.

"So who's going to let me in on the secret?"

Frank looked at his wife. "What secret?"

"The secret of how long you three have been meeting together. I mean, I can't tell you how happy I am! About you, too, Dave. But it's all such a shock—"

"You sound like you think somebody tweaked your nose," Frank teased.

"I don't blame her for feeling left out," Marie stated quickly. Then she turned to Jeanee. "I should have called you, hon. But right off the bat Dave started meeting with us—"

"Oh," Jeanee said with a smile. "Bishop's confidences. Right?"

"That's right," Frank agreed. "But it did start with Brother Winston's visit. I can tell you that."

Marie smiled. "Your husband started coming the day

after Daddy was here, and he hasn't missed a week since then."

"Made a blasted nuisance of himself," Dave added.

"You loved it and you know it," Marie stated matter-of-factly.

"Not when he started pinning my ears back with all that religious stuff."

"Don't you listen to him, Bishop." Marie was smiling. "He's even reading the Book of Mormon."

"Yeah," Dave growled good-naturedly, "and trying to figure out this goofy wife of mine. Mormons!"

"Dave," Jeanee questioned, "what got you interested in the Church?"

"Marie's father," Dave responded. "I was pretty upset to find out what he did. But you know, that man is as humble as anyone I've ever known. I listened to his apology to Marie, and there wasn't one ounce of excuse-making. He accepted full responsibility. That impressed me."

"But what does that have to do with the Church?"

Dave chuckled. "Nothing. But he also told us how he felt about the Church, and about Jesus — Marie called it his testimony. I felt such a warmth toward him while he was talking that it made me want to know more. Since then your husband's been helping me do a little repenting of my own, and I think, well, I'm feeling pretty good about things."

"Jeanee," Marie said softly. "Remember when I said the Church wasn't a place of truth?"

"Yes."

"To be honest, we came tonight because the example Daddy and you two have set in terms of open-minded learning persuaded us to give it another try—"

EPILOGUE

Pillows of fog hugged the hills. Jeanee snuggled next to Frank as he drove, looking out the window at the profusion of October colors that were bathing the valley in bright splashes of crimson and gold.

"Oh look! Is that a deer? It is! It's a deer!"

"Yup, it's a deer, all right." Frank grinned at his wife's childlike excitement.

"I don't think I've ever seen anything more beautiful than—Oh, Frank, I'm so glad we're finally doing this!"

"The scenery outside is almost as incredible as the scenery inside." Frank winked.

Jeanee almost blushed.

"I mean it, honey. I don't think I've ever seen you look more beautiful."

"It's just the color of this sweater," Jeanee teased. "It brings out my eyes."

"It's a lot more than the sweater, although I have to admit the sweater looks mighty pretty, too."

Jeanee smiled and looked out the front window. "Life sure has its rewards," she said with a sigh.

"And how!" Frank grinned. "Speaking of rewards. Do you realize you haven't awakened in the night for months!"

"Nor have I had one of my—oops—I'm not going to claim them by calling them mine ever again. Let me rephrase that: Do you realize I haven't had even one catalepsy spell?"

"Uh-huh." Frank smiled. "Ever since that last major memory."

"Peggy tells me that's a good sign."

"I hope to shout it is!" Frank was more than enthu-
siastic.

"However, I may still have more memories to go
through," Jeanee admitted.

"But none of them will be as difficult, honey. The Lord
let me know in prayer that once that was over, it would
keep getting better all the time."

"And it has been." Jeanee almost squealed with giddy
freedom. "It feels so good to feel good!"

"Have you been writing in your journal today?"

Jeanee looked down at the book in her lap. "Uh-huh,"
she answered reluctantly. "Just a poem."

"Want to share it?" Frank invited.

"You want me to?"

"Absolutely."

"It's kind of—well you know how my poetry is."

"Yeah, deep. Go ahead, read it. I'm all ears."

With an expression of great peace, Jeanee began to
read:

> *Truth*
> *As long*
> *As I hid you*
> *I knew*
> *Suffering.*
>
> *When*
> *I endured*
> *You*
> *I knew*
> *Sacrifice.*
>
> *Once I accepted you*
> *I knew*
> *Joy!"*

There was quiet for a moment. Then Frank spoke.
"Jeanee, honey, do I deserve you?"

Jeanee smiled. "Someone once told me that *deserve* doesn't have anything to do with it. Besides, Terri says that if we got what we really deserved, we'd probably all burn in hell."

"Terri said that?"

"Uh huh!" Jeanee giggled. "And I think there's a lot of truth to it."

Frank pulled at his collar in mock discomfort. "Well, it's certainly true for me. Anything looking familiar?"

"Not so far," Jeanee replied as she looked ahead.

Frank reached over and touched his wife tenderly on the cheek. "You're an amazing women, Jeanee," he stated softly. "You know, you could have become bitter and hateful to your parents."

"I was bitter, once." Jeanee spoke with great reverence. "Before Christ healed me of it. Now He's also healing me of the wrong thinking I've carried around in my mind all these years.

"Frank, darling, I know now that the secrets, the lies my father taught me, were even more damaging than the abuse itself. He took the truth from me. The things he said and did taught me to believe I was to blame for everything that happened."

"And nothing could be further from the truth," Frank stated firmly.

"But the lies were all trapped in those dark little drawers with the memory of what he did. And as long as they were there, they kept influencing the way I thought and the things I did.

"Terri was right! She told me last year that someday I would understand. And I do. I know now that the only reason hell kept coming back is that it was tied to all those lies."

"And you shall know the truth—" Frank smiled.

"—and the truth shall make you free." Jeanee finished the scriptural promise, almost giggling. "And I do feel free!

I do! Even when the sadness comes, it's honest. And it's okay to feel it."

Frank smiled and winked at his wife.

"And something else." Jeanee was almost radiant as she spoke. "Frank, I've been praying about this, and I know now that I don't have to remember everything he did, just the things that the lies are tied to. Those lies are what kept making me sick. Once those lies are all taken out, I'll be fine. I just wish—

"There!"

Frank looked ahead. "Where?"

"That motel up there. Frank, I remember that motel. The road will curve after that, maybe a quarter of a mile, and then we'll come to a lane off to the left—"

"Are you sorry we didn't go to Doug and Terri's place on the lake?"

Jeanee snuggled against her husband. "Not for a minute. I'm sort of nervous, but I'm so excited! It's time, sweetheart. It really is!"

"I think so, too," Frank responded softly as he steered through the curve. "And I'm proud of you, hon. I want you to know that."

Jeanee said nothing as Frank slowed the car to make the turn into the lane Jeanee had spoken of. And looking at her face, lit by the late afternoon sun as it was breaking through the clouds, he was suddenly overcome with the most amazing feeling of permanence.

This little girl-woman that had once held such secrets was even more exciting now that her secrets were being revealed. He knew they had more yesterdays to deal with. He felt certain his sweet wife would again have to face her invisible enemy. But he was beside her now. And with God to help them, they would overcome that enemy together.

"Forever," he whispered to his eternal companion as he slowed the car to a stop in front of her mother's home. "Jeanee, hon, for you and me, it is forever—"

Authors' Note

While the preceding story is fictional, all of the characters we described, as well as their experiences with abuse, have been based upon the lives and experiences of Latter-day Saints. All of these people, both perpetrators and victims, have willingly shared this painful part of their lives and have graciously consented to have their own personal horror made public in the hope that the cycle of abuse thus exposed will begin to lose its insidious power over others.

This was not intended to be a definitive work. There are many avenues to healing, each as unique as the individual's experience. But whether they be beautifully sweet and complete, as was Terri Elder's experience, or deeply stirring and life-changing, as was depicted in the lives of Bob Nichol and Jeanee Greaves, all true avenues must embrace truth and ultimately lead to Christ.

ABOUT THE AUTHORS

Blaine M. Yorgason, who holds bachelor's and master's degrees in history with a focus on the American West, is the author of sixty books and numerous articles and short stories. His novel *The Windwalker* was produced as an award-winning movie; *Chester, I Love You* was filmed by Disney Productions as the made-for-television movie *Thanksgiving Promise;* and his novella *Charlie's Monument,* now in its twenty-fifth year of publication, has been an acclaimed musical production.

One Tattered Angel, the touching biographical account of his family's experiences with their adopted daughter Charity, was awarded the Literary Award for Non-Fiction for 1997 by the American Family Institute. *One Tattered Angel* also received the award for "Outstanding Book, Inspirational Category—in Recognition of the Inspirational Book Which Independent Booksellers Most Enjoyed Hand-Selling during 1996–1997."

Blaine and his wife, Kathy, have seven children and thirteen grandchildren.

Sunny Oaks's life experiences and simple, poetic writing style enhance the dimension and honesty of this collaborative work.

Sunny is the sixth child in a family of fourteen children. She was born in the shadow of the Cardston, Canada, LDS temple but moved to the United States while still a child. Currently she is serving as executive director of the HOME Connection, a family mentoring project building sufficiency skills in families with young children.

Ever since she can remember, Sunny has been writing poetry and music, and in 1987 she released a collection of her music entitled *Sunny's Song.*

She and her husband, Michael, have eight children and eighteen grandchildren, three of whom they are raising.